Drift

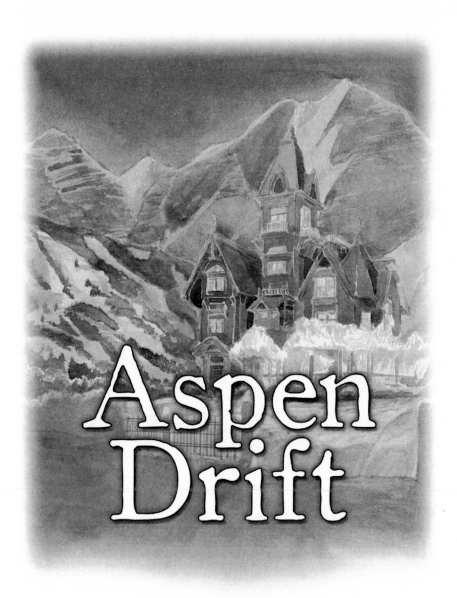

Aspen Drift

ANDY STONE

LAST DOLLAR PUBLISHING
ASPEN, COLORADO

Published by Last Dollar Publishing,
A division of Last Dollar Media,
El Jebel, Colorado

ISBN: 978-0-692-71488-1 9/2016

Cover and title page illustration
by Tom Southwell

Cover design by Laura Duffy

Book design by Karen Minster

Printed in the United States of America

For Linda,

my light in the dark.

Mi media naranja.

REQUIRED DISCLAIMER

This book is entirely a work of fiction. Got that? Fiction. Entirely. Names, characters, businesses, places, events and incidents are either the products of the author's sometimes-fevered imagination or used in a fictitious manner. Any resemblance of any characters or events to any real persons or events is entirely coincidental—a comment, it must be noted, that was not infrequently made about the author's news stories when he was a reporter at The Aspen Times.

ACKNOWLEDGMENTS

All the blame, of course, is entirely mine. But if there's some credit to be given, let's be sure it's properly spread around. So, my thanks to:

Nancy Elisha, a wonderful woman and wonderful reader who really knows Aspen.

John Colson, a reader, writer and editor who knows Aspen and newspapers inside out (and, often enough, upside-down).

Tom Southwell, a brilliant artist and a great friend.

Victoria Skurnick, my agent, who gave me a dose of confidence in the book, helped me shape it and did her level best to sell it.

The three Aspen Times editors who, each in his or her own way, kicked me around and taught me so much: Bil Dunaway who, for unknown and unknowable reasons hired me as a reporter and changed my life. Mary Eshbaugh Hayes who taught me that you can run a newspaper and still be a wonderful, warm human being (a lesson I may not have learned all that well, through no fault of hers). And Loren Jenkins, who gave this small-town reporter a close-up look at a real world-class journalist.

All the men and women who worked with me over the years at The Aspen Times. Like any newspaper, the Times is a family—and like any family it can get pretty rambunctious, but it's still home.

And finally, the entire population of the town of Aspen over the past 40-odd years, for being an endless source of amusement, inspiration, challenge, friendship, outrage, support, love and, of course, the occasional dose of loathing. All good for the soul.

Aspen Drift

1

DECEMBER 21, 1988.

Deep winter. Deep snow in the high mountains. Dawn over the Continental Divide.

The first rays of the rising sun slice deep into the valley, to a grove of evergreens perfectly positioned to catch the first light every year on exactly this day, the Winter Solstice. At the center of the grove, that frozen light explodes in color as it passes through a crystal the size of a man's head, set in a disk of hammered copper atop a granite column. And all of it—crystal, copper, granite and trees—placed very exactly and very expensively beside a mansion that looks out over the old mining town in the valley below. "At the Solstice, we honor the ways of the Ancient Druids," the proud owner loves to explain. He paid for the grove, the crystal, the house, the jet and all the rest of it with the runaway success of his book, "Investment Wisdom of the Ancients." His own investment career had been a spectacular failure, but as an author—and, thereafter, a lecturer and TV personality—he was a smash.

He was not in residence on this particular Solstice. An attack of gout, an affliction unknown to the ancient Druids, had sent him to St. Bart's for the holidays. But if he had been here and had been awake to witness the dawn, he would have smiled with pride at his sunrise.

Directly across the valley, a ski patrolman who owned neither house nor jet nor grove of evergreens, turned his face into the same sunrise as he rode the chairlift to work, dangling in the frozen morning air. Eager to begin his work day with a run through the fresh powder snow that had fallen overnight, he looked down at a lone figure, skiing fast, staying close to the trees, politely leaving the powder in the middle of the run undisturbed.

The patrolman knew the skier. Her name was Astrid and she was fourteen. Their paths crossed like this all winter long as he rode up to work and she skied down to school from the mountaintop restaurant where her parents were caretakers. The patrolman looked at the snow and the sunlight and the evergreens that lined the runs and smiled with pride at his mountain.

That same rising sun was, if not beautiful, at least a source of light and a promise of warmth to come for the man clinging to the back of a garbage truck, lurching through a downtown alley, hauling away the traces of yesterday's indulgence and last night's excess. The garbage man shared an apartment with five other ski bums, lived on beans and franks and, if he got no other benefit from his degree in sociology, at least he appreciated the irony of waking in squalor to spend his mornings collecting empty champagne bottles. And then skiing the rest of the day, every day, all winter long.

Throughout downtown, the roar of the garbage truck and the glorious fire of the rising sun were equal, unmitigated horrors to those with hangovers. And that was not a small number. But hangovers made no difference: the sun was up and the day would not be denied. This was Aspen, Colorado, and Aspen is too expensive a town for anyone to skip a day's work. Or a day's vacation.

And so it began, with a rattle and a clatter and a buzz.

Skis were sharpened, walks were shoveled. Sore muscles—and pounding headaches—were dragged out of bed into showers hot or cold, wrapped in wool and Lycra and nylon and sent out to ski again with eager delight. Or pained determination.

And, as the skiers headed up the hill, down below in the streets flocks of non-skiing wives and girlfriends cruised the stores, gleefully picking out the perfect piece to complete their ski ensembles. A scarf perhaps. Or sunglasses. Or, never mind the accessories, a whole new outfit. Everything except boots and skis, of course. And, really, not buying skis saves a lot of money, so they certainly could afford a new jacket. That one. The one with the mink-trimmed hood.

A rock star and a movie star, having finished an extravagant brunch, walked through downtown, arm in arm. They woke up in bed together that morning, neither one quite certain how that had come to pass. But there they both were and each had decided after the briefest moment of reflection that being seen in Aspen, the week before Christmas, could only be a good career move. So they notified their publicists and then ventured out to see and be seen, and tried desperately to think of something to talk about.

A former ski racer gave a lesson to a dangerously overweight man and his dangerously attractive, dangerously flirtatious—and dangerously young— daughter. A cab driver with an Ivy League PhD in philosophy parked his taxi outside the airport terminal, counted his cash and figured that with one more fare he'd have enough for dinner or a gram of cocaine. A true philosophical dilemma.

And in the late afternoon, as the sun skidded low and fast to the end of the shortest day of the year, two men stood side by side at the top of a ski run. The taller one, wiry, bareheaded despite the cold, eyes hidden behind mirrored sunglasses, laughed harshly. "I certainly have to admire your courage."

The other, round-faced, bulky in a down parka and a knit hat with a pom-pom, jutted his chin. "I'm not afraid of..." he started, but the first man kept talking.

"Foolish courage, of course. Given all the men *your* wife has been..." He let his voice trail off with a shrug and the smallest of smirks. They both knew exactly what word he was being too polite to say. And then he said it anyway. "...fucking. Given all the men your wife has been fucking"—he cracked the word like a whip—"I would have thought marital infidelity would be the last thing you of all people would want to talk about." He sounded amused. "And yet you come yelping to me on that exact subject. Very brave. Very sad." He leaned closer. "And very stupid." The shorter man licked his lips, about to speak, but the tall man tipped his skis onto the icy trail below them and in an instant he was gone. Fit, athletic, he raced down the slope with the relaxed grace that comes only with a lifetime on skis. Shifting his weight just a little, he cocked his hip, carved a turn across the slope and disappeared into the trees.

Smiling all the way.

The other man stood, suddenly alone at the top of the trail. Bulging goggles covered half his face, turning him into an alien insect, short, fat and forlorn. He had tracked the tall man down, followed him doggedly, determined to catch up, have his say, make his demands. He was going to be heard. He was going to win. But he hadn't won and now he was alone and the hour was late. The sun had dropped behind the ridge; shadows stretched across the snow. He was looking down a trail that was far too difficult for his limited skills and there was no way back, no other way down. Had he known the run was known as Elevator Shaft, it would not have cheered him at all. It was going to be a painful trip. And the spectacular view across the valley, over Aspen to the mountains beyond, was of no comfort.

Far below, the tall man was speeding down the mountain. His smile had nothing to do with the conversation just ended. Skiing this fast on a trail this difficult left no room for other thoughts. He was intent on the terrain ahead, relaxed on his skis, riding the steel edges down the icy slope. Later, he would consider the pudgy man's attempt to threaten him. Later, he would consider the substance of the threat, consider whether his wife really had been cheating on him. Later, he might decide that someone needed to be taught a lesson, a painful lesson. But that would all come later. Right now, skiing had his full attention and he couldn't help smiling, even after a lifetime of this exact pleasure.

Everything else could wait.

2

THE INTERCOM SQUAWKED, GARBLED AS ALWAYS, BUT Jackson got the message. "LJO! Laverne on line three!"

It was code. Jackson was LJO—"Little Jimmy Olson, cub reporter"—and "Laverne on line three" meant Angry Reader in the Front Office. Visits from angry readers were not uncommon at the Aspen Sun. Sometimes they were amusing, sometimes enlightening, sometimes they simply needed to be avoided. Jackson decided this was one of those times. He grabbed a pen and a notepad from the desk, snatched his parka off the hook and headed toward the back door, moving quickly and quietly for someone of his size—he was tall and broad, large but not clumsy. And even as he made his hurried exit, he was glad to know that Stormy, who guarded the front desk at the Sun with unnecessary ferocity, wasn't mad at him any more. She hadn't talked to him in a week, but now she'd given him fair warning, time to slip out the back before the Angry Reader could corner him in his office for a shouting match.

This time of year, the Angry Reader was almost certainly a JHP: Junior Hockey Parent. "If I'm going to get up at two in the morning to drive those kids halfway across the goddamned state, I'm damn well going to see a story in your damn paper!" Perhaps not quite so delicately stated.

Jackson was close to turning 40—old enough that some of the Hockey Parents were his age. He wanted to slap them, just to get their attention, and tell them they needed something better in their lives than fighting to get a story about a kids' hockey game into a small-town newspaper. He was also old enough to refrain from indulging that urge—and old enough to say the hell with pretending he cared about the kids or their hockey games. He didn't have to care. All he had to do was write the stories. Which he did. And, lucky break, he happened to be good at it.

He had taken on the junior hockey beat years ago, as penance for some sin now long forgotten—an assignment blown, a deadline missed. Maybe a heart broken. And, despite his ever-growing seniority, junior hockey had become his forever, along with the usual rag-tag assortment of small-town news beats and, far more important and annoying, whatever the editor decided to throw his way. But the junior hockey was a newsroom tradition: Jackson covered junior hockey. And slipping out the back door when Angry JHPs came in the front was a hallowed part of that tradition. Good entertainment too, as loud voices faded to confused silence and the Angry Parents stood by an empty office, red-faced with rage and no one to take it out on.

Jackson shrugged into his parka as he slipped out into the alley, into the falling snow and gathering dark of the December afternoon.

The snow was falling heavily as he walked across town. Street lights flicked on, even though it was barely four o'clock. He pulled the hood of his parka over his head and marched through the gloom.

He didn't share in that gloom. Not at all. Jackson's nearly forty years hadn't left many scars. He'd been in Aspen a decade and a half, and it seemed that a life of partying and skiing—combined with a job that kept him on his toes—suited him perfectly. Even a brief failed marriage hadn't turned anything sour. No gloom there. That was behind them now, and PJ, his ex-wife, was a great friend. At last.

His hair was a little long, light brown and straight, no gray; his eyes dark and quick. The broken nose he got in college when a pick-up basketball game turned ugly had marred the boyish good looks he'd been so proud of in high school; but over the decades he'd found that crooked nose had added a twist of character that some women found more than merely intriguing. A little blood, a little pain and, after that, years of success in the bars. All in all, a fine trade.

He moved through the snow, balance solid. He'd been an athlete of sorts through high school; not quite a star, he'd relied more on his size and determination than on any real athletic gifts. Football had been his game, but even with a well-padded helmet, he'd never grown fond of being kicked in the head—which, from his experience, seemed to be the defining characteristic of the game. And when it became clear that he was nowhere near talented enough to expect a college scholarship, he'd quit the team and focused his determination on the classroom.

That determination had been rewarded with admission to a college he couldn't afford.

From the outside, his family might have appeared middle-class in its best years, but they were faking it even then, and by the time Jackson graduated from high school his father was years gone and even the appearance of middle-class was as long gone as the old man. Still determined, Jackson had worked nights and weekends and every day of every vacation and somehow he'd scraped through college. He'd even done well enough to get into law school. Which he absolutely couldn't afford.

So he'd hitchhiked the thousand miles back home for the first time in years, to see his mother and ask if there was any way—any wild unexpected way—she could help him out, if only with a view to having a successful son who could help her out in turn. He found the shabby house looking even shabbier than he remembered. And a family of equally shabby strangers living there. They'd never known his mother and had no idea where she might have gone after the bank took the house and tossed her out.

That night he'd gotten drunk with an old high school friend and even though they spent most of the night laughing, it was clear to Jackson that there was no happy ending waiting for him in any story set in that small town. Unlike his friend, he'd been lucky enough not to get his high school girlfriend pregnant during their extended bouts of late-night backseat grappling and he wasn't going to stick around and give bad luck another shot at him.

The next morning he was out on the highway with his thumb in the air. Over the next few years, he found a lot of places and a lot of jobs he didn't like, and then, almost by accident, Aspen. And now, here he was. In a town he loved, with a job he loved.

His biggest regret was that he hadn't started skiing until he found himself in Aspen. Not that that was surprising. He'd been raised in the flattest of flatlands and when he was growing up, the only thing going downhill had been his family.

Anyway, by now he could ski. Well enough. A friend in a bar had once said, more loudly than necessary, "You ski like a football player. Looking for someone to knock down." Still, if not being a better skier was as bad as the regrets got, Jackson could handle it.

OK, sure, he had regrets about his marriage, too. He never had a chance of being a great skier, but maybe he could have been a great husband. Good anyway. And he hadn't been.

And then he stopped thinking about it. No point.

The driving snow stung his face and froze on his eyelashes. He was surrounded by hulking mansions, looming in the dark. The original Victorians of Aspen's West End had been buffed and puffed—inflated to two or three or ten times their original size and renovated to meet the most demanding tastes of the most demanding people on the planet. Old miner's cabins had been restored to a glory they had never known when actual miners lived in them—and, in all that new glory, they were still just the entryways, the mudrooms, for the enormous mansions that loomed above them.

Aspen had been born as a silver-mining town, enjoyed a sudden wild burst of prosperity and then gone bust almost overnight when the silver market crashed in 1893. For decades, Aspen had slumbered, almost a ghost town. Now those old ghosts had been banished by the living dead. There was something eerie in the scene, the dark buildings, the empty streets, the swirling snow.

Jackson grinned. He was dressed for the storm—solid boots, warm parka—so why not take pleasure in the worst that winter could throw at him? It made him feel a little closer to the original Aspen, a rough and tumble silver mining camp a century ago. He knew he was ridiculous, but it got him in the mood for his assignment. He was going to the Aspen Historical Society to look through the back issues of the newspaper from December 1888, exactly a century ago, to find stories for "100 Years Ago Today."

"100 Years Ago" ran on page two of the Sun every day. Brief bits from stories that had run on that same date a century before. Small town news, mining news, gossip, bar fights, arrests in the red light district—whatever caught his attention when he was leafing through the old papers archived at the Historical Society.

Like junior hockey, "100 Years Ago" was Jackson's beat forever. But unlike junior hockey, he loved it.

He'd settle down in the archives and slip into a warm bath of the past, paging through the endless pointless details of life in Aspen back when it was a mining camp with mud streets and delusions of grandeur. Reading the papers, he'd begin to feel he was following the news when it really was news. Hot off the press, day by day. And the news then wasn't really so different from what was going on still: fortunes made and lost, broken hearts and broken noses, big shots and petty crooks. He'd follow their stories from week to week, forgetting that they'd all been dead for most of a century.

A gust of wind swirled the snow around him as Jackson marched up the walk of the over-wrought Victorian mansion that was the home of the Aspen Historical Society. Harkney House had been grand in its day, but that day was long past. Now Old Lady Harkney was showing her age, amid the new painted floozies.

Inside, Maggie at the front desk looked up as Jackson walked in. He nodded to her and she gave him a look—careless and dark, a backhanded slap—that made him wonder what he'd done to earn that. Had he asked her to go home with him when he shouldn't have? It was that kind of a look... but, no, he hadn't. He was certain. He'd made that mistake too often, but never with her. Though he had thought about wandering up to the desk and asking straight out if she happened to share his fantasy about after-hours sex in a darkened library. He'd had that particular fantasy since junior high school. He even remembered the name of the librarian: Miss Brown.

Maybe he'd ask Maggie today. Worst he could get from her was a nasty look and he'd already gotten one—for no reason he could think of. Then he remembered: It had been Maggie's roommate he'd hit on. And he definitely should not have done that. For a lot of reasons. And certainly not at Michael's Bar, where everybody knew both of them. But after a long night at Michael's, mistakes came easy.

Back in the archives, he tossed his notebook on a table and pulled a thick volume off the shelf, two months of newspapers from a hundred years before. The pages were yellowed, but still readable. He opened to late

December 1888 and began reading—though he couldn't keep himself from thinking about a threesome with Maggie and her roommate.

With that on his mind, he naturally assumed the worst when he read a bold-face paragraph about Reverend and Mrs. James Osgood. Jackson was familiar with Reverend Osgood. From time to time he'd pulled out samples of the Reverend's over-heated sermons to run in "100 Years Ago." Mrs. Osgood had mostly kept herself primly and properly out of the news. But now here she was, accompanying her husband on a visit to the newspaper office to chat with the editor, who reported how charmed he was to witness "a blissfully wedded couple so deeply in love." In the course of the visit, both the minister and his wife professed their abiding affection for one another and commented on how happy their marriage was.

Of course it was. That's exactly what happily married couples always do: run downtown to talk about it with a newspaper editor. Jackson was suspicious.

The Osgood Exemplar of Marital Bliss had wafted into the editor's office, arm in loving arm, on a Wednesday. Jackson flipped the pages ahead to the next Monday's paper and saw a note that Reverend Osgood hadn't led the Sunday service. Reverend Duckett had filled in and preached a fiery sermon on the wages of sin.

Jackson smiled. Had to be a story there.

He thought about skipping forward a week or two to see how it all played out. Skipping ahead was against his rules. He liked to let Old Aspen unfold in all its timely glory, week by week, just the way it had happened. What was the hurry? They were all dead now. But this time he couldn't resist. He paged ahead a week and the names leaped off the page: Mrs. Juliet Osgood, wife of the Reverend James Osgood, had left town unexpectedly to see her mother Back East.

There you go.

And under the item about Mrs. Osgood leaving town, there was a subhead, "In other church news" and a paragraph that said, "Amid turmoil, the choir held a special meeting before rehearsal. No refreshments were served." The story gave no further details. But still, "turmoil." And no refreshments. Grim news indeed.

Jackson skipped forward again and found this note: "Miss Ernestina Rose, whose voice has been such a welcome addition to the choir ever since her arrival in town, is leaving to return to her sister's home in Kansas City."

He'd seen that name before, maybe a month ago, in an item he'd pulled out and used in the paper. He flipped back until he found the story.

It was about the ladies of the choir at Rev. Osgood's church—their beautiful voices and their good works and, because sometimes there's space at the bottom of a column that must be filled, a paragraph about the new soprano who had joined the choir. Miss Ernestina Rose. A young woman who had come to town for the funeral of a cousin, killed in the mines. "Entranced by our booming camp," the paper reported, she stayed on, renting a room from Mrs. Bellamy and singing beautifully in the choir. Like an angel. And the women were so glad to have her bright young face join their sewing circle. And she had dinner out every night. And she delighted everyone who met her. And at last the column was filled and the story could end.

OK. The characters were in place: a happily married couple and an angelic young soprano. Jackson jumped ahead again, past Miss Ernestina's sudden departure and found a boxed notice, saying that Rev. Osgood had left to attend to family business and the congregation would be led by Rev. Duckett until further notice.

The wife gone to see her mother. The soprano gone to see her sister. And the man in the middle just gone.

Jackson closed his eyes and smiled. This could be a story. An Old West Melodrama. The Reverend and the Fallen Angel. He liked the sound of that. A story with depth and scope. A picture of the Old West.

He started leafing back through the pages of the old papers. He pulled down another volume. Then another. The Reverend James Eagleton Osgood had come to town three years before the drama broke out. Moved "from Back East" with his wife. Preached the usual Sunday sermons, which the paper reported faithfully every Tuesday. He seemed to prosper. An upstanding citizen. Jackson wondered if he could track the minister to his Back East roots. He was thinking big.

Then Miss Ernestina Rose showed up. Jackson found scattered bright references to her. She seemed to have caught the editor's fancy, as well as the minister's. But the editor had political aspirations and he wasn't about to risk it all on a fling with a soprano. The minister apparently had no such scruples.

Then the lights flicked off and on, twice. Maggie was closing and he hadn't really started on "100 Years Ago." He was going to have to come back on Monday.

On his way to the door, he passed Maggie who was straightening papers on her desk. He thought about his Sex in the Empty Library fantasy and— what the hell—started to ask, "Did you ever…" Then he caught himself and stopped, because he wasn't a complete idiot. But before there was any silence at all, she said, "No. Definitely not."

Whatever Jackson's question might have been, her answer was clear.

3

THE JET DANCED A MULTI-MILLION-DOLLAR BALLET AS
it made its way through the lesser planes on the Aspen tarmac. Anyone,
almost, could come to Aspen, of course. Almost anyone could fly there and a
distressingly large number could fly in their private planes. The real dividing
line was between those who could and those who could not afford a significant plane. Serious hardware. Heavy metal. Big enough to matter. Bigger
than the sad little planes the commercial airlines flew to Aspen, for sure.

Roger Randall Dictu was not a man to settle for less than he could
afford; and it was no small point of pride to him that he could easily afford
a jet that settled him solidly among those who mattered. But even as his
more-than-big-enough jet made its way into the take-off queue, Roger Randall Dictu was not pleased.

The immediate cause of his displeasure was strapped into a seat too close
to Roger Randall, chattering away too nervously. The source of this annoyance's nervousness was irrelevant. Fear of flying, fear of his host or the
general fear of life that one would expect from such a sad person—Roger
Randall didn't care. The little man was clearly verminous. Was that a real
word? Roger Randall decided it must be. It described too many people far
too well. How could such a useful word not exist? Verminous, yes. The man
was verminous and the best that could be hoped for was that he would shut
up, so he could be ignored.

This... creature... had been imposed upon Roger Randall by his wife.
Marybelle Dictu was an enthusiastic participant in the social whirl of
Aspen's non-profit organizations and she had insisted that Roger Randall
provide a free ride back to New York for "her" executive director, a man
with the unlikely name—no, the impossible name—of Saxby DuPont.

It had been a singularly unwelcome request. Unwelcome because Roger Randall (as he insisted everyone address him, even his wife, even in their most intimate moments) hated sharing his jet. He loved to luxuriate in the cabin that could easily hold more than a dozen, but was, by his choice, reserved for himself alone. And when he did share his plane, he did so only with those he considered to be of his status—people who would not actually need to ride in his plane because they had planes of their own.

But most of all, Roger Randall was raging over an attempt to blackmail him, just the day before, when a different verminous (definitely a word) cretin had interrupted his skiing and threatened to reveal that Marybelle Dictu was having an affair.

Roger Randall's unhappiness over that incident was not relieved by the fact that he had slapped the suggestion down with a reference to the toad's own slut of a wife. Nor had he been much cheered when he learned that the toad had finished his trip down the mountain on a ski patrol tobog-gan. Emergency surgery followed. That counted as a satisfactory result, but nothing could touch Roger Randall's seething rage at the thought that his wife, Marybelle Dictu, could be even suspected of having an affair. If she wanted to have an affair that was her business. But for her to be careless was unthinkable. And to have that toad dare to approach him on the mountain to demand that Roger Randall withdraw his black-ball at the Metropolitan Club and then, when that demand was quite rightly scorned, to have the toad threaten to expose Marybelle's "adulterous indiscretions"… well, that was outrageous.

And outrage was something Roger Randall Dictu was very good at.

His rage was large. There was rage for his wife, for her supposed lover, for the would-be blackmailer. And still more than enough rage to encom-pass this latest imposition, this Saxby DuPont, this fake human being with a fake cleft in his fake chin, breathing air that Roger Randall was paying for as the jet angled into the sky.

And now the worm was unbuckling his seat belt, crossing the cabin and settling into the seat next to Roger Randall himself. This was intolerable.

"Roger," he said. "First of all, thanks again for the ride."

The silence that greeted this remark stretched out as Roger Randall pondered whether to correct the unwanted guest's grievous sin of addressing him as "Roger," without the required "Randall," or to allow him to continue in the error and so dig himself an even deeper hole. The excrescence pushed ahead.

"So, Roger, I thought I would take advantage of our time together to discuss an opportunity that might well have some benefits for you. Significant financial benefits."

Roger Randall greeted this with continued silence. He let the words buzz by while he studied the sweaty face, the obvious plastic surgery.

Meanwhile, Saxby DuPont was convinced he was on a roll. Painting a glorious picture of the future and certainly never looking back. Not for an instant. He knew the past was right there, right behind him. But if he never looked back, he never had to see it. And neither did anyone else.

Certainly no one needed to know anything about the past—about his past. Most particularly, no one needed to know there had ever been a person named Arnold Firkin. And no one needed to know about the frenzied scrambling that had led that person up from the outer reaches of the Borough of Queens to his present position as executive director of the Aspen Historical Society. He never discussed his personal history. Indeed, he would have denied all of it under oath. Denied he had ever so much as visited Queens, ever known anyone who lived there, ever lain awake at night and cried about schoolyard jeers of "Firkin the Gherkin." He had considered legally changing his name, leaving all things "Firkin" completely behind. But then he'd decided, no, he would be known as Saxby DuPont—"Not one of *those* DuPonts," he would modestly insist—but legally he would remain Arnold Firkin, as a reminder of what he'd overcome and what was always lurking, eager to swallow him again, to suck him down into the depths. Besides, the name-change paperwork was daunting.

But other than his name, he left his past behind and he would have denied it all so fervently and meant that denial so deeply that he could have easily passed a lie detector test. And for some episodes in his past, a lie detector test might have been appropriate. That upward scramble had not been pretty or painless—for him or, most of all, for anyone who got in his way. Scrabbling claws can leave scars.

But Saxby DuPont's reticence about his past was irrelevant. Roger Randall Dictu knew it all anyway, had known it instinctively from the moment he laid eyes on the man. He reeked of desperation. And Queens.

Roger Randall focused on the little man's eyebrows, which twitched from the vigor of his sales pitch. Caterpillars in orgasm, thought Roger Randall Dictu. He was amused at his own cleverness.

Without listening, Roger Randall knew that he was being hustled. He liked that. He liked being lied to. It gave him wonderful freedom when responding.

DuPont held a finger in the air. He was going to make an important point.

"Now, Roger, I will have to insist that everything we discuss here must remain completely confidential."

Roger Randall cut him off. "You are on my plane. As my guest. I will respect the obligations of hospitality." DuPont began to shape up a smile in response, but Roger Randall kept going. "Of course, you are only here because you have asked for a free ride across the country, so you are absolutely not in any position to 'insist' on anything." There was a brief silence as the half-formed smile died. "But, please, do continue."

DuPont stumbled. He'd lost his place.

Roger Randall watched the little man struggling, trying to get back on track, mustering the courage for some particularly outrageous lie. He stared the weasel right in the eye, daring him to go ahead and tell that lie. Not that he cared; it was just what he did.

The noises began again. And suddenly, although his face did not betray the slightest hint of interest, Roger Randall was paying attention. The intruder was discussing the Historical Society, its grotesque Victorian museum in the West End and his plans for a new museum of some sort— and he needed just the right...

Roger Randall held up his hand, invoking silence. DuPont stopped, reluctantly; he had so much more to say. Roger Randall stood and strode to the front of the plane, opened the cabin door and bent over to talk to the pilot. A few moments later, the plane banked sharply and began to descend. Roger Randall strapped himself into a seat at the front of the cabin, his back to his suddenly nervous passenger.

"What's happening?" asked DuPont.

"We will be landing a matter of minutes. You will be getting off."

"Where?" DuPont voice was almost a squeak. He couldn't see—nor would he have been encouraged if he could—the smile on Roger Randall Dictu's face.

"I'm sure they'll tell you once you're there."

ROGER RANDALL DICTU breathed a sigh of pure pleasure. Getting rid of that creature was an excellent way to open negotiations. But even more than that, he was delighted to have his plane to himself again. He had some serious planning to do.

He had two separate battles ahead in this complicated campaign he was waging and now he could see the clear path to victory on both fronts laid out in front of him.

One part had been clear for some time and his thoughts touched on it briefly, pausing in amused satisfaction at the image of himself—Roger Randall Dictu—as David on his way to battle Goliath: David—in no way an underdog, simply a hero not yet revealed—picking up random stones from the fields, trusting his instincts to find exactly the right one, the perfect size and shape and weight to slay a giant.

Roger Randall had invested time and money on one particular obscure stone long before the true worth—its weight and sharp edges—became clear. But now it was going to pay off.

He nodded, smiled. It was bulletproof.

Then his mind skipped ahead to the second front in his campaign, where, astonishingly, the so recently and delightfully departed excrescence actually had sparked an idea that would be of significant benefit. Sometimes an investment of a mere million or two could tip a hundred-million-dollar deal the right way and Roger Randall Dictu had an exquisite sense of leverage, coupled with a predator's feral wisdom.

Roger Randall smiled wolfishly. He really loved this game.

He indulged in a moment imagining that absurd creature, DuPont, desperately trying to find his way home from wherever the hell it was in the middle of nowhere that they had shooed him off the plane.

A great way indeed to open negotiations.

And he could see his strategy, already complete in his mind, rolling out smoothly: clear, simple, inevitable. Some government fool thought a thousand acres of wolf habitat wasn't valuable enough? Fine. He'd throw in a museum.

Perfect!

Who could resist a museum?

He allowed himself a brief smile. Then he put that aside and focused. He had work to do. He had to review the speech he was going to give tonight— just a brief speech, a few words humbly acknowledging the Humanitarian of the Year Award he was going to be so deeply honored to receive. It was an easy speech to write and even easier to give. Roger Randall Dictu could be brilliantly humble

4

"JACKSON, GET YOUR BUTT IN HERE."

Great. Jackson slouched into the editor's office. He knew what was coming. Fester needed to yell and Jackson needed to listen. He didn't need to pretend to care. Under other circumstances, when professionally appropriate, he could pretend to care quite convincingly—pretending to care is a necessary skill for a reporter—but here and now in Fester's office they both knew exactly what was going on. Jackson had heard Fester's phone conversation and Fester knew he'd heard it. No secrets in the newsroom.

"Where's the goddamn story about the goddamn hockey game?"

"Right where it belongs. Nowhere."

"You trying to get us all canned?" Fester liked to talk as if he was a tough guy from an old movie. He wasn't tough enough to pull it off, but Jackson liked him for trying.

"Come on, Felster." He was careful to pronounce the "L" very clearly. Tall, skinny, bald, with a permanent squint from trying to look tough, Jacob Felster knew everyone called him Fester, but dropping the "L" in his presence was considered bad form. "No one's going to get fired over a junior hockey game that no one cares about."

"Jackson, you take all the goddamn fun out of this job." Fester lowered his voice. "Prince Hal's chewing my ass." Hal Feasance was the assistant publisher and executive editor—meaningless titles for the half-bright son of King Harold, owner, publisher, real boss, and, as he liked to tell everyone, getting way too old for this business. "He says Dictu's threatening to start his own newspaper if we don't do a better job of covering junior goddamn hockey. Apparently some of his friends are upset that their precious children's athletic triumphs are not appearing frequently enough in our newspaper."

"Bullshit. Rich guys don't throw away money. That's why they're rich. Hal knows that. He's just too chickenshit to stand up to the rich fucks." Fester winced, but Jackson kept going. "Fucking R2 Dictu's not going to waste any of his millions just to screw with us."

Fester's lip twitched. In the normal course of arguments, this would have been the time for him to lecture Jackson on the R2 Dictu issue. Roger Randall Dictu was known in the newsroom as R2 Dictu, in honor of R2D2, the "Star Wars" robot. There was an informal competition at the paper to see who could slip a Star Wars reference or the word "robot" into a Dictu story. Jackson was the all-time leader, by a wide margin.

Fester lived in deep—and quite reasonable—fear that Dictu would catch on and wreak some horrible vengeance. Putting an end to the R2 Dictu game was a priority, but right now he needed to keep the conversation focused on junior hockey.

"I agree that Mr. Dictu"—a touch of formality to counter Jackson's disrespect—"does not want to spend his money starting a new paper. I'm certain he realizes it would be cheaper to hire someone to kill you. And dispose of your corpse in the foundation of his next shopping center. I believe he's building one in Florida right now."

"Florida's nice this time of year. A little warm weather might be just what I need."

"Your choice. In the meantime, you will be writing more junior hockey stories. Starting immediately."

Jackson nodded. Writing stories was his job after all. Fair enough. He'd been yelled at, cursed at and threatened with violent death. That ought to be penance enough to cover the sin of skipping a hockey game for nine-year-olds. It was time to move on.

"I've got a great story idea."

"If it's not junior hockey, I'm not interested."

Jackson ignored that and launched into a pitch for The Minister and the Fallen Angel, a real-life Old Aspen Wild West Soap Opera, complete with Hot Passion and Burning Disgrace. He'd been thinking about it ever since he stumbled over the story in the Historical Society archives and now he sketched out a multi-part series: a respected minister, a solid marriage, the beautiful soprano, the temptation, the fall, the disgrace. It would take a lot of research, but he could do it.

Fester leaned in close, stared into Jackson's eyes. "You will write stories about junior hockey. We will print stories about junior hockey that you have written."

"Let the goddamn parents write the stories."

"We will print professionally written stories that have been written by a professional reporter who works for this newspaper. And that professional reporter is you. Clear enough?"

"OK, how about this?" Jackson knew he'd lost, so what the hell. "Suppose I weave the hockey stories into my soap opera? You know, the minister battles his demons by taking a long walk, stops to watch some kids play hockey on a frozen pond. I'll use the kids' real names so the parents can still clip it out and put it in their scrapbooks. Great idea, right?"

"Go cover a hockey game. Write a story about it."

"No games tonight." That could have been true.

"Then write about a practice. Nice tight, bright feature, five hundred words. For Monday. I'll put it in the budget."

Game over. You can't refuse an editor's direct assignment. Asshole.

Fester leaned back in his chair.

"Take Beast with you to get pictures. I'll put you down to lead off the front with a photo." He smiled. Then he added, "Good job on the Johanssen obit."

That was Fester's way of apologizing for being a jerk. It wasn't much of an apology, but it was as good as Jackson was going to get. And he had done a good job on the obit. Gustav Johanssen had been the last surviving member of the three-man crew that had cut some of the first ski trails on Aspen Mountain. The other two men from that crew had died a few months before, within a week of each other. The two of them dying so close together after all those years had been a good story: two men born in Aspen just after the mining boom went bust, sticking around into the new era and playing a part bringing skiing to the town. Working on that story, Jackson had picked up a lot of good details, so he'd gone back to his notes when Johanssen had died and put together a solid story about the End of an Era. Everyone likes

End of an Era stories—and this was a good one. Someone else's misfortune is a reporter's chance to shine. Even a misfortune as commonplace as dying.

Jack the Jackal, he thought. That's me.

WALKING ACROSS TOWN to the ice rink, he tried to tell Beast about the Minister and the Fallen Angel.

"Come on, Beastie. You gotta love it. A Sweet Young Thing comes to town. A Tasty Tidbit. Joins the choir. Falls for the preacher. Hot and heavy—but he's married. They get caught. It turns ugly. Great stuff."

Beast wasn't interested. He hitched his camera bag higher on his shoulder and kicked at a clump of snow. "Screw that. It's Friday night. I was on my way to get a burger. I need to have something solid in my stomach before I start drinking for the weekend. You know that. Anybody knows that. But now I'm going to this thing… this hockey thing. Freeze my ass. Freeze my camera. Surrounded by kids. You know I fucking hate kids. And now I won't get a chance to eat before it's too late and I'll have to start drinking without any dinner. And when I start a weekend that way it never works out well. You know that. Remember when…"

Jackson didn't bother to join the conversation. Beast didn't need or want any help.

Beast was a hometown boy, born in Aspen, the unintended son of one of the hottest women in town. She was a ski instructor in the winter, white-water guide in the summer, always ready to party and most definitely not ready to have a son. But she did—accidents happen—and she wasn't the kind to back off from any challenge that came her way on the mountain, on the river, in bed or anywhere else. So she did her best to be a mother until Beast was old enough to be sent away to school. Then she persuaded the most likely candidate for fatherhood that sending the boy to boarding school back East was in everyone's best interest. That lasted a few difficult years and then Beast was back, understanding that his mother loved him, but he was on his own. And even more so a year after that, when she got caught in an avalanche heli-skiing in the Buga-boos. They say she almost outran it.

After that, Beast lived with friends whose parents felt sorry for him, moving every couple of months when beastliness outweighed pity. That went on until he turned 17 and got his own room in an apartment he shared with five ski patrolmen. One of the patrolmen had a camera and Beast borrowed it one day when he was bored. From that moment on, his life's course was settled.

He got his job at the paper when he was 18. He'd been hanging around the office a year before that anyway. That was more than a decade ago and despite everything he was still living like any other young ski bum who'd just bounced into town—partying hard, never planning more than his next meal, his next drink, his next joint. And he loved it. He was thirty now, but he still looked the same as he ever had: long arms, a sham-bling gait, eyes that were bright when you got a glimpse of them through the frizzy black hair that drooped in a curtain across his face, a look he'd adopted as a teenager to keep people from staring, trying to guess which local stud was his father. It gave Beast his characteristic gesture: tossing his head so his hair flipped back, just for an instant, as he slapped his camera up to his eye. And it gave him a wild-child look that a surprising number of women found irresistible.

Jackson had figured Beast might like the Fallen Angel story. Local color and all. But Beast's Aspen didn't extend back any further than tales of his mom in the late '50s. Jackson let him rant.

When they got to the rink, Beast stopped complaining and got to work, immediately serious, completely professional. Jackson talked to the coach, who gave him a hard look and said, "About goddamn time." That didn't help. But, like Beast, he focused on the job. It wasn't the kids' fault that their parents were jerks. And as long as he had to write the story and put his name on it, he might as well do his best.

JACKSON AND THE BEAST marched up Aspen Street to the bottom of Lift 1-A, snow shovels over their shoulders. The hockey practice was over and, when neither of them felt like plunging straight into Michael's Bar, Beast had led the way, stopping to grab the shovels from a condominium complex at the bottom of the hill.

At the chairlift, they cut across the slope and headed uphill, along the trees at the edge of Norway Slope, a steep run with big bumps and more than a few rocks sticking out through the snow.

Halfway up, prudence and stupidity reached a perfect balance and they stopped.

"Like this," Beast said, sitting on the blade of the snow shovel, the hickory handle sticking out between his legs. He grabbed the handle and raised his feet high off the snow. In an instant, he was sliding down the run, riding the shovel like a toboggan, laughing wildly, careening off the bumps, until one huge bump shot him into the air. The shovel flew one way, Beast another. He landed hard and then lay there, motionless, for way too long, while Jackson leaned on his shovel, stared downhill and wondered why he wasn't more careful when it came to choosing his friends.

Beast still wasn't moving and Jackson wondered if this, finally, was the time when he was going to have to haul Beast—unconscious or worse—to the hospital. And he thought, as he often did, about the time Beast had saved his life. The story was simple enough: Backcountry skiing, over-confident or unlucky, Jackson had been caught in an avalanche. Not a big slide, but big enough to carry him a hundred feet down the hill and leave him buried, one arm trapped below him, the other thrust upward, immobile, hopeless. There was a tiny air pocket around his face, but he was already beginning to lose consciousness when he felt—miracle? hallucination?—a hand grasping his. Then he must have passed out.

The next thing he knew, he was waking up and Beast was kissing him. No, Beast was breathing him back to life. He coughed and Beast pulled back. He started to say something, but Beast put a hand over his mouth and whispered, "Still sketchy. Rest of it's just waiting to break loose." Beast dug quickly but smoothly with the small folding shovel he always carried into the backcountry for exactly this purpose. When most of the snow was cleared away, Beast made sure Jackson could move his hands and feet, whispered, "Lucky motherfucker," and pulled him out of the hole where he should have died. He dragged Jackson into the safety of the trees and said, "I ought to make you walk down, you clumsy fuck." Jackson's skis were long gone, buried somewhere above them. He never did find them. Beast pulled off his own parka, wrapped Jackson in it and skied down for help.

Jackson spent a cold couple of hours, staring up the hill at the chute Beast had skied down to save him. A huge cornice was indeed just waiting to break loose and, not long after Beast left, it did exactly that, thundering down the mountain, sweeping everything away. Stupid as Jackson might have been to get caught, Beast had been twice as stupid to ski down the heart of the chute and rescue him. There might have been a safer way, but it wouldn't have gotten him to Jackson in time. Later on, Jackson had tried to thank him—as if there could be words to express that kind of thanks—but Beast just hugged Jackson tight, one time, and said, "Forget it, amigo. Next time I'll let you dig your own way out."

And now, below him in the night, Beast leaped to his feet, covered in snow, let out a whoop and shouted, "That was incredible! Come on!"

The only way out was down and the only way down—with any shred of pride—was sitting on the shovel. Besides, saying no to the Beast was not allowed. Not now, not ever. How could he say no to that much crazy enthusiasm, that much wild spirit? How do you say no to your best friend? So down he went.

And, as it turned out, Beast was exactly right. It was incredible.

And, as they discovered on the next run, even more incredible if you started much higher on the slope.

THE VIEW OVER ASPEN from Red Mountain was stunning: the lights of town cupped in the palm of the valley, an icy slash of moonlight gleaming across the ski runs and, above, the infinite black sky. Some would argue that the spectacular view was part of the reason for the equally spectacular cost of a Red Mountain house—and yet, tonight, very few of the guests seemed to appreciate the view. Not for its beauty anyway. Those who noticed there was a view seemed impressed only by its value. "Worth every dollar he paid for it."

But most were too busy—talking, hustling, eating, drinking—to even glance out the windows that stretched from the Brazilian hardwood floors to the hand-hewn beams thirty feet above. One young woman did stand by the glass, staring out at the night—but her appreciation for the view was also open to question. Her name was Jennifer, though she might have had a hard time coming up with it in a hurry if she'd been asked. She was unsteady on her feet and, with no one nearby, chattered and giggled to herself. A waiter cruised past with a tray of champagne flutes filled with Roederer Cristal. The young woman reached for a glass, teetering at the edge of her balance. The waiter swerved smoothly, keeping the tray out of her reach while steadying her with his free hand.

"Easy, darling," he said with cheerful familiarity. "You're losing it."

"Fuck you on toast," might have been her reply. She was slurring so badly it was impossible to tell what she was trying to say. Or what she might have meant.

The waiter set down the tray and took her arm. "My dear," he said as he led her away, "I think you need a bump." He tapped the side of his nose and raised an eyebrow. She followed him without an instant's hesitation.

Five minutes later, when they walked back into the room, they laughed together like old friends. He swept up the tray of champagne and resumed his rounds with new snap to his step. She rubbed her nose, semi-discreetly, sniffed once, crisply, and marched across the room, bright-eyed, ready to plunge into the ocean of chatter.

"So I got it for half of..."

"They said she had no idea what..."

"Well, if she's sleeping with him, then who's he..."

The conversations swirled.

"We had lunch at the club, but by the time we finished I was too high to even..."

"I was waiting for them to call, but Paris is eight...

"He couldn't do anything about the ligament or the cartilage, so they just replaced the whole..."

She spun around and crossed the room again. Looking for her chance.

"So I bought it."

"So I took it."

"So I said the hell with it."

She charged at the billows of conversation, brimming with things to say: keen observations, interested questions. But there never seemed to be a gap in the chat. And when she sensed a moment and tried to jump in, her mouth was dry and her lips stuck to her teeth and nothing came out, except a tiny squawk that no one heard—or acknowledged. And eventually she was back at the window. Talking to herself.

Few if any of the guests noticed that their host, their great good friend, Roger Randall Dictu, had left the party early. Few knew him well enough to know that this was not where he lived. He kept this house for entertaining only. His actual home, in Aspen's West End, was more tasteful, more comfortable and much more private. He certainly was not about to share it with this assemblage—most of whom smugly considered themselves close friends and honored guests.

On his way to the door, Roger Randall had stopped to talk briefly with the woman in charge of the bar. Her hair was an untamed mop of black curls, her eyes dark blue. She had an unlikely splash of freckles across the bridge of her nose. He gave her quick instructions: Stop pouring the Cristal and switch to the Moët, the White Star. No more Chivas. Just Johnnie Walker. Red. And shut the bar down by 10. They can drink on their own after that. He finished with a crisp, "I'm sure you can handle everything without any problems." He paused for a moment. "As always." Another pause. "Am I correct?" Something in her look said, yes, he was correct. He slipped her a hundred-dollar bill, as crisp as his voice, and she raised an eyebrow in appreciation.

And, as the front door closed behind him, his wife, Marybelle Dictu, stopped to talk to the same bartender, issuing her own orders. As long as Marybelle was there, Cristal and Chivas would be poured. And the bar would stay open. And, again, the bartender nodded that she understood.

But this time there was no unspoken communication. And no hundred-dollar bill.

By midnight, Marybelle was long gone, as were most of the guests. The babbling blonde was still staring out the window, chattering on. Eventually, the waiter, her new best pal, came by, with his parka on and hers over his arm.

"Come on, sweetheart. I think it's time to leave."

As she tried to walk, she almost fell, so he guided her on a quick detour through a back room. When they emerged, she was bright-eyed and eager again. Still unsteady, but ready for anything.

On the way to the door, he nodded to the bartender with the wild curls. "Night, Peej."

She looked up, gave him a brief narrow-eyed nod in return and then shot a longer look at the woman by his side. The blonde gave a sloppy, happy smile in return and the bartender murmured "Jennifer!" under her breath and went back to cleaning up for the night as the happy couple headed for the door.

THE PHONE had to ring a dozen times before Jackson opened his eyes. It had taken a lot of tequila to fight off the dangerous chill he and Beast had been facing after their snow-shovel runs down Norway Slope—you can't be too careful when you're dealing with the dreaded chill.

Once he was awake, Jackson let it ring few more times before he dragged himself out of his warm bed and stumbled across the cold room to dig the phone out from under a pile of clothes.

And for all that, what he got was a voice he didn't recognize, slurred by alcohol or, more likely—Jackson was a bit of a connoisseur in these matters—a heavy dose of painkillers.

"Gotta keep eye on Dickhead. Roger. Randall. Dickhead."—the voice fought for that desperate precision that only the truly twisted could think sounds sober—"Up to something. Fucker gets away with ev'thing. Gotta get 'im."

The voice paused. An answer was called for.

In general, Jackson agreed with every slurred word and he responded like the dedicated hard-working reporter he was, the way he always handled anonymous late-night hot tips. He hung up and crawled back to bed.

WHEN JENNIFER WOKE, it was dark. She had no idea where she was. Her mouth tasted like bad choices. She was naked and she wasn't certain who the man in bed with her was. His name was… She'd remember in a minute. A party. Red Mountain. A waiter with a tray of champagne and a vial of cocaine. She stared at the man next to her. Must be him. And his name… No idea. No matter.

Her hangover was already thumping, but she managed a smile—a small one, but a smile nonetheless. Just a brief moment to celebrate waking up on another day. Whatever it might bring.

She'd been here before. Not here in this room, but here in a strange bed, with a strange man and a nasty hangover. Familiar territory. All she wanted to do was find her clothes and leave. And once she was out the door and in the street, she'd figure out the rest.

Her party dress—a flimsy, flashy thing—was crumpled on the floor beside the bed, along with the rest of her clothes. Her parka was on a chair across the room and—now a real smile—she could see the strap of her purse sticking out from beneath the parka. The purse was much too bulky to be elegant, because it was large enough to hold clean underwear, a pair of jeans and a sweatshirt. Waking up in a strange place is bad enough—if in fact it's really bad at all—but however you feel about waking up strange, it's great to have a change of clothes. Walking home in the morning in your party dress with your butt hanging out is a drag.

She slipped out of bed and got dressed quickly. She didn't worry too much about making a little noise. She was pretty certain the guy in bed—she gave him a glance, not bad looking, that was nice—was just as eager for her to be somewhere else as she was. He snored and she smiled again; he was faking it.

On her way across the room, she glanced at a stack of mail and saw his name: Derek. It didn't sound familiar. Not that it mattered. He'd called her Suzy all night long, and she hadn't bothered to correct him. Suzy, Jennifer. What difference did it make? He didn't care and neither did she.

Then she was out the door, closing it quietly behind her. No harm, no foul, and she was on her way home.

5

WHEN JACKSON WALKED INTO THE NEWSPAPER OFFICE,
Stormy was vigorously insulting a customer who had the nerve to ask for a
back-issue of the paper. Her glare was a stiletto, her voice the steely edge of
the blade. It was weeks after Christmas and she was wearing a Santa Claus
hat, which only added to the menace.

"October?" Utter disbelief. "Two months ago?" Such behavior could not
be tolerated.

The customer looked prosperous, well-groomed, decent enough. His
expression was stuck halfway between bewilderment and anger, with an
edge of shame. It was a look that Stormy often evoked.

"Well, I thought..." he managed, but that was as far as he got.

"You thought?" she snapped. "Whatever you might have done, you most
certainly did not 'think'!" Freezing him with a glare, she turned to Jackson
and said, quite pleasantly, "Double-L alert." Then she turned back to her
victim.

Jackson hurried on into the depths of the building. Stormy's tirades
were never pleasant. Besides, as she had just alerted him, he had someone
waiting in his office: Double-L.

Double-L stood for "Loony Lars." No one called him that except
Stormy. It was her secret code name. Stormy loved secret codes. And, as
promised Double-L was sitting in Jackson's office. Looking like a pioneer,
smelling like a snowmobile.

And Jackson was glad to see him.

His real name was Gunnar Magnusson, but Loony Lars was a perfect
fit. He was far from young and far from big, but he had the wiry strength
that a small man can have at any age and his short bowed legs gave him the

cocky walk of a man a quarter his years. His face had weathered to an age-less leather, with a little red in the cheeks when the temperature went below zero. His eyebrows were crags and the eyes under them were busy, darting, checking everything. And then there were his ears. Unremarkable, except for being several sizes too big. "Create their own weather," Gunnar liked to say and Jackson had once put it in a story. And all of it topped—today as every day from Halloween to the First of May—by a green ski cap with a white snowflake design and a long red tassel. Gunnar would tell anybody who'd listen that the cap had come down to him through the generations from his Swedish great-great-grandwhatever. But in fact he had snatched it out of the donation box in the alley behind the Thrift Shop, one spring evening—just moments after a woman in a Mercedes had dropped it off, stuffed in a box with a half-dozen cashmere sweaters. Gunnar didn't care about cashmere, but he knew he and that hat were meant for each other.

He was the son of a son of a son of an Aspen miner. From a family that had never gotten anywhere despite generations in a town that had twice exploded into wealth. When the mines were booming, the Magnussons never hit pay dirt. When the mines closed and you could have bought a square block of downtown Aspen for a hundred bucks, Gunnar's grandfather could barely scratch together ten. And, later, when you could still buy a Victorian in the West End for a couple thousand, the Magnussons couldn't dream bigger than a couple hundred. And now it had come down to Gunnar, end of the line, living in a cabin on a mining claim on the back of Aspen Mountain, well past 70 and needing a snowmobile to get to his home seven months of the year.

None of that bothered Gunnar at all. He was proud of his hard-luck family history. He loved those snowmobile trips to his tiny cabin. And if he was a little bit crazy—maybe more than a little bit—that wasn't unusual for anyone living alone in a cabin. Was it living alone in the mountains that made people crazy? Or being crazy that made people live alone? Either way, Loony Lars was a good name. Stormy's nicknames were cruel and percep-tive in equal measure.

Gunnar had a paranoid streak and he lived looking over his shoulder to see who was lurking in the shadows. But he balanced his obsessive secrecy with a human need for friendship, someone to talk to when he came off the mountain. And for reasons that were never clear, he had focused on Jackson as his link to humanity. Tag, you're it!

It was part of Jackson's job to listen if someone had a good story, and Gunnar's stories were always good, usually a little strange and, often enough, bewildering, filled with secrets and word games, puzzles inside riddles, and Gunnar always challenging, daring, insisting that the puzzles had to be solved. Jackson liked the challenges, even when he had to shrug and surrender to Gunnar's laughter. "Too bad, college boy!"

The two men had developed a real, if odd, friendship—spending more than a few summer nights sitting and drinking on the porch of Gunnar's cabin. The cabin had been built in a hurry a century before by a miner more interested in finding his fortune than in careful construction of a home, but Gunnar had lived there long enough to turn it into a sturdy shelter. Inside, the walls were lined—floor to ceiling, virtually every inch that wasn't windows or doors—with books. Thousands of books. Gunnar swore they were just for insulation, but he could walk to the shelves without hesitation and pick out exactly the book he needed to support his point in an argument. And he loved to argue.

On one of those late nights, Gunnar had confided the tale of a girl he'd loved who had broken his heart. For a moment, Jackson thought the old coot was going to cry—but then, as if realizing he'd gone too far, Gunnar had twisted the story into a tale of how that young girl's older brother had plotted to murder him in an abandoned mine and run his body through the lixiviation mill. Jackson was drunk enough to scoff.

"That's just another damn Gunnar story."

Gunnar had made a noise that could have been an imitation of a wounded elk and walked unsteadily across the porch to wrap Jackson in a fierce hug.

"You're like a son to me, boy." And before Jackson could even consider an answer for that, the old coot added, "The son I never wanted."

He cackled and wandered back inside to get another drink.

But today there was fear in his voice.

"Why did you put him in the paper? You think they're not paying attention? They killed the others. Now they're going to kill me."

It sounded like another one of Gunnar's Mystery Tales. Jackson was ready to laugh it off, but something really was wrong.

"What are you talking about?"

The words came tumbling out.

"I'm talking about Reverend Son of a Bitch. You put him in the paper. Happy marriage my ass!"

So now he understood at least one shred of what Gunnar was talking about. The Reverend and Mrs. Osgood's visit to the editor to brag about their wedded bliss had been in the paper that morning. When Fester wouldn't let him chase down the whole story, Jackson had given up and put it in "100 Years Ago Today"—ignoring the fact that by now the date was off by weeks. Can't let trivial facts interfere with a good story. Especially one that's a century old.

But by the time he got that clear in his mind, he'd missed something else, because Gunnar kept going. And now he was talking about things that didn't have anything to do with Reverend Osgood.

"…so proud of themselves. First Trail Crew. Fine. To hell with them. I had another job. I just went up to help them out when I had time. But I was there the day they found it. I know what happened."

Jackson tried to break in and start to untangle the story, but then Fester shouted, "Damn it, Jackson! What part of deadline don't you understand?" It was one of the editor's favorite lines and Jackson had never figured out an answer to it. Probably because there wasn't one. Fester wasn't waiting for an answer in any case, "I need that goddamn school board story and I need it half an hour ago."

"Gunnar. Maybe later. I have to …" But the old man was already stomping away, leaving a scent of rage and snowmobile oil in his wake.

"SCHOOL BOARD'S FILED—and I've got a lead on a great story, boss."

Fester hardly bothered to look up.

"If it's not junior hockey..."

"Come on, I'm serious. Word is Dictu's working on something big. I've got a great source." Just the slurred midnight caller, but Fester didn't need to know that. "If you give me some time, I can catch R2 Dictu with his pants down."

It was pure sport. Staying in the game. Paying Fester back for the junior hockey assignments. But part of the game was knowing when it was time to stop. Which was right now. The look on Fester's face was pure Elmer Fudd, ready to explode after Bugs Bunny tied his shotgun in knots, stole his pants, and locked him outside in the middle of a blizzard. Jackson had to get out of earshot before he burst out laughing.

Now he had to get busy and find a real story or Fester really would explode—and unlike Bugs and Elmer, Jackson wouldn't be able to just slap a Band-Aid on it and blow his editor back up like a party balloon.

ROGER RANDALL DICTU set aside the thick sheaf of legal papers and the two maps—one very old, one quite new, each with a small area out-lined in red ink. It was all exactly right. Perfect. He straightened the edges of the stack of papers. All squared away.

Yes, one player still puzzled him and Roger Randall didn't care for mys-teries; but he had done what he had to and everything was under control.

6

JUST ANOTHER NIGHT AT MICHAEL'S. THE FAMOUS novelist was in his place at the end of the bar, knocking back shots with a carpenter, a network news anchor and a large-breasted woman a third his age. A ski instructor and a real estate salesman—he handsome, tanned and successful; she blindingly blonde, tanned and beautiful—carried on an awkward conversation, neither certain of the other's name, both trying to remember if they'd ever spent a night together. They had.

And all around them, people swirled, stopped, cruised and eddied. The noise rose and fell—waves in the ocean of another damn good time. Drinks were bought, promises made and lies told, as conversations drifted up to the ceiling through clouds of perfume and sweat. And everyone knew that right here, right now, was exactly the right place to be. And they were all right there.

Jackson was hunkered down on a bar stool. A few nights ago, PJ had been filling in behind the bar. He'd wanted to talk to her, but she'd spent the evening flirting outrageously with Gunnar, and Jackson couldn't get a word in. She was too busy buying the old coot drinks while he ranted about a lost mine. Worth millions! Eventually, Jackson had given up and gone home. Tonight, PJ wasn't there and Jackson was drinking alone.

The bartender was depressed because his girlfriend had dumped him, so Jackson tried to cheer him up with a story from municipal court about a man who had been arrested for disturbing the peace on Halloween. That wasn't easy to do in Aspen, but this guy had been running stark naked through the heart of downtown in the middle of the year's first snowstorm, cradling a bright blue hundred-pound tank of nitrous oxide in his arms, screaming about werewolves. There was, in fact, a pack of werewolves—and vampires and ghouls and mummies wrapped in bloody gauze—on his heels, but they weren't naked, so they got to go back to the party, while Tank Man spent the rest of Halloween in jail. Jackson loved that story. Especially the way it had ended, just that week, when Tank Man came back to town from California to be sentenced to time served and take a bow as the entire courtroom stood and cheered.

The bartender didn't crack a smile. His heart really was broken.

Just then, someone grabbed Jackson's arm. "You hear about Gunnar?"

HOSPITALS ALL SMELL the same. A mix of antiseptic, tears, fear and guilt.

The man in the bed was snoring loudly, his head swathed in bandages, his right arm in a bright pink fiberglass cast. Jackson decided that this would be a reasonable time to turn around and go home. He'd been there and now he could leave without disturbing the patient—and without having to endure whatever hell Gunnar would undoubtedly unleash if he were awake.

But before he could turn and head for safety, a nurse brushed past him, with a cheery, "Gunnar! Time to take your temperature!"

The figure in the bed began to grumble, but the nurse popped a thermometer into his mouth which shut him up immediately. Jackson was impressed. This was the best—in fact, the first—method for silencing Gunnar he'd ever seen. And then it was too late. The thermometer was removed and the uncorked Gunnar shouted, "Villain!"

By Gunnar's standards it wasn't much of a shout, more of a squeak, but the intent was clear—and even more so when he followed with, "Remorseless, treacherous, lecherous, kindless villain!"

The nurse giggled. "Don't take him too seriously. He's on heavy meds. Woke up after surgery singing 'Happy Birthday.'"

"Surgery?"

"It took some work to put that arm back together, but he'll be all right."

"O, vengeance!" Still a squeak, but a squeak with an edge.

"And" said the nurse, "he got a good whack on the head. A concussion for sure. Maybe worse." Her voice shifted into medical mode. "Intracranial bleeding. Danger of subdural hematoma." Then back to her normal voice. "We're keeping a close eye on the old guy. You can go in, but don't let him get too excited and don't stay too long."

Jackson had a strong feeling he had already stayed too long. Gunnar fixed him with a stare whose ferocity was in no way diminished by the fact that he had only one eye on the job, the other buried under bandages. And, for all that, Jackson could hear a certain touch of sly satisfaction as the old man whispered, "I told you so."

"Come on, Gunnar. That was no conspiracy. It was a tree." Jackson had talked to a friend at the sheriff's department. He knew what had happened. "You ran your snowmobile into a tree."

"They were after me! Hell-hounds!"

"Take it easy." Pause. "Tell me what happened."

The fierce gaze wavered. The one eye blinked.

"I... don't remember." A little muffled. Then picking up steam. "I hit my... my... you know!"

"Head."

"That's what I said!"

"Sure. OK, Gunnar. You go back to sleep. I'll come see you tomorrow."

"Wait!"

Jackson waited.

"I know what I know, damn it. I just can't remember."

"That doesn't make any sense."

"Neither do your damn news stories. But I read 'em anyway. Jack, they're trying to kill me. I can prove everything. I just need a little... help." Gunnar twisted his face—what little of it showed—into what he must have considered an appealing look and he lifted the shocking pink arm off the bed, a crippled flamingo trying to fly. It was so absurd and pathetic, Jackson couldn't help laughing. And with that laugh, he knew he was signing up for whatever strange ride Gunnar had in mind. You can't laugh at a banged-up old man—an old man with a broken arm and a bandaged head and a pretty good claim to being your friend—and then just walk away. Only a real jerk would do that. With a sigh and a shrug and, finally, a smile, Jackson was in. After all, that was his job: Finding out what people didn't want anyone to know and putting it in the paper for everyone to see. Jack the Jackal.

Gunnar saw what was happening and kept rolling. His memory might have been scrambled, but his instincts were still solid.

"I know the whole story. I will when I remember it anyway. But we have to get the proof. And we have to be careful. They got the others. They almost got me. If you're not careful, they'll get you too."

"Wait a minute. What others?"

Gunnar didn't answer. The silence stretched out long enough for Jackson to regret having laughed his way into this. Long enough for him to consider just admitting that he really was a jerk and walking out. He'd done worse things. But Gunnar started up again and the game went on.

"I'll remember. Tomorrow. I'll tell you all about it tomorrow."

"Jesus, Gunnar! Is there anything you actually do know?"

"July 19, 1946. I know that. We need the newspaper from July 19, 1946. July 19, 1946." Having grabbed one solid fact, Gunnar wasn't letting it get away. "You come back here tomorrow with that newspaper and I'll show you what you need to know."

"Sure thing, Gunnar."

"July 19, 1946. Do you want me to write it down?" He waved his busted right arm in the air, as if he was scribbling a note.

"Easy, Gunnar. Don't worry about it. I'll go find the paper over at the Historical Society."

Gunnar snorted. "If it were that easy I wouldn't need you, newsboy. It's not there."

"How do you know that?"

"Doesn't matter. It's not there. They wouldn't have left that where anyone could find it. It's... what's his name? What's his name? What's his name!"

Suddenly Gunnar was shouting and Jackson was thinking about subdural hematomas and intracranial bleeding. He didn't know what to say, but Gunnar kept going.

"Anyway. That whaddayacallit, that… newspaper's not in that archive. And it's not down at the Denver Historical Society either."

Jackson didn't bother to ask how he knew that.

"Bet you can tell me where I can find it."

"Damn right. In a box I saw over at Johanssen's place, week before he died." His voice dropped. "They killed him too, newsboy." Then he was full-volume again. "Box sitting in the middle of his kitchen table. Cardboard box. Had a bright red apple on it. We were talking and he pulled that newspaper out. He was careful with stuff. One of the prissy ones. Saved everything. Get me the box and I'll get you the best story you ever had. Johanssen gave everything to the Historical Society. So that box is over at Harkney House. Down in the basement. Cardboard box with a bright red apple on it."

Right then, the nurse came in and chased Jackson away. But he was more than ready to leave—and he fumed all the way back across town. Harkney House basement. Son of a bitch!

7

JACKSON'S EYES WERE STILL WATERING FROM THE BITE of the tequila when Lucy—great buddy, great waitress, the Queen of Michael's—waltzed up with three more shots on her tray. She took one, Jackson and Beast took the others, they clinked glasses and knocked 'em back. Then she was gone and they were trying to remember what they'd been shouting about.

Jackson thought of it first. "Harkney House basement! Crazy old fucker. Sending me on this impossible goddamned errand like it's no big deal."

Beast shrugged. "I can get you where you need to go. You don't have to be such a dick about it."

Jackson didn't hear any of it: the offer of help or the reprimand. He wasn't done with Gunnar yet.

"Running me around for his own amusement. Tomorrow he'll have forgotten the whole damn thing. Fuck him."

"Said that already."

Yes, he had. And it sounded so good that he said it again. "Fuck him."

"You reporters are all such sweet-talkers." Lucy angled by on her way back to the bar. Jackson leaned over and whispered in her ear. She laughed and disappeared into the crowd. Minutes later she reappeared, a tray heavy with drinks floating high overhead. At the end of the bar, the famous novelist was embracing three off-shift waitresses at once. They were all howling with laughter. One of the waitresses was married. One was gay. The third would go home with the writer once or twice a year, but always wished she hadn't. She was laughing, but her eyes were on a ski instructor across the room. and it didn't look like this was going to be one of the writer's lucky nights. Didn't matter. They were all having fun.

Lucy swirled past them, a booze ballerina, dipping gently and snorting up a small pile of coke from the writer's thumbnail. He patted her butt, she kissed the top of his shaggy head and twirled on into the crowd, cocktail tray never wavering.

An Austrian ski racer and a Swedish ski instructor talked, never looking directly at one another, peering over each other's shoulders into the crowd, eyes darting around the room. He'd won three World Cup races, she'd modeled for a ski calendar, but neither could quite be certain there wasn't someone better to talk to.

Just another night at Michael's.

Beast shouted something in Jackson's ear.

"What?"

Beast dragged him into a quieter corner of the room. "I can get you into the basement."

Jackson was still not in the mood. "You can't find anything down there. You ever been down there?" Beast shrugged. Of course he had. Beast had been everywhere.

"Why not take a look?"

"What do I do? Ask Saxby Fuck-You DuPont to let me just rummage around?" Jackson knew he'd be a better reporter if he didn't have quite so many enemies, but some of the people he had to write about just pissed him off. Saxby DuPont, executive director of the Aspen Historical Society, was one of them.

Beast sounded like he was about to become another one. "Mother fucker!" he shouted—shouting was really just normal conversation level in Michael's at that hour on a Friday night. "I told you. I can get you in there. I've got a key."

"What?"

"I. Have. Got. A. Key. Asshole."

There was a long silence. Not really a silence. There was never a real silence in Michael's until an hour after last call. But a long moment passed when other people were making all the noise and the two best friends didn't say a word. Finally:

"How did you get it?"

"A good photog always has a key." It was one of Beast's rules, which he invoked as he found ways into any place that caught his attention. "Besides, I'm living there."

"What?"

"You keep saying that."

"What?"

"That. You keep saying 'What?'"

"How are you living in the basement of the Historical Society? Asshole."

"Much better."

"So...?"

"Remember when Nikki caught me with someone else and threw me out of the apartment?"

"Yeah?" Nikki had lasted longer than most of Beast's girlfriends—maybe six months, if Jackson remembered right. Hard to keep track. The life of the Beast was complicated.

"That someone else was Roxanne."

Jackson didn't know how to respond to that. There was only one Roxanne: Roxanne Mariana. Executive assistant to Saxby DuPont. Famously hot. Famously out of reach. Roxanne and the Beast? Not possible.

"She gave me the key. Said I could sleep in the cellar after Nikki bounced me."

There was just too much wrong with that story. Jackson began with the obvious. "No way, Beastie. Roxanne's way too hot to be sleeping with you. Maybe like one time—if she was really drunk. But there is no way she'd be doing you twice, much less risk her job by giving you the key to anything."

Beast just smiled. "Yeah, well, no accounting for tastes." He smirked. "You're jealous. Be patient. Wait your turn." Then he laughed. "As if that would ever happen."

Jackson almost blurted out that he'd already had his turn. Sort of. He and Roxanne had spent one night together. Not memorable. Not even close. They were both drunk and it was bad enough that they both agreed it had never happened. And to never try again. Agreed without a word being said. Nothing more than a look that sealed the silence.

And while he was still thinking about that, Beast was dragging him out the door, into a serious snowstorm. Jackson balked, insisting on one more round of tequila. Two shooters for protection against the cold. And then—fortified—they marched out into the storm. The mountains were getting a solid coat of snow. No more early-season bare spots. Jackson had been skiing a couple of dozen times already and he could feel the season starting to settle in. It was going to be a great ski year.

SNEAKING INTO Harkney House wasn't as dramatic as it might have sounded. Even now, with ski season in full swing, Aspen's West End was very much like the ghost town that Aspen had almost become after silver crashed in 1893. The difference was, after the silver crash there was no one in town because they all went broke and left. Now it was the opposite: The neighborhood was deserted because everyone was so rich. Anyone who could afford a West End house was too rich to spend any time there, except for a few weeks a year: Christmas and New Year's, maybe Spring Break, Fourth of July. Tonight the neighborhood was dark. Everyone had been in town for Christmas, then flown away right after New Year's. But they'd all be back. They seemed to know exactly the day they were supposed to fly in—billionaires, it seemed, were at least as intelligent as the swallows that flock to Capistrano.

So Beast and Jackson didn't have to even pretend they were sneaking. They just walked across the lawn to a side door; Beast pulled out a key, unlocked the door—and there they were.

The basement was a bad dream: dark and damp and dangerously old. Beast reached up and yanked a cord and a single bulb flicked on, a puddle of light that emphasized the darkness beyond. Cardboard boxes and broken pieces of furniture piled against the walls. Crates and cartons and rolls of carpet. Brass-bound trunks and old leather satchels. All exuding the unpleasant scent of antiquity. The beams that supported the first floor were close overhead, sagging under the weight of the years; some were cracked, supported by questionable collections of timbers and rocks and screwjacks. And below the beams was a low-hanging chaos of pipes and wires, cracked, leaking, bent and sagging, the result of decades of haphazard attempts to bring modern civilization to a century-old house.

Beast was grinning, a little embarrassed at how proud he was. He'd found the ultimate Beast Hole.

Wherever Beast lived was the Beast Hole. It could be an apartment or a girlfriend's apartment or someone's couch—or the backseat of his car. Beast's living arrangements were always uncertain. The only constant was Beast himself. Beast in the Hole.

It had been months since Beast reported that Nikki had thrown him out of her apartment. Since then, he'd just say, "Back to the Hole!" and slide away. A man of mystery. It was his standard exit line. So if his story was true, he had somehow been hooked up with Roxanne for all that time. And his key to the basement door seemed to support his story, as did the fact that Beast rarely bothered to lie. But it was still hard to believe. Roxanne had come to Aspen straight out of a high-powered job in New York, spent a year cocktailing, just for fun, then decided to find a more stable situation. Which she did, easily. And now she was the executive assistant to the executive director of the Aspen Historical Society. She was smart and beautiful and she'd managed to make the transition from Big City Beauty to Rocky Mountain Hottie without losing a step. She was always her own kind of perfect.

Except, it seemed, when it came to men. There was no way sleeping with Beast counted as a successful move. As a photographer, he was a near genius. As a buddy, unbeatable. As a step up any ladder Roxanne might want to climb... unimaginable.

Beast grabbed Jackson's arm, leading him deeper into the basement. "Watch your head." He flicked on another light. The basement broke up into a warren of small rooms. More old furniture. Piles of steamer trunks. Racks of old clothes. Rusted pieces of machinery from the mines and the early ski lifts. The stone walls were thick and solid, rocks piled up years ago by men who were skilled with rocks, whether they were busting them to dig for silver or stacking them to build a rich man's mansion.

Beast led the way through the clutter, around a corner, ducking beneath a beam that sagged alarmingly. Beyond that, some of the historic debris had been cleared away and an Oriental carpet unrolled. A couple of armchairs, a couch and a big brass bed, a nightstand, a lamp on a table. Beast grinned. "It was all here. I just rearranged it a little."

He opened a drawer in the nightstand and pulled out a small tin box, popped it open, took out a joint and struck a match. He took two hits and passed it to Jackson, who took two himself. They flopped down in the big armchairs and laughed, passing the joint back and forth.

Time passed, as did at least one more joint.

Then Roxanne showed up.

"Shit! Beast! I told you..."

Beast handed her the joint. She took a toke, still angry. Her eye caught Jackson's and in that instant—again without a word—it was very, very clear that a certain night had never happened.

She glared. "You can't be here. Beast, I told you..."

Jackson broke in. "I just need to find something. Let me dig for it and then I'm gone. I need..."

"No! I don't want to know. I don't even know you're here. Just do what you have to do and get out."

She turned on Beast. "And no one else. Not ever. This isn't your clubhouse."

There was a short uncomfortable silence. Roxanne took another hit on the joint. It was down to a roach, glowing in the dark where she stood, just outside the pool of light from the lamp.

She offered Jackson the roach, he took it, burned his finger, winced, and saw her smile. "Help me out a little. So I don't have to come back. Where should I start looking for stuff that's been donated within the last year?"

Stoned at last, she waved her hand vaguely back the way they'd come. "That room right inside the door. They just dump everything. All that historical crap." She grimaced. Then she stared at Jackson. "Go find what you want and get out."

Just to show that he could, Jackson grabbed the tin box and rolled up one more quick joint, a fat, sloppy one. He lit it, took a deep toke and passed it to Roxanne. She took it, took a drag, passed it to Beast, then looked back at Jackson. "Well, go on!"

Smiling in spite of himself—who could resist the charms of young love?—Jackson threaded his way back through the historic morass.

The room next to the door wasn't big, but it was crammed full. Jackson stood, shaking his head. In the dim light, the piles of cardboard boxes were overwhelming. He didn't know where to start. He didn't want to start.

Far behind him, carried on the drafts that meandered through the basement, there were whispers and a laugh. He smelled the smoke from the joint. He groped around in the dark, found the light cord and started digging into the roomful of discarded history. He worked his way through the piles of boxes, looking for that bright red apple Gunnar had described.

Now the sounds from the dark changed. Unmistakable sounds: sighs and creaks and Roxanne making noises that she definitely had not made on that night with Jackson that never happened. Loud noises. Focus, damn it! He thought how easy it would be to decide he'd done enough. And then he saw a flash of red. Could be a red apple. On a box at the bottom of a pretty big stack. He was going to have to move a lot of boxes to get at it. The noises peaked and then quieted. Jackson grabbed a box. Then another. Then there was a giggle and the noises started again, and Jackson focused on moving fast. Roxanne and the Beast. He still couldn't believe it, but there you go. He forced himself to keep moving boxes, digging for the bottom of the pile. Focus. Nothing damaged. Nothing spilled. He was a professional journalist doing research. Roxanne screamed. Jackson kept working

He got to the box—and, yes, there was a red apple on the side and "Johanssen" neatly printed on the top with a felt-tip pen. He opened the box and saw some newspaper clippings. Then Roxanne gave a particularly enthusiastic shriek, and Jackson grabbed the box and ran.

"MOTHERFUCKER!"

The stocky man in the black raincoat kicked the car as hard as he could—and screamed with pain.

Shit! Broken toe for sure. Son of a bitch! Dead battery in the middle of the fucking night in the middle of a fucking blizzard and now a broken toe. Fuck you!

He went to kick the car again, realized how much it would hurt, tried to stop, lost his balance, slipped and landed hard.

"Mother! Fucker!"

Shouting made him feel better. And from where he sat, he could see the dent he'd put in the car door. That made him feel better yet. Let the cheap cocksucker pay for that! His pants were starting to soak through. He scrambled back to his feet—still unsteady. He didn't have the right shoes for this fucking weather. Hell, none of his clothes were right for this fucking shithole. They sent him to the North Pole, they should have given him … whatever the fuck you wear at the North fucking Pole. Who did they think he was? Nanook of the fucking North? And then that cheap fuck gave him this piece of shit pink faggot Cadillac with a fucking dead battery.

He took a deep breath. He wasn't supposed to call attention to himself. Screaming "Motherfucker" at the top of his lungs at three in the morning wasn't professional.

But, goddamn it! He'd done his job. Then he'd gotten the hell out of there and walked halfway across town with the snow caking on the back of his raincoat, away from the big mansions, across the river, to this ramshackle neighborhood where he'd stashed the car. He'd been counting on the heater in the car to keep him warm until it was time to go back to the airport. Now he was freezing in the dark and he didn't have any way to get to the airport in the morning. He should have stayed around to watch the fucking house burn. At least it would have been warm.

Looking around, he spotted the lights on the second floor of a fake Swiss chalet half a block away. As he limped closer, he could see at least half a dozen people through the window. Three more were walking in the front door.

Whatever was going on in there, it was certain to be better than freezing to death outside.

Just inside the front door, two guys were smoking a joint. They gave him a quick look and then ignored him. Whoever he was, they decided, he wasn't a cop.

No one had ever mistaken Viktor Yaroshenko for a cop.

He went upstairs and the first person he saw was a slightly bedraggled blonde with a runny nose and bloodshot eyes. Not the most attractive combination, but she was still a real cutie. He knew instinctively that the red nose and eyes were not the signs of a common cold. And he also knew, with the same instinct, that he had exactly what she wanted—what she really, really wanted—in the glass vial in his jacket pocket.

He smiled at her and she smiled back. He didn't look like anyone else at that after-hours party. They were all younger, tanner, healthier. But just as his instinct had made him certain she didn't have a cold, her instinct made her certain about the glass vial in his pocket.

And they both decided this was all going to work out perfectly.

He did have a moment of doubt a little later, when he made his third trip back to the car to refill the glass vial. He'd suddenly made a lot of new friends—and these fucking kids might look tanned, fit, and healthy, but they were hoovering up his blow at an impressive rate.

With the blonde cutie leading the way.

WALKING HOME, cradling the cardboard box, Jackson cut through an alley, past PJ's place, an apartment above a garage behind another vast and vastly remodeled Victorian. It was late, but the lights were on. She was probably just getting home from a last-call shift behind the bar. He thought about knocking on her door, but he knew he couldn't. He thought about what she was probably doing right now. He glanced at his watch. Last call was at two. Give her time to throw out the drunks, count the cash, lock the door and walk across town. She'd been home maybe half an hour. So she must be ... And he realized he had no idea what she must be doing. They'd been divorced ... hell, three years, going on four. No kids.

No problem. They just couldn't live together without killing each other. So he was out here in the dark and she was in there. Maybe alone. Maybe not. So it was all different. And by now he was a block past her place and crossing the street.

He got home, pulled off his clothes and fell asleep. Maybe he woke when the sirens went off. He might have. A good reporter doesn't sleep through a siren in the middle of the night. Fifteen years ago, he'd have been dressed and out the door with his notebook. Ten years ago, he'd at least have been on the phone. But now, at best, he maybe opened one eye. If he did, he must have glanced at the clock and seen that it was well after 4 a.m. The press was already rolling and the sirens didn't matter. Not now. It was tomorrow's news. And then he rolled over and went back to sleep and forgot he'd ever woken up. If he had.

8

THE PHONE. THE HEADACHE. THE PHONE. FESTER SHOUTING.

"Where the hell are you?"

"You know where I am. You called me."

"Get in here!" Still shouting. "Now!"

"It's Saturday."

"Harkney House burned last night. To the ground. How the hell did you sleep through it?"

"Harkney House?"

"That's what I said. Now get over there."

"Where's Beast?" Wide awake now.

"If he knows what's good for him, he's already there. Wondering where the hell you are."

Jackson had already hung up.

HE COULD SMELL the fire as soon as he was out the door. Cold weather had put a lid on the valley. Low clouds filled the sky. The mountain disappeared into the mist right above the top of Corkscrew and Super 8, steep narrow runs that twisted down into town. Looking toward the West End, he could see black smoke rising to join the clouds. He was almost running. Then he was running, ignoring the ice underfoot. Beast was certainly already there, taking pictures. Nothing to worry about. Jackson was only running because it was news.

And then he was there. The mansion that had stood for a century, proud and pretentious, was gone. Turrets and gables, porches and balconies, all gone. Four blackened chimneys stood in the midst of the wreckage, as did a few charred walls—and, as Jackson watched, one more wall collapsed with a rush and clatter. Three fire hoses sent arcs of water onto the smoldering pile. A dozen firemen stood by in yellow slickers. A handful of cops patrolled the edge of the property, keeping people a safe distance away.

Waving at one of the cops as he walked by, Jackson scanned the crowd. No sign of Beast. He spotted George Junker, chief of police, a remnant of an earlier age when small-town cops were supposed to be red-neck tough. The Junkers had been in Aspen for generations: solid, polite and neighborly, with an inbred mean streak that popped up once in every generation. George was one of the mean ones, but instead of torturing cats the way his grandfather had, he became chief of police. He was big and bulky, with a shaved head that might have concealed his impending baldness but left him sunburned in summer, shivering in winter and displaying an unfortunate lopsided skull all year round. He and Jackson shared a reciprocal loathing, one more enemy Jackson didn't need and couldn't resist.

When he saw Jackson walking his way, Junker became immediately busy talking to one of his men. He gave Jackson a tight smile to freeze him in place and went back to talking, lowering his voice. Jackson spun around, looking for a friendly face. He found a fireman he'd gotten drunk with—often enough to consider a friend and drunk enough that Jackson couldn't remember his name. The name didn't matter right now. The fireman stood out in the crowd: tall, with an impressive handlebar mustache. But today he looked ragged, face smeared with ash, sagging with fatigue.

Jackson didn't ask the only question he cared about. Beast was going to show up any minute. No point in getting things stirred up. So he asked the news question instead. "What happened?"

He got a shrug. "Who knows? These houses, seems like sometimes they decide they've had enough. Old wiring. Old wood." He shook his head.

"What time did it start?"

"Call came in right at four. First truck was here in ten minutes. Time they got here it was full-on. Never had a chance. Old stuff burns fast."

"Any idea what started it?"

"Were you listening? No idea. Nothing." He gestured at the scene around them. "Springtime in the Rockies. Où sont les neiges d'antan?" A fireman with a degree in French Lit. Around the smoldering rubble, there was indeed an unlikely mid-winter springtime. The snow was gone, melted clear out to the curb by the heat of the blaze. The lawn was a mass of churned mud. Springtime in the Rockies, exactly.

Jackson knew that the longer he waited the worse it would be. Then he saw Roxanne heading their way, walking fast, and he knew he had to say it before she got there. He didn't want to. Saying it would make it real, but he had to. Right now.

"Beast might have been in there."

"What!" All fatigue gone.

Roxanne was almost there.

"He was sleeping there. He told me last night when we left Michael's. Right around last call. Said he was coming back here to sleep."

Now Roxanne was there. No need to drag her into it.

"He had some way to get in. Broken lock or something."

They looked at the remains of the building. Another section of wall looked ready to collapse.

"Shit." The fireman hurried away.

Roxanne was standing next to him. They looked at the fire, not each other. "I wouldn't have told anyone," she said. Jackson didn't answer. "If they find him, that's that. But maybe they wouldn't." Jackson turned to her, sharply, but she kept going. "Wouldn't it have been wonderful if the Beast just disappeared? Like a wizard. You know he'd want it like that if he could. Sha-zam! All gone." Her voice was small and sad. "He was sound asleep when I left. I kissed him goodnight and..." She didn't say anything else for a while. A swirl of sparks rose into the sky. "Jackson," she finally said, "don't take this wrong, but I think I'm going to enjoy my life a whole lot more if I just never talk to you again. OK?"

And not waiting for an answer, she walked away.

WHEN JACKSON got home at last, long after dark, the first thing he saw was the cardboard box with the bright red apple. He had a strong urge to kick it, throw it out the door, into the snow. If he hadn't gone there with Beast, hunting for that box... who knows what might have happened? Beast might not have smoked that last joint and passed out. He might have stayed at Michael's until last call and then... then what? Then nothing. Then who knows what? Everything leads up to whatever happens. Change one thing, any one thing, and it all works out some other way.

But it hadn't. It had worked out this way. And they'd found Beast's body late in the day, deep in the charred wreckage.

Jackson stood there with the box in his hands. He couldn't throw it away. If it was somehow to blame, then it had to count for something. If it wasn't to blame—and he knew it wasn't—then he still didn't know what to do with it. He didn't want it. He didn't want to look at it.

Finally, he crammed it deep into the back of his closet, where the dirty laundry piled up.

9

HE STARTED WITH THE HEADLINE: "EXIT THE BEAST."
Definitely inappropriate, but that was the point. Start out in the wrong
direction and you might get where you're going. He couldn't be cold, clear
and professional writing his best friend's obit. But he couldn't go all soft
either. Not for the Beast.

So Jackson wrote the truth. The Beastly truth. Full speed. Full volume.

He touched on the tragic peaks and dug into the heroic depths of Beast's
storied career. Highs and lows both necessary to give the lay of the land—
and the lows, of course, made much better stories. He could only tell a tiny
bit of what he knew. So what he tried to find was Beast's spirit, the spirit
that made him a hero to Jackson—and more than that, a hero to Aspen. To
part of Aspen anyway. Jackson's Aspen.

Jackson knew as well as anyone that there was a lot more to Aspen than
that. He wrote stories about every corner of town and everyone in it. But
Jackson's Aspen mattered—and Beast, of all people, had been an unlikely
shining light to that crew. Waiters and waitresses and bartenders. Ski tuners
and ski instructors. Shop clerks and cab drivers and carpenters and dish-
washers. And school teachers and lawyers too. All of them living like they
skied: a little too fast, balanced on a thin edge, no time to worry, because
when you worry you crash. Working hard, then partying hard in the bars,
and after the bars closed, after Last Call when the bartender shouted, "You
don't have to go home, but you can't stay here." Landing hard and bouncing
back. Out on the town and out in the mountains, summer and winter. Trying to live up to a spirit that might have been theirs, might have been the
town's. Might have been the mountains'.

Faster and faster.

And loving it.

Until, suddenly, it ended. Just like that.

Eventually, Jackson stopped typing and sat at his desk. He didn't know if he'd gotten it right, but he was done.

He didn't want to file the story. But he had to, so he did.

And then he went home, got drunk, stopped himself from making two or three or six phone calls, passed out and woke up the next morning, bright-eyed and full of energy to start hunting down all those great Junior Hockey stories he'd been ignoring for so many years.

"SO WHAT ARE YOU doing about it?"

"About what?"

"Cut the crap, Jack."

PJ was angry—and her version of angry came with a nasty edge. She'd cut him with that edge before. Especially in the months leading up to the divorce. He'd never enjoyed it and he wasn't enjoying it now, but even under the circumstances, he couldn't help thinking that she was looking great. Never exactly beautiful, PJ made a blend of toughness and freckles work out to pretty much the same thing. A strong nose, high cheekbones. Blue eyes so dark they were almost black, especially right now. Her mouth just a little crooked, an upward tilt that kept threatening to turn into a smile, no matter how angry she was. Even now. All together, angry or not, better than merely beautiful. And beautiful without being beautiful, she was big without being large: a little over five and a half feet tall, with an uncombable mass of curly black hair that she pulled into a ponytail when she was skiing and sometimes held down with a rhinestone tiara when she was working behind the bar. Jackson had seen her hair in pigtails, seen it piled high in a costume-party Texas Beauty Queen beehive, seen it wet in the shower, seen it tousled in the morning.

For a moment he was remembering one of those mornings. Then her voice slashed through anything as flimsy as a memory.

"Beast is dead. What are you doing about it?"

"Nothing I can do, Peej. Jesus! It's only been two days. Anyway, Junker's probably right. He's saying Beast started it himself. Passed out with a joint. How many times have you seen that?"

"That's bullshit, Jack. I thought he was your friend." Jackson tried to object, but she rolled right over him. "He was better than that and you know it. He wasn't some fucking amateur. Some tourist who didn't know how to handle it."

"We all get too high sometimes. You do. I do."

"Not Beast. Not like that." She narrowed those almost-black eyes. "He was different." Then she said it again. "He was better than that."

"Geez, PJ. Almost sounds like you were sleeping with him."

The moment he said it, he wished he hadn't.

Now those eyes were wide open.

"You know what, Jack? That's one more thing that will never be any of your goddamned business."

He knew better than to apologize.

"OK. You tell me. How did it start?"

"Arson." She said it so simply.

"Who? Why?"

"You're the goddamn reporter. You figure it out."

And then she was crying and Jackson knew he wasn't allowed to comfort her.

JACKSON SHOULDN'T have answered the phone. He should have known better. PJ had just left the office, tears of rage wet on her cheeks, and he was still trying to figure out which part of what had happened was his fault. And whether he was angry at her or himself or Beast. But he was in the office and he was a reporter and so when the phone rang, he answered it.

"You worthless lazy son of a bitch!" Great.

"Look, Gunnar…"

"Don't give me that crap! You didn't do anything and now it's too late. We needed that newspaper, that box and it's gone!"

Jackson heard something ragged in Gunnar's voice, something ready to tear. He knew he should break in and tell the old son of a bitch to calm down, that he had the damn box. But he felt his own rage ready to explode. If it hadn't been for Gunnar, he never would have been down in that basement with Beast and maybe none of this would have happened. And even if it had, none of it would have been his fault. Goddamn it! The hell with Gunnar and the hell with his missing newspaper!

"I don't give a shit about your newspaper! Beast died in that fire! Fuck your newspaper!"

It was ugly, but it felt good. Jackson waited to hear what Gunnar had to say.

But all he got out was a screech: "I need…" His voice turned into a howl and a choking garble and then silence. And Jackson could hear the machines in Gunnar's hospital room beeping, then screeching their own animal howls. And a nurse shouting, "Gunnar!" and the line went dead.

ROGER RANDALL DICTU enjoyed doing business on the phone. He loved negotiating the way he was right now: sopping with sweat, his shirt and shorts clinging to his body after a fierce workout in his home gym. He loved to picture the men on the other end of the line, dressed up in suits and ties, like the businessmen they thought they were—never knowing they were up against a real predator, sweaty and moving in for the kill.

All they knew was what they heard over the phone: his steely voice, calm, cold, never raised in anger. Never betraying the excitement he felt. Or the contempt.

"Fix it!" he snapped, breaking into the other man's litany of excuses. "I explained it once. Don't ever make me explain things twice." He kept going, even as the other man tried to answer, "If you let me down, I will take whatever steps I feel are appropriate." The voice on the phone tried again, but Roger Randall Dictu wasn't finished. "Whatever steps I feel are appropriate," he repeated, clearly and distinctly, adding, "And you do not want that to happen."

He hung up, gently, and glanced down at the nylon shorts sticking to his sweaty body. He had become aroused by the sheer joy of the negotiation. He checked his watch. A young woman who called herself Bethany would be here soon, but his arousal would not last until then. He had time for one more phone call. One more triumph. His wife was at one of her luncheons. She would be home in 90 minutes, exactly. Bethany would be gone by then. His household ran so very smoothly.

He considered his next call. Bethany was always punctual. With careful timing, he could manage to hang up the phone just as she walked through the door. That would add a little more spice to the game. She would be there and he would be ready.

But before he could make a call, the phone rang. He let it ring three times. Never be eager.

"What?"

He listened, started to smile, then stopped.

"The money came with a very clear stipulation. No dogs were to be put to death. Not. One. Single. Dog. Is that clear?" Roger Randall Dictu's fondness for dogs did not extend to those human beings whose job it was to protect homeless dogs.

Hanging up the phone, he sat and thought for a long minute about the collie who had been his only companion through the long, lonely years of his childhood. A typical all-American childhood: loved his dog, hated his parents.

There was a discreet knock at the door. Damn. He didn't need to look down to know that Bethany was going to have to work just a little bit harder.

WHEN JACKSON got to the hospital, Gunnar wasn't dead. He was propped up in bed, semi-conscious. The nurse said she didn't know exactly what had happened. He was shouting. Then he stopped. The machines went crazy. And now… this. Jackson didn't feel the need to fill in any of the gaps in her knowledge. He figured that clearing up his role "would not be medically useful," as a hospital administrator had once said when explaining why no details on the hospital CEO's bonus would be released to the newspapers.

Suddenly, Gunnar lurched bolt upright and started singing, "Daisy! Daisy! Give me your answer do." Then he broke off, cackled with laughter and fell back against the pillows, gone again.

No visitors were allowed, but the Aspen hospital could be a wonderfully informal establishment and Jackson wasn't alone, standing in the hall, looking into Gunnar's room. A man about his height and probably ten years younger, with a full bushy beard, was wedged into the doorway next to him.

The bearded man snorted. "Pretty much normal." Jackson gave him a glance and the man stuck out his hand. "I'm Winston. Gunnar's neighbor."

Jackson knew that "neighbor" had a pretty flexible definition up on the back of the mountain. Gunnar's century-old miner's cabin was one of an uncounted number of wildly assorted structures up there—with an uncounted number of wildly assorted people living in them. Miners, artists, drug dealers, school teachers. People waiting for the end of the world. People waiting for the statute of limitations to run out. People waiting for rich relatives to die or for grudges to be forgotten. Aging hippies and neo-hippies. Probably a stock broker in a yurt somewhere up there. They were scattered through thousands of acres of near-wilderness, some living legally on mining claims, some just squatting where they figured no one would find them—or no one would care.

"We're in a cabin about half a mile uphill from Gunnar," the neighbor continued. "Close enough to hear the dynamite when he's having a good time."

That made Jackson smile for what felt like the first time in a long time. He thought about summer nights, sitting out on the porch of Gunnar's cabin, drinking shots, telling tales, watching the stars, shouting poetry and lobbing dynamite into the dark. Jackson wasn't much for poetry or dynamite, but Gunnar loved them both, gleefully mixing Shakespeare, E.E. Cummings, Bob Dylan and high explosives. He'd throw his arms wide and cry, "What I want to know is how do you like your blueeyed boy Mister Death?"—and then heave a lit stick of dynamite into the night.

Jackson shook Winston's hand.

"I'm Jackson."

"Yeah," said the man with the beard, in a tone that meant, "Know all about you." Jackson was used to that.

Gunnar was singing again. Jackson didn't recognize the song. Gunnar's version of singing—even at his best—didn't involve anything that might actually be classified as a melody. And the words weren't familiar. Gunnar squawked, "Ashes to ashes. The ghost is clear."

Jackson looked at Winston.

"You know that one?"

"The old coot never could get the words right. It's 'Ashes of laughter.'"

Jackson shook his head. "Still don't …"

Winston tried singing, but his version of melody wasn't much more melodic than Gunnar's. Finally he shrugged. "'Ophelia.' The Band. Gunnar loved Robbie Robertson. Tried to get him clued into Jim Morrison, but he just didn't get it."

Jackson had always through Morrison was a no-talent faker, but somehow this didn't seem like the time or place to be debating Great Rock Poets of the 1960s.

"All right, boys! Time to go. No visitors."

The shift had changed and the new nurse vigorously herded them away from the door.

"Follow the drift!" Gunnar's voice was suddenly loud and clear. "The Liberty Drift!"

Jackson stopped and looked back into the room. Gunnar's head had fallen back on the pillow and his eyes were closed.

A drift was a mine tunnel; the Liberty Drift had to be a mine. The mountains around Aspen were filled with old mining tunnels. And hearing Gunnar shout about a mine stirred something deep inside Jackson—a moment of unease, a shiver at the thought. A trap: dark and deep. When he was just a kid, after his father took off, his mother had started locking Jackson in a closet, sometimes as punishment, sometimes just to keep him out of trouble while she went drinking. More than once, she'd forgotten he was there until the next morning—and then punished him for the mess he made. That all stopped when he got old enough to kick a hole in the door, but the terror of those dark hours still came back too easily.

Jackson shook his head. Nothing Gunnar said made any sense—and if Gunnar didn't have to make sense, Jackson didn't have to pay attention.

JACKSON PUT GUNNAR out of his mind long enough to write two quick junior hockey stories—making progress on his new personal goal to write more junior hockey stories than anyone in the history of the world.

Fester had decreed that Jackson was not allowed to write about what had happened at Harkney House: not the fire, the death, the impact on the Historical Society. None of it. Not even—and for this at least Jackson was grateful—the tight, bright little feature on the no-doubt-fascinating history of Harkney House and the quirky old-timers who had lived there. No tragedy would be complete without a story like that. But everyone knew Jackson was too involved to touch any part of the story—even if no one suspected how involved he really was. So he was turning himself into a junior hockey machine. Doing his job, doing a little penance, and avoiding at least one major irritant. Jackson was in no mood for complaining hockey parents. He might have strangled somebody.

But now today's quota was filled and Jackson was going skiing. He closed the door to his office, changed into his ski clothes, jammed his feet into his ski boots, clomped out the back door, and in fifteen minutes, he was on Lift 1A, heading up the mountain. This late in the day, the lift was almost deserted. A good thing. He was in no mood for cheerful chat with a stranger. Or a friend. At the top of the lift, he skied down to the Ruthie's lift and, again, rode up alone. He made a point of enjoying the ride. The cold air. The silence made only more intense by the clatter of the lift.

He skied off the chair and headed straight down the short steep pitch below the lift, then across the flats to International, a narrow trail filled with small sharp moguls. The trail steepened and he snaked through the bumps his skis cutting the hard-packed snow. He couldn't ski nearly as well as a lot of people—the arts reporter, who wasn't worth a damn as a reporter but had been a racer in college, or R2 Dictu, or, hell, hundreds of others who skied this mountain every day—but that didn't matter really. Sometimes he cared, but most often he just enjoyed the physical act of skiing, the cold air, the beauty of the mountains, the—damn! He caught an edge, crossed his tips and hit the snow hard. You can't take time to enjoy the glory of skiing while you're skiing.

Jackson was back on his feet in a moment. He skied the rest of International, then raced down the catwalk past the Mine Dumps, steep trails that dropped out of sight into the trees. Once he passed Last Dollar, he was committed to Silver Queen, where, on one memorable day, he had fallen almost all the way from top to bottom of the pitch known as Elevator Shaft. Today he skied it fast and ragged.

At the bottom he checked his watch. There was time for one more run. He skied to the Bell Mountain lift and rode up out of the shadows into the late afternoon sun, picturing the line he was going to carve down the Face of Bell.

10

THE SHRINE JUST APPEARED ON ASPEN MOUNTAIN, THE same as all the others—the shrines to Elvis, Hendrix, Bob Marley. One day it was there, not much really, a handful of Beast's great pictures tacked onto the trees in a sheltered spot a little way down S-1. It was a tough place to get to—a steep drop and then a sharp turn into the trees—which was the least the Beast deserved. At first only a few people knew about it: the ones who ought to know. But word spread fast, as word about a legend does. And soon, people who hadn't known Beast were eager to demonstrate that they knew the shrine—mostly by pointing to it, standing safely back from the edge of the icy drop, peering into the trees below, and then following the catwalk to the safety of easier runs. That's the way it is with a legend: Those who can't follow, stand back and point.

At first it was just the photos. And then people added clippings from the paper. More of Beast's photos and newspaper stories about Beast's own exploits and disasters. Beast stories from the police blotter. Beast stories from the sports section. Beast as hero. Beast as victim. Beast as hapless dupe. Sometimes all three. And hanging from the branches of the trees, a wild array of bits and pieces: broken stuff, lost & found stuff, precious stuff some of it. At first, stuff that made sense, hung there by people who knew Beast and knew how to honor him. Then came stuff that didn't have anything to do with Beast, dead or alive, real or imagined, because people wanted to join the club, so they hung up random objects and pretended they knew why. But, again, that's the way it is with legends. Everyone wants to play. Anyway, it was all in his honor and how many people get anything in their honor?

Jackson stayed away from the shrine. He also, as Fester decreed, stayed away from the story. He hadn't told anyone that he—or Roxanne—had been down in the basement that night. No point. It wouldn't change anything. Certainly not George Junker's conclusion, as gleefully quoted by the cop-loving police reporter: "The damn hippie passed out, dropped a marijuana joint and burned the place down."

The reporter wanted to put that exact quote in his story and Jackson offered to kill him if he did. So the story stuck with the bureaucratic jargon of the official report, but the message was still the same. "After careful investigatory forensic procedures in detailed depth, it is our official and inescapable conclusion that the young man who was inhabiting illegally in the basement of the subject premises started the fire after falling into unconsciousness while feloniously smoke substances of an illicit nature."

The fire was Beast's fault. Case closed.

Jackson didn't want to add any weight to that judgment, so he never told the cops anything. He knew he was withholding what Junker certainly would call "vital law enforcement investigatory information." But Jackson didn't really care. Nothing he said could change what had happened. So he kept what he knew to himself and he kept what he felt to himself. Because he knew it wasn't his fault and he still felt so guilty he couldn't stand it.

ASHES. ALL ASHES. Marybelle Dictu could have screamed. She could have cried.

Not long after the Dictus settled in Aspen, a woman Marybelle didn't know hugged her and declared they were absolutely going to be best friends. Later that same day, that same woman cackled to another of her countless best friends, "Marybelle?" Her hand fluttered. "Just the average wife of your average billionaire." Marybelle wouldn't have been flattered to hear that "average," but the "billionaire" definitely flattered Roger Randall Dictu. He wasn't even halfway there.

That was five years ago and things were better now. Much better. The shopping center business had boomed and the Dictus, husband and wife, had prospered beyond any halfway reasonable dreams. But money alone was never going to be enough for Marybelle to slip into Aspen's social order where she wanted to be: somewhere near the top.

More than a few bright young wives had tested Aspen, persuaded their husbands to dip in a careful billionaire's toe—a nice little condo for a few million—had seen what the situation was and quickly decided to look somewhere else: a town where a billion dollars still meant something. Aspen wasn't easy.

But Marybelle had decided Aspen was going to work out very nicely for her and she wasn't one to give up on anything she had decided. Sharp intelligence, dangerously wrapped in a perky blonde high school cheerleader all grown up: hitting her forties and not losing a step. Pretty in that small-featured, sunshiny, all-American way, with the sharp eye for human nature that a cheerleader—head cheerleader, thank you very much—would wield ruthlessly in high school and ever after. And leading the way was her smile, a smile that flattered and welcomed, excited and threatened.

Marybelle quickly figured out how things worked in Aspen. Non-profit boards were the steps on the ladder leading where she wanted to go. She studied the Aspen Board Mafia, who shuttled from board to board, swapping seats, swapping favors, writing checks. Theater, dance, art, music, books, stray cats—wherever there was a need, the Board Mafia was ready to leap in, take charge, raise money and do a little good along the way.

Eventually Marybelle settled on the Aspen Historical Society.

To some, that might have seemed an odd choice. The Historical Society was solid, stolid, old-time Aspen, a maiden aunt among the newer groups, with their aura of arts and intellects. But Marybelle saw that the society might be ready to bust out. The maiden aunt smashes a teacup, slams a tequila, and dances on the table. And Marybelle was there to lead the way. First, she snagged a seat on the Oversight Committee, which gave the executive director his annual review. She gave him his review and, when the dust from that had cleared, Marybelle quite naturally emerged as chair of the Search Committee to find a new executive director. Someone more "dynamic," she explained when she told the board they were going to hire Saxby DuPont. And with that taken care of, she became chair of the Vision Committee and, in remarkably short order, drafted a new mission statement. Then, as newly elected chairman of the board (no politically correct "chairwoman" for Marybelle, "Madam Chairman" would do nicely), she launched a $50 million fund-raising campaign to build a state-of-the-art mining museum, a Disney class—no, world class—mining museum. With history. Featuring an authentic recreation of a ride in an ore cart through a rocky fiberglass mine shaft.

Stand back, Aspen! Marybelle Dictu was on the scene.

So, in a whirl of parties—dinner parties and cocktail parties, skiing parties and costume parties, picnics and concerts and whatever it took—Marybelle swanned irresistibly into the front ranks of Aspen society.

And now it was all ashes. All her planning and maneuvering, alliances built, friendships forged and, when necessary, ruthlessly betrayed (but always with a smile). All ashes, like Harkney House itself. It was a tragedy.

To her surprise, Marybelle realized she was heartbroken. And not just for the social setback. Indeed, not even mostly for the social setback. Brisk, efficient and, she liked to think, unsentimental, Marybelle had developed an unexpected attachment to all that history. The Historical Society was her path to a proper spot in the Aspen social order, but that didn't mean she couldn't care about it. And now that it was all gone she realized how much that history—"all that dusty history," as she now bitterly regretted having referred to it—really meant to her.

She hadn't realized how upset she was until she met with Saxby DuPont after the fire.

"What a tragedy," he started. "That poor young man." His face was under careful control, but his voice threatened to get away from him. "But what a lucky break," packing a shout's worth of excitement into a whisper. "We're home free."

"What are you talking about?"

The edge in her voice should have slowed him down, but his mind was overflowing with plans for the new museum, now a glorious double museum—the mining museum and the Historical Society's Aspen museum

ANDY STONE

combined in one brand new building at the base of Aspen Mountain on a site donated by… well, no need to mention that. Marybelle must know. And if she didn't, well, that was none of his concern. And his mind was filled with the glow from his dreams of what his next leap upwards would be. After Aspen.

Saxby DuPont had come to Aspen from a third-rate private museum, in a mid-size Midwest city. Switching, on the fly, from world art to local history was no problem. He didn't care about history, but he'd never cared about art either. He wasn't going to fall into that "content" trap. Running a museum wasn't about what was in the cases or on the walls. Running a museum was all about vision. Or, as he preferred: Vision!

At his job interview, he didn't waste time chattering about history. He tilted his surgically perfected chin in the air and angled his head so they could see his impressive and expensive Museum Director profile as he sketched a picture of the Historical Society on the cutting edge of… something. Details to come.

DuPont saw the mining museum as a powerful boost on the ladder leading up, up and ever further away from Queens. But his joy had soured whenever the dark shape of Harkney House floated across the surface of his thoughts. The Society's great treasure. Too old, too dreary and too expensive to maintain. Foundering in an ever-rising tide of trunks and boxes and barrels and crates, an invasive fungus of history growing in the damp basement. Mired in history, they would never make any progress.

"History has to be modern!" he had lectured the board. He argued for making that the society's motto. He'd lost, but the vote had been close and he still dreamed of victory.

"Saxby?" Marybelle demanded an answer.

"We're rid of Albatross Acres." DuPont had been peeved that no one else would pick up his clever name for Harkney House "The albatross has flown." At least he didn't flap his arms. "From now on, every penny goes straight to the mining museum. What an incredible stroke of luck!"

He thought of one final point. "This will be the perfect time." His smile grew even wider. "History has to be modern!"

Marybelle began to scream.

INSIDE MICHAEL'S BAR, a knot of prosperous men in tuxedos thought they had established a beachhead; but they were actually being walled off, like an infection. The crowd that surged around the infection had no time for the tuxedoed few; nor did they notice Marybelle Dictu as she marched into the room, her bright raptor's smile leading the way—delighted, delightful and dangerous—hunting that exact tuxedoed cluster. It was only a few weeks after the Harkney House fire and, even though the big money wouldn't be back in town until it was time for spring skiing, the first Historical Society Recovery Benefit was about to begin and these men were not going to be allowed to shirk their duty.

Marybelle spotted her prey and waded into the crowd. She plunged into the heart of the cluster, a needle into an abscess, draining her men out the door and down the block to the fund-raiser where they were meant to be.

As the little group departed, the crowd filled the space and no one noticed they were gone—or had ever been there. The night was young, but it was well on its way towards being yet another night at Michael's. Voices were loud, laughter was louder. Drinks were disappearing at a brisk clip. Lies were told and accepted, if not believed. Lovers and enemies and strangers leaned close to catch a murmured word. The bar was alive, even though one of its own had died just a few nights before.

You can't keep a good bar down. And Michael's was a great bar, with an obligation to recognize the healing power of a good time. So a good time was being had.

JACKSON WAS SPENDING the night at home. A rare event, even though he really liked his apartment. It wasn't much: up a flight of stairs to a second story studio, a view of a few trees and a patch of sky and if he didn't look down he didn't see the half dozen cars in the cracked asphalt parking lot. Not much at all, but that was all he needed. Nice enough to bring someone home for the night. Nice enough that he didn't have to feel like a loser because he lived there. And he was mostly just there to sleep. The newspaper office was home and clubhouse during the day. He loved being there and he got paid for it. An excellent arrangement. Michael's was his living room—and it was a great living room, a magic living room, with friends dropping by to party every night and beautiful women bringing him drinks. And he never had to clean up.

Apartment, newspaper, Michael's—it added up to not just the best home he'd ever had, but really the only home he'd ever had. The house he'd grown up in had never been anything close to a home. Even in the years when they'd tried to pretend, the pretense never made it inside the front door. The lawn got mowed. There was a picket fence that got a fresh coat of paint every few years. But inside, nothing fit. Certainly not Jackson, not his parents. Pieces from different puzzles. Even with carpet on the floor and furniture in all the rooms, the house echoed as if it were empty. If his parents had friends, Jackson never met them. No one ever came to visit. And it never occurred to him to bring any of his friends home. Because it wasn't home.

But this one room apartment looking out over the parking lot was home. And tonight he was staying home, looking at the box he had taken from the Harkney House basement. The box with the bright red apple on the side. It had been sitting, untouched, since he brought it home that night, since waking up to hear about the fire, since coming home again after a long terrible day, since he stuffed the damn box in the closet because he couldn't sleep with it in the room. He hadn't looked at it since then, as it disappeared under a pile of dirty laundry.

But now he felt he owed it to Gunnar to dig it out and dig into it.

The old coot was getting a little better every day. Sooner or later, the subject of that box—and the newspaper that was supposed to be in it—was going to come up again. And when it did, Jackson wanted to have an answer that didn't involve another screaming fit.

So here he was.

The box was filled with a welter of papers and keepsakes. Photos, diplomas, postcards and clippings. One of probably twenty boxes that had come out of Gustav Johanssen's house, the last traces of three generations of stalwart Norwegian miners, a family history that dwindled and ended with a childless old man who had once cut trees for a ski run.

Jackson sat next to the bed on his one decent chair and searched through the box, looking for that July 19, 1946, edition of the Aspen Sun, peeling back the layers of paper delicately, placing each item on the bed. Now that he was accepting that he had the box, he was proud that he'd rescued at least this small slice of history from the fire.

He found the newspaper near the top. It wasn't the whole paper, just the front page. The lead story, top of the front, was about problems with the city water supply: old pipes, rusty water. Below that, something about people dumping trash in the Glory Hole, an open pit at the edge of downtown left over from the mining days—perfect for trash and so much closer than the county dump. The story he was looking for was at the bottom of the page. Not big news even in those slow years.

The headline was "Sad Find on the Mountain." A trail crew had discovered a collapsed cabin, a shack really, deep in the trees. Inside the wreckage, they found a skeleton. The coroner had gone up with a couple of deputies to bring it down. He told the newspaper it was the skeleton of a woman and she had been dead a long time and that was about all he could say. The story cut off in the middle of a sentence and was "continued on page 5." But Jackson didn't have page five, just the front page. There were two rust-edged holes at the top left corner of the page and a thin tear in the paper between the holes. It had that trace of rust too. Maybe page five had been clipped on there. Now it was either somewhere in the box or lost forever.

The box was almost full. He considered turning it upside down and dumping everything out on the bed. But still trapped by that flash of pride in his act of historic preservation, he emptied the box carefully, one fragile item at a time. It was slow work, but he'd officially dedicated the night to this chore. He had plenty of time.

The page five continuation was another half hour deep into the box. Not much, one column of type, a few inches long, neatly clipped out of the paper. Saying no plans had been made for the remains. And then going on—there was space to fill—it talked about the ski runs the crew had been clearing that day and the town's hopes for prosperity as a ski resort. And at the very bottom, a note that the grim discovery should serve as a reminder to owners of mining claims on the mountain that they needed to inspect their properties for potential hazards. Everyone, it said, should remember the tragedy just two years before when young Joseph Nygaard was killed by a cave-in while exploring the long-abandoned Liberty Drift mine.

The Liberty Drift.

Jackson sat for a long while. Untangling knots.

Everything felt sticky. And nothing made sense.

There was the fire. The fire had nothing to do with Gunnar—even though Jackson had only been in the Harkney House basement because Gunnar had sent him there looking for this newspaper in the box with the red apple on the side, so the fire and Gunnar kept sticking together in his mind. But there was no connection.

And there was the Minister and the Fallen Angel, Jackson's Wild West soap opera. And that didn't have anything to do with the fire either—even though he had stumbled across the story in the archives in Harkney House, the archives that were gone now, burned in the fire. So the fire and the soap opera kept sticking together. But there was no connection.

And there was Gunnar, ranting about the minister—Reverend Son of a Bitch—and raving in the hospital: "Follow the drift. The Liberty Drift!" It hadn't meant anything, but now suddenly it did. Jackson had no idea what, but here it was, in the story Gunnar sent him looking for—the story about the skeleton in the cabin. But the Liberty Drift was on page five, the jump. He could have found the paper and still missed that. So maybe it didn't mean anything. Maybe it was only the skeleton that mattered. And Jackson wished he had asked Gunnar right at the start why he thought a passing mention of the long-dead Reverend Osgood in the paper was going to get him killed. But he hadn't asked because he knew Gunnar was just being his usual crazy self. And Gunnar never answered questions. Never straight-out anyway. Everything was always a riddle, another one of Gunnar's mysteries. So why worry about it? Son of a bitch. Both of them: Gunnar and the Reverend.

Gunnar was tied to the Reverend. And Gunnar was tied to the Liberty Drift. And the Liberty Drift was tied to a skeleton on the mountain.

And so was Gunnar, because he was there the day they found it. The skeleton. And that's why they were trying to kill him. Whoever "they" were. But none of that had anything to do with the fire. And maybe none of it had anything to do with anything. Maybe it was just coincidence, crossed wires—like the short-circuit that had probably started the fire in the first place.

And why couldn't the damn chief of police have simply blamed it on the wiring? Old wires, dry wood, a random spark. That would have been the end of it. Jackson could have let it drop. Even PJ could have let it drop. They could have mourned Beast and gone on. But now he had all these pieces that kept sticking together and not making sense.

So he rolled a joint to help him think and smoked it, sitting on the floor, pushing puzzle pieces around in his mind. The joint didn't help. When he thought about the fire, he thought about PJ telling him he had to find out who started it—and then he just thought about PJ and why all that had to work out the way it did. And he thought about Gunnar—and he had to work to remember that Gunnar hadn't been sabotaged by a mysterious agent working on behalf of a conspiracy linked to a skeleton in a shack on Aspen Mountain. Jackson couldn't have stopped anything by tracking down Gunnar's paranoid conspiracy. And he couldn't have saved Beast by not smoking that joint with him in the basement. And he couldn't have stayed married to PJ without one of them killing the other.

11

JACKSON WOKE UP FACE-DOWN ON THE FLOOR WITH A nasty headache that he knew too well and a mouth full of lint from the carpet. He desperately needed to swallow, but he knew the life that carpet had led and he wasn't about to swallow whatever was stuck to his tongue. There was a half-empty bottle of tequila next to him. The sight of it jogged something ugly deep in his memory, but he had more than enough ugliness on hand right now, so he pushed memory aside, focused on the bottle and took a slug of tequila to cleanse his mouth—pulling himself upright to spit it out into the sink. Hygiene first.

Leaning against the counter, he surveyed the room. The cardboard box was off the bed, on its side on the floor, contents scattered. He remembered—a foggy memory—smoking a joint to help him think and then deciding that a little tequila would clear the marijuana haze from his mind. It hadn't. One more lesson he had consistently failed to learn over the years. And he remembered trying to crawl into bed at some unknown dark hour, which would explain the mess. He didn't remember missing the bed and hitting the floor, but that fit right in with all the rest.

His first good sign of the morning—he took it to be one anyway—was when he realized that the incessant whining deep within his skull wasn't the result of brain damage. It was the protest of a telephone off the hook. Not surprising, considering the rest of the domestic carnage. He found the phone eventually, hung it up and moved on.

The next good sign was that he managed to take a shower without drowning. At times like this, you take your good news as you find it. And as he walked over to the newspaper office—walking slowly, keeping his head carefully balanced to avoid the dreaded intracranial sloshing—he realized that the noise he was hearing now was himself. Humming. And eventually he recognized the tune: "Ophelia." The song Gunnar had been singing. "Ashes of something. Something is clear. Dah-dah-di-dah-dah... whatever... whatever... Ophelia... dah-dah-di-dah."

Jackson actually loved that song. Gunnar's neighbor... what was his name? Winston. Wow. Jackson's mind was working. Unlikely and impressive. "Ophelia.... la-dah-dah." Except now that tune was stuck in his head and he began to worry he might catch whatever Gunnar had.

Jackson chased The Band away with a rousing version of "The Star-Spangled Banner" and—head still carefully balanced—marched to the office.

He paused in the sunshine outside the front door, struck by one more memory from the night before. The phone ringing endlessly, finally answered. That same damn voice that had done the same damn thing to him before.

"Dickhead. Fuckin' Dickhead. Lettin' 'im ge' 'way with it. Gotta get 'im."

He'd handled this call the same way he'd handled the one before. Well, almost the same. His aim, not surprisingly, wasn't as good—which explained why the phone had been off the hook. A mystery solved! He was on a roll. Doing fine, thank you.

WHEN JACKSON walked into the Aspen Sun, a man was standing at the front counter, yelling at Stormy. Never a good idea. She slammed her hand on the counter, drew herself up to a level of towering outrage that might have seemed impossible for someone so short and plump, and let fly. "The publisher is *not* in the office. The publisher does *not*, in any case, proofread the classified ads. And even if he did, neither the publisher nor anyone else in this newspaper office could possibly be expected to know that the misspelling that resulted when *you* filled out the advertising form in *your* illegible handwriting"—she was waving a slip of paper in the air—"turned the name of your lost dog into an obscenity in Dutch!" Stormy turned her baleful gaze briefly in Jackson's direction and immediately returned to abusing the unhappy customer. "You are *not* going to get a refund. You are *not* going to get an apology. You are going to get *out* of this office. Right now!"

The man scurried out the door without a word.

Stormy smiled triumphantly.

It wasn't a good day at the newspaper. A sales rep was crying because a full page real estate ad had a picture of the wrong house. The head of circulation was pleading with the police to let one of his drivers out of jail and, on a different line, negotiating a price with a tow service to get that same driver's car out of the river. Back in the production department there was a trail of blood spattered across the linoleum floor, the result of an accident with a razor-sharp Exacto knife—a not-uncommon occurrence, but today it was a real tragedy: the blood had splashed across the page and it was all going to have to be typeset again.

Things were better in the newsroom, where an aggressive game of office-chair basketball was underway. Reporters in their chairs scooted across the floor, trying to shoot a crumpled page of the paper into a trash can. It was a popular game—and only once had someone wound up in the emergency room as a result.

A radio tuned to the police communications band squawked in the background. Someone was getting arrested for a mid-morning DUI. An ambulance was being dispatched to the base of Aspen Mountain to pick up a skier with a broken leg. The entertainment reporter sat at his desk with headphones on, eyes closed, bobbing and weaving to music only he could hear, typing furiously. The political reporter guided a nervous candidate for governor through the middle of the room—fortunately he was quick on his feet and managed to avoid a reporter hurtling by in his chair, making a fast break for the trash can. The ear-splitting wail of the town's fire siren cut through the din, calling out the volunteer fire department. Mikey, Beast's long-time understudy, now chief photographer, raced into the room, screaming, "Where's the fucking fire!"

Home sweet home.

Jackson grabbed a notebook and headed off to interview a Hockey Mom. He figured he was on track for a World Record and he wasn't going to let it slip away just because the thought of writing another Junior Hockey story made him seriously consider suicide.

THE LATE AFTERNOON SUN was in Jackson's eyes as he drove down the valley. The hangover had ebbed by the time he filed the Hockey Mom feature, studded with subtle twists that would leave the Hockey Mom herself feeling strangely annoyed, even as her fellow Junior Hockey Parents celebrated her good fortune to be featured in the newspaper.

It was while he was giving that story one last quick read that Jackson noticed that "Ophelia" was running through his mind yet again and he had a sudden flash of insight—the kind of bright flash that, earlier in the day, would have made him certain that the hangover or the constant repetition of that damn tune had brought on the same kind of stroke that had befuddled Gunnar.

But now he was strong enough to realize that he wasn't succumbing to whatever had felled Gunnar, he was understanding him. The thought of finding meaning in Gunnar's raving from a hospital bed, probably should have made Jackson drop everything and head to Michael's, where he could drink his way back to sanity. But after hearing Gunnar shout about the Liberty Drift and then finding the Liberty Drift in that newspaper story buried in the box from Harkney House, Jackson was ready to find meaning wherever he could and follow it wherever it led. And right now it was leading him to Ophelia: Ophelia Grace Fields, one of the few remaining links to Aspen's past.

Ophelia Fields was always worth visiting. She was born in the 1890s on Durant Avenue, in a Victorian house that had been part of Aspen's original red light district. Her mother, Sadie Jinks, was another flower that had blossomed in that same disreputable district. Sadie was the daughter of one of the town's best-known, best-loved madams, Augusta Jinks, who ran "a clean house for clean girls" offering Aspen's working men the kind of relief that only working girls could provide. But when the Midland Railroad came to town and built its station uncomfortably close to the houses of ill-repute on Durant, the prostitutes were asked to move to a different neighborhood—which they cheerfully did. Except for Augusta. Seeing the handwriting on the parlor wall, she decided it was time to change her ways instead of changing her address. So she changed the sheets, changed the décor, hung out a Boarding House sign and started renting rooms by the night instead of the hour, no companionship included. Augusta's daughter, Sadie, made the transition from washing sheets in a brothel to washing sheets in a boarding house. And Sadie gave birth to her daughter, Ophelia, in 1893, just in time for the Silver Crash.

Jackson had interviewed Ophelia half a dozen times. She was hard of hearing and tended to ramble—but rambling was fine as far as Jackson was concerned. Once he'd shouted a question loud enough for her to hear, she'd rattle on until he had enough for three stories. His only problem was writing fast enough to keep up.

Living with her great granddaughter Louise on the Fields Ranch, halfway between Aspen and Glenwood Springs, Ophelia was always glad to see Jackson—or anyone else who wanted to stop by and chat. So, soon enough, he was sitting in the late-afternoon sun on a glassed-in porch on the south side of the old ranch house, ignoring the spectacular view of Mt. Sopris, the massive broad-shouldered peak that dominated the mid-valley, and listening intently to Ophelia's tales.

Jackson started by mentioning Gunnar and that set her off. "Spoiled brat! Used to baby sit for him. Locked me out of the house one night, middle of winter. Wasn't but about five years old, the little shit." Ophelia's language was a source of embarrassment to her family and amusement to Jackson, who always cleaned it up when he wrote his stories. "Took me most of the night to get him to let me back in. Said I had to guess the secret password. Barely got back inside before his mother got home. Hated that kid. Always had secrets. Talking in riddles. Thought he was smarter than anyone."

Ophelia began to mumble to herself, so Jackson tried another topic: a skeleton in a cabin. That did it.

"Oh, I remember when that happened. Sure I do. They were cutting those ski trails. Gustav and those other boys. Made a big fuss about that skeleton, like it was a mystery, but everyone knew all about it. Grandma Augusta knew, that's for sure. She was here when all that was going on. Grandma Gus—we only ever called her that when we knew she couldn't hear us—used to talk about the poor girl, died in a shack up there on the mountain. That girl the preacher got in trouble. Preacher ran off. Never heard from him again. But that poor girl had nowhere to go. Proper ladies drove her right out of town. So she hid up in that little shack. Some of the girls who worked for Augusta snuck food and blankets up to her. Middle of winter. Colder'n you know what. Begged her to come back to town, but she just wouldn't do it. Snow finally got too deep for anyone to get up there and that was the end of it. No one knew, no one wanted to know, no one cared what the whores said. Everyone decided to just forget all about it. Like it never happened. Grandma Gus must have told me that story a hundred times, sitting in front of the fire, middle of the winter, killing cold outside and she'd tell me about that poor crazy girl. Got to where I could say it right along with her." Ophelia's voice shifted into a strange register—a 95-year-old woman imitating a child's imitation of another old woman a lifetime ago. "Just think on that poor little gal up there in a shack on a cold night like this, shivering and crying, all because she let some preacher preach her into perdition. And then leave her there for the Devil to play with." Ophelia nodded sharply. "That little girl should have come in out of the cold and made a good living down on Durant Street. But she was too good for that. Damn fool. Died for that preacher's sins. And her own pride."

She paused for what might have been dramatic effect—and began to snore.

Jackson sat for a while, listening to Ophelia snoring. There it was. Gunnar's big mystery: the skeleton in the cabin. And it was Jackson's Wild West Melodrama: The Minister and the Fallen Angel. The story Fester had killed. Son of a bitch. Jackson got up quietly and slipped out of the living room and into the kitchen, where Ophelia's great granddaughter Louise was cooking dinner.

She looked up and smiled. "Grammy can talk, can't she?"

A pot of stew was bubbling on the stove. Knowing his dinner wasn't going to be much more than a slice of pizza, Jackson lingered a while— not hoping for an invitation, just enjoying the aroma, looking around the kitchen of the century-old house, crammed with the odds and ends that collect over generations.

And watching Louise Fields as she worked. Dark-brown hair. Pretty with no make-up. Tan and strong from working outdoors all her life. She smiled and got even prettier. Jackson wanted to keep talking to her. He knew who she was. He'd seen her around town a few times and always thought she was good-looking. But somehow he'd never actually met her before, in all the times he'd been out to the ranch to talk to Ophelia.

"Well, I'm glad to talk to her. She knows what Aspen used to be like back in the mining days and there aren't many left who do."

"I heard her going on about that girl who died up in that cabin, about the skeleton they found."

"I guess you've heard that story before."

She laughed and Jackson liked her laugh.

"Only about a thousand times. It might be Grammy's favorite story."

"Gunnar sent me up here to ask her about it."

"Gunnar sent you? I thought he was in the hospital. Out of his mind or something like that."

"Yeah. Something like. I went to see him in the hospital and —" Jackson hesitated "— he was singing."

"Gunnar can't sing. And I can't think that smacking his head into a tree would help that." She started to laugh again and then smothered it, embarrassed to be laughing about someone in the hospital. Jackson liked her embarrassment as much as he'd liked her laugh. He smiled to let her know he thought it was funny too.

"'Singing' probably wasn't the right word. More like what you'd get from a cat with his tail caught in the garbage disposal." Good, Jack. Clever.

That'll impress her. Moving on. "Anyway, he thought he was singing. And it was the song 'Ophelia.' You know, The Band."

"So you came up here. Kind of a leap."

Jackson considered saying he'd just come up because he'd been looking for a chance to meet her, but after the garbage disposal line he figured he better avoid another stupid mistake, so he just shrugged. Always a safe answer. Then he had to fill in the silence.

"Ophelia made it pretty clear that she doesn't much like Gunnar. 'Little shit' was the term she used."

"Gunnar teased Grammy about her name."

"Sounds like Gunnar."

"Get thee to a nunnery! He liked that one, but it was a little too easy. Sometimes he'd do 'There's Rosemary, that's for remembrance.' The whole speech. That'd make Grammy just about spit."

"Um… I don't get it." It occurred to Jackson that maybe he shouldn't admit that, but he wanted to keep the conversation going.

"That was Ophelia. You know, in 'Hamlet.' When she was raving mad. Just before she drowned herself." She raised an eyebrow. "I thought you reporters all went to college. I figured you knew all about Shakespeare."

Jackson wasn't sure if he was being insulted or teased. He decided it had to be teased. He was enjoying talking to this woman who looked so strong and healthy and pretty and smelled of home cooking.

He smiled and kept the conversation going.

"Where's all the Shakespeare coming from? Naming kids Ophelia? Gunnar quoting from 'Hamlet'? Does everyone around here recite Shakespeare by heart?"

She smiled much too sweetly. "Don't they do that where you come from… college boy?" The smile changed into a real one. "Aspen's always been a little crazy for Shakespeare. They had a women's Shakespeare society back in the mining days. The Swans of Avon. Touring companies would put on his plays at the Opera House."

She walked into the living room and pulled a large leather-bound book off the shelf, gilt letters "The Compleat Works of Wllm Shkspr" on the broad spine. "My version of the family bible." She looked at the book for a long moment. "Grammy Ophelia was fascinated by him when she was little. Because of her name, I guess. And she passed that on to her daughter. My grandmother used to read Shakespeare right here in the living room Sunday mornings, instead of going to church with Grandpa. Us kids got to choose. Church or Shakespeare. I stayed here."

She raised an eyebrow. "In fact, Gunnar would come up sometimes and read too."

"Gunnar?"

"He was some kind of Shakespeare whiz in high school. Grammy said he won a prize for reciting 'Hamlet.' At the Opera House."

"Gunnar? At the Wheeler?" Jackson realized he was right on the edge of sounding stupid, but he couldn't think of anything else to say.

Ophelia rescued him, calling from the next room.

"Louise?"

"What, Grammy?"

"Is that reporter fellow still here?"

Louise looked at Jackson and raised an eyebrow. He shrugged. She shouted, "He's gone, Grammy!"

"Good. He was annoying me."

Louise laughed, more of a snort than a laugh. Jackson liked women who snorted when they laughed. They walked out onto the back porch.

"Don't worry about Grammy. Next time you're here she'll have forgotten how annoying you are."

"I'll keep that in mind."

They stood for awkward moment. Jackson wasn't ready to head back to town for his slice of pizza.

"You know anything about a mine called the Liberty Drift?" As good a question as any, he thought.

"Why are you asking about that?"

"Gunnar was shouting about that too. Same time he was singing about Ophelia."

"Grammy talks about it. Says it's haunted. Cursed."

"You serious?"

"Grammy is. I don't believe any of that, but she's dead flat serious about it. If you'd asked her about that, she'd probably still be talking—or she might have spooked. Thrown you out."

"Great. A skeleton in a long-lost cabin and a cursed silver mine. I'm not sure I know what to do about any of that."

"You should talk to Skip Olsen. You know him, right?"

"Sure. Sheriff's Deputy. But why would he know about the skeleton?"

"Trust me. He's my cousin. He's weird about all those old sheriff's records. His dad, my uncle, was coroner back in the '40s and '50s. Skippy'll know how to dig up the coroner's report from back when they found that skeleton. Tell him I sent you." She smiled.

"Great. And the haunted mine?"

"I'll ask Grammy. Call you if I find out anything."

Perfect. Jackson was happy enough to hug a Hockey Mom. He had a great story with a haunted silver mine and a woman he liked who was going to call him.

"So..." He had a sudden urge to kiss her and knew it would be a really bad idea.

"See you."

As he turned to step off the porch, Jackson glanced down to check. She wasn't wearing a ring. He knew that. He just wanted to make sure.

12

FOR JACKSON, THE COUNTY RECORDS VAULT WAS A PLACE
of refuge. Over the years, he had spent countless hours hiding in the dimly
lit room lined with volumes dating back a century or more. He'd hidden
from work; he'd hidden from the cold rain and mud of November and
May; he'd hidden more than a few times from having to face the mess he'd
made of his marriage. The records of mining claims were a swamp, a jungle,
endless entries from the days when Aspen had proudly called itself a mining camp: claims staked, worked, bought, sold, traded, abandoned, cross-
referenced from one volume to another, paper trails leading here, there and,
in the end, nowhere.

After an hour or so hauling heavy books back and forth across the room,
Jackson found what he was looking for: the Liberty Drift. Just one line, one
entry among thousands. Each one of them someone's dream. Someone's
disaster. Back-breaking work in terrifying conditions ending with nothing
more than scars and debts and broken bones.

Having found that one record, he spent another hour back-tracking
through history, stumbling into blind alleys, dead-ends, one after another
until he finally located the papers of incorporation for the Liberty Drift
Bountiful Mining Company. It was mostly legal boilerplate. A few para-
graphs of jargon, an impressive engraved design on the certificate, implying
solidity and vast wealth and, finally, the names of the company sharehold-
ers. Jackson scanned the list.

James Eagleton Osgood.

Son of a bitch.

Make that Reverend Son of a Bitch.

The Reverend Osgood didn't just have a sweetie from the choir. He had himself a mining claim too. And the dreams of glory that must have gone with both of them.

Armed with the name of the corporation, Jackson went to the assessor's office to check the tax records and find out who owned the claim now. Of those thousands of claims staked a century ago by men of infinite optimism, almost all had run aground on the shoals of reality and their wreckage had drifted through foreclosures and tax sales. Most of those drifted all the way back into public ownership; many others eventually wound up in the hands of the ski company, which amassed old claims to affirm its control of the ski areas, built on a mix of pubic land and private mining claims. If Jackson was going to follow the Drift, the tax records would be a good clue where to pick up the trail.

He spent an hour going through the records and then, realizing he was running late, dropped everything and ran to City Hall to cover a design review board lunch meeting. They hated his being there and he shared the feeling. The meetings were boring and everyone was busy eating, stuffing sandwiches into their mouths, talking while they chewed, as if neither their appetites nor their vitally important thoughts could wait. Big guys, talking loud, spraying a little lunch as they argued. And Jackson alone couldn't eat. No one offered him anything, but he couldn't have eaten anyway. Watching them closely, trying to figure out what they were saying through the wads of food, left him queasy.

When that meeting was over, Jackson went down the hall to talk to a city planner about a law suit. Someone had taken deep offense at a city ruling on the height of the two-story gazebo behind his renovated Victorian and was determined to have the outrage overruled, no matter what it cost. Based on the paperwork in the file, it had already cost a lot. The suit cited "an expert evaluation of the visually effective slope of the hand-split redwood shake roof." Whatever that meant.

Jackson hurried back to the office and filed two quick stories—trying not to think about that lunch meeting and the airborne spray of half-chewed sandwich. As he was finishing up, Fester stuck his head in the door.

"Good work on that Hockey Mom story."

"Yeah. I sure hate those people."

"Well, keep it up."

"Hating them?"

"Writing about them. I don't care if you hate them. That's up to you."

"Gee, Felster. You're the bestest boss a boy could ever want."

Fester stepped all the way into the office and lowered his voice.

"Dictu had had lunch with Hal today."

"What's that supposed to mean?"

"Just that he's breathing down my neck. Our neck. Our necks. Whatever."

"You sound flustered, Felster. Hah! Try saying that ten times fast. Flustered Felster. Flustered Felster. Flustered…" Jackson let it go. He was in danger of getting tongue-tied and switching "Felster" to "Fester." No point in stirring up trouble. Never fuck with a flustered Felster.

"Screw it, Jack. I'm just saying, Dictu's got his eye on us and he's getting buddy-buddy with Hal. That can't be good. Keep those hockey stories coming."

"I'm on it, boss."

"Sure. And one more thing."

Jackson raised his eyebrows to show he was listening.

"Harbuck's been complaining."

"That tight-ass is always complaining."

"You're filing too many late stories, pushing production back. The pages are getting to him late."

Jackson didn't have an answer to that—because it happened to be true.

Jackson mostly got along with everyone at the paper. He and Fester had a good time yelling at each other, but it was all part of the game and they both understood it. And Jackson had what he considered an entirely appropriate genial contempt for the cop-loving police reporter who unquestioningly transcribed—and even believed—every lie the cops told him. But they still managed to get along perfectly well, complaining about deadlines and editors and proofreaders the way reporters all do. But Harbuck and Jackson never got along and never would.

Harbuck was the late-night production chief. He ran the enormous camera that took full-size pictures of the finished pages from paste-up. Then he used the negatives from the camera to burn the plates for the press. It was painstaking, exacting work and Harbuck was exactly the kind of perfectionist who was perfectly suited to the job. Which made him exactly the kind of perfectionist who loathed Jackson's relaxed attitude toward things like deadlines. And the feeling was mutual.

But in this case, Harbuck was entirely right. Not only was Jackson busting deadlines, sometimes he was doing it on purpose.

He knew that if he filed late enough, no one was going to screw with his story. By the tail end of the late-night shift, the proofreader was doubling as the copy editor. And while she was a brilliant woman with an astonishing grasp of spelling, punctuation, grammar and syntax, she really didn't have much judgment when it came to news.

Slipping something past her that a real editor would have pounced on was a dodge that Jackson tried to resort to as rarely as possible. He considered it one of the privileges of working for a small-town newspaper and he didn't want to abuse it. Over the years, neither one of them had ever gotten into too much trouble for it. And when there was trouble, Jackson stood up and took the blame.

This was clearly not a point to discuss with Fester, so Jackson settled for a simple, "Sorry, boss. I'll try to mend my ways."

And then he was off, on his way back to the county clerk's record vault. There, alone in the room, he had a chance to think about what he had found that morning at the assessor's office. The Liberty Drift mining claim had never fallen into the typical swirl of failure and loss. The ownership was clear, an unbroken line from the mining days right up to the present, unclouded by tax liens or sales on the courthouse steps. Not unheard-of, but rare. The taxes were paid right on time every year. By the LD Trust of Chicago, which wasn't particularly revealing. Still, there was something there. Something that continued from a hundred years ago straight through to the present. Something that wasn't a figment of Gunnar's paranoid imagination.

So Jackson needed to keep digging.

His first step was tracking the Liberty Drift back to the very beginning. Finding the tax record had been a surprise. He didn't want to miss anything else. So he went back to the heavy books, hunting for the location notice, the very first record for any mining claim, specifying a 20-acre rectangle of land, as called for by federal law. It was the miner's official, legal declaration that "Right here. This is where I will find my fortune."

After the usual drudgery, he finally found his way to an index listing the book and page for the Liberty Drift location notice. With a little smile, he hauled the book out of the shelves, laid it on the table and flipped it open to the proper page. And there, tucked tight between the ledger pages, was a folded sheet of paper. With a crude skull and crossbones drawn on it in pencil.

He stared at the piece of paper for a long time, fighting the urge to open it. He didn't believe in hauntings or curses—but still. No need to rush into things. He scanned the filing itself. A simple map with basic information establishing the borders of the claim. He wrote it all down.

Finally he unfolded the note. In the same blunt pencil as the drawing on the front, it read, "Nygaard. Rosie. Daisy… You?"

Jackson considered being scared, but he settled on excited instead. Nygaard was the kid in the old newspaper story. The one who'd been killed in the Liberty Drift. By a cave-in. Rosie and Daisy? He smiled. Sounded like a bad vaudeville act. Ophelia might be a good one to talk to about Rosie and Daisy. Ophelia and, maybe, Louise. He smiled again.

But, as long as he was at the courthouse, Jackson figured he'd start with a source that was close at hand—so he headed for Lorena's office.

Lorena was an assistant county clerk, a job she'd nailed down when she graduated from Aspen High School more than thirty years ago and held onto with determination and hard work. She had no desire to move up the ladder. The county clerk got more money, more respect and more responsibility—and, as an elected official, could find herself out of work at the whim of the voters. Lorena had seen county clerks come and go while she toiled happily in her own secure niche.

She had a round face, a little short on chin, a little long on nose, a face without distinction, except for her eyes. Jackson was fascinated by her

smoky green eyes—despite the severely tweezed eyebrows, scary twin daggers standing guard above the smoky green.

"Hey, Lorena, got anything for me? Any hot tips?"

She raised her eyebrows, the daggers ready for action, and shrugged.

He meant to start right in on Rosie and Daisy, but somehow the late-
night slurred phone calls pushed to the front of the line.

He moved a step closer, lowered his voice. "My pal Dictu up to anything? Buying? Selling? Building?"

In Dictu's line of work, all roads led through the county clerk's office—
and Lorena was the eye-in-the-sky traffic reporter who knew all, saw all and
was specifically supposed to reveal absolutely nothing. Her face tightened.
The twin stilettoes lowered. Jackson waited. Lorena hadn't held onto her
job all those years by talking to the wrong people, and, as a newspaper
reporter, Jackson was pretty much by definition the wrong people. But he
could tell Lorena had something to say.

"Dictu?" Her voice was loud and clear. "Nope. Nothing at all." She
smiled and managed to keep talking, almost without moving her lips, looking down, shuffling papers, dropping her voice to a whisper. "His lawyer's
been here. Lot of action, bottom of the mountain." Her voice was so low he
wanted to lean over the counter.

Then she raised her voice again. "Anything else?" And lowered it. Back
to her ventriloquist act. "There's a problem. Look at the map." Her face
went blank. Daggers back to neutral position. Conversation over.

Jackson smiled. Stretched his back. "Well… what can you tell me about
Rosie and Daisy?"

Lorena's face loosened up. "So Gunnar's doing better?"

Jackson raised a non-threatening eyebrow of his own.

"If you're asking about those two, you've been talking to Gunnar. So he
must be doing better."

"You got that."

Lorena smiled.

"Rosie and Daisy were a couple of old miners."

"A miner named Daisy?"

"Oscar Daisy."

"Daisy, Daisy, give me your answer true."

"Oh yeah. Daisy hated that one. He caught you singing it, he'd go off." She shook her head. "Him and Rosie were maybe the last leftovers from the old days. Gunnar's pals. Lived on mining claims somewhere up the Pass. Gunnar used to go up and get drunk with them pretty often. They always said there was still plenty of silver in the mountain if anyone'd just go look for it."

"Lost mines worth millions, right?"

"Something like that." She shook her head. "Old coots. I kind of miss 'em." A pause. "Kind of."

"What happened?"

"Got killed. Both of them. Messing around in an old mine. Pretty sure Rosie was first." She to think. "Yeah, Rosie for sure. Rock got him. Not a real big rock, they said. But big enough. Happens in those old tunnels. Gunnar came in after it happened. Said he knew it hadn't been an accident. Murder for sure." She paused again. "Gunnar was pretty nutty about that. Someone killing anyone who messed around in that mine. You know that, right?"

"Which mine was that?"

She went on, as if she hadn't heard him.

"Then Daisy got himself killed. A couple of months after Rosie. Same mine. Cave-in. Blocked the drift completely. Gunnar about went completely crazy after that."

Jackson waited a moment before he asked again.

"Do you know what mine it was?"

This time she answered.

"Sure." She blinked those smoky green eyes. "The Liberty Drift."

"WHILE U WERE OUT." Jackson had always hated those notes, a syntactical abomination that should be banned from a newspaper office. There were already too many typos in the air. But this time he didn't mind. The note said, "Louise" and under that a phone number.

He smiled when he heard her voice on the phone and he tried to think of something clever to say, but he came up empty, so he settled for, "It's Jackson." Then he couldn't help adding, "Remember me?"

There was a tiny silence. He should have quit while he was ahead.

"I called you," she said.

No clever comeback to that.

"So… what's up?"

"Is that how you professional reporters talk?"

"As long as a source is friendly. Don't make me play rough."

Another silence. "Anyway, I asked Ophelia about the Liberty Drift and she had a lot to say. Pretty much what I told you. It's haunted. Cursed. She had a list of people who died up there."

"Rosie and Daisy, right?"

"Boy reporter's on the job."

"And Nygaard too."

"There you go. And she swears there were others. Anybody goes up there winds up dead."

"Go back to the mining days and they're pretty much all dead by now anyway."

"I'm not going to tell Grammy you said that."

Uh-oh.

"Except her, of course."

"Too late."

He was trying to stay on his toes. This wasn't like chatting up a drunk cutie at Michael's.

"Did she say why it was cursed?"

"It's all about the Reverend."

"Osgood, right? It was his mine."

"OK. Now I am impressed. So, yes. His mine. He ran out on that girl and left her to die."

"Sounds like a good reason for a curse."

"Let that be a lesson to you."

"Hang on. I've got a lot on my conscience, but no dead bodies. No one knocked up and left to die."

"Sure about that?" Suddenly serious.

"Yes, ma'am. I'm sure."

"Good thing. Girl can't be too careful these days."

After they hung up, Jackson wondered if that last line of hers was a good sign.

Then he started trying to untangle everything one more time. He didn't believe in haunted mines or a secret conspiracy to kill Gunnar. But people who poked around that mine had a tendency to wind up dead. And Gunnar wasn't dead, but he'd come pretty close.

He needed a story, but his choices weren't looking good. Haunted mine or Looney Tunes conspiracy. Or another junior hockey story.

Jackson called an old friend in Chicago.

It took four calls. The first was to the Tribune. That's where she'd gone from the newsroom in Aspen. Mostly on the strength of her police stories. Rebecca had done one hell of a job covering the Aspen cops. In her own special way. For sure, she never should have been allowed anywhere near the police beat. She had a dangerous weakness for men in uniform—especially men carrying guns. When it came to Aspen cops, she had a few quick crushes and a couple of long-term boyfriends and a reputation that triggered at least one fist fight and cost a pretty good cop his job.

Police work can be risky and Becky liked things risky. Drunk at Michael's one night, she told Jackson how one cop boyfriend handcuffed her to the steering wheel of his patrol car. Naked. And left her there for an hour. Just a block from the middle of town. To teach her a lesson. She admitted she loved that. And she loved being on the inside, hearing about cops from cops. "I don't screw cops to get stories," she said. "I screw cops *and* I get stories. Big difference."

She was a hell of a good reporter, too. Even fully dressed.

She'd left the Sun the way she did everything: all of a sudden. One afternoon, she got a phone call, talked, hung up, let out a whoop and ran straight out of the building. The next morning, hung-over but radiant, she came in early—for the first time ever—and started cleaning out her desk. When someone asked where she was going, she looked up and answered as if, of course, everyone already knew, "Chicago. To the Tribune." And then she went right back to work on her desk, throwing almost everything in the trash—including a stapler, a tape dispenser, and, probably just for fun, the telephone. In the end, with nothing but a small cardboard box under her arm, she headed for the door, stopping to kiss half the reporters goodbye. Some of them with passion. Men and women alike. Fester, who'd been watching from his office, followed her, slowing to rescue the telephone from the trash.

"Rebecca," he said and she turned around. "Aren't you going to give me any notice?"

She laughed. "I start on Monday. It's a two-day drive if I don't break down. I'm late already."

"You at least have to quit."

She smiled bright as the sun. "Yes, I do," she said. Then she giggled. "'I do.' Just like a wedding." That big smile. "I now declare us woman and ex-boss. I'll call to tell you where to send my last paycheck."

And she was gone.

Now she was gone from the Tribune too. And gone from the next two papers after that. But Jackson found her on the fourth try, still in Chicago, at an alternative weekly. She was happy to hear Jackson's voice and started right in. Before he could say much at all, he'd learned that she'd been married twice and divorced twice in just five—was it really five?—years and now she was wondering why she ever thought it was a good idea to leave Aspen but she'd started taking Ritalin again and she thought it was helping her and really she never should have stopped taking it and did Jackson think maybe there was still a place for her at the Sun?

"Well, I have an assignment for you."

"An assignment?"

"Sort of." And then he told her about Gunnar and about his last visit to the office and his accident and the Liberty Drift and how the taxes were paid out of Chicago.

"So you want me to go chasing off after some obscure company that pays taxes on some obscure mining claim because some crazy coot says someone was out to kill him because he was poking around in —" she made an eerie woo-woo sound "—a haunted mine."

"Sharp as ever, Becks. Yeah, that's pretty much exactly what I want." Then he told her about the Minister and the Fallen Angel. And how Reverend Osgood—a.k.a. Reverend Son of a Bitch—had hustled his cheating ass out of town. "Back East on family business. And I'm thinking Back East probably meant Chicago, because that's where the taxes are getting paid."

"Sounds like a true romance story. Jesus, Jackson, you've gone all soft in the head. And how do you get from the Cheatin' Reverend running out of town to Gunnar running into a tree?"

"I don't know. But that's the way it is. Gunnar says Liberty Drift and Liberty Drift says Reverend Osgood. We need to fill in the blanks. I was thinking you were still at the Tribune and you'd have some connections. I'm guessing maybe you still do. So can you help me out here?"

"Why should I?" A teasing tone of voice.

"You still owe me." He couldn't resist. "For not telling Prince Hal about that time in his office ..."

She started laughing and tried to shout over him "Hey! Hey! None of that!"

But Jackson just had to finish. "You and that cop. The big guy. On the prince's desk."

Now they were both laughing.

"I straightened up all the papers after we were done."

"Way out of line, Becks."

"I never told you about the time in your office, did I?"

"Jesus! Don't! I still have to work in here."

After a moment they both stopped laughing and caught their breath.

She said she still knew some people at the Trib and she'd see what she could find. He told her if she found anything to make copies and mail them to him. He didn't want anything lying around, out on the newspaper's fax machine.

"A super-secret hundred-year-old scoop. That's some hot shit, Jack."

They laughed one more time and hung up.

It wasn't until much later that he realized he hadn't told her about Beast. How could he have forgotten?

He turned off the office lights, waved to the night editor and headed out. He had one more chore to take care of.

"DAMN IT, JACK!"

The message PJ had left at the paper said to call her, but, after talking to Becky, he walked across town to catch her at work at the hotel bar that was her regular gig. He knew she was going to yell at him and he thought fighting in person was so much more rewarding. Fighting over the phone, you don't get the real flavor—not to mention the flying spittle. Plus, if she was working, he might get a free drink out of it.

Right on all counts. She was behind the bar and as soon as he sat down she slammed down a shot and a beer in front of him, spilling a little of both to make it clear that she wasn't glad to see him. Then she kept him waiting half an hour. He spent the time watching Jennifer who was cocktailing, high as a kite, spilling drinks on her customers and giggling helplessly. At last PJ took her break and now she was yelling, close and personal—spitting mad, if not quite spitting.

It's not always satisfying to be right.

They were standing in a hotel hallway. They'd spent a lot of time together in hallways, grabbing moments while she was on break. Some of those moments had been memorable. This was not going to be one of them—not one of the memorably good ones anyway.

"What the fuck are you doing, Jack?"

He didn't say anything. He knew where she was heading, but he could wait until she got there. No hurry. And not much of a wait.

"You get anything on the fire?"

"I don't know. No. Nothing."

"The ace reporter strikes out."

"That's why you called me? To tell me what a worthless jerk I am."

Somewhere down the hall, two men laughed and tried to sing, a woman's voice joined in: wrong key, wrong song. They all laughed. There was the sound of something heavy hitting the wall and glass breaking. It was only ten o'clock. If they didn't slow down, they were going to miss the best part of the night.

"I shouldn't have to do your job for you, Jack."

"Then don't."

Two women hurried past, heads together, one smothering a giggle.

"Look, Peej," he said after a moment. "Fester says I'm not allowed to work on the fire. Nothing about Beast. I'm off that story. I'm working on something about Gunnar." He didn't know why he mentioned it. Maybe just to show he was busy. Her eyes narrowed and locked on him. Unexpected, unsettling. "He said someone was trying to kill him. I'm trying to figure out for sure what happened."

"That's bullshit. There's nothing to that. Gunnar was just an old drunk who ran off the trail and hit a tree."

"Jesus, Peej..."

"Get your shit together, Jack. If you don't want me to do your job, then do it yourself." The hall was quiet. PJ waited a little while, then said, "I called you because one of the girls here, when she's not cocktailing, works catering for the private jets."

"And?"

"And she says the morning after the fire, she was bringing breakfast out to the airport for one of the jets and there was a guy who flew out, first thing, as soon as they opened the runway. First light. She said he looked big-city. Black raincoat. Some kind of black hat with a skinny little brim. Said she noticed that because he looked like he was auditioning to play a thug in a movie or something. Way out of place here. Said he looked rough." PJ laughed a little, which was better. "And that girl knows rough. Anyway, he was coked up, half-drunk and rude as hell. And no luggage."

Jackson smiled. "What else?"

"Isn't that enough?"

It was something, but he could tell she had more. So he waited. Even if he still loved her—which he didn't—he knew how to interview someone who was holding out. Shut up and wait. But PJ was good with silence. So they slipped into a silence contest and stood there for a while, knowing what they were doing, which finally made them both almost smile. Jackson let her win. "What else did you find, Ace?"

"I asked her if anyone else saw him and she said maybe the guy handling baggage. Timmy, you know him. Real tall. Great skier. He works the door here sometimes. I asked him about it last night. And he said he'd seen that same asshole – 'asshole' was his word."

PJ was enjoying herself. Over the years, she'd been fond of telling Jackson that she was a better reporter than he was. Sometimes he was inclined to agree.

"Remember to say 'thank you' very nicely when I'm done. He'd seen, Timmy had seen, that same asshole—still his word—fly in the night before. Black raincoat, weird hat, black city shoes. Timmy said he kept waiting for the guy to slip and fall on his butt. Came in real late, right before they shut the runway down. Timmy's working a lot of back-to-back shifts. Clean everything up and shut it down at night, then open back up before sunrise. Gets about six hours off between shifts. Does that every weekend. Says the fuckers who run the place won't give anyone a decent schedule because they're too busy kissing billionaires' butts to give a shit about the people who work for them." She took a deep breath. "He said the newspaper ought to do a story about that."

"I bet."

"Says he can't talk to you and you can't use his name. He doesn't want to lose his job. He makes a lot of money working those doubles and has all day free to ski. But he says it just isn't fair."

"And the extra money goes up his nose because he needs a bump to keep going. End of the season he's broke again."

"News flash!" she said.

"I'll get right on it." A short silence, not uncomfortable. "So that's all you've got?"

"Oh fuck you, Jack. Come on. There was some guy here that night, some guy who didn't belong here. I'm saying he started that fire. He killed Beast. And you better care about that as much as I do."

Jackson had to admit she was right. He cared about Beast. And if PJ's hot tips meant that maybe Beast hadn't killed himself by accident—No.

Stop. Killed himself by accident with Jackson's help; he could still see himself ordering one more round from Lucy, still see himself rolling up one more joint before he went to search for that damn box—then Jackson was going to be glad to track it down.

So he nodded. "Thank you, PJ. Thank you very much." He could see she was pleased he'd remembered to do as he was told.

13

GOODWIN "GOODIE" RAWLINS STARED AT HIS NAKED image in the mirror and smiled benignly at his protruding hairy belly. He stroked it with satisfaction. Here in Aspen, land of slim athletic gods and goddesses of every age, it certainly wasn't fashionable to have an enormous belly, so it gave Goodie an extra measure of proud pleasure to know that, despite that belly, he was rich enough—no, correct that, significant enough—to enjoy a steady stream of slim young goddesses. Goddesses indeed. He'd had more than his share—no, correct that, he'd had his fair share, which happened to be an enormous share. To match his enormous physique. And the faces and bodies that appeared in his memory were all first rate. No sleaze. No skanks. No hard-faced hookers. And, he thought without blushing even a little, no fatties.

He'd had what he wanted and he'd wanted nothing but the best. His belly was, in its own way, a work of art. He'd achieved those extra pounds—50? maybe more, certainly more—on a diet of nothing but the very best. No gobbling cheap fast food for Goodie Rawlins. His was a high-class Old World belly, built with caviar and foie gras and thick-cut slabs of well-aged beef.

Nothing but the best. And lots of it. Certainly that was something a man could be proud of. And Goodie was the man to be proud of it.

But now he had a problem—and it was barely past nine in the morning. A problem this early in the day didn't seem fair. Goodie hated wrestling with problems. He hated wresting with anything except those slim young goddesses. He liked things—again, like those goddesses—that performed as expected and then went away.

The problem was not particularly demanding, but Goodie's frustration threshold was extremely low. The problem was the shamrocks. Big green shamrocks. That much he knew for certain. But how big? What shade of green? What should they be made from? Who would make them? How many would he need?

Goodie didn't deal with details. He was an idea man. He hired people to take care of details. And that was the heart of the problem he was facing right now. Jennifer, his personal assistant, the woman who had taken care of details like this, was gone. She walked out—without giving notice—a week ago. Or was it two weeks? A month? It seemed like yesterday. It seemed like forever. The only time that mattered to Goodie was right now—which was when he wanted whatever he wanted. And what he wanted right now was someone to handle the damn shamrocks.

Goodie was justly famous for his annual St. Patrick's Day Party. When guests arrived at his Red Mountain house, they were required to strip naked, right there in the huge front hall. And everyone was given a shamrock. One bright green three-leaf clover, with a piece of string attached. They could wear that one shamrock anywhere they wanted. And that was all they could wear. One shamrock. No more. No exceptions.

It made for a great party, fueled by champagne, cocaine, Irish whiskey, and Goodie's own constant thundering cries for "More!"

And so questions about the shamrocks were very important. Too large, no fun. Too small, no mystery. (Not much mystery in any case, but still...) And should they be stiff fabric or soft? Absorbent or water-proof? No one wants a soggy shamrock. Durable or tear-away? It made Goodie's head ache.

And even as he worried, he stared at the mirror, absentmindedly stroking his vast belly. Wondering, idly, if Jennifer had really been serious about rape charges.

As if anyone would believe that! He was Goodie Rawlins. He traced his ancestry to aristocrats of every sort: counts, dukes, even a prince or two. Centuries ago, one adventurous Lord Rawlins had sailed to America, bought up vast tracts of land (elbowing a few upstart Pilgrims out of the way), and then fled back to civilization as swiftly as possible to live on the profits of his New World holdings. Succeeding generations had moved to the New World once civilization seemed to have gained a permanent toe-hold, but stayed very much moored on the East Coast, ready to follow their ancestor's example and flee at a moment's notice. Their children were born in New York, educated in England, raised by nannies and ignored by their parents. Goodie had broken with tradition when he moved to Aspen, the first member of his family to venture so far west. But one family tradition he would never surrender: He always got whatever he wanted. Just for asking.

Rape? Not possible. Not for Goodie.

Jennifer's work had been shoddy for months. And then that last day, she had come to work late, clearly hung-over and just as clearly not having been home since the night before. Goodie didn't approve. Late-night debauchery was inappropriate for those who had to show up to work bright and early the next morning—especially when they were showing up to work for Goodie.

When Jennifer finally did drag her cute little ass into work, their discussion of her behavior hadn't gone well. Cross words were spoken and then, after he thought he had very generously found a way she could express an apology, things got worse.

But when she had first uttered the word "rape," clearly misinterpreting his generosity in finding a way for her to apologize, he had stopped the discussion. Stopped it once and for all, the way he stopped anything that annoyed him: with money. Lots of money. Goodie hated haggling. He just produced cash in an amount with enough zeroes to make the problem go away. Which she had.

But now he had to deal with the shamrocks all by himself. It wasn't fair.

And that was when the doorbell rang.

With his gaze fixed on his own image in the mirror, Goodie got to see a mixture of puzzlement and annoyance wash across his face. He had no idea who might be ringing his doorbell or why—it was Jennifer's job to keep track of that. Goodie concentrated on getting the annoyance to fade from his face, leaving just the puzzlement. He always thought his puzzled expression was particularly charming.

And the doorbell rang again.

Who could it be? Yoga instructor? Financial advisor? Massage therapist? Conveniently, all three were the same person. A very flexible young lady with strong hands and an MBA. Of course, it could be the police. Or the gardener. The gardener would be a good person to ask about the shamrocks. He knew all about plants.

The doorbell rang again.

Well, thought Goodie, let's just consider it an adventure. He tore his eyes away from the mirror and, still absentmindedly stroking his naked hairy belly, he marched down the hall, down the stairs, past the fountain, across the foyer, and threw open the door.

And there, instantly hiding the flash of irritation with which she had been about to ring the doorbell a fourth time, stood Marybelle Dictu. And as quickly as the irritation disappeared it was replaced by surprise, followed by amusement, the slightest of downwards glances, and finally an arch outrage.

"Mr. Rawlins!" she exclaimed.

"Goodie," he interrupted. He stood with the relaxed arrogance of a Caesar, his right hand spread wide across the upper slope of his stomach.

"You are naked," she observed.

"This is how I dress at home," he replied.

"I'll bear that in mind." She stifled a smile. "Nonetheless, I believe we have an appointment to discuss the future of the Aspen Historical Society."

"The future of history," he said. "So fascinating." And he offered her his arm. "I'm afraid the girl who was in charge of my appointments has let me down badly. She is no longer in my employ. So hard to get good help in the mountains. Please do come in."

She took his arm and they crossed the foyer together: she in a superbly tailored casual outfit and he clothed only in the thick mat of hair that covered most of his body.

Marybelle smiled as she thought of how viciously disturbed her husband would be if he'd had any inkling how deeply she was aroused by this fat hairy man. Roger Randall Dictu spent hours in the gym. He skied, he bicycled, hiked and climbed mountains. He was trim and fit and sleek and he assumed that made him supremely attractive. It would be inconceivable to him that she might prefer someone like Goodie. But Marybelle's father had been a round hairy man and, somewhere deep within, she knew that this was how a man was supposed to look.

As Goodie waved her into the living room, she stopped. "You'll have to put a bathrobe on," she said. "We have business to discuss."

Goodie smiled, but made no move to get a robe.

Marybelle smiled virtuously. "My mother taught me never to discuss money with a naked man."

Goodie caught her glancing down. "Business first," he said.

"Exactly," she replied.

He went to get a robe.

"JACKSON!"

Damn. That was Fester's assignment voice. Jackson knew it all too well. He had his parka on and if he'd been a little bit quicker he would have already been out the door. But it was too late now. He was trapped.

"Got a great story for you."

Double damn. Fester's "great stories" were notorious. The newsroom code for them was "DDT": Dull, Dreary and Trivial.

Might as well make the best of it.

"What have you got, chief?" Fester hated being called "Chief," but Jackson couldn't resist. It was all part of the game. And Jackson had to stay in the game. Professional pride.

"Somebody desecrated a grave in the Ute Cemetery." Jackson cocked his head. This was better than the usual DDT. "Guy called. Said someone busted the top off a couple of gravestones."

"Busted the top off? Sounds like a lot of work."

Fester shrugged. "Said they maybe stole a third stone completely. He sounded confused. You know how people are. Get all excited."

"How'd he know about it?"

"Said he was skiing—or snowshoeing or something—in the cemetery. Nice place to spend the day, right? Christ, we've got a million acres
of fucking mountains. You'd think he could find someplace better than a
cemetery."

"So… ?" Jackson needed to steer Fester back onto the topic.

"So just that. Desecration. Get on it."

"Right, chief." Fester winced. "I'm on it. But right now I have to go over
to the courthouse." He didn't mention that he was going there to check into
the story that turned Fester into Elmer Fudd—R2Dictu's possible deal at
the base of the mountain. If Fester wanted to know, he should have asked.

TWO HOURS LATER, Jackson was back out on the street. Smiling,
but puzzled. He'd found the land deals Lorena had hinted at, each carefully wrapped in a corporate name or an LLC or a trust or some other
legal device whose ownership was certain to be hidden, in turn, inside yet
another shell and another and another and on into the distance, until, as
one local lawyer liked to say, they disappeared up their own corporate asshole. Maybe some other day—some other lifetime—Jackson would settle
down to trace all those threads. But not today.

As much as Jackson had hated English class and ignored Shakespeare,
he had always loved Greek myths. Heroes and villains and gods who got
laid on a regular basis. His kind of stories. And confronting those endless
twisted paths of hidden ownership reminded him of Theseus in the labyrinth—following its endless twists and turns only to find the man-eating
Minotaur lurking at the center. Jackson didn't have to spend dreary hours
of research to be certain that the vicious creature at the center of this legal
labyrinth would be named Dictu.

He couldn't prove it, but that didn't matter, because he had also found
the problem Lorena had mentioned. The patchwork that Dictu seemed to be
assembling was split by two chunks of land. Neither one large, but both in
exactly the wrong place. One belonged to the Skiing Company. Snatching

that property up would be difficult. Dictu might be ruthless, but the Skico was the big predator in this particular jungle. It could be an interesting battle. But the other parcel was the deal-killer. It belonged to the U.S. government. And although it was under the control of the government in its cute Forest Service Smokey the Bear disguise, the real government was exactly as friendly as a real bear. It was hard to believe that Dictu's maneuvering could add up to a major development. The territory was fractured and looked certain to stay that way. A couple of multi-million-dollar houses at most. Barely worth a story. And that was the puzzle: If it wasn't worth a story to Jackson, how could it be worth all the legal wrangling to Dictu?

PJ WAS WALKING OUT of Gunnar's hospital room just as Jackson got there. She gave him a look and kept on walking without a word. A few days ago, she'd told Jackson that Gunnar was just an old drunk who ran into a tree and Jackson shouldn't waste any time on him. Now she was Florence Fucking Nightingale. Jackson guessed he had never understood PJ. No reason for that to change now. He watched her walk down the hall, remembering happier times, when not understanding her somehow seemed like a good thing.

"Jack, damn it! Get in here!"

Gunnar was in a great mood.

"I'll be getting out of here soon," he insisted. "I'm heading back home."

Jackson doubted it. There was no way Gunnar could take care of himself with his arm in a cast and his brain still half-scrambled, but there was no reason to argue about it. Gunnar had certainly been getting better by the day: stronger and saner every time Jackson visited.

In fact, he was looking strong enough and sane enough for Jackson to talk about the box with the red apple on it and the newspaper clipping inside—and the fact that he'd found the box and brought it home before the fire. So he told Gunnar everything and hoped for the best. Gunnar rewarded him with a big smile.

"That's great, Jack!"

His memory of the screaming fight that had triggered his stroke—or whatever it was—had apparently been wiped clean. That bridge crossed, Jackson talked about his search through the county records, about the Reverend Osgood and the Liberty Drift; about Nygaard and Daisy and Rosie; and about Jackson's call to Rebecca. But in his enthusiasm for his own investigation, Jackson didn't notice that Gunnar was getting maybe a little too excited. Then he looked up and saw Gunnar waving his pink flamingo cast in the air. There was something wrong with his eyes.

Jackson switched gears in a hurry, trying for calmer tone.

"I guess that's it for now," he crooned. "I'll keep working. You just get some rest."

But it was too late for soothing.

Gunnar sat bolt upright, face bright red, eyes bulging, and shouted, "She should have died—" he dropped his voice to a hoarse whisper "— hereafter!"

It sounded familiar. Shakespeare probably. Not for the first time, Jackson wished he had paid a little more attention in high school English. But there wasn't time for that particular regret right now, because Gunnar was ready to explode again.

Certain he was doing exactly the wrong thing, Jackson shouted, "What the hell is that supposed to mean?"

The pink flamingo circled and Gunnar howled, "Out! Out, brief candle!"

It was too late to change course. Jackson was committed to fighting fire with fire, screech with screech.

"What are you talking about?" Leaning in, shouting right in Gunnar's face.

And somehow it worked.

The flamingo crashed. Gunnar fell back, his eyes went quiet and soft and then filled with tears.

"I don't know," he said. "I don't know." The tears spilled down his cheeks. "Get me out of here, Jack. If I'm going to die, I want to die at home. In my own bed."

AS ALWAYS, one drink led to another, which led to a joint that Jackson shared out in the alley with a house painter and a guy who had climbed Everest twice and had trouble holding the roach because he'd lost most of his fingers to frostbite. It was bitterly cold outside, so they slipped into a back hallway, where the climber fumbled open a tiny white paper packet and offered each of them a healthy snort of cocaine, balancing the powder on the point of a knife, that he held wedged between the stubs of his fingers. "Razor-sharp," he said, his words slurred, his hand shaking as he stretched the blade out toward Jackson's face. "Handle's carved from the thigh-bone of a Buddhist monk. Smuggled it out of Tibet in my underpants."

Jackson eyed the wavering blade. The etiquette was clear: If he wanted the bump, he had to take the risk. He moved quickly, swooping down to the blade, inhaling sharply and darting away with an appreciative snort. The rush was worth the danger. And the danger was part of the rush.

Jackson had headed straight for Michael's after leaving the hospital. A nurse had come in and seen Gunnar crying. She'd given Jackson a dirty look and Gunnar a sedative shot. Visiting hours, she announced, were over.

As Jackson, the painter and the climber helped one another back into the bar, he reminded himself that this was not just mindless partying. He was on the job, investigating, and right now he was trying to understand what Gunnar had been shouting about. If singing "Ophelia" and "Daisy, Daisy" had both turned out to be relevant—relevant to what he wasn't certain, but relevant—then "She should have died hereafter" and "Out, out brief candle" needed to be figured out. The "candle" one was definitely Shakespeare. And "died hereafter" sounded like it was too. But that didn't help understand what any of it meant to Gunnar. So Jackson was committed to getting his brain sufficiently addled to match up with Gunnar's traumatized cerebral cortex. Gunnar went head-first into a tree; Jackson went head-first into Michael's. A good reporter goes the extra mile for the story, danger be damned. Like that damned spot. Out, out damned spot! No, candle. Brief candle. Out, out brief candle. Focus!

So. Another shot and then back to the alley again.

When the joint was too small to hold, Jackson pinched off the burning ember and swallowed the roach.

"Ashes of laughter!" he declared in Gunnar's honor.

The climber, apparently not a devoted fan of The Band, wagged what was left of a finger as he corrected Jackson. "Ashes to ashes." He unfolded the little envelope, licked the paper clean, smiled and added, "Dust to dust."

Then he passed out.

Jackson and the painter had to carry him back inside where it was warm, so he didn't lose any more fingers.

And the night was still young.

JACKSON WAS SITTING on a bed, naked, staring into the eyes of a naked woman. He knew her name. Lorrie. That was good. Once you're naked, it's a little late to start asking names. He'd seen her around town for a couple of years. She was young and strong and he'd always thought she looked a little wild. Square face, eyes that could have been golden in the right light, tipped up at the corners. Her hair was light brown, cut short— never looking combed and always catching his attention.

They'd crossed paths on the mountain and she was a great skier, fast and smooth. They smiled when they saw each other. They'd talked a few times at Michael's. But this moment was a whole new story and Jackson wasn't entirely comfortable with it. In fact, he was seriously uncomfortable. It was her eyes. The color that could be gold had disappeared completely. There was only the raging black of her dilated pupils.

That was the drugs, he knew that. But the drugs weren't what bothered him. He'd taken as big a dose as she had and his eyes almost certainly had that same bottomless-pit look. What was making him uncomfortable was the way those black holes were fixed on him—and the question she was asking. One question. Over and over. And again.

"Who are you?"

The path to this particular hell had started after Jackson and the painter had revived the climber and propped him up on a bar stool where the bartender could provide whatever further treatment seemed necessary. Jackson had ordered another shot and was considering what to do after that one was gone when Lorrie—her golden eyes looking perfectly respectable at the time—had wandered over, picked up the shot he had just ordered, knocked it back herself, leaned against him and started to talk about… something. What she was talking about was irrelevant. What mattered was the simple fact that they were talking. And that she was leaning against him. And that they were both at least halfway drunk. In short, things had been looking good.

Then Maria wandered by. Maria the Bombshell Bartender—some people called her 'Shell for short, but she didn't like it. She wasn't working tonight. She'd just stopped in for a drink before heading off to do whatever a hard-partying bombshell bartender does on her night off. She had jet-black hair and an attitude that frequently scared Jackson. She'd sidled over to Jackson and Lorrie, opened a small plastic jar half full of a disturbingly purple powder, held it out to both of them and raised an eyebrow. "Lick-em Aid, anyone?"

Jackson looked at Lorrie. Lorrie looked right back at Jackson. He thought, Here we go again, licked his finger, dipped it into the purple powder and then popped it into his mouth. Lorrie did the same. So did Maria. Then they all had another round. Then a third.

Here we go again indeed.

Lick-em Aid was simple enough: grape Kool-Aid powder with an undetermined amount of mescaline mixed in. The fake grape flavor, reeking of childhood, covered the vile taste of the mescaline and the undetermined nature of the dosage added a vibrating edge of uncertainty. Whether it was really mescaline or some modern synthetic, LSD most likely, was another unknown. But grappling with unknowns was the point of the game, so Jackson took one more lick for good measure.

Lorrie grinned, said "Don't want to risk the dreaded underdose," and took two.

And now it was hours later. How many hours he didn't know. What had passed during those hours was also a mystery. The evidence—the two of them naked, sitting on a bed—was circumstantial at best and the thought of trying to remember was scary. He was having trouble getting a grip on what was happening right here and now; loosening his hold on the present in order to go wandering around in the past was too big a risk.

But that all faded into background noise when Lorrie buried her hands in his hair, gave his head a shake, which seemed dangerous—something could come loose if she shook too hard—and demanded, "Who are you?"

The first time she asked, he thought she'd simply forgotten. He knew how that could happen, so he just said, "Jackson. I'm Jackson. You know me."

But she dismissed that with a shake of her head. And asked again. "Who are you?"

He tried to laugh it off. "You know. Jackson. Cub reporter. Aspen Sun. Aspen, Colorado."

"Who ARE you?" Again. "WHO are you?" And again. "Who. Are. You?"

It wasn't a fair question. Not at a time like this. No existential crisis needed right now, thank you. But she sounded desperate, so he tried to answer anyway. Again. And then again. Any answer. Name. Address. Astrological sign. Favorite color. But every answer got the shake of her head and her hands even tighter in his hair.

"Who are you?"

This was bad. Very bad. They were stuck in a loop. Circling the drain. He could see the black hole waiting. Black as her eyes. He took her hands out of his hair as gently as he could and ran for it—snatching up his clothes and trying not to stumble and fall as he pulled on his pants, shirt, shoes and socks, and parka, before he lunged into the icy cold outside.

When he hit the street, he was hopelessly lost. He could have been a block from home. Or on a different planet. Wherever he was, it was four in the morning on a dark winter's night and everything had a bright edge of rainbow colors. He started walking, figuring the freezing air would clear his head.

He wondered if Lorrie would even notice that he'd gone. Either way, she'd be all right. The mescaline would wear off eventually. She'd sleep and sooner or later she'd wake up and feel normal. Or close enough to normal to see it glimmering on the far horizon and know what direction to head in.

Toward it or away from it, that was her choice. For himself, Jackson knew he'd be awake straight through till dawn—and then go directly to work. He had a school board meeting in the morning. Terrible luck. That bunch knew a hang-over when they saw one.

He marched through the dark; if he kept moving he wouldn't freeze. Shimmers of color gnawed at the edge of his vision as he navigated the alleys and back streets. The roads were plowed, but there were banks of snow along the curbs and occasional cars, buried in drifts. The alleys were deeper in snow, unplowed, rutted. The slush at the bottom of the ruts melted during the day and now, in the hour before dawn, the water had frozen into smooth ice, small perfect mirrors in the chaos of the alleys.

As he picked his way through the scattered landscape—familiar and alien, welcoming and threatening—his mind searched for something to fix on, something stable to keep him from lurching back into the madness. And the memory of Beast was what it found. A good friend. A solid friend who had always offered the stability of being reliably crazy. A valuable companion at times like this.

He tried to picture Beast's face, a face he knew so well. But the image was blurred. He could see that curtain of black hair, but the face behind it was fading. The more he tried to focus on the image, the more elusive it was. He went looking for other memories—those moments of solid friendship that were the anchor he needed in the shifting dark. And those were blurred too. No, not blurred: missing. He could remember the famous stories—the ones everybody knew. The building blocks of the Legend of Beast. But, even though Jackson had been there for so many of them, they weren't real memories any more. They were just stories. What he couldn't find were the real moments between two friends. Not stories, not exploits, just the quiet moments that were the heart of a friendship. The moments that made him love Beast.

He knew he loved Beast—had loved him, still loved him—but he couldn't remember those moments. And it wasn't the drugs in his system that got in the way. In fact, it was the drugs he'd taken tonight that pushed him to recognize what he suddenly and certainly knew: that his memories of Beast were fading into the fog that had settled over his life, a freezing fog, not heavy as rain, not cold as snow, delicate as it settled and froze, gossamer but persistent, layer after layer, until it was solid and heavy enough to snap tree trunks, erase memories, break bones. That fog had been settling ever since he and PJ split up. The drinking to get through it. Then the drinking to forget it. And then the drinking just because he was already drinking and what else was there to do? But it wasn't the drinking. Not exactly. He'd been drinking for years. Drinking happily for years. Aspen was a party town. And Jackson loved that party.

But in this moment he could see, too clearly, the difference. He suddenly remembered waking up face-down on the floor with a mouth full of lint from the carpet, a half bottle of tequila by his side and the contents of the box from the Harkney House basement scattered everywhere. Something had nagged at his mind for an instant that morning and now he knew what it was: the memory of finding his father lying that same way, passed out, face-down, drunk, on a filthy carpet.

That was the difference.

And Jackson realized, with sudden absolute clarity, that he needed to stop drinking. Stop smoking dope too, for that matter. Not forever. Certainly not forever. But right now. Right now for certain.

He wondered exactly what that was going to mean. He took a moment to mourn whatever it was he was leaving behind. He shivered in the freezing dark. Then he stopped and looked around. And he wasn't at all surprised to find himself looking down the alley toward PJ's apartment. Aspen's a small town. For a moment he thought maybe he should knock on her door and tell her what he'd just figured out. And even as he thought what an overwhelmingly bad idea that was, he saw a faint gleam of light in PJ's window. And then it went dark. It could have just been a reflection. Or a last hallucination. Or PJ and someone who wasn't Jackson waking for a moment in the dark and turning on a light to reassure themselves who they were and where they were and … Stop it!

He was going to have to stop that, as surely as he was going to have to stop drinking.

And right then—even as, despite his best intentions, he was still looking for that lost flash of light in the darkness—he heard the voice of his tenth-grade English teacher, Mrs. Battles. English was never Jackson's favorite subject and Mrs. Battles was one of his least favorite teachers: a severe woman who seemed to lack all traces of humanity until she read Shakespeare aloud, when the full force of her otherwise absent emotion burst out, embarrassing in its intensity. He would sulk in the back row of her class, doing his best to answer her dark cloud with a darker one of his own. And because she loved Shakespeare so shamelessly, Jackson let his loathing for her turn into an equal dislike for Shakespeare. Stupid, of course; but that was high school. Yet now, he heard her voice. "Out, out brief candle!" Mrs. Battles loved that speech and loved to recite it, from "Tomorrow and tomorrow and tomorrow" all the way to "sound and fury, signifying nothing." Somehow that speech had stuck in his memory, buried deep enough that he didn't know it was there. But tonight, there it was. And it began, "She should have died hereafter."

His cerebral cortex trauma project seemed to working. At least a little anyway. He knew where Gunnar's quotes came from—even if he still had no idea what they meant.

MARYBELLE DICTU was giggling wildly, almost hysterically. Submerged in a foaming hot tub, she caressed Goodie Rawlins in a distinctly intimate place and now he was returning that caress. In a moment of complete abandon, she thought "The hell with my hair-do" and dived under the water to do something that made her companion howl his favorite word. "Goooodie!"

And when Marybelle came up for air, she started giggling all over again at the thought of her husband seeing her now. At the thought of him finding out, after all these years, what she really liked. The splashing got frantic.

"Goooodieeeee!"

And even as Goodie's howl still echoed against the Italian tile of his spa, Roger Randall Dictu was crawling out of a tent pitched beside a frozen lake halfway up Mount Sopris. By the light of the moon, he could see his companions getting their gear ready. They planned to be on the peak at dawn, to ski down the narrow fingers of the chutes below the summit and into the vast snow-filled palm of the bowl below. Dictu grabbed his skis. He liked the challenge, the danger, the sense of accomplishment. And ski mountaineering was an excellent item to drop into business conversations when he was looking for an edge.

The predawn cold bit into him as they headed up the mountain. This was the fifth year he'd done this and every time he thought it was the hardest thing he'd done all year. But now he knew for certain he could do it and so it occurred to him as he pushed ahead in the dark that he might need to find a new challenge—but he couldn't think about that until after he'd survived this one.

14

THE BEDROOM WINDOWS LOOKED OUT OVER THE
mountains, etched into the black sky by the full moon, a span of icy peaks,
from the high ridge of the Continental Divide to the east, sweeping west
past Aspen Mountain and on to Pyramid Peak and finally Mt. Sopris
more than twenty miles down the valley. It was a view of almost mythic
proportions, yet nicely encompassed by the windows, which were equally
impressive, in their own way: an expanse of glass, forty feet high, a series
of individual windows, each unique, irregular, all shapes and sizes, form-
ing a wall that bulged and zigzagged across the southern side of the room,
stretching out into the mountain air like a creature yearning to fly. Or so
the architect had said. The house—built with aluminum from World War
II B-17 bombers recovered from the jungles of Okinawa, lumps of anthra-
cite coal from Outer Mongolia and rough chunks of slag glass from the fur-
nace of an abandoned factory in Bombay—was a work of art, he explained,
the bedroom was the incandescent core of that creation, and the wall of
glass was the culmination of the artistic act. Certainly, he admitted, a million dollars was a lot to pay for a window. For a window—but not for a
work of art. Yes, that art leaked when it rained. And, yes, the art was drafty
and the room was impossible to keep warm, but there's a price to be paid for
living in a work of art.

Arnie Bing had nodded when the architect talked about "living in
a work of art." Six foot six, hulking and bald, Arnie considered his own
life a work of art: escaping from the Soviet Union, erasing his past—
especially his KGB career, shedding his accent, accumulating a fortune
in trash collection in Cleveland, finessing a federal racketeering charge,
and then risking it all for a big payoff on porn. That was art. And if his

architect—a prize-winning architect, the best that money could buy—guaranteed that this window was "art," well, Arnie Bing the Trash King was in a position to pay whatever it cost. As he already had for other works of guaranteed art. The living room in his Chicago apartment boasted several Monets. Unless they were Manets. Hell, as Arnie liked to say, they could have been Mayonnaise, but they were definitely Art. The price tags alone made sure of that.

Arnie loved his bedroom window. His wife, the lovely movie star Princess Lily DeField, hated it. She hated the strange shapes. She hated the leaks. She hated the drafts. And, though she never mentioned it to anyone, she really didn't give a shit about the view.

She'd complained. Oh yes, she had complained. Lily was not shy about making her feelings known—or about much of anything else, for that matter. But there was nothing to be done about it. Arnie loved his window, his house and his time in Aspen. So Lily sulked every night they spent there; but, sulk though she might, she was there every winter. For they were joined in holy matrimony and wheresoever Arnie went, there too would Lily go—at Arnie's sole discretion, as required by the terms of the marriage contract. As far as Lily was concerned, the only redeeming aspect of those Aspen weeks was Arnie's determination to ski every day—anyway he said he was skiing and, whatever he did, he left her alone to do whatever she wanted. And she definitely wanted. Lily wanted a lot of things and she spent her days getting the things she wanted. Then at night, every night, she displayed her unhappiness with the drafty bedroom, shivering with goose bumps beneath the naughty nighties, which were also required by the terms of the marriage contract. She could even bring a slight tinge of chilly blue to her famous lips, to keep him at bay. Unless contractually obligated otherwise.

So Arnie was immediately suspicious when he found her lounging across their bed, with her gown flung open and that nightie artfully arranged the way she knew he liked it. Smiling at him with that famous come-here-lover-boy smile. Hmmm. He hadn't told her he was going to exercise an option. That's what he liked to call it when he demanded the services specified in the marriage contract. And he was always the one who made the demands.

She never initiated physical contact of any kind. She could, but she didn't—contact she initiated did not count against her contractual obligations. So tonight he was on his guard when she let the gown slip off her shoulder. No gooseflesh. No shivering. Just that smile.

Then she lifted her sweet naked shoulder slightly, tucked her chin down just a little and gave him The Look. The look from her famous movie poster, the look that had stared down from countless dorm-room walls and inspired countless adolescent masturbations. And earned her not one red cent of royalties. Too bad, but she was collecting her rewards now. And she knew he couldn't resist The Look.

But still he stayed away from the round bed with the silk sheets. "It isn't February yet," he said. She laughed and let the nightie slip even more, baring a breast. The laugh was giddy, flirtatious, warm. The breast was surgically perfected. She was certain he couldn't resist. No man could. And as long as she didn't touch him first, he would owe her $10,000 when they were done, because he'd already had his January fuck. He reached out and touched her breast. Yes! She'd won. Once they were finished.

But first he had to get it up, which was neither quick nor easy and required a fair amount of help on her part. She didn't mind. What else was she going to do? Look at the fucking scenery? And eventually—God it really did take forever to get him up for it—they completed the task. They both managed convincing performances by the end. Although she was, as always, distracted by the need to make sure he didn't crush her under his mountainous bulk.

When they were finished and lying in bed, lights dimmed under the sweep of chilly sky, she said, "I'll need the money in my account first thing in the morning."

"What money?" His voice was blankly innocent.

"The ten thousand for fucking you. You said it yourself. It isn't February yet."

"But it is, Lily, my sweet," he said. He gestured to the fancy electronic display that gave day and date and weather information. It had slipped past midnight. It was February.

"It was January when we started, I saw it." A child's triumph in her voice.

"Forgive me, my darling"—an endearment he enjoyed exactly as much as he knew she hated it—"but it was February when we had actual penetration."

"That was your fault! You took so goddamn long!" An ugly rage was building.

"The contract is clear," he said. "Penetration is the defining moment."

He wanted to gloat, but she was so damn cute. Not quite as cute as the poster, but cute—and she would never know that he, through an amusingly convoluted chain of corporate ownership, was the one collecting all the royalties from that poster's still impressive sales. And he could have her at his will. For free. Once every 30 days.

"Asshole!" she hissed, as she drew her robe tight.

"My darling Lily."

She marched away. Eventually he heard a door slam shut in the distance. She'd be back. She couldn't sleep anywhere else. That was in the contract too. He lay on the bed and admired the view. He was pleased. A decent fuck—which was as good as it ever got with her—and a clever bit of business to top it off. She could stay mad if she wanted, but she had to uphold her part of the contract next time he wanted to get laid. And do it well. Her screen credits might have been porn, but she was a movie star and her skills as an actress were also part of the contract.

As was, of course, her title: Princess Lily. And it might—might—have even been legitimate. The reckless daughter of a small-town Midwest socialite, Lily had moved to New York and hung out with the best of the worst and the worst of the best and not much in between; she'd even had a bit part in an Andy Warhol movie. When that thrill had started to fade, she'd married Prince Egon of Somewhere or Other—details of his "royal family" were fuzzy, as was his "royal family fortune," which eventually turned out to be mostly the result of some very risky drug transactions. And once Lily was his "princess," he'd turned his entrepreneurial attention from dealing drugs to draining her bank account, which didn't take long—especially after her devout Catholic parents disowned her. After that, her trajectory was relentless: steep and down. It ended with a front-page picture in a tabloid of Lily at her worst: hopelessly stoned, sitting on a New York curb, having just thrown up on her shoes, looking like a candidate for a homeless shelter. The headline: "From pantie-less heiress to penniless airhead."

That was when Lily pulled herself together, cleaned up her act, pumped up her boobs, put her best talents to work and launched her career in porn as Lily DeField. In her own way, she was quietly proud of everything she'd accomplished. And her parents could go fuck themselves.

And Arnie could go fuck himself, too. Except—under the terms of that damn contract—he didn't have to.

"JACKSON!"

Damn. It was a variation of Fester's assignment voice: his "Where's that story?" voice. Jackson was pretty certain he knew which story was on his editor's mind.

"I'm on it, chief."

"On what?"

A tricky moment. If he named the wrong assignment, then there'd be two he'd have to deal with. But, again, that was part of the game.

"The Ute. The grave desecration."

"So where's the story?"

He'd guessed right.

"I'm working on it."

"Don't work on it. Write it."

"I've almost got it. It's getting tricky. But it's going to be great." Damn. Now he'd have to come up with a great story. With something tricky in it. "But right now I have to go up to the hospital."

And before Fester could object, Jackson raced out of the office.

LILY GAVE FRANZ "the look" and he just laughed. Her famous movie poster ("Lily DeField... Lily defiled... in Pink Passion") hadn't made it to the Austrian village where he'd spent his boyhood, so he'd never soothed his adolescent frustration with fantasies based on that Look and that elusive nipple, barely showing, but obviously there under the gauzy robe for any teenage boy to see. Besides, he was too young to have seen that poster unless he got it from his older brother. Lily liked her boyfriends young, but sometimes that meant they were too young to appreciate her fame—or their good fortune to see her famous Look in the flesh. It annoyed her when Franz laughed. The Look was not something to laugh at. The Look was supposed to be something Franz couldn't resist. Not that he ever showed much resistance. She might have been a decade—or two—older than him, but she was still seriously sexy in her perfectly engineered fashion. She treated him well, bought him extravagant little surprises, and kept him pretty well satisfied on the afternoons they spent together—and what he did on other nights and afternoons was none of her business.

But today Franz Gernhofer was not happy. Lily had just told him she was not going to be able to make the "loan" she had promised him. And he needed that money. He had a trip to Cabo planned. With a woman his own age, which meant he was going to have to pay his own way; so he really needed the money. And now Lily was telling him no. So he sulked. Lily sulked strategically; Franz sulked just because he was still a young brat who didn't know what else to do when he didn't get his way. When she saw him pout, she'd flashed him The Look without thinking and his laugh touched off her simmering rage.

"Fuck you, Franz! It's bad enough putting up with my limp-dick husband without you getting nasty."

Instantly, Franz gathered her in his arms and kissed her hard. If he had been able to change directions with that same agility in his ski racing days, he never would have been dropped from the Austrian Junior National Team. He knew Lily could find another young lover any time she wanted, but he wasn't going to find another rich bored Aspen wife anywhere near as desirable as Lily. He'd struggled to make love to more than a few who fell

far short and he knew that Lily—despite her temporary shortage of cash—
was a trophy to be cherished.

For the next half hour, the room was filled with the sounds of passion
and neither of them was acting at all.

Later, as they lay side by side, legs still entangled, Lily said, "God, that
almost makes up for having to fuck that cheap son of a bitch. Even if it is
just once a month."

Franz had already heard all about how Lily had been cheated out of the
$10,000 and he knew better than to point out that now, at least, she had
the rest of the month off. So he kept quiet and let her run on. And she did.

"And he's too cheap to get my car back. The fuck."

Franz knew that story too—how Lily's car had gotten stuck and been
towed and the door had gotten caved in, and her limp-dick husband was
fighting with the tow company and refusing to pay the bill... and Franz
had stopped listening long ago. He knew more than she thought he did
about what really had happened to that car. As part of his assortment of
grade-school skills, Franz was excellent at eavesdropping while pretending
to be asleep—and Lily had never really learned how to whisper. Especially
not when she was gossiping with her girlfriends on the phone. He had been
saving what he had overheard for a time when he needed it, but this wasn't
the time. Revealing what he knew and ending with the barbed threat to
tell Arnie might get him what he wanted, but it would almost certainly get
him thrown off the Lily DeField gravy train. And just thinking the words
"gravy train" made him think about the cute puppies in the Gravy Train
dog food commercial and he'd always wanted a puppy, but his father... and
just as his thoughts were about to wander off, as they so often did, Franz
had a bright idea—or what passed for bright in the dim cavern of his mind.

"Hey, suppose I get you the car back. That ought to be worth something, yes?"

And the thought of getting her car back and getting one up on Arnie at
the same time, got Lily so excited that she knelt by the bed and started to sat-
isfy Franz in the way she knew he liked best. But he stopped her and insisted
on a cash deal for the car—and Lily promised him five hundred, which

would at least cover his plane ticket. So he agreed. And then he pushed her head back down so she could finish what she'd started.

GUNNAR LOOKED around the cabin, nodded with satisfaction, gave a surprisingly sane smile and said, "Thank you." Quiet and sincere. Jackson, Winston and Ella May all smiled back.

Jackson had been trying to figure Ella May out all afternoon. Winston had first referred to her as "my old lady," when he'd called Jackson and said they were going to the hospital, bust Gunnar out of there and get him back to his cabin. Given that Winston was living in a cabin up on the back of Aspen Mountain, the term "old lady" and the name Ella May had left Jackson expecting a hippie mountain mama, but that certainly wasn't this lady.

She was a mix of fashion model and mountaineer: a tall, willowy red-head with serious cheekbones, dressed for serious backcountry work in well-worn gear. She handled the process of getting Gunnar out of the hospital with cool professional focus, which continued as she supervised loading him, on a stretcher, into the back of Winston's battered Jeep Wagoneer and getting him strapped in and settled down. She maintained that focus all through the drive up Castle Creek and then the snowmobile trip up the mountain and then, finally, the short haul carrying Gunnar's stretcher up the stairs and into his cabin, when she showed she had the physical strength to back up all her other qualities.

And then, after Gunnar closed his eyes and began to snore and Winston said he was going to ski up to their cabin and bring back some supplies, Ella May stood out on the porch with Jackson and revealed one more qual-ity: She loved to talk. First she surprised Jackson by lighting up a cigarette and then, with great good cheer, she began to chat. In short order, Jackson learned that Ella May was a beauty queen—an actual beauty queen, Miss Something-or-other—from Mt. Shasta, California, who'd been a rising star in the world of TV weather, looking to make the jump from a local station to the big time when she'd gone to Aspen on a whim, to get a taste of the high living she figured was in her TV-star future, but she'd fallen in love: first with the mountains, then with Winston. "Met him in a bar. He brought me up here that first night and I never left." That was ten years ago. Now she was a trained EMT and led backcountry search & rescue teams and, yes, she smoked and Winston could go screw himself if he thought he could get her to stop.

By then, Winston had returned with a backpack full of supplies, including a bottle of good whiskey, which gave Jackson a serious opportunity to face the fact that he wasn't drinking. But there was a good fire going in the wood stove and a cup of hot tea gave Jackson something to hold and sip while Winston and Ella May enjoyed the whiskey and the afternoon passed easily.

Gunnar woke as the sun was setting. His smile was still calm and his eyes clear. He wanted to know if Jackson was tracking down who had sabotaged him and run him into the tree, and, by the way, what had happened to the newspaper he'd sent Jackson looking for—in short, everything all over again.

So Jackson filled him in again, treading carefully as he talked about the Liberty Drift and the Reverend Son of a Bitch. He feared another meltdown, but the old man's attention never wavered. His eyes looked fine, clear and calm. So when he got to the end, Jackson decided to take the chance and said, "Out, out brief candle."

Gunnar gave him a puzzled look. "What's that supposed to mean?"

"It's 'Macbeth.'"

Gunnar's eyes widened and Jackson feared the worst, but it wasn't another fit, it was righteous anger.

"I know that, damn it! Act 5, scene 5. I'm not a fool. But why are you yammering about that?"

"It was what you said to me. At the hospital." Gunnar raised a questioning eyebrow, so Jackson, because he couldn't think of anything else to say, quoted the entire passage, with Mrs. Battles' voice in his ear, from "Tomorrow and tomorrow and tomorrow" all the way to "a tale told by an idiot, full of sound and fury, signifying nothing."

Gunnar smiled. "Well done, college boy. Didn't think you knew the whole thing. Except—" he raised an admonishing finger "—you skipped the first line. 'She should have died hereafter."

Jackson laughed with relief. "Good point, you old coot." Fair response to "college boy," he figured. "So what's it all mean?"

Gunnar shook his head. "Hell if I know." Then a sly grin. "You figure it out."

"YOU GUYS ARE GREAT."

The three of them were standing out on the porch. Winston shrugged.

"Gunnar may be crazy, but he's kind of a hero to me. And I know how easy it is to get crazy living up here alone." He looked over at Ella May. "I got a pretty good dose of that before Ella showed up."

"The crazy was the best part of you." She laughed. "Still is."

Inside the cabin, Gunnar roared, his voice was getting strong again. "The one-eyed undertaker blows a futile horn!"

"Shit!" said Jackson. "What's that supposed to mean?"

Winston grinned. "'Shelter from the Storm.' Gunnar loved Dylan. Don't worry about it."

VIKTOR YAROSHENKO NEEDED a moment to catch his breath, to calm down, for fuck's sake! His heart was beating double time, he was cold, he was sweating. There was something he needed desperately to say, but his mouth was so dry that nothing came out but clicks. He glanced around the room. Everyone was staring at him. No, everyone was ignoring him. He wanted to scream, but he couldn't catch his breath. He wanted to run, but there was nowhere to go. Too cold outside. Too hot in here.

He glanced at the mirror on the wall. That couldn't be him looking back. It was a one-way mirror. Someone on the other side was watching him. He threw a glass and the mirror shattered. Now everyone really was staring at him. They were laughing. "Always hated that mirror!" someone shouted. It was OK. They were all his friends. Best friends. No they weren't. He didn't even know them!

He could hear police helicopters outside. Circling. The other night he'd run outside with his hands in the air, surrendering. They'd all laughed at him and he'd almost shot one of them. He could still feel his fingers twitching, yearning to pull that trigger. That would have shut the little pricks up.

Viktor knew he had to calm down. Deep breath.

Fuck! These kids did a lot of blow! He was going to have to score some more. Find a connection here. He couldn't go back to Chicago yet.

Too many loose ends.

Fuck!

JACKSON STRUGGLED through knee-deep snow in the dark, floundering, cursing, hating every step. It was bitterly cold. But he had to be there. After his last conversation with Fester, there was no way he could show up in the office tomorrow without some notes on the desecrated graves. He headed straight here after Winston dropped him back at the hospital.

The Ute was a slice of Aspen history, the first rude burial ground of a mining camp, where people died hard and fast and young. It was the graveyard of the poor, the hard-rock miners, their wives and their whores. The shopkeepers and the bankers and lawyers and the men who owned the big mines were buried on higher ground. Their cemeteries were in much better shape. The Ute had run to ruin decades ago.

Jackson fought his way through the snow-packed tangle of aspen trees and brush, picking his way across the crusted snow that supported him. Until it didn't. Every few steps the crust would break and he'd plunge knee-deep into the snow beneath. His jeans were soaked and freezing to his legs. People died pulling stupid stunts like this. He should have stopped at the apartment for his skis.

He reminded himself that he was an idiot—and Mrs. Battles was glad to join in from the deepest darkness of his freezing mind. "It is a tale told by an idiot."

He wanted to shout at her to shut up. Shut up! But she was certainly dead by now and this didn't feel like the time or place to pick a fight with the dead.

He flicked the beam of his flashlight out into the night and saw a weathered chunk of marble in the snow, a gravestone. A name he didn't recognize and two dates. Birth and death. One day apart: Oct. 17, 1892 – Oct. 18, 1892. Under that it said "Beloved Son." Life was hard in old Aspen. Hardest, he supposed, on the very young, born into a world of pain and escaping—some at least—almost immediately.

Out, out brief candle.

Pleasant thoughts for a man who might have tricked himself into freezing to death in a cemetery. Good work, Jackson.

He fought on, breaking through the crust again and again. His shoes were filled with snow. He couldn't feel his feet. The trees around him were twisted, stunted, menacing. Graves were scattered, headstones tilting, some barely poking up through the snow, some standing as tall as Jackson. A stern angel looked down, marble eyes glaring. He really needed to get out of there, no matter what kind of hell Fester would rain down on him. Better unemployed than dead.

And then he realized he was there: a gravesite with two stones broken off, raggedly, a foot or so of stained marble sticking up from the snow. No names or dates to be seen, just the rough edges of broken stone. And the third grave, he supposed, just a hole in the snow, the right size and shape to have been left if someone had indeed stolen an entire gravestone—which seemed a strange thing to do, even given the evidence of the two broken stones.

Jackson was more than ready to flee in search of warmth, but he didn't have anything yet to tell Fester. So he knelt and dug into the snow where the missing stone had once stood, pounding his fist through the crust and shoveling with both hands.

A foot or so deep, shivering uncontrollably, fingers freezing—thinking of the mutilated hands of the mountain climber at Michael's—he found the stub of the third stone. It too had been broken off, just closer to the ground. And on that broken stub was a single line, five words, carved deep a century before: "She should have died hereafter."

"Me too," thought Jackson. And he ran for it.

LATER, after a long hot shower, as he collapsed into life-saving sleep, Jackson's last thought was of Mrs. Battles, declaiming passionately. "Out, out brief candle! Life's but a walking shadow, a poor player that struts and frets..." He wanted to stay awake for the last part, "It is a tale told by an idiot," to see if maybe she'd add, "I'm talking about you, Mr. Jackson." But he didn't make it. He fell sound asleep as the voice in his head proclaimed, "And all our yesterdays have lighted fools the way to dusty death."

15

JACKSON WAS AT MICHAEL'S, CONTINUING RESEARCH
on what his favorite bar was like when he wasn't drinking. His first insight:
It wasn't as much fun as he remembered. His second insight was directly
related to the first: Drunks aren't as charming or clever as they think they
are. He kept a club soda in his hand, so no one would buy him a drink,
and after an hour of sipping he needed to go to the bathroom. He climbed
off the bar stool and headed out the door. No point in braving Michael's
bathrooms. The men's room at Michael's had a lot more character than a
bathroom ought to have. As Beast had declared, "At Michael's, you piss in
the alley. The bathroom's for blow." When you went into the men's room
and actually bellied up to the urinal, you got questioning, hostile looks from
the men—and, often enough, women—who were there buying, selling and
snorting cocaine. Taking a leak marked you as some kind of pervert.

Tonight was too cold for the alley, so Jackson hurried down the block
to the newspaper office and used the bathroom there. Then, ready to head
home—where he could be bored quite nicely all on his own—he was pulling on his parka when the phone in his office rang. A telephone ringing in
an empty office is a sad sound, and he couldn't stand the pain, so he picked
it up. It was Louise.

"Hey, I just talked to Cousin Skippy about digging out the coroner's
report on that skeleton and he's a little skittish. He comes from the chickenshit side of the family. I'm thinking maybe I better walk you over there
and introduce you."

"Well thanks, but"—he needed to be careful here—"I think your phone
call will get the job done. If that keeps him from hating me the minute I
walk in the door…"

"He hates you already."

"Thanks for sharing."

"Come on. You knew that. Everybody at the sheriff's department hates you."

"Hazard of the profession. Cops and reporters. Cats and dogs. Write a couple of stories about guys sleeping on the job and they never forgive you. Anyway if your phone call helps him get over it, even just a little, I bet we'll be just fine."

"Don't want me holding your hand?"

"'Please, Miss Fields, can I ask the nice man about the dead body.' Doesn't come off all that professional."

"It's your funeral." A brief pause. "Don't forget. He carries a gun."

"I'm not afraid. I've got my pen. Mightier than the sword and all that."

"Didn't someone say, 'Never bring a pen to a gun fight.'"

"Don't worry, Miss Fields. I'm sure we'll get along, me and Skippy."

"He really hates that name."

Before Jackson could ask about that, the night editor rushed into the office. He waved his hands to get Jackson's attention, grabbed a piece of paper and scrawled "PJ on 4. Something WRONG!!!"

Jackson considered ignoring him. Considered ignoring PJ. Knew he couldn't.

"Hey, Louise," he said, "Got a bit of an emergency here. Let's talk about this later. I'll call you."

"Sure thing, college boy."

Deep breath. Forget about joking around. Pick up line 4. The night editor was right. Something was very wrong.

PJ almost never cried. She got angry instead. Over the years, Jackson had seen her cry a few times, very few; he'd seen her angry more times than he could count. But when he picked up the phone, she was crying. Worse than that: She was scared. And PJ never got scared.

She was talking so loud, so fast, he couldn't understand a word she was saying. He hung up and ran across town to her apartment. He saw the broken window as he came up the stairs, then she opened the door and he saw the mess inside.

"What happened?"

She gestured at the chaos behind her. "What the fuck do you think happened? That's what happened."

"Come on, PJ. I'm not the one you're mad at. I didn't do it."

She took a breath and balled her fists. Jackson watched her exhale. The fear was gone. No more crying.

"Came home from work and found this… fucking mess."

"Glad you're taking it well."

"Yeah, well, fuck you too." She picked up a large piece of broken glass from the window. "And this…"

Scrawled across the glass in lipstick—PJ's lipstick, Jackson knew the color too well—was "Mind your own business."

Then she told him why it was all his fault. She'd been doing his job, doing what he should have been doing—trying to find out who started that fire and killed Beast. She'd been trying to find out more about that guy who flew in the night of the fire. She'd asked everybody at the airport, but no one would talk to her. She rattled off a long list of people who should have talked to her, people who could have talked to her—but none of them would talk to her, goddamn it! She took a deep breath, but not to calm down. And maybe she wasn't getting anywhere, but at least she was trying. And that's what Jackson should have been doing and maybe they would have torn up his place instead of hers, except that he was such a slob he wouldn't have even noticed.

And then she almost smiled. PJ yelling at Jackson for being a slob had been a regular part of their relationship. Now it was short-hand reminiscence, nostalgia for even the bad parts of the good times.

So he hugged her and they stood that way for a long time. Then they swept up the glass and fastened cardboard over the broken window. He helped her straighten up the apartment. He knew it well enough. She'd lived here since she moved to town and he'd moved in when they first got together. Then he moved out when everything fell apart. Make that "blew up"—when the marriage ended, it wasn't nearly as gentle as "falling apart" might sound. Maybe not as gentle as "blowing up" might sound either.

It made sense that neither one of them had any idea how to be married. PJ's family history was maybe worse than Jackson's. She never knew her father. He'd disappeared before she was born. She never knew who he was—and maybe her mother wasn't entirely certain either. Her mother had married fast after PJ was born; then she died before PJ's first birthday, so PJ was raised by her step-father and, for a little while, his second wife. She'd moved out before PJ was really old enough to remember. As far as PJ was concerned, her step-father was her entire family. And her step-father had always hated Jackson—maybe because the first time they met, he and PJ had already been married for six months. Her step-father thought that was rude. And that was it for Jackson and PJ's family.

Working to clean up the apartment reminded Jackson of what it had been like to live there when they thought maybe they could actually be a family—just the two of them. He remembered some of the good times. He got the feeling she was remembering them too.

When the apartment was looking close to normal, she got a couple of beers and they sat on the couch long enough for him to lose track of how long it had been. Eventually it got dark.

"Jack, please stay."

"MR. JACKSON, are you planning on actually filing any stories for the paper this week? Or this month? I don't mean to pry. I just want to be able to alert the rest of the staff so they can be ready. In the event."

Fester's super-polite act was an earful of broken glass. That's why he did it. But he had a point. It had been days since Jackson's by-line had been in the paper. He hadn't been focused on his job. He'd been hard at work on other things, but he couldn't say that. He looked around his desk for something he could turn into a story, but Fester beat him to the punch. "The Historical Society's having a fund-raiser tonight. It's a dinner, but you can show up afterwards." Meaning the paper wasn't going to pay for Jackson's dinner. "It's a big deal. Kick off the Historic Recovery. That's what they're calling it. 'An Historic Recovery.' It's going on the front tomorrow. So get right back here and file."

"But I have to..."

"No, you don't. You have to go to the fundraiser and you have to file a story."

"Come on, Felster. You know I hate that stuff. And I hate all those people."

"It's an assignment, Jackson." And he was gone.

Jackson called PJ. He'd been thinking about her all day. About spending the night, sure. But also about the way everything had gotten very real in a hurry. She'd been pushing him hard to find out who set the fire—and he'd been blowing her off, because, despite her clues about some mysterious thug flying in that night, he was clear that no one had set that fire. It was Beast's fault. Jackson's fault. No one's fault. But now, all of a sudden, PJ's impossible ideas were looking frighteningly real. Someone really had wrecked her apartment, really had called to threaten her, and it really did seem to be tied to her chasing after that mysterious thug. Maybe she was right. Maybe it really was arson.

Jackson had been planning to go by her apartment and make sure she was all right. And, yes, maybe spend the night. But now he called and told her he had to work and wouldn't be able to come by.

She said, "That's OK, Jack. Nothing to worry about. Skeeter's here. I'll be just fine."

Skeeter was on the Aspen Mountain Patrol and PJ had dated him pretty heavily a year or two before.

"I didn't know you and Skeeter..." He left it hanging. PJ left it there too.

"Thanks, Jackson. Really. You're my hero." She used to say that a lot. And sometimes she meant it. But back when she used to mean it, Skeeter wasn't there.

Walking across town to hear what Marybelle Dictu had to say at the Historical Society benefit, Jackson pushed thoughts about PJ out of his mind. They weren't married anymore. Her life was none of his business.

Instead, he thought about Louise—and what he knew about her life, which was probably more than she might want him to. Louise's parents had split up a few years ago and it had been ugly. Old ranching families fall prey to the same foolish lusts as ski bums. Maybe not as often, but when they do, the stakes are higher. Louise's father, Everett Fields, moved out when he got caught playing around and the marriage went bust. It was his family's ranch, but he figured it was time to put a little distance between himself and all of that. So he moved into an apartment in town with his girlfriend. His wife, Louise's mother, headed for warmer elevations and never looked back.

Jackson knew all that without even meaning to. And he knew about Louise and—what was his name? Jeffrey. They used to live together. Like her parents' marriage, that hadn't ended well.

So he knew a lot of things Louise would rather he didn't know. But part of what he knew was that Louise came from a real family. Broken, but real. Nothing like his family. And nothing like PJ's. Their homes weren't broken—they were road kill.

Sure, Louise had secrets. But right now, he didn't want to know them.

He thought about a dinner party a few years ago when he'd looked around the table and realized he'd slept with every woman there. As had at least one other man at the table. And he knew that at least one of the women had slept with every man. And all of them knew all about it.

No secrets there.

He wondered how much Louise knew about his past.

It isn't necessarily easy living in a small town.

ROGER RANDALL DICTU was eating alone. Marybelle had some damn thing she had to go to tonight. She'd told him what it was, but he didn't care. Now he leaned back in his chair and looked up at the waiter. His manner was perfect, his service excellent, but there was a flash of insolence hidden inside his perfection and they both knew it. The waiter knew who Roger Randall was—of course he knew—and that made the insolence outrageous.

The waiter bent slightly at the waist as he spoke. His posture was perfect, humble, but still, damn it, insolent. He was tall, ruggedly handsome, with curly black hair and gleaming white teeth that he flashed in an annoying smile.

"Would you care for dessert, sir? Our desserts are famous." He was treating Roger Randall as if he were a tourist, as if he didn't know everything about this restaurant. Intolerable. "You really should try our homemade New Orleans Pecan Praline Pie."

Roger Randall pounced. "Homemade? New Orleans? Which is it? Homemade or New Orleans?"

The waiter smiled. "New Orleans *style*, sir. But homemade, of course. All our desserts are homemade."

"Really? And whose 'home' are they made in? Cooking at home for a restaurant is illegal. You do know that, don't you?"

"Well, really, sir..."

Roger Randall knew he had only the thinnest advantage to work with, but he wasn't going to let go.

"Perhaps you bake these pies in *your* home. I certainly hope not." He narrowed his ice-blue eyes. "I can picture the kind of place you call 'home.'"

That, he thought, ought to set things straight. But instead of accepting defeat and showing proper deference, the waiter just smiled. His attitude remained absolutely perfect, but his voice still held that undetectable, but obvious, edge. Just like Roger Randall, he was good at what he did.

"Well, sir, as you wish, of course. I could bring you a slice of our famous homemade New Orleans Style Pecan Praline Pie and you could decide for yourself, sir, whether to eat it." A tiny pause. "Or shove it up your ass." His perfect smile never wavered. His perfect teeth gleamed.

"Greta!" Not wasting an instant on astonishment or outrage, Roger Randall spotted the owner of the restaurant and shouted her name. In a moment she was at the table, a tall blonde, fit and trim and just a few years past 40. She'd gotten the restaurant in a divorce settlement and made it into the success that her drunk of a husband had only dreamed of. She sensed trouble and there wasn't any hint of insolence in her manner as she looked from waiter to customer and inclined her head inquiringly.

"This young man's behavior is unacceptable."

"Well really, Mr. Dictu. Michael's one of our best..."

He cut her off. "You need to get rid of him. Right here. Right now. If you ever want to see me in this restaurant again." This should be fun.

But the waiter was still smiling. He was bored waiting tables. His girl-friend, a former Bunny from the New York Playboy Club, had a great job cocktailing. He could take the rest of the season off and let her pay the bills. Or maybe he'd dump her and head up to Jackson on his own. Great skiing up there. He pulled off his apron—he'd always hated those aprons—and tossed it on the table, knocking over a glass of very expensive wine. The glass shattered. The red wine flooded the pure white tablecloth.

Roger Randall was, for once, speechless. The waiter grabbed the woman who had, up until that instant, been his boss and gave her the deep passion-ate kiss they'd both been considering since the day she'd hired him. He let her go and walked to the door, turning back to shout, "Dick you, Fuck-tu!" and then laughed gleefully as he strolled off into the night.

MARYBELLE DICTU stood up and clinked a spoon against her wine glass. The crowd showed no signs of quieting down. Perhaps the open bar before dinner hadn't been the best idea—but liquor early helped with con-tributions later. This boisterous enthusiasm should translate to generosity in the end, but for now it was annoying. Marybelle finally got their attention when she gave the glass an extra hard whack and it shattered. People who had ignored the polite clinking immediately stopped to look around. Even in the best circles, the sound of shattering glass is often a prelude to deli-cious drama. But in this case, it was just Marybelle—surprised but then proud at her success in taming the mob.

"Forgive me for 'breaking' in on you!" Her voice was clear and confi-dent, not even a hint that she hadn't meant to shatter that glass. Let those who doubted her resolve take that as a warning. This woman would do whatever was necessary. She could grab a shard of that broken glass and start slashing throats if that's what it took to get those pledges rolling in. Better get on the winning team right from the start. "Thank you all for coming out tonight! I just know this is going to be the start of something big! An Historic Recovery!" The woman knew her exclamation points. The crowd couldn't deny her the applause she demanded.

Marybelle went on to talk about the Spirit of Aspen. She invoked Walter and Elizabeth Paepcke, the almost mythical founders of Aspen's modern day renaissance, and the "brave soldiers of the Tenth Mountain Division" who had come to Aspen after the war, and the "tough citizens of Aspen" who had all joined together to bring "this magical town back from the brink of desolation" with their hard work and creative genius. She talked about "rising from the ashes" and how the Aspen Historical Society was committed to restoring what had been so tragically lost.

Standing at the back of the room, sipping a beer—he'd caught the tail end of the open bar—Jackson thought none of it really meant anything. Except that she never mentioned the $50 million mining museum. That was mildly interesting. Jackson was already planning on leading his story with "Back from the brink of desolation..." and seeing where that took him.

Then, after a surprisingly short speech, for which Jackson was deeply grateful, Marybelle introduced the rest of the board—an impressive assemblage. In the past weeks of crisis, Marybelle had found it prudent to trim away deadwood, get the board in fighting shape for the campaign ahead. The new board members displayed good cheer and seriousness of purpose as they were introduced. And the last to be named, the newest board member, sitting at Marybelle's right hand and rising to acknowledge the polite applause, was Goodwin "Goodie" Rawlins. The applause had a certain surprised quality to it. This was not Goodie's normal social circle. Those who knew him had assumed—with a certain amusement—that he was just there as Marybelle's escort for the evening. Some of the audience hadn't recognized him at all. Either because they'd never seen him before or because they'd never seen him wearing clothes. In any case, there was an element of general astonishment as they gazed at the beaming new board member.

Goodie reached out and took the microphone from Marybelle. For an instant, surprised, she seemed to resist, but she was gracious at all costs and let it go. Goodie thanked her and, grinning wildly, announced that he was kicking off the fund raising with a personal pledge of one million dollars. Marybelle parted her lips in well-controlled amazement. The applause was deafening. "But!" Goodie held up one finger and, unlike Marybelle's earlier efforts, the silence was immediate. "My million dollars—and I will write a check tonight—is a challenge grant. Those of you right here, tonight, have to match my million dollars. The entire one million dollars. Before we go home. Or the deal is off!"

And there was silence.

JACKSON LOVED writing that story. He still got to use "brink of desolation."

"Supporters of the Aspen Historical Society heard fulsome praise for the 'heroes' who brought Aspen 'back from, the brink of desolation.' Then they peered over the edge of another brink and decided that, while desolation has its drawbacks, it has one major advantage: It's cheap.

"Society President Marybelle Dictu opened last night's fund-raising gala by spelling out the organization's difficult financial situation as it seeks to recover from the disastrous Harkney House fire. Then potential white knight Goodwin Rawlins tried to jumpstart the fund-raising with a challenge pledge of $1 million—valid only if it were to be matched 100 percent by the assembled cross-section of Aspen society before the end of the evening.

"Unfortunately for the society's coffers, those attending the event may have deep pockets, but they couldn't reach deep enough to make any significant progress toward that $1 million goal. On-the-spot pledges in response to Rawlins' challenge barely passed the $100,000 mark before the giving stalled.

"'Deep pockets, short arms,' muttered a member of the wait staff.

"Although the black-tie affair was supposed to run until midnight, the crowd thinned dramatically in the quarter hour after Rawlins made his pledge. By 11, the only people on the dance floor were dressed in blue jeans and seemed to have wandered in to fill the void left by the swiftly departing guests, who were disinclined to dance—having perhaps pulled a muscle ducking Rawlins' challenge."

Jackson thought long and hard and then took out the "pulled muscle" line. It had no place in a news story. Actually, most of what he'd written had no place in a news story, but that line went too far. Then he put it back in. Then he took it out again. But "deep pockets, short arms" definitely stayed.

It was after midnight by the time he finished the story, long past deadline. Even the proofreader had gone home, so he handed it directly to the typesetter, who was sharp enough to catch any major errors. Jackson knew Harbuck would be outraged. And he knew he'd catch hell from Fester in the morning, but maybe that would make him would think twice before sticking Jackson with another assignment like that.

Then he sat at his desk for a while, thinking randomly about PJ and Louise. And Gunnar. Finally, he picked up the pad he'd been looking for when Fester was demanding a story. It was the one he had carried into the Ute Cemetery. It's pages were wrinkled, crumpled from getting soaked in the snow and jammed in his pocket. The ink had fuzzed out through the wet paper. On it he had scrawled, even as he was seriously worried about collapsing in the snow and freezing, five words: "She should have died hereafter."

16

HOW LONG HAD IT BEEN SINCE HE'D THOUGHT ABOUT Beast? About him dying. He thought about Beast every day. But he thought about him alive or he thought about him dead. He never thought about him dying. That moment. The whole building falling in flames, coming down on top of him in the dark. He needed to keep that exact terrible moment very clear in his mind.

He was still at least half certain it happened because Beast got high, passed out, knocked something over and burned the place down. No, wait—he needed to be more exact, always: It happened because Beast got high with Jackson, passed out, knocked something over and burned the place down. And that sounded more likely than an arsonist flying in on a private jet to torch a historic Victorian. But if it had been Beast's own stoned fault, then who was threatening PJ? Who had trashed her apartment?

Whoever it was, Jackson had to make it stop.

If PJ was right, then she was in the cross-hairs for trying to track down the guy who had flown in the night of the fire. And that would mean the best way to get them to leave her alone was for Jackson to step up and make it clear that he was the one chasing the story. You want to scare someone, thought Jackson, scare me.

Which meant he needed to actually get on the story.

Jackson decided to start with the plane that flew the thug in the black raincoat to Aspen. There had to be records of that.

Jackson drove out to the airport. He didn't know anyone who worked there, not really. Not since an old girlfriend had gotten fired by Aspen Scareways for sending some aggressive jerk's luggage to Damascus, instead of Dallas. An innocent mistake. Really.

So he took his chances, headed to the private terminal and explained to the man behind the counter that he needed some information on the last plane that flew in on a certain night. And flew out the next morning.

Jackson did his best to be very polite, but the guy behind the counter started with a laugh and after that he didn't want to say anything except, "Fuck off!" Which he said loud and clear. Then he couldn't help adding that he hated this rat-shit town and everyone in it. And he couldn't wait to move back to the city. And that he wouldn't piss on Jackson if he was on fire. And, finally, that this wasn't any two-bit local operation, the guys who owned the company were from Chicago and Jackson had better watch his ass.

That sounded promising, so Jackson followed up in kind.

"I need to talk to your boss and he needs to talk to me. What's his phone number?"

That got him another serious "Fuck off!"

"Yeah. Right. Then you tell him to call me. Jackson at the Aspen Sun. He needs to call me. He'll know why. And you need to do some serious work on your customer service skills, dipshit." Then he spun around and marched away, before the guy behind the counter could get in another Fuck off! And before he could see the broad grin plastered across Jackson's face.

That should do it. Word would get where it need to go. It was Jackson working on the story. Not PJ. No point in hassling her.

Now he was having fun. He'd made someone angry, he'd been threatened and now he was looking over his shoulder, being careful, because PJ would kill him if he got careless and anything happened to him. And that's what made it fun. He was on an adventure with PJ again.

He thought about calling PJ, to tell what he'd gotten done. And then he thought about Skeeter.

And just like that, it wasn't quite such an adventure anymore.

"JACKSON! MY OFFICE. Now."

That wasn't good. Fester's efficient boss voice meant he was doing something he didn't want to do. Never a good way to start the day for anyone involved.

"Sit." Jackson thought about woofing, panting with his tongue out. He decided not to. "Are you still screwing around with the Harkney House fire?"

"What do you mean 'screwing around'?"

"Cut the crap, Jack. You know exactly what I mean." Jackson had nothing to say. "So knock it off. Drop it."

"Wait a minute. I've got…"

"Forget it!" Fester paused for a moment. "I've been cutting you a lot of slack ever since… you know, the fire."

"Bullshit."

"What?" Fester was getting angry. Jackson didn't care.

"You never cut me any slack. You never had to. I've written more junior hockey stories in the last couple of months than anybody's ever written in the history of the world. And you know it."

"OK. But you know what? Now you're going to write even more."

"Fuck it, Felster. That's not fair."

"A fair is where they have a Ferris wheel and pony rides for kids. No one said anything about fair." Fester decided to try honest instead of angry. "Look, Dictu is…"

"Fuck Dictu!" The anger in Jackson's voice surprised both of them. "He doesn't even have any goddamn kids."

"Fine. Forget Dictu. This is about the newspaper and I'm saying, Prince Hal's saying, we're going to start running those stories. And…"

"I know. I'm going to write them."

"Exactly. So forget about the damn fire."

"Wait a minute. What's the connection? OK, I'll write more junior hockey stories. But why do I have to stop trying to find out what happened with that fire?"

"Because I say so."

"That's the way you're going to run this newspaper?"

"That's the way I'm supposed to run this newspaper. I'm the editor. And I'm telling you to stop wasting time on that damn fire. It's over. Let it go." A moment of silence. Fester went on, quietly. "Jack, I know Beast was... I know it hurts. But you've got to get over it. And sooner would be better."

There was honesty in his voice. He really did care about the paper and the people who worked there. But Jackson still didn't like what was happening.

"What else are you working on?"

Fester was trying to steer the conversation back to normal. As if everything was settled. He'd shown a little emotion and everyone was happy. The discussion was over. And now Jackson had to come up with a story, so he started talking about the Ute Cemetery.

He still hadn't written the grave desecration story, but that was OK, because now it would be the foundation for something much bigger.

He explained how the Ute was a real slice of Aspen history, how it had been neglected all these years, fallen into ruin. And here was the big idea: Save the Ute. It could be a great crusade for the paper. Get the town worked up, raise some money, make everyone look good.

And Fester loved it.

"All right! That's what we ought to be doing. Something for the community."

"You're making me all teary-eyed."

"So what's your plan?"

And to his own surprise, Jackson realized he did have a plan. "We'll ease into it. I'll write a few stories about the cemetery before we start campaigning to save it." Now he was on solid ground. "I'll start with that desecration story."

"Wondering if you were ever going to get around to that."

"Hey, I've got it. Almost got it anyway. There's something strange going on there."

And he told Fester about the missing gravestone and the inscription, "She should have died hereafter."

Fester knitted his eyebrows which, as always, looked like a cornfield after a raid by a flock of crows. "I don't get it."

Jackson explained the quote, carefully finding the right tone to show that, of course, he knew this quote well, but, of course, he wasn't smug about his knowledge.

"Anyway," he concluded, "that's all that's left."

"So we've got a mystery."

Fester was smiling. Everybody loves a mystery.

And Jackson had been working on the story over at the county record vault, so he had more to add.

"I found the cemetery records. They're sketchy, but near as I can figure that plot is registered under the name 'Finch.' No indication who the three graves are, but the way they're laid out—two stones about the same size, side by side, and then the third, set off to the side—I'm thinking maybe two parents and a child. That fits with the inscription too: She should have died hereafter. There are a lot of real young kids buried there. A few days old. A week. Maybe two. So maybe that's what we've got here. Mr. and Mrs. Finch and their little baby."

"Makes sense." Fester nodded, agreeing with himself. "But why would anyone bust up the stones? Why cart the kid's stone away."

"That's the mystery."

"Solve it. Or you don't have a story."

"One problem."

"What's that?"

"The fire ..."

"Forget the fucking fire!" Jackson couldn't help smiling.

"Easy, boss. Just that I would have used the archives at the historical society for research. It'd all be there. In the old papers. But that's all gone now."

"Yeah, well, that's your problem. That's why they call it work. Did I mention that?"

Jackson didn't bother to answer.

"Great," said Fester. "Glad we got that cleared up. Now find me something for tomorrow's paper."

Tomorrow's paper. There was always tomorrow's paper. The demon had to be fed. Feed it or be fed to it. That was the only choice.

Jackson started calling around. The county manager was out of his office. The school superintendent was too busy to take his call. The city planner was more than glad to chat, but managed to take up half an hour without saying anything of even minor interest. The county manager didn't have anything, but he mentioned that the head of the Road & Bridge Department was seriously proud of his new snowplows. Jackson thought he'd rather slam his hand in a car door than write about new snowplows.

Then he remembered he'd promised to call Louise back. Two days ago.

He felt a little guilty. Just a little. This was still Aspen, after all. But he'd been focused on her, then he'd hung up and run off to rescue PJ—and spend the night. And since then it had mostly been PJ on his mind, which was dangerous under any circumstances.

"Hey, college boy."

She recognized his voice right away. Instead of going back to the subject of her cousin Skip who apparently hated his own name as much as he hated Jackson, he went off on the tangent of the day.

"Hey, do you know anything about a family named Finch?"

"Mrs. Finch? Oh yeah. Why?"

"Working on a story and the name Finch turned up."

"Only one Finch that I know of in Aspen. She was the English teacher. And she's famous around our place. She and Great Grammy couldn't stand each other. They had a pretty serious disagreement over 'King Lear.' Lear blinding Gloucester. Grammy had some strong feelings about that scene and Mrs. Finch had a very different opinion. You know how some people get about Shakespeare." No, Jackson didn't. But he didn't want to get into that right now. "Anyway, Mrs. Finch came to tea one day and she tried to bully Grammy." A pause. "That's the way Grammy tells the story anyway. 'Tried to bullyrag me right there in my own parlor.'"

Jackson smiled. "Ophelia's tough."

"So was Mrs. Finch. She got so mad when Grammy argued with her. Grammy told her off and, way she tells it, Mrs. Finch never crossed her threshold again."

"All right, great stuff for my story."

"Don't quote me."

"Come on. That was a good line."

"Don't be lazy. You should be getting all this from Ophelia."

He felt as if women were always telling him to stop being lazy and do his job. It was annoying, especially when they were right.

"OK. I'll do that."

"Why don't you come out to the ranch for dinner tonight? Grammy drinks a glass or two of wine just about every night. We'll get her talking about Mrs. Finch and she'll tell you everything you need to know."

"Sounds great."

"Dinner's at six. Won't be any food left if you're late."

JACKSON SPENT the next hour making one more stab at getting a story about Dictu putting together a deal at the base of the mountain. He was on deadline, running late, and Fester had forbidden him to work on that story. How could he resist? Besides, if he couldn't figure out who killed Beast—or if no one killed him and it was all just a series of accidents and misunderstandings, which was, he knew, the way the world usually worked—then at least he could shine a bright light on whatever secret project R2Dictu was working on. And if the bright light sent the cockroaches scurrying for cover, well then, he would count that as a blow for justice.

But Jackson didn't make any progress on getting that bright light to shine. Lorena at the county clerk's office managed to communicate a totally uninterested shrug over the telephone. Then Jackson called his friend, Brian, at the Forest Service, a pretty good friend and an even better source, a guy who was usually eager to talk—hard to shut up, as a matter of fact. But this time he wasn't any more helpful than Lorena. His voice was flat. "Nope. Nothing going on."

And then it was almost four o'clock and Jackson still hadn't written anything for tomorrow's paper. So he sucked it up and called the Road & Bridge Department. If he had to write about snowplows then, damn it, he would write about snowplows.

But the head of Road and Bridge, instead of talking about his beautiful new plows, gave Jackson a story about the city's plan to start plowing the alleys early this year. That didn't sound like much, but the good part was that they were going to be aggressive about towing cars that were parked anywhere in or even too close to the right of way. All those cars buried in the drifts all winter were going to have to be moved or they would be towed.

That was going to make a lot of people angry. And Jackson loved writing stories that were going to make a lot of people angry.

THERE WERE steaks and baked potatoes and some kind of casserole and beer and wine and a dozen people around the big table. Jackson knew most of the names because that was his job, but he didn't know many of the faces. These weren't people he interviewed. They weren't people who showed up in the newspaper and he got the feeling they liked it that way. But they seemed glad enough to have him there and they included him in the conversation as they passed the food around, ate and drank and laughed and argued. It was a family dinner. And, aside from maybe Thanksgiving, when someone always included Jackson and other Aspen "orphans," it had been a long time since he'd been at any kind of family dinner. In fact, Jackson had never had many dinners that fit that description. Not with his family. He never knew what had happened to his father—the old man had just disappeared—and his mother might have tried to do the family thing, but she hadn't tried very hard. Most days, getting out of bed was more than she could manage. Family dinners, family anything, just weren't on the agenda. He'd tried to track her down after he moved to Aspen, but, in the end, by the time he'd heard she was dying, she'd already died. A gust of laughter broke out at the ranch table and Jackson realized he didn't want to miss this family dinner by brooding over dinners he'd never had.

So he cracked open a beer, cracked a couple of jokes, and dived right in.

By the time the meal was done, Grammy was sipping her third glass of wine and giggling.

Louise raised an eyebrow at Jackson. This was his chance. "So, Ophe-lia"—they'd been on a first-name basis since the second glass of wine—"do you remember Mrs. Finch? The English teacher?"

Ophelia carefully finished her sip of wine and set the glass down on the table. "Mrs. Finch." She cocked her head and smiled. "Birdie Finch. Called her that behind her back. And then one time someone called her Birdie right to her face and she turned red—red as Woody Woodpecker and I swear if that wasn't the funniest..." She was silent for a moment. "That bitch!"

Louise burst out laughing. "Grammy!"

"She sat right in my parlor, my own parlor and told me I didn't under-stand anything at all about King Lear. Sat right there on my couch and said it was nice that I was 'fond of the Bard,' but she was the teacher, so I was going to have to admit she knew better. Said that right to my face. I showed her the door, I guess I did!" Then, one more time, just for good measure, "Bitch!"

Ophelia was smiling, enjoying the outrage. Then her face collapsed. "Wasn't very Christian of me. She had a hard enough life, I guess. Maybe a little Christian charity..." And she began to cry. It reminded Jackson that there was a reason he didn't go to family dinners.

LOUISE WALKED him to the door. "I guess three glasses of wine was one too many." In fact, Ophelia had been laughing by the time the dishes were cleared, but Jackson wasn't going to ask about Mrs. Finch again.

They stood inside the door as he shrugged into his parka.

"Sorry about your story."

"Never mind. That was the best meal I've had in a long time."

"It was good to have a new face at the table. I get to see this crew pretty much seven nights a week."

"You have got to get out more."

"Are you asking me out?"

Jackson hadn't meant to. But now that he was halfway there... "Well, maybe I am."

"Call me when you get it figured out better than just 'maybe.'"

He thought maybe he ought to kiss her goodnight, but he wasn't sure. He was pretty certain the rules were different out on the ranch than in the alley behind Michael's. He stood there for a moment, not knowing what to do, so she kissed him.

"That was nice."

"Call me."

He thought about the kiss halfway back to town. The rest of the way he wondered how he was going to find out more about Mrs. Finch. He had a story to write.

17

"TWO SKELETONS?"

Jackson squinted at the faded ink, the scrawled handwriting.

"That's what it says." Skip Olsen had dug out the report, but he wasn't happy about it. Louise said he hated Jackson and apparently she knew what she was talking about. Lots of people Jackson wrote about wound up hating him. Particularly cops. It used to bother him.

Jackson shook his head as he puzzled over the handwriting. "One young adult female. One infant. Possibly ... ?"

"Foetal. A fetus. The woman might have died in childbirth. Or right after. Maybe the cabin collapsed under the snow and killed her."

"None of that was in the paper."

"Everybody already knew. That's the way it was back then. Everyone knew everything. The paper just printed the parts people were supposed to know."

Jackson read a little more. "OK. So what's this? 'Items held in evidence.'"

Cousin Skip almost smiled. "Waiting to see if you'd notice that." He pulled out a small metal box. "Crazy to keep it this long, but that's what we do."

He opened the box and showed Jackson the meager contents: a few scraps of cloth, a small piece of bone and a tarnished thin silver chain with the back half of a locket. The deputy reached into the box with the stub of a pencil and flipped it over. The back was engraved with a scrolled flower design. "That's it," he said. "Don't know what kind of story you can get out of that. Mother and child. Dead a hundred years. No clues. End of story. Unless you want to make something up."

Jackson thought about getting annoyed. "Let's just leave it at that."

"Leave well enough alone? You never do that, do you?"

Jackson decided again not to get into it, but the deputy didn't want to let it go.

"No scandal, no story. You need something bad to happen or you're shit out of luck. That makes this one a dead end for you, right?"

Enough.

"I guess. Unless you have something you'd like to confess. Skippy."

He leaned extra hard on the name—knowing the deputy hated it, but having no idea why.

Skip's face turned bright red and Jackson remembered—not for the first time in these offices—that he was dealing with a man who was carrying a gun.

The deputy opened a desk drawer, slammed it shut, opened another. After a moment he looked up. "You still here?"

Jackson couldn't just let it end like that. He had to say something. Something that wouldn't get him shot.

"Were you working the day Gunnar had his crash?"

A question out of nowhere. The deputy seemed to accept it as a peace offering.

"Sure."

"Anything strange about it? Out of the ordinary?"

The deputy snorted—his snort wasn't as cute as his cousin Louise's.

"Just Gunnar. He was nuttier than squirrel shit." He thought a moment. "Otherwise, no. He was heading up the mountain and went off the trail."

"That's it?"

"Yup. I saw the tracks. Lucky he wasn't killed outright. Doesn't take much to get killed in the mountains. Night. Winter. Hell, any time." He narrowed his eyes and stared at Jackson. "It's just that easy —" he snapped his fingers "— to wind up dead. One small mistake. End of story."

Jackson decided it was time to leave.

Roger Randall Dictu gazed out at Pyramid Peak, while the two dogs from the shelter, not winded at all by the dash up the mountain, ran in circles and rolled in the snow.

Today even the hard-edged magnificence of the 14,000-foot peak didn't quiet his annoyance.

Roger Randall was proud of his self-knowledge—no need for self-help seminars—and he knew exactly what was bothering him. He could still hear the echo of that damn waiter's laughter. Not being a fool, he knew he was being foolish. He was almost embarrassed that he'd taken the time to make inquiries and had discovered that there was nothing he could do to bring that insolent little shit to heel. The man—no, not a man, just a boy—was too small to crush. He had nothing but his skis and his beat-up old Jeep and his beautiful girlfriend, which he apparently valued in exactly that order. Roger Randall had grown up in the 1960s, and he'd listened to Janis Joplin singing "Freedom's just another word for nothing left to lose." But now he was learning what that really meant—from someone who had that kind of freedom. And Roger Randall hated it.

He knew what he needed: a new challenge. Not another weasel to crush. A real challenge.

He thought about his ski descent of Mt. Sopris and remembered the thought that had crossed his mind when he was starting the final climb to the summit in the dark. Sopris was hard, damned hard, but he could do it and he knew it. It was time for something wilder. A real challenge. And as he thought about that, the echo of the waiter's laughter faded. Screw Janis Joplin. Roger Randall Dictu was free because he had a lot to lose and because he was a real man, willing to risk it all.

He gave a sharp whistle. The dogs rushed to his side. He was the bright spot in their lives. As they were in his.

JACKSON SAT at his desk waiting for the phone to ring. He needed a story. He was thinking about what Skip had said. Jackson wouldn't have a story until something bad happened. Sometimes that bothered him. It really bothered him when a jerk like Skip pointed it out.

The phone rang. Jackson looked heavenward in an unspoken prayer for bad news.

It was worse than bad. Three skiers buried in an avalanche deep in the backcountry.

Jackson grabbed his parka, excited and hating himself for it. But before he got out the door, Fester burst into the office.

"Damn it, Jackson! Where the hell have you been?" Jackson started to say he'd been right there in the office, but Fester didn't even slow down. "We've got a dead movie star who hit a tree on Ajax. And some family up on Red Mountain just filed a law suit against the elementary school principal for saying their brat has to take Ritalin. Pick one and get on it. I'll hand out the other."

"Fuck that," said Jackson. "I'll take both of them and yell for help if I need it." He wasn't going to mention the avalanche to Fester, but he had a sudden fear that someone else might steal the story. So, like a dog pissing on a juicy tidbit, he shouted over his shoulder as he ran out the door, "I've got an avalanche too!"

Jack the Jackal, on the job. He'd hate himself later. Right now he was too busy.

He ran to the sheriff's office to find out about the missing skiers. The story was clear-cut and real bad. They were half of a group of six and the others had seen them swept away by a massive slide that boiled down the hillside and across the trail. Jackson saw the names of the three who had survived and his heart sank. He almost certainly would know the three who had been lost.

He jogged across town to the base of Aspen Mountain and found a ski instructor who gave him the names of the patrollers who brought the dead movie star down the mountain. Not really a movie star, in the end. TV, not movies. And a bit actor, not a star. But a name and a face some people would recognize—and, in the end, a human being who skied into a tree and died. Front-page news. Shut up, conscience.

Then he raced back to the courthouse to get the file on the elementary school law suit. He recognized the names of the parents and he knew he could get some good information—OK, juicy gossip about their brat—from the woman who lived in their caretaker apartment.

Four hours and fifteen phone calls later, he finished the last of his three front-page stories. That ought to keep Fester off his back for a couple of days. Take that, Skippy.

THE NEXT MORNING, Jackson headed up the mountain before work. But on his first run, he lost a ski in the heavy powder at the top of Last Dollar and tumbled a long way down the steep slope. He landed hard on the top of a mogul and lay there a while with snow down the back of his neck and the back of his pants. He looked up the slope twenty feet to where his sunglasses were—and then much farther up to his hat. No sign of his ski. Finding the ski took a good half hour—floundering uphill, sweating and cursing; then digging through the snow, freezing and cursing.

He skied down and went to work.

By late afternoon, his shoulder was stiffening up and his knee was aching somewhere deep inside. He was working, without any real enthusiasm, on a story from the Planning Commission when Fester came into his office.

"I'm thinking maybe we could shake loose fifty bucks for some research on that Ute story. That missing gravestone."

"What?"

"We need a good story to kick off our Save the Ute campaign. We can spend a little money."

Jackson was astonished. Fester never spent any money on anything. Beast had once suggested "We're not paying for that," as the paper's motto. Printed on the front page, right under the Aspen Sun flag. And now Fester was spending half a hundred just for research. He must be feeling guilty about junior hockey.

Jackson hurried to spend the money before Fester could change his mind. After a few calls, he found a journalism student at Denver University who said he'd gladly put in a couple of hours going through the State

Historical Society archives for fifty bucks and a by-line. Jackson said the by-line wasn't going to happen, but he'd give the kid a "researched by" credit if he got anything good.

He trudged through the rest of the Planning Commission story and was getting ready to go home and put some ice on his knee when his phone range.

"Get over here right now!" It was PJ. "The ambulance is on its way." She hung up before he could ask what the hell she was talking about.

When he got to her apartment, the door was open and he could see PJ inside, bending over the couch, wrapping someone in a blanket. Blonde hair.

PJ looked up, bewildered. "She was on the porch. Jennifer. Unconscious. When I got home."

"What ... ?"

"I don't know."

"Did she walk here? Did someone dump her here? How ...?"

"Goddamn it! I don't know! I don't know!"

The ambulance raced up the alley and stopped, siren dying in the thin air. The alley was dappled with mud and frozen trash and stubborn drifts of dirty snow. A still life: Springtime in the Rockies. With ambulance.

The EMTs raced up the stairs. They took Jennifer's pulse. Shined a light into the tiny pin-pricks of her pupils. Slapped an oxygen mask on her and carried her away.

PJ grabbed her parka and headed down to her car. Jackson was right behind her. PJ's car usually spent the entire winter buried in the snow. Once the lifts started running, she never left town until the season was over and it was time to head somewhere warm. It always took jumper cables to get Griselda—PJ named her cars—running. But before she could get the car door open, a pick-up with red lights flashing skidded to a stop in the alley. It was a volunteer fireman, answering the emergency call.

PJ yanked the truck's door open and climbed in with Jackson right behind her.

"Hospital," she gasped out. "The ambulance's already gone."

The fireman threw the truck into gear and raced out of the alley.

The ski day was over and the streets were jammed with college kids on Spring Break, already drunk and looking for action. The driver ducked the heavy traffic on the Castle Creek bridge, driving down into the gorge on the steep, icy Power Plant Road and crossing the creek there. They fishtailed wildly on the ice coming back up, forced their way into traffic on Cemetery Lane, ran the stop sign at the highway and got to the hospital just behind the ambulance.

Then they stood and watched as the gurney was rolled into the emergency room.

PJ AND JACKSON sat in silence. Time passed the way it does in hospitals: too slowly to bear, too quickly for everything that might be happening. Hospital visits weren't unusual. People got hurt all the time: skiing, kayaking, climbing. There were always friends to visit with torn ligaments and broken bones. But visiting Gunnar and now, worse, waiting to hear about Jennifer—this was different. Those other visits were about life, about living maybe too much. These visits were about...

And before he could finish the thought a doctor walked out of the ICU, shaking his head.

Jackson and PJ were on their feet.

"You can't print anything until we notify next of kin," the doctor told Jackson.

Next of kin. End of story.

"Does she... did she have any family" asked PJ. Calm now that it was over. After a moment of silence, she said, "Tracey was her roommate. Maybe she knows."

"What killed her?" Jackson had to ask.

"You can't print it," the doctor insisted. "But I'm pretty sure it was heroin. The eyes. Blue fingernails. Heroin and whatever else. You know Jennifer." Jackson realized the doctor was almost crying. When he mentioned that to PJ later on, she told him that the doctor had lived with Jennifer for a couple of months and she'd broken up with him when he told her that he was going to lose his license if he kept giving her pharmaceutical drugs. Broke his heart. She left him for a ski instructor with good coke connections. Then left the ski pro for a rock star. And after that, who could remember? You know Jennifer.

But the doctor kept rattling on. "We can't do that kind of testing here. Have to send it out. I don't know. That's up to the sheriff." He stopped short. Then he walked away fast.

"SOMETHING'S WRONG. Everything's wrong. Jenn didn't do smack."

"She did anything anyone put in front of her face. You know that. Partying too long, too late, too wired to sleep, someone offers her smack... why not? She'd put anything up her nose."

PJ knew he was right and she didn't care. "Then who gave it to her? How about you, Jack? Was it you?"

"OK, PJ. Take it easy."

"Screw that. Someone killed Beast. They tried to kill Gunnar. Now they've killed Jenn. They're killing my friends? Who did it? Who?"

Jackson didn't say anything. They were standing outside her apartment after walking back to town. It had been snowing hard when they left the hospital and it was snowing even harder now.

"Never mind, Jack. I'll find out myself."

"No!" He surprised himself by how sharply that came out.

But PJ suddenly smiled. "There you go. One more item on that list of things you don't get to tell me. Let's make it number one on that list. You don't get to tell me No. Not now, not ever. How great is that? And Jack"— her smile seemed real—"you know I'll love you for the rest of my life."

"Come on, PJ. This is my story."

"Too bad. Everyone thinks you're cool, Jack. But this is my town too. I'll let you know what I find."

He walked home through the spring storm—big, wet flakes falling with a kind of desperation, as if a thick coat of white could erase what had just happened.

THE NEXT DAY, Jackson stayed away from the story. The cop reporter asked him what he knew about it and he said, "Nothing" and left it at that. The reporter went to the press conference with an FBI agent who came up from Glenwood to explain the dangers of drugs and Jackson went to a zoning board meeting to listen to a fight over the color scheme for a new hotel.

"I know you would prefer that our guests fly in and arrive at a building constructed out of mud and wattle," said the hotel's attorney. "But my clients are quite reasonably insisting on a more welcoming appearance."

While they haggled over a precise legal definition of the required "muted earth tones," Jackson stared out the window at Red Mountain, where the scrub oak poked through patchy late-spring snow. Jennifer could have been careless enough to let someone kill her, but it was hard to know who would have wanted to. You have to take someone seriously to hate them enough to kill them. And no one took Jennifer seriously. Most likely, she'd killed herself. By accident for sure—though some day she might have gotten around to killing herself on purpose. Jackson didn't think about it much, but he knew some kind of a bad ending had always been one of the possibilities for Jennifer. Feel good and party hard right now and there'd be plenty of time to get your life on track later. And later could so easily become much later—and much later could just as easily become too late.

He thought about Louise. The enormous distance between her life and Jennifer's. Not that Louise's life was all worked out. Her parents had gone through an ugly divorce, some of her cousins were idiots and Louise herself was deep into her thirties and still hassling with drunk boyfriends who cheated on her—but there was something solid underneath. She had family and history to fall back on whenever "later" finally came around. Jennifer didn't have any of that. But none of that mattered, because "later" never came for Jennifer. She died the way she lived: right now. An easy accident. Too easy.

Jennifer and Jackson hadn't been close. Jackson didn't really even like her much. Once when they were both pretty drunk, she'd asked him to go home with her and he'd turned her down—which was pretty rare. But still, she was part of his Aspen. Someone who wasn't really all that young but still liked to joke about living fast, dying young and leaving a good-looking corpse. She'd managed that. Didn't seem like much of an accomplishment.

"Are we keeping you awake, Mr. Jackson?" Two of the board members snickered. The chairman liked to catch him dozing, but he wasn't—not this time anyway.

He glanced up. "Don't worry. I've got it." He pointed at the hotel's lawyer. "Mud and wattle. Right Brian?"

The lawyer smiled, thinking that quote would almost certainly show up in the paper. He was proud of it. He'd thought of it in the shower that morning and he was eager to see it in print.

"That's right. Mud and wattle. And that's a shameful situation to be imposing on this world-class resort community where we know we need to ..." And he was off. The chairman glared at Jackson; Jackson smiled pleasantly and nodded. You started it, asshole.

And Jennifer? Jennifer was dead. Like Beast.

"IF YOU'RE LOOKING for more money, forget it."

Jackson had finished the mud-and-wattles zoning board story and all he wanted to do was go home. But first he had to deal with the college kid on the phone from Denver, telling him how hard he was working on the Finch story.

But the kid surprised him. "Forget the money ..."

"Really?"

"Hell no. I need the cash. But I'm telling you there's something weird going on. I'm looking for those files—anything on the Finch broad —"

"Stop trying to sound like a reporter."

"— and everything's missing. Pages torn out of the newspapers in the archives. Rolls of microfilm disappeared. A couple of those big bound volumes just gone missing. You don't just tuck those fuckers in your pocket and slip out the door. Someone's working hard to kill that story."

"Probably my boss. Doesn't want to shell out the fifty bucks. Keep looking. Try the state records. Department of Health or something like that. They must have been keeping of births and deaths even back then."

"How about that byline?"

"Get me the story and we'll talk about it."

Why would anyone care about the Finch family? Bust up their graves. Try to erase them from the archives. It didn't make any sense—but neither did anything else that was happening. Jackson was sick of things that didn't make sense.

But everyone loves a mystery—so he wrote a teaser for the Ute Cemetery story: "The Forgotten Cemetery and the Missing Gravestone." He hyped the series and he hyped the story. "The Tragic Mystery of Widow Finch." He talked to the night editor and got him to run it in a box on the front page.

Then he went home.

THE CHURCH was Catholic, not Orthodox—but that didn't matter. The calm was what Viktor craved.

He fought for some shred of control. Was he there to mourn? He didn't know if he was. He didn't know if he could. He might have been sorry. He couldn't tell. He couldn't think. His heart was a rabbit, zigzagging down the middle of the road, looking for a speeding car to throw itself under.

A woman across the aisle got up and moved further away. Was it his breathing, rasping through his ruined nose? Were the voices in his head so loud that she could hear them? He wanted to run after her, drag her back to her seat.

There was a blonde two rows ahead of him. He couldn't see her face. No matter. He couldn't stand the sight of that blonde hair. He closed his eyes and his vision filled with whirling dots of color against the black of his rage.

Fix it! The son of a bitch had told him to fix it!

A curtain of red swept down across the whirling colors. He opened his eyes in panic.

The blonde turned around to stare at him. Was he shouting? He had to get out of there.

Fix it? He'd fix it.

He raced out into the night. A light snow was falling and, for the first time, the sight of snow made him smile. A thick coat of snow would help.

He'd fix everything.

"JACK, take a long lunch. Let's ski a run."

Jackson smiled. It almost sounded like the old PJ.

"Don't need to call it lunch. Counts as work time. Interview on the chairlift. Adds authenticity. 'Swinging over the Ridge of Bell, the hot-skiing bartender said…' Prince Hal loves that."

"Fuck you, Jackson."

"Well that would definitely have to be on my lunch hour."

"You wish. Gondola. Half an hour."

It wasn't the old PJ, her voice was tight, but the words were right so he didn't worry about it.

It was one o'clock by the time they got to the gondola. The noon rush of people trying to get the most out of a half-day ticket was long over, so they had a car to themselves.

At first they rode in silence. Jackson had nothing to say, so he followed his instincts and said nothing. Eyes safely hidden behind mirrored sunglasses, he studied PJ. He didn't recognize the look on her face. She wasn't angry. She wasn't scared. She wasn't happy—that was certain.

The gondola angled up the mountain, the cable whirring, chattering and clattering. They crossed over Jackpot and Jackson studied the icy moguls, the way he always did, thinking it didn't look that steep from up here, trying to pick out a good line to ski, knowing he'd never find it when he was actually thrashing his way down the run.

They cleared the last of the trees and suddenly they were dangling high above Copper Bowl. The gondola car rocked in the wind. Jackson watched the skiers coming down the bowl. Some were fast and graceful. Some were slow and careful. Others, fast or slow, were awkward and dangerous. The bright colors on the awkward skiers fascinated him. Why work so hard to be noticed if you're going to look that bad? The car stuttered and jerked to a stop, rocking even harder.

"It's time to drop it, Jack. The whole thing."

PJ's voice was sudden and harsh.

"The whole…"

"All of it. The fire. Beast. Gunnar and his stupid conspiracies. Just drop it."

"I don't get…"

"It's over. Beast is dead. Gunnar's brain-dead." She stopped for a moment. "Jenn's dead. Let it go."

"You were the one who said…"

"Forget what I said! Forget everything. Just fucking forget it!"

"How about the guy in the black…"

"Let it go."

The car shuddered and swung and started moving again.

They rode the rest of the way in silence so thick that Jackson thought even if he shouted he wouldn't make a sound.

As they neared the top, he tried anyway.

"Jesus, Peej…"

"Forget it, Jack!"

The car lurched into the top station and the doors slammed open. PJ hurried out, grabbed her skis, kicked into the bindings and took off. Jackson stayed close behind. PJ raced down the easy runs at the top of the mountain, dropping into a tuck and then veering onto the narrow trail that cut through the trees high on the back of Bell Mountain, skiing fast through the bumps across the top of Bell and then disappearing into the trees on the Face. PJ was a little awkward on her skis, but somehow that disguised how fast she was going. Jackson had long ago given up trying to keep up with her—especially when she was as upset as she was now.

He skied the Face and forgot about PJ—about catching up to her, about trying to understand what had just happened. He simply skied, looking ahead for the best line through the bumps, catching a glimpse of the low afternoon sun burning through the trees above Spar Gulch, but not letting the beauty break his focus.

When he emerged from the trees and stopped to catch his breath, he could see PJ far below, near the bottom of Spar, moving fast, weaving through a crowd and disappearing toward the catwalk to Kleenex Corner and Little Nell. He skied down by himself and walked back to the office. Not thinking about PJ. Not thinking about Gunnar or Beast. Not thinking about what, if anything, really separated him from Jennifer anyway.

JACKSON WOKE UP in the middle of the night to the sounds of a party. No, not a party. With a party there would have been loud voices, laughter, music. And there should have been cheers. Wait. Why cheers? He shook off the fog of sleep and tried to think. There should have been cheers because what he'd heard was a string of firecrackers going off. And people always cheered after they set off firecrackers. So it wasn't a party and it wasn't firecrackers.

He struggled out of bed and went to the window. Everything was quiet in the moonlight. Normal. Except for the bullet holes in the windshield of his car in the parking lot below.

Well there you go. PJ was right. And he'd done the right thing. He'd made a lot of noise, gotten people angry, put his stamp on the story and—bam!

thank you very much—he'd been noticed. And now someone was trying to scare him, instead of her. Well done.

And his beat-up old car had a flashy new detail: bullet holes. He liked the look. Very Bonnie-and-Clyde.

Curiously pleased with himself, Jackson went back to sleep. An hour later, he woke with a start, tangled in the sheets as he fought to escape a dream of someone chasing him with a machine gun. And after that he didn't sleep very well at all.

18

JACKSON ONCE HAD A MARATHON-RUNNING, COKE-SNORTING, yoga-addicted real estate saleswoman girlfriend who settled all her serious life decisions—including the vital question of where to eat dinner on any given night—by consulting the "I Ching," the Book of Changes, an ancient Chinese oracle that offered cryptic advice based on tossing three coins.

The "I Ching" frequently advised what the prudent man would do, but to the best of Jackson's recollection, it never said, "The prudent man doesn't sleep deeply when someone's out there with a gun." But it certainly should have.

Jackson hadn't been sleeping well since the night someone had used his car for target practice. The bullets had gone right through the windshield and out through the rear window, scattering shards of glass across the front seat and the trunk lid. Whoever did the shooting had been standing right below Jackson's apartment window.

Under the circumstances, waking up every half hour was prudent—he liked the word, even though prudence had never been one of his strong points.

When Jackson wasn't sleeping, he had plenty to think about. The gunman—and Jackson assumed it was a man, assumed, in fact, that it must have been PJ's favorite suspect, the thug in the black raincoat—had only shot the passenger's side of the windshield. Did he do that on purpose? Did he mean to keep the diver's side clear so he could lure Jackson out onto the road and finish him off? Was he just being polite in some strange fashion? Was he a bad shot? Was it completely meaningless? All good questions.

The Aspen cops had already noticed the bullet holes and pulled Jackson over for a chat. They'd smirked and asked if he'd been robbing banks. He told them he was doing ballistics tests for a story and had gotten a little carried away. They let it go at that, but Jackson had decided he didn't really care for the Bonnie-and-Clyde look. But new windshields were expensive.

Tonight he gave up on sleep early and sat looking out the window—watching the stars wheel across the black sky above the blacker mountain. He thought about Jennifer and Beast. And Gunnar. And Louise. And most of all, damn it, about PJ going from "I'm on it. Get the hell out of my way" to "Forget it. They're dead." What had happened?

And while he was at it, he thought about the things that always flooded his mind in the dark night: failures and mistakes, large and small. Why was it that triumphs—he must have had a few, he was certain—never came to haunt his thoughts when he couldn't sleep?

When the moon began to rise and its glare swallowed the stars, he pulled on his cross-country ski gear, grabbed skis and poles and headed down to the car. He needed to talk to Gunnar. Maybe a half-crazed coot with a head injury could give him some answers.

He drove up Castle Creek, keeping his mind empty, focused on the road in the dim cone of the headlights, until—around a curve, out of the dark—headlights! Blinding him, in his eyes, careening down the middle of the road… Jackson yanked on the steering wheel and lurched off onto the shoulder as the car sped by, its lights turning the bullet holes into a glittering series of halos. A flight of angels sliding across his windshield.

It was four in the morning. Any drunks should have been heading the other way: uphill, out of town, home from the bars. Jackson pulled back onto the road. He glanced in the mirror, half expecting to see taillights veer off the road and down into the creek. But instead he saw a reckless U-turn and suddenly those bright lights were heading back towards him. Even from far behind, the lights were fierce, flashing through his rear window. For a moment the car was flooded with light: Jackson winced, the bullet holes in the windshield flared again. Whoever was behind him had recognized the car and was coming to finish the job.

He floored the accelerator and his car responded with its usual indifference. The road crested a small rise and ran down to cross the creek. There was a series of downhill turns leading to the bridge and, as the car picked up speed on the downhill, Jackson took the curves without letting up on the gas—all he had going for him was momentum and the fact that he almost certainly knew the road better than whoever was chasing him. But after the crossing the creek, the road started uphill again. Relentlessly uphill.

Jackson glanced in the mirror. No headlights behind him. Nothing but the black of a valley too steep for the moonlight to reach. Maybe the son of a bitch had missed the turn onto the bridge and was upside down in Castle Creek right now, drowning. A pleasant thought, but not one to count on.

He saw salvation ahead and, without time to think, killed the lights, yanked the wheel sharply to the right and went rattling and clattering down the steep dirt road to Conundrum Creek. At the bottom of the hill, he skidded the sharp turn and headed for what he hoped would be shelter: a bizarre wooden stockade, a fake Fort Apache that a half-bright millionaire had built to be his wilderness getaway. But the millionaire—or, more likely, his wife—had realized the vast foolishness of the project long before it was finished and all work on the fort had stopped abruptly. Jackson had written a story for the paper when the Wild West Stockade Company had filed suit in county court, demanding payment for "Two thousand logs, 'Ft. Apache Style.'"

He jammed on the brakes. The stockade loomed in the dark, at least ten feet tall, the logs sharpened at the top: giant pencils to sign the giant checks for this giant waste of money. He half fell out of the car and scrambled to the main gate—tall enough for a stagecoach, wide enough for the cavalry to ride out four-abreast—and… Yes! It wasn't locked. The owner was probably hoping someone would burn it down.

He swung the massive gate open, drove his car inside, closed the gate, dropped the thick crossbar in place and collapsed against the logs. It was designed to keep out blood-thirsty Apaches, it could probably handle whatever thug in city shoes was chasing him. He leaned back to see if flaming arrows were coming his way.

Brief moments passed and then he heard—a hundred feet above, on the main road—the growl of a powerful engine, as a car raced past, heading up the valley. Jackson allowed himself a smile. But it wasn't long before he heard that same engine returning, moving more slowly. He heard tires crunch onto the gravel at the top of the turn-off and then come slowly down the dirt road towards the fake fort. The engine dropped to an idle and the car stopped right outside the gate. The car door opened and slammed shut. Footsteps on the gravel. Feeling like a fool, Jackson held his breath. The gate creaked and rattled as someone tested it. The crossbar held. Take that, Apaches!

There was a watchtower at the corner of the stockade and Jackson thought about running up to the top and—what? Shouting obscenities? Even he wasn't that foolish. He did allow himself to starting breathing again. He was that brave anyway.

The car door slammed, the engine roared, gravel scattered. Then a terrifying crash as the car slammed into the gate. The logs shuddered—but the crossbar held. The engine roared again. Another crash. How many more could it take? Apaches were never like this.   The gravel crunched again as the car backed up. The engine roared—but this time with a screeching noise. Something seriously wrong.

Would the lunatic behind the wheel ignore the mechanical howl and keep slamming into the gate until the engine exploded?

No.

The car door opened again, but this time with the protesting creak of dented sheet metal. Footsteps on the gravel—and then the sound of someone kicking the log gate. Again and again. And shouted curses in a language Jackson didn't understand. One tiny part of him wanted to laugh. The rest wanted to survive. At last, the kicking stopped, the protesting car door slammed shut, the gravel crunched and the screeching engine faded into the night.

Jackson sat and waited as darkness changed, ever so slowly from black to darkest gray. No flaming arrows. No screech of the car returning. In the vast silence of the mountain dawn, there was only the sound of Conundrum Creek, running down toward its confluence with Castle Creek and then on, still farther, to join the Roaring Fork and eventually the Colorado, chuckling all the way in endless amusement at the fake fort by the side of the tiny creek and, no doubt, at the brave reporter hiding inside.

JACKSON CLIMBED the watchtower. No sign of Indians or thugs by the dawn's early light. Not knowing whether danger was waiting upvalley, lurking downvalley, or long gone, he decided he still needed to talk to Gunnar.

He opened the stockade gate. Outside, the ground was littered with shards of glass and plastic and broken chrome. And a small oval medallion that said "Land Rover." Famously tough, but not tough enough for Fort Apache on the Conundrum.

Jackson finally got to laugh. He started his car, steered carefully around the broken glass and drove back up to the Castle Creek Road and on up the valley to the ski trail leading up the back of the mountain.

Time for advice from the mad man.

GUNNAR'S CABIN was cold. No fire in the stove, no sound, no sign, no scrap of life. Just the thousands of books, staring back at him from the shelves—the cabin so much emptier for being so full of one man's life. All those books with no one to read them.

Gunnar had seemed stronger, saner, that first day back at the cabin. That had been… what? Two, no, three days ago. He should be stronger now. Living at home. Peace and quiet. With Winston and Ella May taking care of him.

And so… So what? So he should still be right here.

Jackson considered Gunnar's lunatic insistence that someone was trying to kill him. Damn it, you old fool, this is no time for you to be right.

He went back out onto the porch. It had started snowing while Jackson was skiing up to the cabin and now the storm had turned into a full-on blizzard. Huge, wet spring snowflakes blotting out the morning. He shouted Gunnar's name because there wasn't anything else to do. Maybe the old fool had decided to go for a walk and was lying helpless somewhere close. The falling snow swallowed the sound and the wind blew the shreds away. New snow blanketed the ground, burying signs of what might have happened.

Still, he could see the almost covered trail of a snowmobile coming up from below, right to the cabin, and then on up into the trees. Could have been Winston and Ella May bringing supplies up from town and then heading back to their cabin. Except the track cut across the bowl below the cabin instead of following the trail. Neither of them would have done that. Unbroken powder was for skiing.

It wasn't much to go on, but Jackson had to do something. And even if he was wrong—if it was Winston or Ella May on the snowmobile—they'd probably taken Gunnar back up to their cabin. So he got his skis back on and headed uphill, following the fast-disappearing tracks in the snow.

It wasn't Winston or Ella May. Those two were pros on their snowmobile, whoever was driving this one was a rookie—veering one way, then the other, cutting across obviously dangerous open areas where the snow could easily slide.

It was closing in on midday by now, but the storm had the mountain wrapped tight. There was no sign of the sun—no sign of the sky, just thick low clouds and blinding snow.

Jackson worked his way uphill, following the tracks. Whoever was driving the snowmobile might not know what he was doing, but the machine could chew its way up the mountain tirelessly. He stopped and held his breath for a moment to listen for the engine, but there was only the thin edge of the wind that drove the snow against his face. And beyond that, silence.

Endless silence, endless snow, endless mountain, there was no sense of time passing—just Jackson's breath and the growing heaviness in his legs. And the tracks he was following filling with the new fallen snow.

Then the tracks, which had been heading steadily uphill through scattered aspens, turned sharply and headed across a steep, wide-open field. Jackson stopped. The open area was at the bottom of an avalanche chute, where a gully opened into the wide meadow and sliding snow tore away the trees. In the middle of a storm like this, that chute could slide at any moment. Only a fool would cross that field right now and the fact that one fool already had made it across just stacked the odds even further against the next fool who might try.

If he didn't want to chance an avalanche—and he definitely didn't—Jackson would have to ski down, skirt the open area, then head back up and try to find the tracks, already almost erased. He looked across, then down. And then he saw, heading up through the trees, a different set of tracks—someone on foot.

Jackson followed those tracks—and they painted an ugly picture. Someone floundering, falling into the deep snow, getting up, staggering on. They couldn't go far. And they didn't.

GUNNAR HADN'T made it far. He was wearing pajamas, socks on his feet. Almost impossible he'd made it even this far. Even more impossible: He was still alive.

Jackson tore off his parka, wrapped it around Gunnar, put his hat on the old man's head. Then, not knowing what else to do, he picked the small body up and cradled it in his arms. Gunnar moaned. He was surprisingly light.

Everything had changed. There were no good choices. No choices at all. He had to get Gunnar inside. Winston's cabin was closest—if he could find it in the storm. And he was going to have to carry Gunnar.

It was impossible. But he didn't have any choice, which made it easy.

JACKSON WAS HUDDLED in front of the woodstove, wrapped in a blanket, clutching a cup of hot tea, still shivering. It had been a hellish trip through the woods in the storm, trying to find a cabin he'd only been to once before, not knowing if Gunnar was going to die in his arms. Not knowing if maybe they were both going to die.

Then he'd heard the whine of the snowmobile. It could have been whoever had dumped Gunnar, coming back to finish him off. Jackson thought about hiding, but didn't have the strength to do anything but stand and wait.

It was Ella May.

And now, while Jackson shivered in front of the fire and Winston sat in a big armchair, looking relaxed, but ready if there was anything for him to do, Ella May was in charge.

"I got him awake enough to get some hot tea into him," she said. "He's tough. But damn, I don't know." She managed a smile. "He kept saying 'Told you! Told you!' Over and over. I gave him something to calm him down. He needs to sleep." The smile was gone. "I don't know." She shook her head. "Just don't."

There was a noise from the bedroom, more a squeak than a shout.

Gunnar was sitting up, thrashing against the pile of quilts that engulfed him.

"Follow the Drift!" he squeaked. "Millions!" Jackson put a hand on his shoulder to calm him. Gunnar looked directly into his eyes, squawked, "Idiot!" and fell back, gasping.

Ell May took over, stroking his forehead. Smoothing his wild hair.

Jackson and Winston retreated to the living room. Elle May joined them a few minutes later.

"Out again. Not much we can do." She gestured toward the windows. The storm still raging outside.

Jackson nodded. "He said he wanted to die up here."

Winston shrugged. "Yeah."

"So we just wait?"

"No way! We're going into the mine." White teeth gleamed in the dark beard as Winston smiled.

Jackson didn't.

"What mine?"

He knew exactly what mine, but he had to say something other than what he desperately wanted to, which was NO!

Winston raised his eyebrows. "You heard Gunnar. The Drift. The Liberty Drift."

"But it's ... I don't ..."

This sounded like the worst idea Jackson had ever heard. Winston's smile disappeared and he cocked his head.

"Gunnar was pretty clear. Follow the Liberty Drift."

Jackson thought he might throw up. Dark tunnels, rotting beams and unmarked shafts. He did not want this assignment.

Nothing to say. He just stood there.

Winston smiled again. "It'll be fun."

A gust of wind rattled the windows.

"Maybe we should wait out the storm."

Winston was already heading for his parka. "Storm doesn't matter once we get underground. That's the thing about a mine."

Jackson was certain he was going to throw up.

"We can't just leave Gunnar like this."

Winston refused to stop smiling. Jackson considered hating him.

"Come on, Jack, there's nothing we can do. And no one could take better care of him than Ella May."

"Don't worry, Jackson. I've got it."

And Jackson knew she did. He was out of excuses. Except to just admit the truth: He was terrified. But once he did that, then what? Admitting you're scared doesn't change anything.

Gunnar chimed in from the bedroom.

"Idiot!"

That made it unanimous.

WINSTON SKIED into a tight cluster of spruce trees. Jackson followed, fighting through the thick, overlapping branches.

Winston stopped next to a tall rock outcrop in the heart of the cluster, snapped open his bindings, stepped off his skis, wedged himself past one last tree and disappeared into a narrow black gash in the side of the mountain. His hand reappeared out of the darkness, grabbed his skis and disappeared again. Jackson stared at the jagged black hole. He'd pictured something he could walk into, standing up: an opening in solid rock, with timbers framing it. That had scared him. This was terrifying: a place you go into and never come out of. Winston's head popped out, that same big smile on his face. "Bring your skis."

By the time Jackson had gotten out of his skis and scrambled down into the darkness, Winston was nowhere to be seen. His skis were leaning against the rock. The space was small, cramped. A low opening led off into deeper darkness. He could hear Winston ahead of him, so Jackson put his skis next to Winston's, bent way down, pushed his fears aside and followed. After a few awkward crouching steps, he sensed the space opening up around him. A small flame flared in the dark and then the light spread as Winston lit a kerosene lantern. They were in a good-sized room, as big as Jackson's apartment, ceiling high enough to stand easily. The yellow lantern light reflected warmly off the rock walls.

Winston lit a second lantern and the chamber was filled with light. There was a beat-up old couch and a couple of armchairs, a half-dozen pictures hanging from nails driven into cracks in the rock, coils of rope, picks and shovels. "Gunnar's clubhouse," said Winston. "I helped him with the couch. Hell of a time getting it in here. He used to come up here and just hang out. Said all the silver still in the mountain kept him company. He swears there's still a fortune."

"Millions."

"Just waiting for the man who's smart enough to get it

"Sure as hell isn't me. I have nightmares about places like this."

"Time for an attitude adjustment." Winston was excited. "This is where the fun part begins. Gunnar cut a little drift back from here to the main tunnel."

"To the Liberty Drift?"

Winston shrugged and walked to the far end of the room, where some boards were propped against the rock. He pulled the boards away. There was an opening behind them. Low and narrow and pitch black. A sign above it said, "Crack of Doom."

Jackson looked at it. "Ah shit."

Winston laughed—and again Jackson considered hating him.

"That's another one of Gunnar's Shakespeare things. Witches in 'Macbeth.' Something like that."

"That doesn't make me feel any better."

"It does get a little tight," said Winston, as if that was a perfectly reasonable response. "You OK with that?"

"No." Silence stretched out for a long moment. "How could this be the only way in?"

"There used to be a regular adit. Big enough to walk right in, Gunnar said. I'm not sure where it was. Somewhere up here. Had a cave-in years back. Killed a couple of guys."

"Rosie and Daisy."

"Nah. They died in different cave-ins."

This wasn't making Jackson feel any better. He just shook his head.

"Well, you can give up. You know, quit." Winston sounded impatient.

"Thanks."

"Up to you. Ready?"

The only answer was no, but Jackson couldn't say that, so he didn't say anything.

Winston pulled a couple of coils of climbing rope and two flashlights out of his pack. He handed Jackson one of the flashlights.

"You can do this. It's not that bad. Think like a snake."

Jackson stared at Winston, who was his height, maybe a little thinner. Finally he managed to say, "Sure."

Winston dropped to his knees, looked over his shoulder, "And don't freak out." Then he disappeared into the opening in the rock. For a moment, just his boots stuck out, scrabbling against the rock. Then nothing. Jackson considered... no, it was too late. So he took a deep breath, got down on his hands and knees, and crawled into the darkness.

For the first few feet, it wasn't bad. Then the rock overhead slanted down and he was forced down on his belly, pulling himself forward on his elbows. It wasn't OK anymore. He could hear Winston ahead of him, scraping and slithering. The rock above sloped down even more and Jackson had to turn his head sideways and stretch his arms out ahead of him. This was bad. Then worse. Too dark. Too tight. He couldn't do this. His breath roared in his ears. The musty scent of dirt filled his nose. Dirt and fear. He remembered being trapped at the bottom of a pile on the football field, his face pushed down in the mud, feeling he was going to drown, He'd panicked then and this was a lot worse. The fear was rising, flooding. He took a breath and pushed forward. He couldn't move. At all. Trapped. He could feel the entire mountain above him, pressing down, crushing him. He tried to claw his way forward, but his fingers slipped and scraped on the rock and he could feel blood, wet on his knuckles.

Then there was a hand grasping his and squeezing. He squeezed in response. In his rising panic, he'd been trapped and alone. Now, in an instant, he knew better.

"Easy does it," said Winston. "You're almost there." His voice was a blessing, filled the with calm cheer of his smile. Why had Jackson ever considered hating him? "I'm out in the main drift already. No sweat. Just breathe easy for a little bit. OK?" Jackson wanted to shout "Get me out of here!" but he didn't think that would help. So he focused on his breathing. In and out. Like the man said. In. Slow and easy. Out.

"OK," said Winston. "Exhale completely. And then wriggle. Like a snake, remember? There's plenty of room, once you find it."

Jackson took a few more breaths and then forced all the air out of his lungs and began to rock side to side in the tiny space. He felt Winston pulling his arms, gently but firmly—and suddenly he slid right out. Death got bored, yawned, and let him escape. Just that easy. Thank you very much. He felt space expand around him. The world flooded back. In a rush, he remembered a bright summer day up Independence Pass, jumping off the highest rock at the Devil's Punchbowl into the icy pool below, plunging so deep that he didn't think he could get back to the surface before he passed out. And then, with a last desperate stroke and kick, he had broken out of the water, into the light, gasping for breath and swimming for shore. And now here he was again, alive and gasping for breath. But this time there was no light and there was no shore.

"All right!" Winston was gleeful. "No worries. I told you."

Jackson sat up and felt around on the rocky floor until he found the flashlight he had dropped when Winston pulled him out of the tunnel. He switched it on and shined the beam on the impossibly tiny crack he had just emerged from.

"I can't go back in there. No way."

"Bet you can. It's back through there or stay in here. Your choice."

"There's got to be another way out."

"Not really. Cave-in that killed Rosie and Daisy blocked the other end of this tunnel. The only way out is right through there." Winston laughed, held his flashlight like it was a microphone and squawked, "Break on through!"—his version of Jim Morrison, wildly off-key, no real melody— "Break on through to the other side!"

The flashlight lit his face from below, a kid trying to be scary on Halloween. But Jackson was already scared.

Winston lowered the flashlight and laughed.

"You know, I could never get Gunnar to pay attention to The Doors. He got way into The Band. Dylan too. But he just didn't get Morrison." He started squawking again.

"Break on through!"

Jackson couldn't take it any more. The nervous energy was still coursing through his veins and he snapped, "Fuck that! Morrison was a screamer and his poetry was pathetic."

"Bullshit!" Winston was outraged.

Jackson was ready to shout a few lines of Morrison to make his point. And then he stopped himself. He was trapped in a mine, lost in the dark, arguing about poetry with the guy he was counting on to get him out of there. "Hey, no offense. The Doors were great." He let it drop at that.

He shined his flashlight up at the ceiling and then down the tunnel into a dark so black the light lost its confidence and surrendered. Everything was falling to pieces. Timbers rotting. Rock crumbling.

He wasn't ready to move yet. So, talk: "Help me figure things out here. None of this bothers you?"

"Hell no. I love it down here."

"Got to be genetic. Was your father a coal miner?"

Winston laughed. "OK. The short version. I was doing post-doc research at MIT." Of course. That made perfect sense. "Neutrinos. Measuring Theta 1-3 with antineutrinos. Lepton flavor mixing violations. All of that. What was the point?" Jackson definitely didn't have an answer. "I was doing field

work on a neutrino detector. They have to be way underground. You know."
Sure. "This one was about a mile down in an old gold mine. And I loved it. I
loved being down there. I loved turning out the lights and just sitting there
in the dark. I mean, fuck dark matter, right? Dark places. That's where it's
at." Jackson considered disagreeing. Didn't risk it. "So I bagged the physics
gig. And here I am. Here we are."

There was a silence. Jackson let it stretch out until Winston switched
the light back on and said, "So let's go." Jackson flashed his light down the
tunnel.

"The Liberty Drift."

Winston shrugged. "Well… not quite. But sort of. Close enough."

"Wait. We're not even in the right place?"

'This is where we're supposed to be. It's a case of you can get there from
here. Maybe."

"What are you talking about?" Jackson was, once again, seriously considering hating this guy.

"Most of the mines are closed off. Concrete. Steel gates. Cave-ins. You
can't just march in, right? Gunnar loved finding a way. Or making his own
way. Liked to say he was liberating the mines."

Jackson wasn't happy. Winston kept going.

"He cut bandit drifts—like the one we just came through. Called them
all Liberty Drifts. Liberation and all that." He took a step into the dark,
then turned back to Jackson. "Sometimes he'd go shouting in French. 'Lib-
erté! Fraternité! Egalité!' Start singing 'La Marseillaise.'"

Jackson just stared.

"I knew he was fucking with me. His knowledge of post-Revolutionary
French street politics was absolutely zero. He read 'Tale of Two Cities,' and
thought he… "

"What are we doing here?" Jackson was probably shouting. He couldn't tell.

"Like the man said, 'Follow the drift.' And this sort of takes us right to
the original Liberty Drift. You'll see. Come on."

One more time: no choice. Jackson followed.

"Watch your step," Winston called over his shoulder. "There's lots of
ways to get hurt. Killed. Stuff to trip over. Shafts to fall down. Way down.

Bye-bye Jackson." He laughed again and walked into the dark, singing. "Break on through ..."

They walked for what seemed like forever, but was probably less than that. Jackson could feel the dark tracking them, circling, closing, waiting for the light to flicker, even for an instant. Darkness is patient. It has forever on its side.

Winston stopped and waited for Jackson to catch up. He shined his light down a black hole gaping in the floor of the tunnel. "Ventilation shaft," he said. "Goes down a thousand feet. Water at the bottom—but no worry about drowning, you'd be dead long before you got there." He laughed. "Watch your step."

And then, at last but also all of a sudden—because that's the way forever ends—they were there. They ducked through a low, rough opening and Winston announced, "This is it! The Liberty Drift. Starts right here."

Jackson didn't have a comment equal to the occasion, so he followed without a word as Winston marched on into the dark. And then stopped. The tunnel was blocked by fallen rock.

Winston shined his light behind them to the opening they'd come through. "Starts right there." Then he turned it on the rocks filling the tunnel in front of them. "Ends right here. Does now anyway. That's the cave-in that got Rosie. Or maybe that was Daisy. Either way. And the far end, the drift is plugged with concrete. So this is it."

"What are we doing here?"

"Following instructions." He shrugged. "Figured we work it out once we got here. But I got to admit there's not a lot to work with." Winston flashed his light around the walls and up onto the ceiling. The light caught a small metal sign, battered and dented, chipped white enamel with a red arrow. The arrow might have originally been pointing down the Liberty Drift, but now it was hanging by a single nail, dangling, so the arrow was pointing straight up toward the blank rock of the ceiling.

Jackson couldn't help looking up. Just rock.

"So this is it? Gunnar's millions. The reason someone's been trying to kill him. Dead end with an arrow to nowhere."

"Follow the drift." Winston grinned.

"Nothing. Fucking Gunnar."

Winston burst out laughing.

"Gunnar was crazy even before he ran into that tree. You knew that."

"Fuck him!"

"Hey, Jack. He was my hero. But I knew he was loony. 'Follow the drift!' We had to check it out, but come on… why would you be surprised?"

Jackson looked at the arrow again. It wasn't really pointing nowhere. It was pointing up. Out of there. Where Jackson desperately wanted to be.

Winston started to walk back up the tunnel. Jackson followed, then turned around and looked back. There had to be more to it. But there was nothing. The fallen rock, the dangling sign. He turned his flashlight off and stood, very alone in the dark, for a long time. Wondering what he was missing. If there was anything to miss.

Then he turned the light on again and hurried into the darkness after Winston.

IT WAS AS IF the mountain coughed—less than that. As if it cleared its throat. A faint sound, a rattle. And then, an instant later, a rush of stale air.

Jackson stopped. Any sound in this profoundly silent dark had to be bad. He held his breath, listening. Nothing. The silence had returned.

He shouted Winston's name. There was no answer except the echo of his voice. He waited, listening to the silence. In a panic, he started to run, the beam of his flashlight veering wildly. Then he stopped, breath ragged in his throat, and shouted "Winston!" again. And, again: silence.

He wanted to run, but Winston's voice was in his mind: "Stuff to trip over. Shafts to fall down. Bye-bye Jackson."

He moved slowly into the dark. Every step careful, scanning the rocks that surrounded him. He came to the ventilation shaft—"A thousand feet. Water at the bottom"—skirted it carefully and kept on.

He turned a corner and there it was: the end of everything, a pile of rock, new-fallen, blocking the way. He swept his light over the rocks. The passage was completely blocked, sealed. And then he saw the arm. One arm, sticking out from beneath the rocks, hand turned upward, fingers gently curled.

19

JACKSON KNELT, ALMOST AFRAID TO TOUCH THE HAND.
Then he grasped it. It was warm. The fingers clenched, squeezing his hand.

"Winston!"

There was a groan from beneath the rocks.

Still holding the hand, Jackson caged his panic in a far corner of his mind. He'd let it out later, when he had more time.

He scanned the rock pile. He didn't want to let go of Winston's hand, but he had to. He disengaged his fingers—"I'm not going anywhere. Hang on"— and stepped back to get a better view of the rocks. The pile looked oddly stable. Two enormous rocks formed a kind of arch above where Winston was buried; below that, the rocks looked smaller—as far as Jackson could see.

He knelt again and squeezed the hand.

"I'm going to start clearing the rocks." Then, just because he had to, "Break on through to the other side!"

He propped the flashlight up at the edge of the pile and began moving rocks away, trying not to trigger a new collapse, keeping an eye on the two huge rocks, the arch that protected Winston. If Jackson moved the wrong rock, everything could collapse. If he worked too slowly, Winston might die before he got to him. He might die anyway. They both… No. No time for that right now.

He kept working—too slowly and too quickly.

First: blood, bright red against the white skin of Winston's forehead.

Then: more blood, matting his dark hair.

At last: his eyes, fluttering open as Jackson clear the dirt away.

His face finally clear.

The son of a bitch was smiling.

"Break on through." His voice was a croak. His breath shallow. Then, "Thanks."

A large rock lay across his chest. Jackson didn't know if he could lift it.

He took a deep breath, and lifted it. No choice. He could feel it slipping, feel the skin on his fingers tearing, feel his hands slippery with his own blood.

And he didn't drop it. Because he couldn't.

Winston's breath came easier now.

Jackson cleared more rocks away crawling head-first under the arch, deeper into the pile to free Winston's legs.

The last rocks he moved were slick with blood.

"OK, suck it up. This is going to hurt."

He grabbed Winston's arms and pulled—gently, fiercely, slowly and quickly as he could.

Winston didn't make a sound until he was well clear of the rocks. Then he let out a cry that was equal parts pain and relief, as Jackson collapsed on the floor.

"NOW WHAT?"

"Well, just guessing, but I'd say we're going to need a little help."

The pain had to be excruciating, but there was no hint of it in Winston's voice. Jackson had bandaged his leg as best he could, but there wasn't much he could do for the jagged bone sticking out through the torn flesh. Jackson balanced admiration against the anger that made him want to ask Winston if he still thought it was fun to play around in the dark.

And since that was all he could think of to say, he didn't say anything.

"Okee-doke. Since I'm not going anywhere, I'm thinking you're nominated and elected."

Winston's voice was as relaxed as if they were sitting in front of the woodstove in his cabin, sharing an afternoon drink. Jackson had to join in and measure up.

"OK. I'm it. But as far as I can tell, there's no way past that." He glanced at the rock pile. "I'm pretty sure the other end was blocked solid. And I don't recall seeing an emergency exit." An edge was creeping into his voice. He stopped and waited for Winston to jump in.

"Well, there is a way."

Jackson waited.

"The ventilation shaft."

"What!" He didn't mean it to come out sounding the way it did — but still, he could remember Winston's description, ending, "You'd be dead long before you hit bottom."

There was a moment of silence. Then Winston said, "I'd go myself, but I'm a little tied up right now."

Jackson didn't have anything to say.

"There's nothing to worry about," Winston assured him. "Ella and I went this way once, just for fun. You go one level down—25 feet, maybe 30—and there's a cross tunnel that'll take you out onto the front of the mountain. You come out in the trees above Spar. We took our skis and skied down. It was a blast. You'll see. Dig the rope out of my pack."

Winston said there was an iron ring set into the wall right next to the ventilation shaft. He told Jackson how to fasten the rope to the ring and then wrap it between his legs, up, over, around and down and eventually into his right hand. "Nothing to it. Just don't let go. You back off the edge, lean against the rope, and then just walk backwards down the wall. You're standing up, but, you know, horizontal. Right angle to the wall. It's really cool. You feed the rope out through your right hand as you go down. It's easier than it sounds. Really. Just remember: Let go with your right hand and you're dead. Otherwise no problem. No worries."

Jackson had a lot of worries, but this wasn't the right time to talk about them.

"Once you're in the cross shaft, you're golden. It's a long march, but it's a straight shot. Nothing to fall down. No turns. No way to get lost."

Jackson nodded. There weren't any choices. Winston couldn't wait.

"There is one tight spot."

"Sure thing."

"No worse than what we went through to get in here."

That moment of terror seemed a lifetime past.

"The good news is that when you get to it, you're a good halfway to the end. It's another rockfall. A cave-in. The way through is all the way to the left side. It looks better on the right, but don't believe it. The way through is on the left. OK?"

"Let's do it."

He took the coil of rope and the one flashlight they had left. Winston's light was somewhere under the rocks.

"Sorry to leave you alone in the dark."

"No problem. I do my best thinking that way."

"Well…"

"Sure."

Jackson started to walk back down the drift.

Winston called out. "Don't let the rope get away from you. You know…"

"Bye-bye Jackson."

"Exactly."

IT TURNED OUT to be almost as easy as Winston had promised. Almost. Easy as pie—apple pie with a big scoop of terror on top. Backing off the edge of a thousand-foot drop in the pitch dark, relying on a skill he didn't have. No worries.

The worst moment might have been right at the top, before he started down. He tied the rope to the iron ring, wrapped it around himself with a mixture of care and courage and fear, walked to the edge and realized that he couldn't hold the flashlight and still control the rope. He stood for a long moment. No way around it. He was going to have to do it in the dark. He did his best to memorize every inch of the rock underfoot—then turned the light off, stuffed it in his pocket and backed over the edge as the utter black engulfed him.

And then he simply walked backwards down the wall—so easy to say, so terrifying to do. But he did it. The rope was burning his hand, scraping the raw skin he'd torn pulling the rocks off Winston. But he wasn't going to let go. No question. No problem. No bye-bye.

One step down. Another. Then another. And another.

Then the wall beneath him abruptly ended. His feet plunged into the void. He'd reached the opening of the cross shaft, an empty space unseen in the dark. He swung violently at the end of the rope. His knuckles crashed against the jagged rock. His face slammed into the wall. He started to fall and in that instant he knew was falling a thousand feet and he'd be dead long before he hit the bottom. That fraction of a second stretched out to swallow the world: time and distance and darkness all swirled into one.

And then he crashed into the rock floor.

The momentum of his swing had carried him into the cross shaft and he only fell a few feet. And just like that, he wasn't dead—and being alive hurt like hell as he hit the rock with his elbows and his butt and the back of his head.

And even through that white flash of pain he could hear the clatter as the flashlight, jarred loose from his pocket, skittered across the rock and into the shaft.

And in the silent dark, he might have heard it, long seconds later, splash when it hit the water a thousand feet below.

DARKNESS WAS TIME. Darkness was distance. Darkness was everything and the darkness went on forever. And then some.

Holding a hand out in front of his face so he didn't walk into some unseen rock wall, Jackson trudged through the dark. Whether the tunnel was curving or he was veering from side to side was impossible to know, but his shoulders kept running into the jagged walls, tearing his shirt and then his skin. First one shoulder, then the other. But he kept on walking because there was nothing else to do. And he kept trusting Winston's insistence that there was nothing to fall into, no side tunnels to get lost in, because, again, there was nothing else to do.

And he walked forever. He walked under the mountains and under the ocean. And then he walked some more. Spring and summer and autumn came and fled and winter came down again while he walked. And he walked some more. And at last, after another endless chapter in the Annals of Forever, he ran into something in the dark, stumbled and fell. He lay there, thinking long and hard about just not getting up again—because what was the point? Then he got up again. He could give up on himself, that was easy enough, but he couldn't give up on Winston.

After long minutes groping in the dark, he realized the tunnel was blocked. He felt carefully from wall to wall—rocks filled the way. He climbed, painfully, slowly, up the pile until he was crushing himself against the solid rock at the top of the drift. There was no way forward.

And that was good news.

That was what Winston had said so very, very long ago, back before the darkness had become everything and forever. He closed his eyes—and thought how odd it was that even in the depths of this blackness he still closed his eyes to think and remember—and he heard Winston's voice telling him that there was one tight spot, another rockfall, a cave-in, and, "When you get to it, you're halfway to the end."

And Winston had said, "The way through is all the way to the left side. It looks better on the right, but don't believe it. The way through is on the left."

Or had he said the way through was on the right? Had he said it looks better on the left, but don't believe it.

Was that what he said?

Jackson couldn't remember.

Or he could remember—but he remembered it both ways.

And he couldn't see which way looked better so he would know to go the other way. He couldn't see anything. He couldn't see any way.

Better or worse.

Left or right.

He crawled all the way to the right and he thought he could feel an opening, something to crawl into.

And then he crept all the way back across to the left and he couldn't really feel anything at all.

Well, maybe there was a tiny space, a tiny crack to crawl into.

Crawl into and die.

And that had to be the way Winston had told him to go.

Crawl headfirst into a space he couldn't see. Into a passage too tight in a darkness too deep.

And there was nothing else to do.

There was no way to quit.

No coward's way out.

Nothing to do but lie flat on his belly and force his way into that tiny crack that was too small to even think about.

He took a moment for a brief chat with himself.

"I'd rather die than go in there."

"And you'll die if you stay here. Dead either way."

"Thanks, asshole. You're cheering me up a lot."

And then, almost crying, he did exactly what he knew he had to do: lie on his belly and wriggle like a snake, into a tiny hole he couldn't even see.

STUCK.

Just that. No more.

Well, yes, more: panicked and terrified and stuck.

The crack he'd wriggled into had opened almost immediately after the first tight squeeze. He'd taken a deep breath of relief and worked his way forward. Winston had been right. This was the way. And if he could get past this, he'd be almost free, almost out into the open.

And then he was stuck. Again.

Trapped.

He couldn't do this. But he had to. He wriggled forward a little more. Pushing. Forcing his way.

And then it was even worse.

A sharp edge of rock was caught under his ribs, digging up into his gut. It hurt to breathe. He tried to back up, but that hurt even more.

And then it was even worse.

Not back. Not forward.

Breathing faster now. Shallow breaths. Heart thudding.

Winston's voice filled his mind.

"Break on through!"

Fuck you, Winston. He writhed, rocked his body from side to side. The sharp rock under his ribs was a fishhook, digging deeper. He found a way to inch ahead, just a little.

Just a little.

OK.

Just a little bit more.

And he was stuck even tighter. That musty scent filled his nose. It didn't smell like fear this time. It smelled like death.

He couldn't panic. Couldn't panic. His breath was coming faster. He had to calm down. He tried to think of skiing. Cruising powder. Wide sweeping turns. Relaxing, as he floated down the mountain. He let the image fill his mind. His breathing slowed. The tightness in his chest eased. And that endless soft descent turned into an avalanche, swirling and crushing and he was buried under the snow, suffocating in the dark...

In the dark.

No!

He focused on where he was trying to go. He thought about Winston telling him he would come out in the trees, the glades above Spar Gulch. He thought about an aspen glade in the snow. A quiet space. He could relax there. He'd be fine when he got there. He could breathe deeply there and...

He was still stuck. This was really it. He'd done it to himself. He didn't have to be here. Now he was going to die. Right here.

He thought about Winston, dying one level above, while he was dying down here.

He thought about Gunnar, dying in the cabin. He thought about Gunnar in the hospital.

"Out, out brief candle."

A tale told by an idiot, full of sound and fury, signifying nothing.

This was it all right. A tale told by an idiot.

To an idiot.

And Jackson began to laugh. He laughed because he was the idiot. Because he should have known better from the start. Gunnar was crazy. Everyone knew that. A tale told by an idiot. To an idiot.

And he laughed even harder, despite the sharp rock cutting into his side.

And, as his body shook with laughter, he could feel a tiny breath of new space under his ribs. Jiggling past the sharp rock. Twisting through the tightest squeeze and... he was out.

Out!

Not out in the open, but out into a wider darkness. Past the cave-in.

He lay there, sobbing with relief. He knew he had to get up. Knew he had to keep on. But not yet. He was halfway there. That's what Winston said. He said that was the good news, but he was wrong. Jackson had walked forever and he was only halfway.

And then he saw a light. A tiny spot of light bobbing in the distant dark.

Impossible. Couldn't be. But he saw it.

It wondered if he had died somewhere along the way—fallen down that thousand-foot shaft, suffocated in the cave-in, died next to Winston under the fallen rocks.

Couldn't be. He was so sore and miserable he had to be alive.

And the light was still there.

He closed his eyes. Opened them.

Still there.

Moving.

Coming closer.

Jackson shouted.

20

THE CABIN WAS WARM. A FIRE CRACKLED IN THE WOOD-
stove. Jackson sprawled on the sofa, Ella May in an arm chair. Neither one
had anything to say.

Jackson had already thanked her so thoroughly that he had the feeling she'd kill him if he thanked her any more. And they had already been
through all the explanations.

Jackson's had come first, right there in the mine, the moment she found
him there in the dark, filthy and bloody. He blurted out what had happened
to Winston, and that sent Ella May rushing out of the tunnel, Jackson hob-
bling behind her, desperate to not get left alone in the dark. When they hit
fresh air, Ella May called Mountain Rescue on her radio, reporting what
had happened and the response that was going to be required—with a calm
ferocity that could not be ignored.

Hours passed after that. Long wretched, cold hours. Jackson sat huddled in the mouth of the tunnel, shivering uncontrollably, while Ella May
filled in the rescue crew on what they were facing. Eventually, someone sent
him down the mountain on one of the snowmobiles ferrying people and
equipment to the site—and once they got a look at him in the light, they
sent him directly to the hospital. The ER docs cleaned him up and stitched
him up and after a couple of hours wrapped in hot blankets, he was starting
to really believe he hadn't died.

They tried to send him home, but he wouldn't go, so they banished him
to the waiting room where he gulped bad coffee and considered questions
about light and dark and life and death and fire and hell and Jim Morrison
and breaking through to the other side and where the other side was and
where this side was.

And somewhere in there, despite all the bad coffee, he fell asleep.

And when he woke up, Ella May was leaning against him, sound asleep. So he went back to sleep too.

And when they both woke up, it was her turn to explain how she had gone looking for Jackson and Winston after they'd been gone way too long, how she'd gone to Gunnar's clubhouse, crawled through the Crack of Doom into the mine tunnel, found the cave-in, decided they must be making their way out by rappelling down the ventilation shaft and out the tunnel—the way she and Winston had done it that one time. And how, finally, she'd found Jackson, filthy and bloody.

And the next time they both woke up, a doctor was telling them that Winston was stable and strong and in no real danger, except perhaps from the boredom of the lengthy recovery he was facing after emergency surgery to save his leg.

And now they were at Winston and Ella May's cabin—safe and warm and even well-rested. And there was no need to talk about any of it.

And no need to talk any more about Gunnar.

"He died smiling," Ella May had said when they reached the cabin and stood over the body on the porch, surrounded by flickering candles, lying so very still at last. "That's when I left him lying in state out here and went looking for you two fools."

Jackson had found the strength to point out that "lying in state" technically meant that a body was available for public viewing. Which led Ella May to suggest that they'd better do something about bringing him inside, because what passed for the public up here on the mountain was mostly carnivorous and their idea of "viewing" was indistinguishable from what she'd call "eating."

And for some reason that had left them laughing until they were too weak to laugh any more and they lay sprawled in silence as the wood crackled and burned and collapsed into embers.

Jackson stopped at the edge of the snow-covered bowl. He switched off his headlamp and waited as the three-quarter moon rose through the fringe of trees on the ridge above him, spilling silver-blue light into the soft curve of the bowl.

Together, he and Ella May had carried Gunnar's body off the porch, strapped it to a sled and hauled it down to his cabin, with Jackson on skis dug out of the pile of gear at Winston and Ella May's cabin. It would have been a lot easier to use the snowmobile, but they didn't want to disturb the night—or the dead—with the howl of the engine.

They carried Gunnar into the cabin and laid him on his bed.

"One last night at home," said Ella May. "I think he'll like that."

"Fucking Gunnar." Jackson said it with love—but he said it nonetheless.

"Little late to be holding a grudge." Ella May smiled. "He's dead, you know."

"I'll get over it. Just a lot of time wasted on nothing."

"Just because he was crazy doesn't mean it was nothing."

"If that's advice, I don't know what to do with it."

They stood in silence. Then Ella May dug through a cabinet and brought back a bottle of Chivas Regal and three shot glasses. She filled the glasses and said, "To Gunnar!"

Jackson thought about it—separating frustration from fear from friendship, settling on friendship and deciding that this was an appropriate occasion for a drink, even for someone who had given up drinking. "To Gunnar." And he knocked back the shot.

Ella May drank her shot and put the third one next to the body.

"Just in case he gets thirsty."

Jackson walked to the door, saw the sky was clearing and said he was skiing back down.

Ella May tried to insist that he spend the night and ski down in the morning.

Jackson shook his head.

Ella May nodded. "Do what you want. I'm just telling you I'm not going out on another rescue tonight." Then she gave Jackson a hug and a big kiss that startled him. She handed him a headlamp and said what Winston almost certainly would have if he'd been there: "Break on through to the other side."

That could have meant "Go ahead and kill yourself if you want to." Or just "Get over it." Jackson figured in the end it all came down to the same thing: making some good turns in the powder.

And now the moon was over the trees and the bowl was brimming with light and unbroken powder. He could feel the freezing cold starting to seep through the rips and tears in the pants and jacket he had put on... how long ago had it been?

Time to go.

So he carved a series of telemark turns through the heart of the bowl—not perfect, but damn good, which was as close to perfect as he ever got. He stopped at the edge of the trees and looked back up at the tracks in the snow. A few good turns. For Gunnar. Full of sound and fury. Signifying nothing.

Idiot.

21

"GUNNAR GUSTAV MAGNUSSON, SON, GRANDSON AND great-grandson of Aspen miners—and an Aspen miner himself—died Friday as he had lived: in a log cabin on the back of Aspen Mountain."

Jackson stared at the words. It can be hard to write an obituary when you know too much. More than you want to know. More than you ought to know. More than you can put in the newspaper.

Way too much. And still not enough.

So he wrote what needed to be written: the details of Gunnar's life on the back of the mountain, perhaps the last of his kind. He added a few good quotes from the old-timers and some details from past news stories about Gunnar. He finished it off with a story of his own: one of those summer nights, sitting on the porch of Gunnar's cabin, shouting poetry and throwing rocks at the bears who kept raiding the garbage. He didn't mention the guns or the dynamite—it was the poetry that mattered. He ended with the image of Gunnar, standing on the porch, declaiming: "And we are here as on a darkling plain, swept with confused alarms of struggle and flight, where ignorant armies clash by night"—the lines punctuated by grunts, as Gunnar heaved rocks at a determined bear.

He considered mentioning the books, the thousands of books that lined the walls of Gunnar's cabin, but he decided that might tempt souvenir hunters to ski up there and help themselves to the library. And he considered putting in an odd fact that he stumbled over: The snowmobile crash that started Gunnar spiraling down into death was on his birthday. For Jackson, it explained why Gunnar woke up singing "Happy Birthday" after his surgery and for the obit it would have been a neat ironic twist, but it felt like a cheap joke and Gunnar deserved better than that.

When he was done, it was a good sketch of the cranky old-timer who should have mattered more than, in the end, he seemed to. Jackson was reading it through one last time, working on not feeling bad until the day was finished and he could head over to Michael's. Not to drink—he'd had his drink for Gunnar up at the cabin with Ella May—but because he figured there'd be people there who would gladly do the drinking for him. Drinking was required and Jackson wanted to bear witness that it had in fact been done. Then he thought he'd go up to the hospital to check on Winston and head home to sleep for a week. Or two.

The telephone rang. He didn't feel like talking to anybody, but that didn't matter. He let it ring twice, then three times, just to be sure they meant it. Then he picked up the receiver.

"Jackson."

"Hello, Jack. It's Marybelle Dictu."

"What can I do for you?" He skipped the pleasant chat, but still worked to stay as polite as he needed to be.

"Yes. Well. I was hoping to see maybe a few more stories about the Historical Society fund-raising efforts for the Harkney House. You know we need ..."

"I know what you need." He could feel it getting away from him but he couldn't stop it. "You need to leave me the hell alone. Raise your goddamn money and build your goddamn whatever the hell it is and ..."

He couldn't control his voice, couldn't stop shouting. He was already in trouble and it was about to get a lot worse. His hand took charge and saved him—by hurling the phone across the room and against the wall.

The call was over. The damage was done: to professional reputation and relationship, to the phone and the wall. But it could have gotten a lot worse.

For once, the newsroom was silent. Everyone was holding their breath. Jackson considered what he might say to fill that silence. Nothing at all seemed like the best choice.

He put on his parka and headed home. The drinkers at Michael's could get drunk perfectly well without him. He'd get to the hospital another day. Winston wouldn't mind.

JUST ONE DAY after the incident that would go down in Aspen Sun history as the Day of the Flying Telephone, Jackson had already regained his personal and professional equilibrium. After reading Gunnar's obituary, Marybelle had called and said she was sorry she'd upset him right after he'd lost a good friend. Jackson had promised to write a feel-good story about the fund-raising. Fester had magnanimously decided to overlook the entire incident; he didn't even complain about the busted telephone or the hole in the office wall—just one more hole, after all.

That's when the kid from Denver called.

"I got it!"

Jackson had a moment of nostalgia. He'd been that eager once.

"Tell me."

"Went over to the Department of Health, like you said. Vital Records. Dug up"—maybe not the best choice of words, but if the kid realized it, he didn't let it slow him down—"everyone named Finch who died long enough ago to be buried in that cemetery. Records from back then are a real mess. Hard to figure out who was who or where or when. Any of that. And then I figured, that quote ..."

"She should have died hereafter."

"Yeah. That's Shakespeare, you know? Macbeth."

Another college kid.

"Yeah, I know."

"So I figured it must be someone who died young. That's the point of the quote, right? Dying too young. And I found it! A girl, died in 1897, one week old. Just listed as 'Infant Finch.'"

"And... ?"

"I back went to the Historical Society and found the story in the Lead-ville paper. The Herald Democrat. It was an Aspen story, but I guess it was such a great story they couldn't resist running it. And whoever's trying to cover up Finch missed it." Jackson could hear the pride in the kid's voice and he didn't blame him. "It's a great story. I'll fax it to you. You're gonna love it."

And the kid was right. The headline on the story was "Tragedy haunts her." It began, "Today the spirit of this mining camp is draped in black, beneath bright blue Colorado skies, as the town mourns the untimely death of a young angel, taken by a sudden, violent fever. Too young to have known the joys and tribulations of this harsh world, the child had been—too, too briefly—the well-deserved blessing of the middle years of our beloved Mrs. Finch."

Then, almost eagerly, with touches of morbid irony—this was a newspaper after all—the story went on to recount the tragic history: the death of Mrs. Finch's husband just two months earlier, "his hand cruelly mangled cutting timbers after he'd given up work in the mines to pursue a safer livelihood, knowing he would soon have a child to support. And now he and the golden child have both been taken so brutally from the bereaved pillar of our educational system."

Having gotten that off his chest, the writer solemnly reported that the bereaved pillar was showing "her well-known strength, forged in deep sadness."

Finally, the story—that frontier blend of hard news and purple prose—concluded, "At least, as she returns to her career guiding the youth of our community to a greater love of literature, she will still have the laughter of children in her life."

It was enough for a pretty good story, but it didn't shed any light on why someone would have stolen the headstone of an unnamed baby girl, daughter of a widowed school teacher. Still didn't make any sense.

And the epitaph. The only piece left behind. OK, she was the English teacher, a Shakespeare fanatic. But, still, "She should have died hereafter." Pretty cold. Maybe Grammy Ophelia was right about her. Beloved pillar or not.

Never mind. Right now, Jackson had a story to write: the Sad Tale of Widow Finch.

And he had a few little bits of his own to toss in—just so the kid in Denver didn't think he'd done all the work. Jackson had done a little digging at the courthouse and come up with, among other minor details, the Widow Finch's maiden name—Juliet Rasmussen—from the license when she'd married Hershel Finch in 1895.

Still, he was going to have to tip-toe around to keep from falling through the holes in the story. He was pretty sure that everything he was writing was true, but there were a lot of questions that he couldn't answer. About Birdie Finch. About her ill-fated husband. He couldn't get anything more without all those old newspapers that were lost in the fire. Lost along with Beast. Goddamn it. Don't forget the Beast.

He focused on the story. A few holes wouldn't hurt it. This wasn't a doctoral thesis. Just a newspaper feature. His teaser had promised "The Tragic Mystery of the Widow Finch"—and this was heavy on the mystery.

He started with a portrait of the cemetery, half-overgrown, cold and forgotten in the snow. With twisted aspen trees—no, make that tortured, go for it. The sad graves of the children. And the one gravesite wrecked. The broken stones. The one stone almost entirely missing, from the grave of a child. A stone placed by a grieving mother. Now gone. A grave now unmarked. A mystery. A secret.

All that was left of the stone was the curious inscription. A line from Macbeth. And then the story opened right up into the tale of the teacher who taught Shakespeare's tragedies and lived her own. The husband who died when she was seven months pregnant, killed on the job he'd taken for safety's sake. Then the death of the child and the words she'd chosen for the stone. Perhaps convinced that the stark eloquence of the Bard would express her grief better than overblown sentiments.

That was how Jackson wrote it anyway. It fit the facts and it fit the page. It sounded good and it certainly could have been true. He wrapped it up, coming full circle, back to the desecrated graves in the forgotten cemetery. And all the sad graves of the small children. And finally, "Out, out brief candle." He couldn't help putting that at the end of the story. His own little private joke with Gunnar.

And he gave the kid in Denver a share of the byline: By Jack Jackson and Dave Anderson. Fifty bucks and a by-line. What more could a kid from J-school dream of?

SAXBY DUPONT smoothed his hair even though he knew it was perfect. He reached out, then hesitated. He smoothed his hair again. Took a deep breath. No backing down. It had to be done. No time for panic. This was who he was—and as long as he was here, this was who he had to be. The executive director of the Aspen Historical Society could not fail to follow up with Mr. Goodwin Rawlins—none of this "Goodie" nonsense, this was business—on his clever bait-and-switch offer of a million dollars for the Historical Society. Oh, he wouldn't use the term "bait and switch" with Mr. Rawlins, but he'd make it very clear that Saxby DuPont knew exactly how the game was played: straight and hard. Calm and cool. He'd get that million dollars. Yes he would. Rawlins could afford it. And Saxby might even make a new ally when Rawlins saw what a solid character he was.

Marybelle had been dragging her feet, so he had insisted that she set up this meeting. "Face to face," he told her. "A meeting between men to settle the matter."

He smoothed his hair one more time. He was ready. He rang the bell.

A young woman in blue jeans and a T-shirt, barefoot, her oval face framed in wild red curls, opened the door. Beautiful. DuPont tilted his cleft chin, honored her with his smile and said, "I'm ..."

"Saxby DuPont, of course. Come in." She gave him a half-smile, which he accepted as her recognition of his own well-polished good looks. He inclined his head, as if to say, We both have roles to play right now. But maybe later, young lady. Maybe later. Her smile widened, ever so slightly.

She led him down a hallway filled with the delicate chiming of temple bells and soft chanting. The chanting grew louder as they neared a set of double doors.

"The Meditation Chamber." she said. "Go right in."

DuPont hesitated. "Am I interrupting?"

"No, no, no." Her voice was warm, supportive. "You're expected."

He opened the door and took a stride toward the figure across the room.

Goodie Rawlins stopped chanting and smiled pleasantly.

"Mr. DuPont. Welcome."

Saxby DuPont stopped mid-stride, frozen at the sight of the huge round man sitting before him, in a full lotus position. Stark naked and hairy. His face painted bright blue.

But all that Saxby could see was his massive, matching bright blue erection.

"Really, Mr. DuPont. Approach. I believe you wanted to talk about a... major contribution?"

Saxby DuPont thought he heard a giggle. He couldn't see Marybelle Dictu, hiding in a curtained alcove close behind Goodie, leaving bright blue smears across her face as she clapped her hands to her mouth to smother a full-on fit of giggles. He couldn't see her, but he knew.

"Mr. DuPont!" Goodie boomed. "Speak to me. Come to me! Reach out!"

Saxby DuPont turned and ran. The gales of laughter from the Meditation Chamber faded behind him. But he couldn't ignore the wicked snickering of the red-haired beauty as she ushered him out the front door.

By the time he got home, he was shaking uncontrollably.

It was time to get the hell out of Aspen.

JACKSON WAS HAVING a cheerful argument with the proofreader about a comma when Louise called and said she was in town on ranch business and she'd meet him for dinner if he didn't have anything better to do.

And now they were eating burgers in a country-western bar called Honcho's. Louise—a ranch girl at heart—had chosen this bar and the crowd was mostly cowboys: a few real cowboys and a lot of tourists who'd bought ten-gallon hats for their Colorado ski trip. A country-western juke box, lots of free shots for locals and the occasional fist fight provided the necessary Western atmosphere. Jackson didn't recognize anyone in the place. This bar wasn't on his usual circuit. Everybody has their home bar and every bar has its home crowd. Just a five-minute walk from Michael's, Honcho's was a long way away. But the burger was good. And he really did like Louise a lot.

And sitting there in the clattering half-light—the rattle of dishes from the kitchen, laughter and shouts from the crowd, honky-tonk music blasting in the background—Jackson found himself telling her the entire story. She already knew some of it, but now he filled in all the details: from finding the story of the Minister and the Fallen Angel in the archives to Gunnar's visit to the office and on through everything he'd found out about the Liberty Drift. He told her about Gunnar in the hospital and Gunnar left to die out in the storm. He told her about going into the mine and the terror of thinking he and Winston were both going to die in the dark, and about getting Winston to the hospital and carrying Gunnar's body back to his cabin and then, finally, skiing through the powder in the moonlight. He hadn't told anyone the whole story—who was he going to tell?—but now he was telling Louise, a woman he really liked, but barely knew. And she listened. Through three beers and a couple of shots for her and three Cokes for Jackson. She must have noticed he wasn't drinking, but she didn't mention it. Good manners.

The waitress brought over one more round: a shot and a Coke. Louise looked at Jackson, raised the shot glass, and said, "To sound and fury, signifying nothing."

He raised his glass. 'To idiots."

She downed the shot. He sipped the Coke.

"Gunnar said they were going to kill him and maybe they did. Whoever they were. And I still don't have any idea what it was all about—except Gunnar insisting it was the Liberty Drift. But we did what he said— 'Follow the Drift!'—and there was nothing there." He thought about that for a moment. "Damn near got Winston killed." He wanted to add, "And me too," but decided not to.

She leaned forward. "I'm glad Winston's not dead. Glad you both made it out of there. But I'm thinking about that girl. Ernestina Rose. You keep calling her the Fallen Angel. Like she's a character in your soap opera. But she was a real person. And she really died. Think about that girl. Alone. In the dark. Dying. She wasn't even twenty years old."

They sat in silence for a few moments while the juke box played and people shouted and beer glasses rattled. Then she leaned forward again,

"You ought to go up there. Up where she died."

"What am I going to find there?"

"Nothing. There's nothing left. But that's where it happened. That part was real. Not a tale told by any kind of idiot. A girl dying. All alone. You owe her that, after rattling her bones all this time."

Jackson didn't have an answer to that. Louise stood up and headed to the bar. Jackson was impressed. After the beers and the shots, she was still rock steady on her feet. Ranch girls know how to drink.

She came back with an Aspen Mountain trail map—it was a cowboy bar, but it was still Aspen and there were trail maps at the bar. She also had a full shot glass. "To Miss Ernestina Rose," she said, raising her glass. "She deserved better." She knocked back the shot and unfolded the trail map.

"Got a pen?"

"I'm a reporter."

She took the pen, studied the map for a moment and made an "X" in the trees between Corkscrew and Corkscrew Gully.

"The catwalk runs right through there." She tapped the pen on the map where it showed the road cutting through the trees. "There's a path that runs up into the trees. It's a little hard to see, especially in the dark..."

"In the dark? You think I'm going up there now?"

"Hell yes. Right now, before you start forgetting what this was all about. There's a cluster of aspen trees right where the path begins, otherwise it's all firs."

"How do you know all this?"

"Grew up here. Remember?"

"That's a long way up the hill on foot."

"That's part of what you need to learn. It's dark and it's cold and it's a long way up the hill."

He watched her, thinking she was right, he was going to have to do this.

"You go up that trail and there's a clearing. Not much of one. That's where the cabin was."

Jackson nodded.

"I know how you felt when you thought you were stuck in that tunnel," she said. "I would have felt that way too." Somehow he doubted that. "But you go up there in the dark, right now. And think about her being all alone there. No one to grab her hand and pull her out. No one to find her and take her home. Abandoned by that son of a bitch. Thrown out like trash and left up there to die. That's the real story."

SAXBY DUPONT SAT on the floor, huddled in misery. He thought he could hear a jeering echo, children's voices. "Firkin the Gherkin!" Damn it all to hell.

He'd tried to get everything back under control. He'd sat with the phone in his hand while the dial tone droned, then turned to frantic beeping and finally fell silent—but there was no one to call. It was all falling apart and he could see so very clearly exactly where it all was going to end.

Saxby DuPont closed his eyes and the images—and smells—of Queens flooded his mind.

JACKSON KNEW HE wasn't going to freeze. He had a good down jacket and there was shelter and warmth close enough, but freezing was easy to think about when he stopped to catch his breath and felt the icy cold closing in. It was spring in town, but up on the mountain the night was cold and the snow was deep. Everything was the way Louise had said it would be. The path into the trees, the tiny clearing—and the feeling of being absolutely alone. It was late by now and the city was quiet. The trees were thick enough to block the lights from down below. He was alone. He thought about Beast trapped in the basement as the building burned. Alone. He thought about Winston, busted up and lying there in the dark. Alone. And then he thought about Ernestina Rose, not yet twenty and never going to get there. Alone. Knowing she was dying. He stood in the tiny clearing, feeling the darkness wrapping itself around him, tighter and darker, until deep shivers wracked his body. It was the cold, he knew that. Not fear or sorrow. And he carefully made his way back out of the trees and down the trail into town.

HE SAW THE TRUCK idling outside his apartment and he could see by the dashboard lights that it was Louise behind the wheel.

"Thought you might want some company," she said.

"It was lonely up there."

They walked up the stairs to his apartment. She tossed her parka on the one good chair and looked around.

"Nice."

"All I really need."

"Don't guess I could live like this."

"Lucky you don't have to."

"I'm just used to a lot more space, that's all."

"And a lot of family filling it."

"That too."

"Something to drink?" It seemed like a good time to move on.

"Something hot. Cup of tea would be good."

He put on a kettle to boil, got a fire going in the wood stove and pulled out two mugs and a bottle of tequila, just in case she wanted another shot. She sat on the chair, he sat on the edge of the bed, while the heat from the fire filled the room.

"I'm thinking about that box," she said after a long silence.

"The one from Harkney House?"

"There's got to be more to it than just that newspaper story."

"Gunnar said the story was what he needed."

"But he didn't need that old clipping. He knew what was in the story."

Good point. Jackson just nodded. For a moment he was thinking of the days when PJ would laugh and insist she was better at his job than he was. Louise wasn't saying that—she was just proving it.

"But he about went crazy when he thought the box was lost in the fire."

"Sure did."

"So I'm thinking there was something else in that box. That's what it was really all about."

"Why wouldn't he just tell me?"

"Because he was crazy. Because he thought someone was trying to kill him."

"That doesn't make any sense."

"Why does it have to make sense? Who told you everything has to make sense?"

"I thought you ranch girls were the solid practical type."

"Don't pull that college boy shit on me." She wasn't teasing and Jackson realized he might have pushed it too far, but she didn't give him a chance to back down. "I'm just saying Gunnar was leaning pretty heavy on that box. Stop thinking of reasons why it doesn't make sense. Why not just take another look?"

"But…"

"Stop thinking, damn it!"

"I'm just…"

"You're just coming up with reasons not to do anything."

"Gunnar was crazy."

"What difference does that make?"

And he didn't have an answer for that.

They sat quietly, both breathing a little hard.

The kettle whistled and he poured hot water into the mugs and dropped tea bags in to steep.

"You still have it, right?"

"The box? It's here. But I went through it."

"I know. And what did you find?"

"That copy of the newspaper."

"That's what you were looking for. This time we're looking for something else. So maybe we'll find that." He wasn't going to argue any more. "Let's take a look."

"It's almost four in the morning."

"I don't know about what goes on in your newspaper business, but out on the ranch we have to go right ahead and get things done or it all goes to hell."

"You're as crazy as Gunnar."

"I thought you Aspen guys liked crazy women."

"There's all kinds of crazy."

She stood up. "You saying you don't like my kind of crazy?"

He got up and without stopping to think about it, kissed her. And she kissed him right back. Then she pulled away and said, "Bet the tea's ready" Then she kissed him again.

This time it was a longer kiss. Eventually, she stepped back, looked him in the eye and raised an eyebrow. Was that a challenge? Was she daring him to ignore the mystery and kiss her again? She lowered the eyebrow. Never mind. He tossed the teabags in the trash, went to the closet, dug out the box, put it on the bed and opened the flaps.

Inside, on top, were the newspaper clippings he'd stuffed in there with a savage hangover one morning that seemed so long ago he couldn't remember when it was.

Inside the box, on top, was the front page from 1946 with the page five jump. Jackson scanned it quickly and handed it to Louise. He tapped his finger against the headline, "Sad Find on the Mountain." She nodded and started reading. He scuffled through the next layer in the box and then he heard her laugh. There was nothing funny in that story. He looked over. She still had the last of the laugh in her eyes.

She pointed to a story near the top of the front page. It was about a fistfight over dumping garbage. "I know these guys," she said. "Guy who threw the first punch was one of my uncles. Guy he hit was a cousin—from the other side of the family. You'd never want to know either one of them."

Jackson stood up and let her take over. She knew more about all of it than he did. He stretched, went to the stove and poured some more hot water on his teabag. He raised the kettle and gestured to ask her if she wanted a warm-up. She shook her head, said "Tequila," and went back to sorting through the papers. When he handed her the shot, she held up an old Valentine's card and said, "Such a sweet message for someone to send to such a creepy old man."

"Johanssen was a creep?"

She took a sip of the tequila—"You don't want to know and I don't want to talk about it"—tossed the card aside and pulled a photo out of the box. He wandered into the kitchen, rinsed out the mugs and when he looked back, she was holding an envelope. She looked at it front and back, then held it out to Jackson.

"What do you think?"

The envelope, once white, was yellow with age, grimy from someone's dirty fingers. It was sealed, but there was no name or address on the front. On the back, someone had written in pencil—across the sealed edge of the flap—"July 12, 1946." Something inside slid from one end to the other when he tilted the envelope. In the upper right corner, where the stamp would have gone, a rusty straight pin was stuck through the paper. It matched the rusty holes in the newspaper pages. He was embarrassed he'd missed the envelope before. He was about to tear it open when Louise said, "Don't."

"Why not."

"If it really is a clue, then you need to take it over to the courthouse and give it to Skippy. He needs to see it all sealed up. With the date across it like that. Proves nobody messed with it. Preserve the chain of custody."

"Chain of custody?" Jackson was impressed.

She shrugged. "All those deputies in my family. Cousins up at the courthouse. Hell, even a simple ranch girl knows that stuff." A sweet smile as she knocked back the rest of the shot and held the glass out for more. "Question is, how come you don't know? Mr. Hot Shot Reporter and all that."

He refilled the glass. "Didn't I tell you that joke's a bit old? That Hot Shot business. Never was very funny."

She stood up, said "Yeah. You told me. So what?" She took a step closer to him, swallowed the tequila. And then she kissed him.

22

WHEN JACKSON WOKE UP FOR THE SECOND TIME, THE sun was streaming in the window and there were papers scattered all over. The red-apple box was on the floor, crushed flat. Jackson smiled. He was late for work, but he was in no hurry to get up. He lay in bed and let the sun wash over him and remembered what he could. The rush when they both let the kiss run out of control. That was when the box got crushed and the papers went flying, as they collapsed onto the bed, laughing as they grappled and rolled and got naked as quickly as they could, clumsy and eager. And, for a first time, it wasn't bad at all. And then, not long after that, the second time, slower and longer and sweeter. And then, still later, Jackson woke up when Louise kissed him as she slipped out of bed right at dawn. He'd pulled her back and they'd made love one more time, quickly but memorably, and then she was dressed and gone, hurrying back to the ranch to cook breakfast for a dozen before the work day began. While he dozed.

JACKSON WAS FINISHING one more junior hockey story and trying very hard not to think about Louise. He did not want any cross-contamination between Louise and junior hockey.

That was when PJ marched into the office.

"Fuck it, Jack!" Loud enough that he knew the whole newsroom was listening. Maybe waiting to hear if some new piece of office equipment was going to learn to fly.

"Hey, PJ. Good to see you too."

"Fuck that! I told you to drop it. Drop the whole thing. All of it. Can't you just keep your goddamn nose out of everybody's business?" Hardly a fair question to ask a reporter, but fairness wasn't on PJ's mind at the moment. "You've got your hot little cowgirl. Isn't that enough?"

"What's that got to do with ..."

"Don't fuck with me, Jack. Let it go."

It seemed like that was about enough.

"It's my story and I'll decide when it's over."

"Screw you, Jackson!"

"Don't fucking tell me ..."

And that was Louise's cue to come through the door with a smile on her face that died fast. There wasn't any room for smiles in that office.

There was room for a short silence while the two women looked at each other. Then they all spoke at once. Louise said, "Well maybe I better ..." And PJ said, "I guess I ..." And Jackson said, "You two know each other? PJ? Louise?"

PJ said, "Jackson, you can't ..."

And he said, firmly and finally, "Not now."

After PJ left, Louise said, "Brings back memories. Home sweet home."

"You weren't ever married, were you?"

"You know I wasn't. But my parents ..."

"Yeah."

"Just be glad you and PJ never had kids."

"Always am."

Louise walked over and kissed him.

"I was thinking we maybe should go see Skippy. Give him this." She held up the small dingy envelope, still sealed.

"How'd you wind up with that?"

She didn't blush, but she lowered her voice and leaned toward him. "It was tangled up with my underpants. In my purse. I got dressed in kind of a hurry."

Cousin Skip had a smile for Louise and a scowl for Jackson. Jackson ignored it.

"I think we've got a clue to that open case of yours. Those skeletons."

"A little late for clues—that was a hundred years ago."

"You don't..." Jackson started, but Louise cut him off.

"Come on, Skippy. If anything comes of it, you can be the hero. We don't care. Jackson just wants to write the story and I'm just a nosy bitch."

"Um..."

"You called me that plenty of times before. Don't try to back away from it now."

"Come on, Louse. You know I..."

"Don't call me Louse. I swear, Skippy, I'll tell everybody in town how you got a spoonful of peanut butter stuck up your butt at the school picnic."

"Louise!"

"I will."

"Wait. What?"

"Jackson, you stay out of this. Unless *Skippy*"—stressing the name—"doesn't want to help us out here. Then you can ask me how he got that nickname."

"Shit! Louise!"

"OK, deal? Right, *Skippy*?"

Jackson thought maybe he'd move the discussion along.

"Look, Skip..."

"My name's Felton."

"Everyone calls you 'Skip.'"

"Never mind that. My name's Felton. Got it?"

"OK. Easy does it. Like Louise said, you can be the hero here. You've got an open case. Two skeletons." He leaned in. "I can trace it back to the mining days. People love that stuff. And you'll be the guy that solved it. Bet you wind up on TV."

The deputy smiled.

Being a hero on TV sounded pretty good to him. Aspen was full of phony TV heroes. Why not a real one? Why not him?

"What've you got?"

"This." Louise pulled the envelope out of her purse, giving Jackson a glance that said she hadn't forgotten exactly where she'd found the envelope that morning.

The deputy reached for the envelope, but Louise hung onto it.

"Slow down. There's a lot of explaining that goes with it."

She nodded to Jackson who gave Skip a rundown on the box full of old papers. He didn't mention the Historical Society basement, just said he'd gotten the box from Gunnar. Close enough. And explained about finding the newspaper clippings and then, later, finding the envelope in the bottom of the box.

"And it looks like it was attached to the clippings," he said, realizing that he should have brought the clippings and hoping the deputy didn't ask about them.

"And here's the cool part." Louise jumped in, holding the envelope up. "It's got the date right across the back. See? And it's still sealed. Never opened. How great is that?"

She put the envelope down on the desk. The deputy bent down and peered at it. He pulled out a pen and flipped it over to look at the blank front, then flipped it again and studied the scrawled date. He shook it and something slid around. He held it up to the light, but nothing showed.

"Fair enough," he said and pulled out a pocket knife.

"Wait..."

He ignored her and carefully slit open one end of the envelope, leaving the flap sealed. "It's evidence now. I've seen it all sealed up and now I need to examine it. Officially. The chain of custody's clear."

In his mind, Jackson could hear Aretha singing, "Chain, chain, chain .... chain of fools." But he managed to keep from even humming the melody.

The deputy peered into the envelope, then held it over a sheet of white paper on his desk and shook it. Something fell out and bounced off onto the floor. The deputy lunged to grab it, banged his head on the edge of the desk, yelped, shouted an obscenity, regained his dignity, bent a little more carefully and retrieved the fugitive evidence. He stood up and cleared his throat. There was a red mark on his forehead where it had hit the desk.

"Son of a bitch almost got away," he said.

"It's lucky you didn't shoot it," Louise suggested. "Skippy's got one of those medals for shooting stuff. Don't you, Skip?"

"Never mind that, Louse."

Family. They'd been doing this all their lives.

They bent over the desk to look at what had fallen out of the envelope.

It was half a locket, tarnished black, but Jackson could see the scrolled flower design etched into the metal.

"Got to be the other half of the locket that's in the evidence box."

Skip turned around and picked up the metal box. "Still got it right here," he said, beaming. "Had a feeling it might come in handy again."

"Uh-huh." Jackson was certain the box would have sat there for months before Skippy got around to hiking back into the depths of the courthouse to file it away for another half century.

The deputy opened the box. Inside were the scraps of cloth and bone, and the tarnished chain with half a locket. He used the blade of his pocket knife to gently scoop up the half locket from the box and slide it onto the paper, next to the fragment from the envelope. They were a perfect match: two oval halves of the same simple shell, both lying face-down on the table. The broken stub of a hinge on one matched up with a cracked edge on the other. The engraved designs were the same on both.

Skip flipped the back half over, the inside, as before, was bare. He flipped the front over, that too was empty. He swung the desk lamp closer and switched it on. In the bright light, Jackson could see there was something engraved beneath the tarnish.

"Can't clean it," said Skippy. "Might compromise the integrity of the evidence."

"Come on, Skip," said Louise. "You must have some kind of magnifying glass in your super-duper boy detective kit."

Skippy dug a magnifier out of his desk and then, all together, trying not to bang their heads, they pieced out the inscription out through the tarnish.

"To Ernestina Rose, the apple of my eye, on her 16th Birthday, Aug. 18, 1885."

Ernestina Rose. The Fallen Angel. Dead a hundred years. Along with the baby that had ruined her life. It was exactly what everybody had known—and this time, for once, everybody was right.

LIKE KIDS at the drive-in, they were sitting in the front seat of Louise's pick-up, outside his apartment. The truck windows were steamed up, but all their buttons were still buttoned. She had to get home to fix dinner. They'd talked about the locket and Miss Ernestina Rose on the way to his place, then stopped in the parking lot to steam up the windows. Now they were cooling down, talking about Gunnar. Jackson was still holding a grudge.

"Let it go, Jack. Gunnar was a scared old man and he was certain someone was trying to kill him."

"But why?"

"I don't know. But he's dead, isn't he?"

"Being dead doesn't get you a lot of points."

"He was kind of crazy, Jack. You remember that, don't you? You're the word guy. You know what crazy means, right?"

He thought about saying, "Sure do—and I'm crazy about you," but that was way too sappy so he kissed her one more time. She kissed him back. A couple of buttons finally got unbuttoned and then she pushed away.

"Got to go make dinner."

23

"HEY, OK, I'M SORRY I BLEW YOU OFF THE OTHER DAY, all right? My supervisor was right there and he's a real dick about talking to the newspaper. And when he says 'newspaper,' he means you. Specifically. I shouldn't be talking to you. Not now. Not ever. OK? Understand what I'm saying?"

Brian, Jackson's Forest Service friend, sounded defensive—and Jackson realized he needed to back off. Before he'd dialed the Forest Service number, he'd spent a good hour sitting in his office at the Sun, getting more and more angry about everyone telling him what stories he couldn't cover. OK, not "everyone"—Fester and PJ. Really, just PJ. Fester was doing his job. PJ was… well, Jackson didn't know what PJ was doing, but it was making him crazy.

And when he'd thought about it longer than he could stand, he'd grabbed the phone and called the Forest Service and he started way too strong, pushing his friend for something on what Dictu was up to at the bottom of the mountain.

And his friend wasn't happy about Jackson's attitude. It was time for corrective action, before Jackson lost a good enough friend—and an even better source. He backtracked a little, circled around and came at it from a much softer direction. A different tone of voice. A more gently shaped question.

And the answer he got this time was much more helpful. And no help at all.

"It's what I've been telling you. Nothing's happening there. Period. Forest Supervisor said no. No deal."

Jackson grabbed at the vanishing hint.

"No deal? So there was a deal on the table."

A silence. Then a sigh from the other end of the line.

"OK. I'm alone here, so I'll tell you quick. But you can't print this because it's not a story. Nothing happened. This is just so you'll know what's going on. Your buddy Dictu offered a trade—a thousand acres in the middle of nowhere. Wolf habitat. Not worth anything to anyone except the wolves. Wanted to trade it for our land at the bottom of the mountain. He said he was offering us a great deal. A thousand acres for less than one." Jackson was scribbling notes as fast as he could. "Far as that goes, he's right. Our property's small and real narrow. You've seen the maps, right? No one could build anything on it. But it's right at the bottom of Aspen Mountain."

"Must be worth a lot to him."

"I guess. Anyway, Forest Supervisor turned him down flat. No deal. Like I said: no story."

Jackson stopped taking notes.

"Great."

But his friend was on a roll, so he offered one more nail for the coffin.

"Same goes for the Skico."

"What do you mean?"

"Just heard part of a conversation. You know how that is."

"Someone walked by and you had to take your ear off the door."

"Watch it, Jacko."

"Sure thing."

"Anyway, there was something about him building some kind of short lift and a training run for the Ski Club. Must have been more to it than that, but that's all I got."

"That's a lot."

"And the Skico told him to fuck off. Just plain go fuck yourself."

His friend was enjoying this.

Jackson was not.

No story. No justice. No bright light. Cockroaches parading in the dark.

"JACKSON? THIS IS Sara Sue."

"Do I know..."

"I work with PJ."

She had to be the hot blonde who'd been working evening shifts with PJ: long hair, good body, great cheekbones, nice smile. He hoped she wasn't thinking about chasing after him, because she would be hard to resist and there would be all kinds of...

"You need to get over here. PJ needs someone to take care of her."

"PJ?"

"She's getting way too drunk and she's starting to rage—and she can't do that here without losing her job."

"So call Skeeter."

There was a brief silence, then, "That's all over. PJ and Skeeter. I thought you knew."

"Why would I know anything about that?"

"I don't want any part of that. OK? You guys work it out. I'm just saying PJ needs a friend down here or she's going to get into deep shit."

He pulled on his parka and headed downtown, wondering what the hell PJ was up to.

When he got there, the first thing he noticed was that Sara Sue was as hot as he'd remembered. The second thing was that PJ was indeed raging. Over the years, he'd seen her drunk, drunker and drunkest—and right now she was drunker and heading for drunkest. She wasn't unhappy, far from it, she was gleeful, with a desperate edge to her glee that didn't bode well for the hours to come. Jackson's first thought was that whatever was going on, it was PJ's problem, PJ's rage, and PJ was a big enough girl to sort it out for herself—even if it did wind up costing her a job she liked and needed and... hell, there was no way he was going to walk out on her.

So he worked his way over to where PJ was holding forth. This late in the ski season the bar wasn't crowded, but PJ had drawn a crowd of her own. He wedged in next to her—elbowing aside some guy who thought if he stayed close enough to this hot drunk he might get lucky.

Sara Sue raised a lovely eyebrow. "Just in time."

"All right, Jackson!" PJ had noticed him. Even drunk, she'd been carefully not paying attention to the loser he'd elbowed aside. "You came to help me celebrate!"

"What are you celebrating?"

"Ya didn't hear? Rich uncle died. Left me a million bucks." Jackson didn't say anything. PJ didn't have any uncles, rich or otherwise. They both knew it and PJ didn't care. She shouted, "Sa' Sue! 'Nother damn drink!" She was waving her half-empty glass in the air, booze sloshing over the rim.

Sara Sue looked at Jackson. It was time for him to step in.

"Forget it, Peej. C'mon. We're outta here." He let himself slur a little, just to get into the spirit. He grabbed her arm and pulled her away from the bar. More of the drink spilled and the glass slipped out of her hand and shattered on the floor. He tossed Sara Sue a look that said he was doing his best and if she didn't like the results she had only herself to blame.

And then they were out on the street.

PJ was determined to keep on celebrating her mythical windfall from her mythical uncle. She dragged Jackson into Little Annie's. Like the hotel bar, it wasn't crowded, which was a good thing because PJ pounded on the bar and shouted, "Bartender! I'm buying a round!" A ragged cheer went up from the dozen or so regulars, always glad to get a free drink.

Even with a small crowd, it was going to cost her a hundred dollars. She couldn't afford that.

"PJ!"

"Forget it, Jack." Her brittle glee was about to shatter. "If I have to wait for genuine good news to celebrate, I'll never get to celebrate anything at all."

She was only moments from falling apart, so he grabbed the shot the bartender put in front of him, raised it high and shouted, "Here's to rich uncles!"

And the drunks at the bar shouted, "Rich uncles!" Everyone knocked back their drinks and PJ laughed instead of crying.

And, as the liquor burned its way down, Jackson couldn't help noticing he was drinking again.

Well, he was with PJ, so it made sense. It was easy. As was the next shot. And that one didn't burn. Maybe because he'd insisted on top-shelf tequila—or maybe just because the second shot never burns as much as the first.

After that, they kept the party going. They split a joint, which made them laugh louder. PJ pulled out a wad of cash and bought another round. Speaking with the careful precision of someone who knew how close she was to not being able to make any sense at all, she explained that although she wasn't rich, she felt rich right now and she needed to make that feeling last as long as she could—and eventually that meant buying an eight ball of coke, which kept them, and a changing cast of friends, going until well after last call. In the end, as the sky was getting light, they wound up back at her apartment, still laughing. As they stood there, she said, "Jack?"

"Yeah."

Serious for a moment. "Sometimes I just get tired of... you know." And finally, laughing as they fell into bed. "Jack, Jack, Jack. What's going to become of us?"

24

"JACK, I KNOW YOU SPENT THAT NIGHT WITH PJ."

"Shit. I'm sorry. I mean …'"—what was there to say?—"I'm sorry."

"Yeah." There was a silence as Jackson tried to think of what else he should say, could say. Louise said it for him. "Look, this isn't high school, Jack. We're not going steady." She smiled in spite of herself. "You didn't give me your varsity sweater." Then no more smiles. "But I don't sleep with a lot of guys. And that has to go both ways. You can sleep with anyone you want—but if it's me, then it's not anyone else."

Jackson hated this conversation. He was sorry he'd spent that night with PJ. Had been sorry even before this. And he was sure PJ was sorry too. But he couldn't say that to Louise. It wouldn't be fair to any of them.

She wasn't waiting for him to talk anyway.

"I don't want to be with a guy who's still half in love with his ex-wife—definitely not a guy who's still sleeping with his ex-wife. That part of its between you and PJ, I guess. But if you're still with her, then you're not with me. OK?"

Finally he had to say something, so he said, "OK." And then, a moment later, "I'll call you."

She shrugged and walked away.

JACKSON CONSIDERED whether he should get into a new line of work. He knew he was too close to 40 to be a fresh new face at anything—but right now he was feeling like someone who needed a clean start after a lot of bad choices. The night with PJ was an obvious bad choice. But it wasn't the only one he could consider. He could have been thinking about their marriage, from beginning to end. A lot of bad choices there. Or he could have been thinking about deciding to blow off law school. Or about a girl in high school: name long forgotten, regret still remembered. But right now he was brooding in a much more immediate way. He had to have a story filed by the end of the day and if he didn't find something pretty quickly, Fester was going to start lecturing him on junior hockey. And he would have to kill Fester. He looked idly around the office to find the best weapon. Ski pole? Cliché. Letter opener? Not sharp enough. Fist-sized rock Gunnar had insisted was silver ore? Promising. He entertained a mental imagine of crushing Fester's skull with the rock.

The phone rang, but it wasn't the story he needed. It was Rebecca, the wayward reporter, calling from Chicago.

"All right, Jack," she shouted, her normal tone of voice. "I've got everything I'm going to get you and it's more than you deserve."

"I'm sure it is."

"Just so you know. You owe me. It was a lot of work. I had to talk to a lot of librarians, all women—and I didn't sleep with any of them, even though one of them was pretty hot. So there!"

"You have my endless gratitude."

"Lucky me. Here's the deal. I've got your Reverend's will. It's pretty weird, but that's your problem. There's other stuff too. I'm putting everything I've got in the mail and then I'm out of here." Jackson wanted to say thanks, but she didn't even slow down. "I've got a rich new boyfriend, Jack, and he's taking me to St. Bart's. And you can kiss my ass."

She hung up, laughing.

And he still didn't have a story. His options seemed to be murder, suicide or junior hockey.

He picked up the phone and dialed the hockey coach.

"WE NEED TO TALK." The door didn't open any farther.

"Go away."

It had been more than a week since that night and the fact that they hadn't talked meant they both knew it had been a mistake. So there was no real reason to dig it up and talk about it. But Louise had made Jackson feel he ought to play by the rules—that sometimes rules were helpful.

"Come on, Peej. Just for a minute."

"No. Why?"

The door opened just a little more.

"That night was a mistake."

"Why are you telling me something I already know?"

Jackson didn't have a good answer for that, so he didn't say anything. She threw the door wide open. Her eyes were tight, her lips were thin.

"Why are you here, Jack? It's your cowgirl, isn't ..."

"That's not fair."

"Not fair? You being here isn't fair. You can't come here to break up with me. We're not together. You can't ..."

She was right. But it would just make things worse for him to admit what they both knew. Better to just be quiet and take it. He owed her that.

She went on a little longer and then stopped and they stood there.

Finally he said, "I'm sorry. I shouldn't even be here." And then again. "I'm sorry."

He saw PJ's mouth begin to relax just a little, the barest start of a smile. A winner's smile maybe. Or the edge of forgiving him because he really was sorry after all. Or maybe the smile of beginning to see just how funny this all was. Right along with sad.

But in the instant of relaxing her mouth to smile, she lost a little of the strength that controlled her eyes and suddenly there were tears welling up and then tears on her cheeks. And Jackson stood there, wanting to reach out and hold her, knowing he couldn't do that—and knowing that he hated this moment maybe more than any other in his life.

The moment didn't last—too long, but not long at all—and then there was the clatter of a diesel engine and the circling flash of red and orange light.

PJ pushed past him, out onto the porch.

"Shit!"

The tow truck was backing up to the front end of her car. The nose of the car was jutting out into the alley. Only a little, but definitely in the alley. The front lawns of the big houses were already green, but the alleys were still deep in snow. Old snow. Icy snow. Studded with cars and bicycles and garbage cans and all the frozen leftovers of a long hard winter.

"Goddamn it! Howard! Stop!"

The driver looked up at her. "Hey, PJ. Sorry. It's gotta go."

"Fuck, no. You can't fucking do that. No."

"You've been tagged"—there was a red cardboard tag on the antenna—"and you gotta go. The plows are just a couple of blocks away."

"Come on. I'll drive it out of there."

"You know it won't start."

She was already running down the stairs with the keys. "Come on, Howard."

"They pay me a hundred bucks each tow."

"Howard!"

"Just saying."

Jackson stood on the deck, looking down. PJ was in the driver's seat, turning the key in the ignition. There was nothing. Not even a click.

"Damn it, Howard. Get your jumper cables."

He was already going for them. "It's costing me a hundred bucks to jump your car."

She laughed, suddenly gleeful at the challenge. "I'm worth it!"

Howard smiled and clipped the jumper cables to her battery, walked back to the cab of his truck, revved up the engine and shouted, "OK! Crank it!"

PJ shouted, "Come on, Griselda!" She turned the key, the starter whirred, the engine turned over. The car exploded in a ball of fire.

The force of the explosion knocked Jackson sprawling. He scrambled back to his feet. Below in the alley, he could see PJ slumped behind the wheel of the car, engulfed in flames. Without thinking, he vaulted over the rail onto the frozen snow pile below, a winter's worth of plowing and shoveling, freezing and melting. The pile stood a steep ten feet high and he skidded down the ice, directly into the flames.

In an instant, the heat melted his nylon parka and the air around him was filled with flaming puffs of goose down that flew high on the rising wave of heated air and then drifted to the ground, bright embers trailing thin lines of smoke onto the mud and snow of the springtime alley.

25

MAYBE CONFESSION WOULD WORK. EVERYTHING WAS
sideways. The asshole reporter had gotten away from him. And that piece
of shit Range Rover hadn't even made it back to town. He had to ditch it
when the radiator blew and walk the rest of the way. And now that screaming bitch bartender had survived. Everything was going wrong. And he had
been raised to know that a run of bad luck was a sure sign that it was time
to go to confession.

Not that confession in this heathen Catholic church would count.

He could feel his jaw muscles tighten. It never stopped. If he ever got
to sleep at night, the sound of his teeth grinding woke him up. She'd complained about it that last night.

Goddamn it!

He saw a flash of blonde hair in the rows ahead of him. Was it her? Fuck
no. Couldn't be. Was every woman in this town blonde?

It wasn't fair! That bitch bartender was alive. And she… she…

Confession? Had he really been thinking about confessing to God?

It was all God's fault!

Fuck God!

THE BANDAGES on his hands made it difficult to take notes or type,
but going to work was easier than sitting home.

He was on the police beat, taking over for the police reporter, who'd
wrecked his knee skiing out of bounds on the back of the mountain. It had

taken two teams from Mountain Rescue and, in the end, a helicopter to get him out of the backcountry chute he'd skied into. At least the rescue made a good story. And it looked like the cop shop was going to be Jackson's beat for a while. As soon as the kid got out of the hospital, he got out of Aspen—packed up and headed home to that big job with the big paycheck that had always been waiting for him at his father's big company. That happened a lot and now it had happened again. Old news.

Jackson wasn't allowed to cover PJ and the explosion. Fester made that clear. Not that it mattered. The cops wouldn't talk to Jackson about it. Neither would PJ. He might have saved her life, but that didn't seem to mean he could talk to her.

Fester, for reasons that made sense only within an editor's mind, had assigned the arts reporter to cover the story. "I can't spare anybody else," he said when Jackson protested.

So Jackson was stuck with his new beat and forbidden to cover the only story that interested him. But he still had to show up at the cop shop every day and check the reports, trolling for news on drunks, petty thefts and anything else that might amuse the always-bored reading public.

Today's best story was a fist fight over a car—a car that had been towed and was sitting under lock and key because the owner wouldn't pay the towing charges. It was a nasty fight. One guy was in the hospital, the other had just bonded out of jail on a charge of assault with a deadly weapon: a tire iron. What caught Jackson's eye was a note on the report that the object of the fight was a pink Cadillac. Two macho guys fighting over a pink Cadillac sounded like a story—amusing enough anyway. He recognized the name of the guy who'd been in arrested for assault. It was Howard, the tow truck driver who'd been there when PJ's car exploded. The other guy was Franz Gern-something. Sounded German.

Jackson headed over to Howard's shop. Howard was glad to see him. He looked like he'd been in a pretty good fight—and he was the kind of guy who likes talking about his fights. Especially when it's the other guy who winds up in the hospital. Besides, he wanted to get his side of the story on the record.

"He's a big son of a bitch. He clocked me pretty good. Sucker punch. Things were looking a little sketchy—till I called in my old pal, Mr. Tire

Iron." Howard smiled, even though his lip was split. "That calmed him down considerable. Then the cops showed. And the fuckers arrested *me*."

Howard insisted it was the other guy who took the first swing. But he cheerfully admitted he was more than ready to fight somebody over that car.

"Never had so much damn trouble with a car. That was the second guy who took a punch at me over that pink goddamn Cadillac. Plus I had a couple of months of screaming assholes." Better and better. Jackson nodded and smiled and Howard kept talking. "Started back around Christmas. Night of that big fire." Jackson definitely remembered that night. "Got a call some guy was stuck. It was snowing pretty hard, so it figured. I went out there and here's this big pink pig, off the road. Big dent in the driver's door. And this crazy fucking guy. Black raincoat in a blizzard. City shoes." Suddenly Jackson really was interested. "I remember the shoes, because he kept slipping and falling on his ass. Coked to the gills. Couldn't stop running his mouth. Soon as I got there, he offered me a bump. No way —" he smirked "— not when I'm working. Said he hated the car. Couldn't blame him for that. Said he'd had a dead battery earlier in the night. But he got a bunch of guys from some after-party to give him a push-start. Must have been a bitch with all the snow. Probably got 'em so jacked up they could of carried the damn car. Anyway, once they got him started, he didn't get three blocks before he skidded into the ditch. And there we were."

Jackson was scribbling fast, having a hard time keeping up. Howard sounded like he had broken his rule about not getting coked up during working hours.

"So I pulled him back on the road and then the fucker went batshit when I told him it was three hundred bucks. Cash only. Like I ought to come out at four in the morning in a damn blizzard for free. He said he'd pay me in blow. I told him to go fuck himself and he took a swing at me. Hit me pretty good. Fucker knew how to throw a punch. Give him that." He stopped for a moment. "Shit. Sucker-punched twice over a damn pink car." He shook his head. "Anyhow, time I got squared away, he was long gone. On foot." He laughed. "I still had the car hitched up to my truck. So I towed it here, locked it up, and figured he'd come looking for it sooner or later and we'd straighten things out. Fuck me. That was just the beginning.

Couple days later I get a call. Ritchie Rich and Bitchy Bitch. Arnie Bing and that porn queen wife of his. You know her?"

Jackson nodded. He knew her. Knew about her anyway. Everyone did.

"Old Arnie said that big pink turd was his wife's car and he wanted it back. Told him there was a $600 bill that had to be paid first. That was three hundred for pulling it out of the ditch, a hundred for towing it into the shop, fifty a day for storage and a hundred for getting punched in the face—but I didn't go into the details. I just told him six hundred and that rich prick wanted to bargain with me. As if he doesn't spill that much down the front of his shirt every time he goes out for some fancy fucking dinner. And when I told him about the door, he really went off. What the hell was I trying to pull? Said I must of banged up the fucking door myself. Towing his car without his permission and then trying to charge for it? Said he was going to call the cops. Then he hung up on me. So fuck him too."

Split lip, bruises and all, Howard was loving this story.

"Next day I get a call and it's Sweet Tits on the line, crying about her poor little car. Said her producer gave her that car after she made 'Passion in Pink.' You ever see that?" Jackson shook his head. Howard laughed. "Hell, I used to jerk off to her poster in high school and now she's crying on my damn phone. Pretty good, huh? Told her to fuck off too."

And so the car sat there, with Howard charging $50 a day for storage on top of the towing bill. The tab was up in the thousands now. And then that asshole came into the shop and tried to pay him a hundred bucks to let it go. Saying "Us locals gotta look out for each other." And when Howard told him to fuck off—which seemed to be Howard's answer to just about everybody— the guy went crazy. And that was when Mr. Tire Iron joined the party.

JACKSON WENT up to the hospital to get Franz's side of the story but the former ski racer was still sleeping off his encounter with Mr. Tire Iron.

Back at the office, Jackson stared at his notes. It was all right there and it all made sense. Night of the Harkney House fire. Thug in a black raincoat and city shoes. Had to be the guy PJ's pals had seen at the airport. Couldn't be two guys like that wandering around town at four in the morning. And if you weren't convinced that Beast had started the fire himself, then that guy was the prime suspect.

And he was driving Arnie Bing's car. OK: Arnie Bing's wife's car. But Arnie figured to be the one with connections to a guy like that. You don't make money in the trash business unless you know how to play rough.

Jackson took a deep breath and dialed Arnie's number. He was going to play it as just another call on just another cop story. Clearing up a couple of details. Ease into it. Once he got rolling, he could bring up the guy who was driving the car that night. Then the fire.

This was going to be one hell of a phone call.

And even as the phone was ringing, Jackson felt a tiny pang of regret that it wasn't Dictu. He really wanted it to be Dictu. And he knew he needed to give himself a good stiff lecture on jumping to conclusions, on picking the bad guy first and then looking for evidence. But hell, he'd followed the trail to Arnie Bing, so he was doing all right. The lecture could wait.

At first, Arnie had a good laugh. Franz and Howard were two of his least favorite people—in Aspen anyway—and the idea of the two of them slugging it out amused him no end. He particularly liked the idea of Franz sleeping off a concussion in the hospital and Howard looking at jail time. But his mood switched when Jackson asked him about the guy who was driving the car that snowy night.

"How the fuck should I know?" A moment of silence, then, "Dumb fucking broad. Christ!"

"I'm not sure I…"

"The car was stolen."

"Stolen? The police didn't…"

"Never called the police. Look, my goddamn wife left the keys in the car. Out at the airport."

"But…"

"She left something—her sunglasses, I don't know, some fucking thing—on our plane. She's always leaving shit somewhere. So she drove out there. Ran into one of her giggle-brained friends and got a ride back into town. Forgot she even had the car. Didn't remember it for two, three days. Then she went back out and—fucking surprise!—it was gone."

"So you don't know who…"

"No idea. No fucking idea. Some jerk. That's for sure." Arnie laughed. "Who else would steal that piece of shit? Jesus!"

Dead end. Still a good-enough cop story, sure. Tough guys fighting over a pink car. But it didn't get him any closer to who'd started the fire. Or why.

"OK. Well…" Jackson was about to hang up.

"Look, something else I need to talk to you about. Nothing to do with that car or any of that."

Jackson didn't care.

"I'm on deadline." Always a good excuse. "Another time, OK?"

And he hung up.

Jackson cleaned up the colorful language and wrote the story about the pink Cadillac, the fist fight, and Franz Gernhofer's "memorable introduction to 'Mr. Tire Iron.'" He didn't mention the keys that were left in the car, the coked-up guy in the black raincoat or anything about "Ritchie Rich and Bitchy Bitch"—including Arnie Bing's well-considered opinion of his beautiful porn-star wife.

FRANZ GERNHOFER'S Austrian accent might have been charming to the ladies who loved him, but filtered through split lips, a concussion and a broken jaw, it was just about incomprehensible. Particularly over the phone. His anger made it even worse. But he still managed to get his point across: He most definitely didn't care for Jackson's story—which had, in fact, made it onto the front page, under the headline, "Pink Passion and a Visit from Mr. Tire Iron."

Franz had called from the hospital to shout that Howard was the one who'd thrown the first punch. Franz had just gone out there to talk about giving a local a break and that asshole had hit him with that… tire thing.

But then Jackson asked him if he knew that Lily had left the keys in the car and that the guy who'd been driving it the night it got towed had stolen it.

Franz managed something like a laugh and even through the bandages and the wired jaw, Jackson could hear a sly, mean tone creep into his voice.

"Wasn't stolen. She left keys on purpose. Heard her talk about it on the phone. Lending car to some guy. Guy she was fucking. Guy with chin. You know. Museum guy. Ha! She fucks anyone!" Franz did not seem to consider that a comment on his own status.

Then someone said, "That's enough Mr. Gernhoffer" and hung up. Jackson pictured a nurse standing by the bedside, getting splattered in bloody foam while Franz ranted. He didn't blame her for deciding enough was enough.

JACKSON WALKED across town to the base of the mountain. He had work to do, lots of it. But first he needed this moment to stand still, just staring up at the snow-covered slope. Smiling.

He had a name, a real name—not that "Saxby DuPont" could possibly be a real name, but never mind that, he had a real person. Because, damn it, behind the had-to-be-fake name and the obviously fake chin there had to be a real person.

And, with that, all the crazy impossibilities were real.

Jackson had no idea why Saxby DuPont would have hired some thug to burn down his own museum. There was still way too much that didn't make any sense.

But now there was a ring of reality to it all—the off-key, cracked-bell ring of reality.

It was far from rock solid. Sure, Porn Queen could have left the keys for Guy with the Chin and the Thug in the Raincoat still could have stolen the car. But it made more sense for DuPont to borrow a car from a brainless girlfriend to loan to his imported thug.

Saxby DuPont. He could work with that. He could live with that.

Saxby DuPont had killed Beast.

And it wasn't Jackson's fault. None of it. The last drink. The last joint. None of that mattered.

He took an instant to remind himself that he really had to give up trying to make every story work out so that R2Dictu was to blame for everything that was wrong in Aspen. He knew better than that.

But none of that mattered right now. No time for gray clouds. This sky was all silver lining.

Because it wasn't Jackson. It wasn't Jackson.

It absolutely wasn't Jackson!

THE WOMAN at the Historical Society said Mr. DuPont was not in today. And when Jackson called DuPont's home number the answering machine said, "Message box full" and hung up—the way DuPont himself probably would have when Jackson started asking about pink Cadillacs and thugs in black raincoats.

So Jackson walked across town to the Dictus' house, where the well-trained housekeeper tried to send him away. But before she could shut the door in his face, Marybelle's bright smile materialized. "That's all right, Yolanda," she said. "Come in, Mr. Jackson."

They stood for a silent moment in the front hall, which was considerably larger than Jackson's entire apartment and seemed to be as far as even a smiling Marybelle was willing to allow him into the house. Then, no more willing to allow silence in her house than she was willing to allow Jackson, Marybelle said, "I would imagine, of course, that you're here to see Roger Randall. But I'm afraid he's off on a skiing expedition to one of those mountains. In the Himalayas." She smiled again and added, "Why he does that, I can't imagine. But it seems to make him happy—and that's all that really matters. Isn't it, Mr. Jackson?" Bright smile. Fiercely bright.

Jackson refrained from agreeing, since Roger Randall's happiness was nowhere on his list of things that mattered, much less at the top.

"Actually, Marybelle," he said. "I came to see you."

Her smile turned quizzical. "So ... ?"

So he asked her straight-out if she had any idea how the Executive Director of the Aspen Historical Society—her director, her Historical Society—had gotten involved with a porn star's pink Cadillac, driven by a sleazeball who was the prime suspect in the fire that destroyed Marybelle's precious museum. He didn't mention Beast. He didn't want to distract her.

As he talked, he watched her smile grow ever more fixed and ever more fiercely bright. When he was done, he watched her struggle for a moment to relax that smile enough to speak. And when she did, her voice was a miracle of calm control.

"Well, of course, I really wouldn't have any idea how any of this could possibly be correct. Perhaps your 'source'"—making it clear she doubted he had anything so unlikely as an actual source—"is confused. So many people seem to be confused these days."

Jackson didn't say anything. No point in discussing the fact that his source was currently in the hospital, recovering from a head injury.

"In any case, Mr. Jackson, if there really is some mysterious pink Cadillac"—her tone implying bottomless depths of disgust with the very idea of such a car—"being driven by some mysterious thug, I am quite certain that any alleged connection to Saxby DuPont is entirely the result of some ridiculous mistake by some person in the employ of Mr. and Mrs. Bing"—the same tone implying the same feelings about Mr. and Mrs. Bing.

And she walked him to the door and again offered the bright smile, a bird fluttering home to roost.

MARYBELLE WALKED back through the house, trying to absorb what she had just learned. She longed to rush up Red Mountain to Goodie's house, but first she needed to think—and thinking was impossible when she was with Goodie. Indeed, as she considered Goodie, even for an instant, her thoughts began to scatter. She reined them back.

Saxby DuPont had better have a damned good explanation or she was going to rain all kinds of hell down on his empty head. And when it came to raining down hell, Marybelle Dictu had studied with the master.

She dialed DuPont's number, cursing the day she had so confidently decreed that he would be the new Executive Director who would stand by her side and do exactly as he was told as she led the Aspen Historical Society into its bright future.

And then the machine answered, told her it was full, and hung up. And even as she raged—no one hung up on Marybelle Dictu!—she thought how odd that was. Saxby DuPont was almost obsessive about his answering machine: his cheerful greeting was updated daily, he always returned calls immediately.

The pain of losing Harkney House began to churn again inside her and she knew the balm for her pain was waiting, smiling as always, in his Red Mountain home. She shouted to Yolanda that she was going out and might not be home until late and she hurried to the garage, grabbing the keys to her car. Definitely not a Cadillac. And very definitely not pink.

26

IF FESTER COULD HAVE WATCHED JACKSON WITH THE
sound turned off, he would have been impressed by the professionalism, the determination, the ingenuity that his reporter was showing on the hunt for leads. If the sound had been turned on, the editor might have been sorely tempted to fire that same impressive professional on the spot—because the story Jackson was chasing was the story that he had been specifically forbidden to cover: the Harkney House fire. And he was veering even further into dangerous territory by trying to find a link between the fire and Saxby DuPont, a man very definitely under the sheltering wing of Marybelle Dictu—and all things Dictu were off-limits to Jackson.

If any part of it would have brought a smile to Fester's face, it was the fact that Jackson was getting nowhere. Bartenders, waitresses, baggage handlers, doormen—the people Jackson counted on to have a finger on the pulse and an ear on the gossip—all had nothing to offer.

Late in the afternoon, he finally surrendered before he drowned in the breaking waves of nothing. He managed to crank out a couple of stories for the next day's paper—and hoped that Fester wouldn't notice that those rather pathetic stories didn't come close to justifying the intense hours he'd spent on the phone.

He was getting ready to go home when the phone rang.

"Jackson. Arnie. Arnie Bing."

Jackson had been careful with his saga about Franz, Howard, and the Pink Cadillac, but he could easily imagine that Arnie might want to pick a few nits off that story—and that he'd have the best lawyers available to help with the nit picking. Fine. But not right now.

"Look, Arnie. I'll be glad to chat with you. But I'm on deadline"—still a good excuse, always a good excuse—"I'm going to have to call you back later."

And he hung up fast. Not waiting for the outraged squawk.

Then he sat at his desk, staring hard at absolutely nothing. He wanted to call Louise—for comfort, for company—but he knew he couldn't. She'd called him after he dived into the fire to save PJ. She said she was glad he was all right. But the conversation was way too polite. And neither of them could ignore—or mention—the obvious fact that he'd been at PJ's apartment or none of it would have happened.

So now he just sat at his desk and stared.

And wondered if maybe it was time to start drinking again.

JACKSON WOKE in the middle of an ugly dream. Ugly, not surprising. Not one he needed a psychiatrist to figure out. He was lost in the dark. Panicked. Running. Tripping and falling. Hurting himself again and again. Not very long ago, he would have figured it was a dream about his marriage to PJ—and no need for a shrink to explain that one either. But, as it was, the dream was clear. Even trite. Jackson might have hoped to come up with a more imaginative nightmare from his expedition with Winston in the Liberty Drift.

He woke with a start, heart pounding, one last image in his mind: that battered tin sign dangling from the rock wall, the arrow pointing up. Mocking him. This way! This way out! Oh, wait. Too bad. There's a thousand feet of solid rock in the way.

But then, in that state of heightened awareness that panic brings—the dream may have been trite, but it was still terrifying—Jackson flung himself out of bed. He landed on all fours, leapt to his feet, and dressed in a hurry, fighting to keep an idea from fading, as dream inspirations so often do. He forced himself to stop, think it through, repeat it out loud until he was certain he had a firm grip on the idea. Then he raced to the office, dug through his stack of notebooks and found the one with the exact coordinates of the Liberty Drift that he'd copied so many lifetimes ago from the location notice in the county records. He checked those against the USGS Aspen Mountain topo map on the office wall and then he sprinted to the courthouse, lips still burning from gulping scorched coffee that had been on the hot plate overnight.

He was there the moment they unlocked the doors and he had the records vault to himself. He pulled down the huge books, one after another, leafing through them, shoving them back on the shelves. In less than an hour—a record for him—he'd found what he wanted. He took careful notes and then hurried back outside. Blinking in the glare of a beautiful day, he stopped to consider. He was desperate to talk to Winston. But based on recent discussions with Fester—and "discussion" was far too polite a word for it—Jackson knew that if he wanted to continue calling himself a reporter and have that designation confirmed by a paycheck from the Aspen Sun, he was going to have to file several stories before he could do anything else.

By early afternoon, three extremely boring stories were filed and Jackson was on his way up the back of the mountain on a snowmobile, his arms wrapped around the too-tempting waist of Ella May. Jackson reminded himself that he was determined to play by Louise's rules now and he had no leeway for another mistake. Besides, Winston was a friend, an injured friend, so that was another betrayal he couldn't think about. Anyway, Ella May would probably break his arm if he made a move. And by the time he had all that straight, they were stopped at the cabin.

Winston was settled in front of the woodstove, his leg propped up. The doctors had said he'd be in a cast for a couple of months and Winston seemed just fine with that. He beamed at Jackson, surprisingly chipper for someone who had almost lost his leg. Almost lost his life. But whatever happened in the mines was apparently OK with Winston. Jackson really did like him—and he really hadn't seriously thought about trying his luck with Ella May, despite the sweet feel of her waist in his arms and the enthusiastic hug she'd greeted him with at the bottom of the mountain

Jackson spread out the topo map, along with another map he'd copied at the courthouse, and explained what he'd figured out.

"Right there," he said at the end, his finger pinning down an exact spot on the Aspen Mountain map.

Winston looked closely at both maps. Looked again.

"Holy shit."

"OK. No talking about it for now. Right?"

"I've got no one to talk to but Ella May and she never listens to me—"

"Roger that!"

"— and you're the one who makes a living spilling secrets."

"Not this one. Not yet."

"Fair enough. It's your deal."

"I gotta go cover a hockey game."

And while he drove back into town and while he covered that hockey game and while he wrote a story about the thrilling victory—might as well be a thrilling victory if he was going to take the trouble to write about it—Jackson thought about a tiny patch of dirt. A couple of hundred square feet. A shred, a shard, a tattered fragment of a mining claim—the Liberty Drift claim.

When the Aspen silver boom was going strong, people raced to stake claims wherever they thought they might find that lode, that vein of silver that would make them rich. Anyone could stake a claim, wherever they were willing to dig long and hard and deep. A claim was a twenty-acre rectangle of land, its size and shape specified by federal law, and each future millionaire could line up his claim in any direction he wanted, in hopes that it would follow the vein he was certain to strike once the digging began. Claims were scattered helter-skelter across the mountain. Each claim was twenty acres, but where it overlapped an earlier claim, the first claim took precedence. Eventually, overlapping claims formed an impossible jig-saw puzzle of fragments. A late claim could be broken into a dozen or more tiny shards, lost and scattered among all the claims that had come before. The Liberty Drift was a late claim. When all the earlier claims were sub-tracted, all that was left was one large piece of land with an ambitious shaft that never yielded any silver. Plus a handful of scattered fragments. And one tiny fragment in particular, long overlooked.

Winston, with an uncanny sense of direction and distance underground, had stared at Jackson's maps and finally agreed—with no room for doubt—that the spot where Gunnar's ravings had finally led them, was right... there! Right where Jackson had said it was. Directly below that tiny fragment. And he agreed that maybe—not that it mattered, but maybe— the arrow on the wall had not been hanging loose. It had been Gunnar's clue, the answer to Gunnar's riddle—Follow the Drift!—pointing up to the surface, hundreds of feet above, where, as the new maps made perfectly clear, that little fragment, the fifty square feet of private property with all its taxes neatly paid over the years, just happened to be directly beneath the top terminal of the Aspen Mountain Silver Queen Gondola—the multi-million-dollar top-to-bottom lift, the pride of the Aspen Skiing Company.

And if the Ski Company didn't want to move their very, very expensive gondola, they were going to have to buy that scrap of private property.

Gunnar was right.

The Liberty Drift was worth millions.

To someone.

Exactly who that was, Jackson had no idea. Nor did he have any idea if that same unknown person was the one who had killed Gunnar. Or if that same still unknown person was the one who had tried to kill Jackson.

More answers. More questions. Same as it ever was.

JACKSON TURNED the mess on his desk into a mess on his floor, as he dug through the piles of mail and other journalistic jetsam that had washed up in his office in the days after the fireball in the alley. The thick envelope from Becky was at the bottom of the pile. True to her word, she'd sent it out the day they'd talked. He took a moment to be amused that for once she was the responsible one. Then he tore the envelope open and started to read.

Becky was right. The will was weird. And she'd included copies of newspaper clippings that underlined how strange it really was. James Eagleton Osgood—he'd dropped the "reverend," but otherwise his full, real name, as if daring anyone to find him—had done well for himself in Chicago. He didn't seem to make any friends or even enemies; he just made money. He traded stocks and he traded commodities. And he amassed a fortune.

But, for all his money, he lived alone and he died alone and perhaps that was why the newspapers found so little to write about his life after he was found dead in his mansion in the spring of 1929.

Then, months later, his will attracted attention when it came through probate court—and the same newspapers that had scanted him when he died were suddenly eager to write about the deceased James Eagleton Osgood. Even in those high-flying days, careening toward October 28, 1929, newspapers counted on pleasing readers with big sloppy dollops of human interest—better still if there was a touch of mystery involved.

The will was a headache of legal jargon, extensive and complicated. But right at the heart of it was the mystery that got the newspapers. The entire Osgood estate was bequeathed to "any child, or any surviving direct descendant(s) of such child, born between the months of January and March, year of Our Lord 1889, to that particular young woman known as Miss Ernestina Rose, believed to be a native of Kansas City, in the state of Kansas, who was most certainly resident in the City of Aspen, County of Pitkin, Colorado, in the year of Our Lord 1888."

The newspaper headlines got right to the point: "Tiny Tot's a Mystery Millionaire!" or, more simply, "Lucky Baby!" or "Oh You Kid!" All of the stories skipped over the fact that the baby would have been almost 40 by then. If there had been a baby.

And that was as far as the papers cared to go. Even back then, as Jackson noted with a mixture of chagrin and satisfaction, Bright, Shiny and Shallow was the name of the game.

Jackson went back to reading the will.

After launching the mystery-millionaire bombshell, the document descended again into the legal swamps. It set up a trust, the LD Trust, to manage the money during such time as it took to determine whether there

actually was such a child born to Miss Ernestina Rose. And on and on…
and Jackson was beginning to see the allure of Bright, Shiny and Shallow, when he got to the paragraph stating that if it ever could be conclu-
sively proved that there was no such heir born to Miss Ernestina Rose, the
estate would go in its entirety to "such charitable organizations as are specified below, with the exception of the Liberty Drift Mining Claim, which
I bequeath specifically and entirely to the former Miss Juliet Rasmussen,
originally of Winnetka, Illinois."

Jackson sat up fast, banged his knee and spilled his coffee.

"… the former Miss Juliet Rasmussen, originally of Winnetka, Illinois.
And may that mining claim be as unrewarding, cold, and barren to her as
she was to me in our painful years of marriage."

Son of a bitch!

He grabbed a pad and wrote it all down, just to make sure he had it
straight: Miss Juliet Rasmussen of Winnetka became Mrs. James Eagleton
Osgood of Aspen, who had been betrayed for an angelic young woman
in the church choir and—as the Aspen Sun had reliably reported—"left
town unexpectedly to see her mother in Indianapolis." And then, apparently after shedding the stain of her married name with a quick transforma-
tion back to Miss Juliet Rasmussen, she had returned to the scene of her
humiliation and, not long after, married Mr. Hershel Finch and become
Mrs. Juliet Finch. And then was abruptly bereaved. Twice. First husband,
then daughter.

Suddenly, the headline on that story about her death—"Tragedy Haunts
Her"—became a lot more meaningful.

And everyone in town must have known. That's why Ophelia had
backed down so fast—and so tearfully—after telling the truth about "that
bitch." Jackson thought about what Skippy had said: Everyone knew everything. The paper just printed the parts people were supposed to know.

Jackson could have kicked himself—except that would mean spilling
even more coffee. He should have seen it long ago. All those Juliets: Rasmussen, Osgood and Finch. Maybe the sudden flood of Shakespeare—hot
and cold running Juliets and Ophelia and "out, out brief candle" and whatever else—had left him deaf to the whole thing.

But now he knew... something. What?

He knew there was no descendant of that particular young woman known as Miss Ernestina Rose. No tiny tot that was a mystery millionaire. That story had ended a hundred years ago when the roof of a run-down cabin on Aspen Mountain collapsed during the fierce winter storms January 1889.

And he knew that the former Juliet Rasmussen Osgood had become the fearsome Mrs. Juliet Finch, who had at least one child, a baby girl who now lay buried beside her parents, under a broken tombstone that said, "She should have died hereafter."

And he knew that Mrs. Rasmussen Osgood Finch had been the proper legal heir to that unrewarding, cold, and barren Liberty Drift Mine—which he knew was, however improbably, worth millions of dollars.

And he knew that mine seemed to still be under the control of the LD Trust, which had been paying taxes all these years.

But he knew he didn't know—and he didn't know if anyone knew—who really should own that mine right now.

If the Trust was still paying the taxes, it had managed somehow to never discover what everyone in Aspen knew: that Ernestina Rose and her child had died in 1889. And so Mrs. Rasmussen Osgood Finch had never properly been awarded her inheritance.

Still, it should have been hers. And it should have been passed on to her heirs. If she had any.

Did she leave a will? Did someone inherit the mine from her?

He wondered for a moment if this was just one more thing that half of town knew all about—Louise and all her damn cousins anyway—and no one was telling him.

He daydreamed about Louise for a moment. Maybe it was time to call her and see if they could put things back together again.

Then he went back to the will. There wasn't much left, except for the passage at the end in which the former philandering reverend specified that if there were no descendants of Miss Ernestina Rose, all his fortune would go to "the Chicago Civic Opera, which has provided me with many moments of comfort and inspiration."

Comfort and inspiration, thought Jackson. There was a time—not very long ago—when a phrase like that would have sent him directly to Michael's, where comfort and inspiration were always in ready supply.

"YOU'VE GOT IT all backwards. Get your head out of your ass! I've got what you're looking for."

Jackson knew the voice, even if this time it wasn't blurred by painkillers or alcohol. He considered hanging up. Make it three-for-three. But this time he listened.

The voice dropped, the whisper of a conspirator. "This is off the record. I'm not an idiot."

Jackson didn't say anything. No point in making a deal. This guy was eager to talk.

"Here you go. Gift-wrapped. You think it's DuPont who did Harkney House. It isn't. That stupid fuck couldn't burn down a Chinatown fireworks factory."

Jackson could hear the sheer pleasure over the phone as the man said, "Been trying to tell you. It was Dictu. Prick-tu Dictu." Jackson had a passing thought that this jerk showed a fierce lack of imagination when it came to nicknames but he kept taking notes as the man explained how he had been on the mountain, with Prick-tu—it was enough to make Jackson consider abandoning "R2Dictu" forever—just a few days before the fire. And he was brave enough to force Dictu to confront the fact that his wife, Marybelle, was cheating on him. "Turned that prick with ears into a prick with horns." He'd taken a bad fall on Elevator Shaft that day, blew out his knee, but it was worth it to see the look on Prick-tu's smug face when he was told the truth about his cheating wife.

"Oh, he tried to hide it, but he was in a rage. Roger doesn't like wearing the horns."

"And...?"

The voice was exasperated. "That's why he did it. To teach her a lesson. Don't you get it?"

And he hung up.

Jackson was stuck. He'd decided he had to stop trying to hang everything on Roger Randall Dictu. That had seemed like a solid move and it had paid off when he found out about the Pink Cadillac and the Thug in the Raincoat and traced it all back to Saxby DuPont. Solid work. But now he had this anonymous jerk telling him it really was Dictu, a second jerk. And to forget about the third jerk, DuPont.

Three jacks is a pretty good poker hand. But three jerks? Only a fool would bet on that.

"HEY, IT'S SUPPOSED to be a great day tomorrow. Sunny and warm."

"Uh, yeah. I guess."

Brian, Jackson's friend over at the Forest Service wasn't making a lot of sense.

"I was thinking I need to drive out east of town, take a look at Difficult Campground, see if everything survived the winter. That should work into your story, right? That's the kind of thing you're looking for, isn't it?"

"What are you talking about? Is this national Let's Not Make Sense Day?"

"Yeah. I thought you would."

"The green cow sings at midnight." Might as well get into the spirit.

"We need to get an early start. I'll pick you up out in front of City Market. About 7. OK?"

"OK. I'll wear swim fins and carry a blue marmot."

Jackson loved conversations like that.

Difficult Campground seemed in fine shape—as far as they could see from the cab of the truck, where they sat as Jackson's Forest Service friend explained everything he couldn't talk about when he was at the office.

First, of course, came all the usual requirements: Jackson couldn't print any of it. It was all off the record. He hadn't heard it from his friend. He hadn't heard it from anyone. He didn't know anything. It was on background. Deep background.

"Let's make it double-super-secret invisible background," Jackson suggested—and got a sour look for that. It all just meant that Brian didn't want to lose his job and he'd lose it for sure if this got out—but still… it was too dirty a secret to keep. And who else was he going to tell?

So here it was: Roger Randall Dictu was getting it done. He had all the private land he'd wanted and now he was going to get those last two lots from the Forest Service and the Skico. And what he was going to do with that property was exactly the worst that Jackson could have expected. The biggest hotel in Aspen: 200 rooms, with a top floor of multi-million-dollar "penthouse" condominiums. And its own private ski lift, so guests and condo owners could get onto the mountain without mixing with the common folk.

Jackson expressed his opinion with an obscenity.

His friend nodded glumly. "It's ugly. Not an ugly building. I mean, sure, the building's ugly. But who gives a crap? They all are. It's the whole thing that's ugly. It'll wreck the bottom of the mountain."

Jackson repeated his obscenity and embroidered on it. Then it was time to be a reporter.

"So what happened? You said it was dead. No deal. No chance."

"Yeah." Still nervous, even with just the two of them in the truck, Jackson's friend chewed his lip. "OK. Look, I have no idea what happened with the Skico, all right? All I know is that they turned around hard. And fast. From 'Hell no!' to 'Let's go!' No idea why. But they've come so far around, they're not just selling their property to Dictu, they're leaning on us to make the deal for our land. Guess one of the senators they own —" a pause to think about that "— called someone way up the Forest Service food chain to suggest we ought to listen carefully to what Mr. Dictu is offering."

Jackson spent a moment thinking about the Liberty Drift and the gondola. While he'd been trying to untangle legal knots and figure out who rightly owned that multi-million dollar mining claim, R2 Fucking Dictu had somehow jumped to the head of the line and grabbed what he wanted.

He went back to basic obscenities.

"Yeah." His friend wasn't any happier than he was. "Your government in action."

"So that's why you're giving him what he wants? A call from a senator?"

"That's the funny part. Well, not funny. You know. Our guys were already going that way."

"The wolf habitat suddenly looked good?"

"That's still part of it, but now there's something about a museum."

"Museum?" Jackson heard the edge in his own voice and dialed it back. "When did the Forest Service start worrying about museums?"

"They're not talking to me. You understand that, right? But I'm thinking it's a public lands, public access thing. He's putting a historical museum on the property. To replace the one that burned down. I guess they couldn't say no to a museum."

And there it was. Simple as sunrise. Not just who, but why: Roger Randall Dictu, for a 200-room hotel. Forget Saxby DuPont and the pink Cadillac, stolen or loaned, whatever that was all about didn't matter. And forget thinking he had to stop trying to blame everything on Dictu. It was R2 Dictu—suddenly now Jackson wanted to say Prick-tu Dictu because clever nicknames seemed wrong—and Dictu was willing to do anything to get what he wanted. Burn down Harkney House and offer to build them a new museum. That was easy.

No one could turn down a museum.

Jackson looked up toward Independence Pass, the Continental Divide. It was still early and the morning sun was fierce. The sky was a savage blue, the snow glittered in the new day's light. Sky, snow, mountains—they didn't care.

And neither did Roger Randall Dictu.

Arson. Murder. Whatever it took.

All for a real estate deal.

"I THINK YOU HAD BETTER LEAVE RIGHT NOW, MR. JACK-
son."

There wasn't even a hint of Marybelle's smile.

He couldn't blame her. She'd been remarkably polite when she threw him out last time, for suggesting that Saxby DuPont had hired a thug to burn down Harkney House—and now he was back, just days later, saying, OK, she was right, it wasn't DuPont. It was her husband. He considered suggesting she might give him at least a little credit for admitting she'd been right the time before, but clearly that wasn't going to happen.

She had started by telling him that Roger Randall still wasn't home from the Himalayas, but Jackson had insisted on explaining about the hotel project and the Forest Service land and the museum.

Her eyes narrowed and she let him finish, but when he was done, she didn't respond except to say, "Good-bye, Mr. Jackson," as she closed the door in his face.

It was a hell of a way to start the day, but embarrassment was part of the job.

MARYBELLE DICTU headed for the basement as soon as the door closed. The huge house had an equally huge basement and one small room in a distant corner was lined with shelves. And the shelves were filled with tapes, hundreds of tapes.

Marybelle hadn't ever listened to the tapes, but she'd kept them organized, labeled, and very well hidden. She was focused and sharp—except when she was with Goodie Rawlins—and the tapes for the weeks before and after the fire were easy to find. The sound quality was excellent. The best was never too good for Roger Randall Dictu and, as his concerned wife, she had demanded nothing but the best when she arranged to have his office phone tapped. The minor deception had been easy for a woman who had spent years observing Roger Randall himself. "He's been getting threatening phone calls," she had explained, "and we need to keep track of them. Of course, we need to keep it strictly confidential. I'm sure you understand." And she'd paid the not-inconsiderable bill in cash. Which everyone always appreciated.

And so now she could listen as Roger Randall talked with another man whose voice she recognized very well: Saxby DuPont.

And as she listened, she felt rage rising within her.

Roger, she thought. You wretched shit.

"HOW WOULD I know if you left your gloves here? That's not my job!"

Another conversation that didn't make any sense.

Based on what he'd learned from his Forest Service connection, Jackson had stopped at the county clerk's office on the off chance that he might find some kind of hard evidence to hang a story on. He had the story, but he dreaded trying to get it past Fester and into print without something more solid than one double-super-secret off-the-record source. He'd asked Lorena if there was anything interesting going on and she just shrugged, her stiletto eyebrows firmly in the neutral position. Then, not moving her lips, she said, "Call me."

Before he left, Jackson searched through the recent development applications. His only bit of luck was finding plans for a new house on the Ridge of Red Mountain that looked as if it was going to set a new Aspen record for Hulking Monster Mansions. It had nothing to do with Dictu, but he knew he could knock that story out in a hurry and get a little breathing room when Fester came raging around.

Back at the office, Jackson called Lorena and that's when he got yelled at about the gloves he hadn't been wearing and hadn't left behind and hadn't asked about. Another one of those conversations.

"I'm not running a lost-and-found for scatter-brained reporters," Lorena added. Jackson wondered if maybe she was enjoying herself a little too much. Then her voice dropped into ventriloquist mode. "Skico digging around. Mining claim. You know." Then full-voice again. "Walk over here and look for your own dang gloves."

OK. The Skico was checking out the Liberty Drift. So maybe it's not quite a done deal. Maybe they're trying to make absolutely sure who owns that claim. And maybe he should be doing the same. Hell, he might even be a step ahead of them.

Feeling lucky, Jackson called Becky's number in Chicago—and she answered.

"Got fed up with St. Barth's and your rich boyfriend?"

"Fuck him. Dumped me for some blonde slut with bigger tits."

"Always told you to go blonde."

"Came out ahead anyway. I hitched a ride home on a Learjet. Had to fly commercial with that loser."

"Always fail upwards."

"You got it."

"So... I need some help with that story."

"Jesus, Jackson. Get over it."

"This one's getting serious. Really."

"Say 'please.'"

"Pretty please."

"How can I resist?"

"You never could. OK. Remember the trust, from the will? The LD Trust?"

"Jack-o, I found that crap for you. You didn't say I had to read it."

"Becks, it was none of your damn business—so I know you read it."

"Read it and forgot it."

So he laid it out quickly and said he needed to find out what had happened to the Trust over the past year or two. Or five.

"No problem. I'll go back and have a chat with my pal the librarian. The hot one. Who knows what else I might…"

"Becky! Stay focused. And I don't want to know what you…"

"Sure you do. But I won't tell you."

On a roll, Jackson called Saxby DuPont, but his luck had run out.

"Message box full."

And that was when, as expected, Fester came raging through the newsroom, demanding copy, damn it!

So Jackson put everything else aside and spent the next hour on the Red Mountain Monster Mansion story. At least it wasn't junior hockey.

"GIVE ME ANOTHER assignment, Jack. I'm telling you, she's hot."

"No switching teams, Becks."

Jackson was glad Rebecca had gotten side-tracked. She'd been talking non-stop and it sounded like she needed to adjust her Ritalin dosage. He was going to have a hard time deciphering his notes.

But it was worth it.

All the assets of the LD Trust had been bought by a corporation registered somewhere east of Borneo. "East of Borneo. How cool is that?" It wasn't a big-money deal. "Shit, Jack. I almost could have bought it myself!" The Trust had been worth millions at one point, but the money had slipped away. "You know what happens with money. Same as with boyfriends." And in the end all the Trust was left with was the Liberty Drift—and enough money to pay the yearly taxes. And the money was running out fast.

Jackson told Rebecca he loved her—and that she'd better not run off with that hot librarian.

"Sure thing, Jack. My heart's yours forever."

"Isn't it pretty to think so?"

And he hung up before she could tell him not to steal from Hemingway.

Then he spent half an hour with an atlas looking up that tax haven east of Borneo and it really did exist: Labuan. She'd spelled it out for him and she was right.

And that convinced him.

JACKSON KNEW he didn't have everything he needed. And he didn't care. He knew he'd catch hell from Fester—and he still didn't care.

He had enough to stir up trouble and he had enough to be sure the trouble he stirred up wouldn't turn around and bite him. Enough to hope it wouldn't, anyway.

He stared at the note pad and felt like a man juggling chainsaws.

OK.

He had the Harkney House fire and he had the man in black flying in and then out, right before and right after the fire.

OK.

And he had someone trashing PJ's apartment when she was looking into the fire story. And someone shooting up Jackson's car when he started digging. And someone chasing him up Castle Creek, driving like a lunatic at four in the morning. Small potatoes, maybe. But it had happened.

So: Harkney House, fire, thug on the loose.

Got that.

OK

And then the Liberty Drift.

He had Gunnar. Oh yeah, he had Gunnar. He had Gunnar saying someone was trying to kill him and then wrecking his snowmobile, going headfirst into a tree, and claiming—when he wasn't raving incoherently—that he'd been sabotaged. And if you don't believe that, well, he had Gunnar carried off into a blizzard and left to die. So, sure. He had Gunnar. And Gunnar was the man who seemed to know way too much about the Liberty Drift. Pretty sketchy, but there was still something underneath all the craziness.

OK.

And he had that one splinter of the Liberty Drift itself, one tiny scrap of lost land directly under the top terminal of the Silver Queen gondola.

OK.

And he had the skeletons in the cabin and Osgood's will and the missing heir.

OK

And he had a corporation from a tax haven somewhere East of Borneo sneaking in and buying the Liberty Drift mining claim from a bankrupt foundation.

So: Liberty Drift, gondola terminal, sneaky land deal.

Got that.

OK.

And all of that was really just decoration, the cherry on top of the Hot Dictu Sundae, because what Jackson really had was Roger Randall Dictu's massive real estate deal, a deal that depended on two things: getting the Liberty Drift mining claim, before anybody realized what it was worth, and moving the Historical Society Museum to his property. Would Dictu burn down a house to force the museum to move? Would he go to any lengths to keep people from finding out about Osgood's will and the skeletons in the cabin—throwing the Liberty Drift into the kind of legal tangle that would block his deal?

Would he do that?

R2 Dictu would do anything to get what he wanted.

OK!

And now he had a page with "R2 Dictu" written in the middle, circled by notes, and every note had an arrow pointing back to the man in the middle.

He knew that every one of those arrows was either weak or blunt, unproven, unprovable or imaginary.

But he could make those arrows fly.

And then wait to see what he hit.

JACKSON WROTE the story fast. Then he rewrote it slowly—adding all the "allegedly"s and "apparently"s and all the other weasel words and phrases that any editor would insist on—and he filed it well after midnight, after even the proofreader had gone home. No point in dragging her into his particular hell, if that's what was coming. Then he walked home in the dark and spent a sleepless night, imaging what might come next: lawsuits, unemployment, all the usual reporter's nightmares.

He was up early and grabbed a copy of the Sun out of a box on his way to the office, to see how they'd played the story. But it wasn't at the top of the front page, where it belonged. And it wasn't at the bottom of the front. And it wasn't buried inside either. It just wasn't there. Wasn't anywhere.

Jackson threw the paper in the trash.

When he got to the office, Fester and Prince Hal were waiting.

Fester sat silently, looking uncomfortable. Hal took the lead. This was a new role for the Prince, who usually did a fine job of playing the rich kid publisher's son: slapping businessmen's backs, kissing advertisers' butts, and staying the hell out of the newsroom. Jackson didn't much like the old version of Hal. He hated this new one.

"Harbuck called me at three in the goddamn morning!" he shouted. "Took until dawn to fix the mess you caused."

Harbuck. He should have known.

"What the hell are you trying to do, Jackson? Get us sued? Get us shut down?"

No point in holding back. "I'm trying to get us a great story. An important story. Or don't we care about that?"

"I care about this newspaper. I'm not going to let you destroy it. That story is fiction. Wild speculation. That story is dead. Now and forever. Got that?"

"Why are you suddenly so concerned? You never give a shit what we run."

The Prince blew up. "I'm not going to let you ruin everything right now! Damn it!"

Right now? Ruin everything? Where did that come from? But Jackson wasn't going to ask Prince Fuckwit for explanations. He turned to Fester.

"You're going along with this?"

The editor continued to look uncomfortable. "It's his paper, Jack." He shifted his gaze. "I've got a family."

Jackson realized this would be an excellent moment to leave. He was certain no one would mind if he took the rest of the day off. He was pretty sure they wouldn't mind if he took the rest of his life off—and they might go right ahead and take care of that detail anyway.

As Jackson headed out the front door, Stormy shouted, "Jackson! Arnie Bing on line 3!" and, without even slowing down, Jackson shouted something back that made even Stormy wince.

And then he was out the door and gone.

UGLY AS THINGS had been in the newspaper office, life was still beautiful on the back of the mountain. The first sharp edge of spring had cut through the thick hide of winter, right on time, which was, as always, much too late after eight months of snow and ice. The fierce delicate green of the new aspen leaves boasted that the snow was banished for another year— foolish, as the boasts of children always are: some of those leaves would be battered and some of those branches would break under the snows of June. It always snows in Aspen in June.

Jackson focused on the green leaves against the swaths of snow that still covered most of the mountain. He pushed hard, skiing uphill with determination that had his heart pounding and his breath rasping. And between the green and the white and the hot sun and the hard work, all thoughts of the newspaper and Fester and Hal and even R2 Dictu faded from his mind.

By the time he got to Gunnar's cabin, he was smiling almost as much as he was sweating. The view from the porch was beautiful and mean and clumsy all at once: mountains dappled white and green and stained with mud and dirt and scarred with fresh spring avalanches. A prom queen who fell on her face and broke a couple of teeth—but still beautiful. He kicked off his skis and sat on the top step. He considered going inside, but the day was too nice and the sun was too warm.

He let the view fill his eyes and his mind. After the sleepless night and the nearly violent morning, he almost dozed off, but then he saw a figure carving telemark turns down through the trees, elegant and fast. For a moment he thought it was Winston—but Winston couldn't walk right now, much less ski. It was Ella May. And of course she skied as well as Winston. In fact, better.

"Hey."

"Hey, yourself. About time you showed up. Winston needs to talk to you."

"What about?"

"Guess he'll have to tell you. Get your skis."

He couldn't keep up with her, of course. She was just disappearing into the cabin when he got there.

Inside, Winston was in the armchair.

"I'd get up," he said, "but…" He shrugged.

Ella May gave him a kiss, said, "I've got some chores," and disappeared back outside.

Winston leaned back, eyes closed. Then he looked straight at Jackson. "There's something we have to do, right now. Serious business." Jackson had had enough serious business for the day. He shrugged, but Winston insisted. "We need to do this and I need you to focus. OK? Say yes. We need to be that serious about it."

"This is starting to sound like Gunnar."

"Just say yes. Really."

"Yes."

"OK. Listen up. I'm going to ask you a question. You get just one chance. Just one clear answer. Right or wrong. Passing grade is one hundred per-cent —" what might have been the shadow of an apologetic grin "— col-lege boy."

"I don't need this."

"Yes you do. Really."

Jackson shrugged. Winston started to raise a finger and Jackson said, "Yes. OK. Yes."

"Here we go. One question. One answer. No hints." A pause. "Jim Morrison was the greatest poet of the twentieth century. Agree or disagree and give your reasons why."

"What!"

Winston burst out laughing. "Sorry. It was getting a little too heavy. OK. Serious now, here's the question." Again a pause. Then, clearly, almost formal. "What was the inscription?"

Jackson shook his head. Gunnar. Checking up on him from beyond the grave. He was about to answer, quick and easy, the inscription from the locket: "You're the apple of my eye." But, no, that wasn't quite right. He stopped to remember exactly what it had said. To Ernestina? Ernestina Rose? My Ernestina? On the occasion of... was that it? And what was the date? If he was going to answer, he was going to have to get it exactly right. Gunnar was a stickler for details. The silence stretched out and Winston smiled—no hurry for an answer.

And then another thought.

No, not Apple of My Eye. That was too easy for Gunnar.

She should have died hereafter.

That was a crazy answer. It was a random inscription that didn't have anything to do with anything at all. Just a gravestone in the Ute that someone had desecrated, the grave of a child who hadn't lived long enough to get her own name. Infant Girl Finch.

It couldn't be right. It was crazy.

But Gunnar was crazy.

She should have died hereafter.

That's what it was really all about. The whole melodrama, the whole chase. From way before the Infant Finch. Ernestina Rose. Ernestina Rose was too young to die. And if she hadn't—if the Angel hadn't fallen into temptation and sin and then been abandoned, left to die—none of it would have happened.

She should have died hereafter.

He was a reporter and that was the headline. So he looked right at Winston and even though the answer had to be Apple of My Eye, he said, "She should have died hereafter." Loud and clear.

Winston's beard split in a smile and his teeth gleamed. "All right! Didn't know if you were going to get that. Way to go!"

He leaned forward, reached up and gave Jackson a formal handshake.

"So"—everything else that had happened that morning suddenly came flooding back and Jackson wanted to get back outside—"are we done?" He was wondering what he was going to do next. Today, tomorrow, the rest of his life.

"Nope. Not yet." Jackson shook his head in annoyance, but Winston was smiling. "You got the right answer, so here's the prize." A pause. "You're Gunnar's heir."

Jackson just stared at him. Winston filled the silence.

"You get everything he owned. The cabin. And everything in it. Free and clear."

Jackson didn't have anything to say. It took him a moment to realize he was smiling and he didn't want to stop.

An image of the cabin filled his mind. The room flooded with light. All the books on their shelves. Quiet. Neat. Precise. Then he thought about going up there with Louise. He realized it was time to call Louise.

And that kept him smiling for a long time.

28

JACKSON WALKED PAST FESTER'S OFFICE. THEIR EYES met, but nothing passed between them: no apology, no anger. Nothing. Now, sitting at his desk, he let the phone ring. There was no one he wanted to talk to. He heard the intercom, garbled as always. He made out his own name—Jackson—even Stormy seemed to realize that this was not the time for cute codes like "LJO." Maybe all of that was over forever. And he could make out another name: Dictu. R2 himself? Not likely. Probably his lawyer. Prince Hal must have shown R2 the story. That seemed about right. Jackson didn't care.

Then Stormy marched into his office. "Jackson! I've been paging you. Marybelle Dictu..."

"Is here to see you." Marybelle herself finished the sentence, gliding around Stormy into the office. "Thank you, Miss Storm."

Jackson just looked at her.

"Are you feeling all right? You don't look well."

Jackson knew he had to rally. He managed a shrug. "Late night." Always an acceptable excuse in Aspen.

Marybelle's lips tightened. No smile.

"Jackson, I need you to pay attention. I have something important to tell you."

That reminded him of Winston—was it really just yesterday? And with that came the thought of the cabin and the realization that life was going to go on. And it wasn't so terrible. Not all of it anyway.

So he smiled and said, "I'm OK."

Her smile fluttered down upon him in return and she reached into her bag and brought out a large manila envelope.

"Read this very carefully. I promise you, it's genuine. You can't print it. You can't quote it. You can't say you have it. If you do, I'll say it was stolen. I'll say it was forged. I'll say whatever I have to. Do you understand?"

"Marybelle. How the hell can I ..."

"If you can't get a story out of this, give it up and get a job waiting tables."

This was a new Marybelle. She paused.

"If you do write a story and play by my rules and you wind up in court, you can use this in your defense."

Jackson didn't know what was going on, but he thought he might like it.

Marybelle added, "But you're not going to wind up in court."

And she was gone, leaving the ghost of her smile hanging in the air.

He opened the envelope and thumbed through the pages. Typed transcripts of telephone conversations, dated, well-organized. Between Roger Randall Dictu and a number of men—none identified by name, just "Male Voice 1," "Male Voice 2."

Jackson took a deep breath and started reading.

Marybelle had been right—and he wasn't going to have to get a job waiting tables. He had the story. He'd already pretty much written it. But now it was rock solid.

Roger Randall Dictu had been the force behind it all. He had backed Saxby DuPont into a corner and applied intolerable pressure on him to get rid of the Harkney House Museum. He had tracked down the Liberty Drift claim and the maps that showed that one remaining vital fragment of property. He had discovered the trail of bad investments that had destroyed he foundation that controlled the claim. It was all there in the tape transcripts.

When Jackson was done reading, he went to Fester's office. They talked—heatedly at times—and then Fester took Jackson to Prince Hal's office. Jackson explained what he had.

"Goddamn it!" Hal exploded. "I told you no. I meant it. No! Not now. Not ever. How stupid are you? I don't care what kind of super-secret evidence you have. I swear, if you can't understand me now, you're too stupid to work at this newspaper."

Jackson was about to agree, when a new voice came raging into the office. "What the hell is this!"

It was Harold. Hal's father. The man who had owned the paper for 40 years, brought it back from near bankruptcy and nurtured it into prosperity—and had been threatening to sell it for years.

He was waving a sheaf of papers. "What the hell do you think you're doing?"

Jackson wondered if someone had given him a copy of Jackson's never-printed Dictu story from the day before. But Harold barely glanced at Jackson. He threw the papers on Hal's desk.

Hal looked at the papers.

"That's a contract, Dad. To ..." Then he stopped. "Jackson, get out of here."

"No!" Harold thundered. "I want witnesses in case I have to strangle you."

"Dad?"

Harold snatched the papers off Hal's desk and tore them savagely in half.

"I will never sell this newspaper to Roger Randall Dictu!" He kept his voice down, but Hal recoiled as if his father was swinging a machete. Harold might like to say he was getting too old and feeble to run the paper, but he was strong enough to terrify his son. "I will shut down this paper. I will burn this building and I will shit on the ashes before I sell this newspaper to—" his gaze swept over to Jackson and a shadow of a grin might have slipped across the old man's mouth "—R2 Dictu!"

He fixed his son with a fierce gaze.

"Is that clear? Is that absolutely goddamn clear? Or do I have to say it again?"

Hal nodded.

"Say, 'Yes, Father.'"

"Yes, Father."

And again, Jackson thought of Gunnar's little games and then he said, "Harold? Can we talk?"

Half an hour later, after Harold had read the story and Jackson had run through the new evidence that couldn't be part of the story but confirmed everything and could be used in court, the publisher slammed his hand on his desk and said, "Print it!"

And when they walked out of Harold's office, Fester actually gave Jackson a hug.

AFTER SOME CAREFUL editing, there was one more thing Jackson had to do before he filed the story. He had to get a comment from Roger Randall Dictu. He had tried before he'd filed the story the first time, but he'd been told, icily, as always, "Mr. Dictu is unavailable." Now he had to try again. He got ready for whatever might come—but before he could dial, the phone rang.

"Jackson! How ya doing? It's Arnie. Arnie Bing. Look, we really need to talk about..."

"Not now!"

Jackson slammed the phone down, steeled himself again, and dialed.

Roger Randall Dictu answered.

Jackson took a breath and outlined the story that was going to run on the front page tomorrow..

"Do you have a comment, Mr. Dictu?"

"I have no comment whatsoever." The developer's voice didn't quiver, but the dog whose ears he was scratching sensed the ferocity in his touch and slunk away, perhaps wishing he was back in the safety of the shelter. "But—and this is strictly off the record, not for publication in any form, just a word of advice for you, young man—if you print that story, you had better have your attorney on speed dial."

And then he hung up.

Jackson sat and waited for calm to return. After a minute, he said a brief prayer to Marybelle Dictu and filed the story.

Then he called Louise.

Jackson slept late. He'd been up until four in the morning. He'd known he was being too careful—paranoid, the press crew called it—but he just had to wait and see the first copies of the paper roll off the press. He wasn't going to wake up and see his story killed again.

And then the press was running and the head pressman fiddled with the ink keys until the headline was black and bold enough for a blind man to read by touch: MURDER AND ARSON: ALL FOR A REAL ESTATE DEAL.

The press crew cheered and slapped Jackson on the back.

Then, at last, he'd gone home to sleep.

And now it was deep into the morning, the sun was high and he was just waking up. And Louise was right there next to him. She gave him a kiss and said, "They can cook their own damn breakfast."

ROGER RANDALL DICTU kept himself from tearing the papers into tiny pieces and stuffing them in the trash. It wasn't easy. He knew that kind of impotent rage was for lesser men, but it was hard—so very hard—not to give in.

He even kept himself from shouting at Marybelle, although the gleam of triumph in her eye almost drove him to violence.

Marybelle hadn't said a word, just smiled, nodded toward the copy of the Aspen Sun that was on his desk and dropped the sheaf of tape transcripts on top of the newspaper.

He glanced through them and realized what was happening. His face didn't betray the sinking feeling, but it was there. Everything seemed perfectly clear in the transcripts, even though none of it was really what had happened. He hadn't caused any of this. He had simply allowed that miserable DuPont creature to make his own despicable decisions. If Roger Randall had really been giving the orders, none of it would have happened the way it had. It was all too ugly, all too messy.

He knew that. DuPont knew that. But the voice on the tape, being oh-so-careful, oh-so-discreet, didn't make any of that clear. Because Roger Randall Dictu never made anything clear, except to the poor fools he was talking to, who knew exactly what he meant.

He knew that. And Marybelle knew that. But she didn't care.

And that was when she laid the divorce papers down on top of the transcript.

"You won't contest this," she said. The dog that had been lying under his desk got up and quietly moved to the far corner of the office, keeping a wary eye on the two humans. Taking Roger Randall's silence for assent, although it was closer to strangled rage than any kind of agreement, Marybelle added, "And, just to be clear, Roger"—no "Randall," not even a hint, the game really had changed—"I get Aspen. You can find yourself another nice little mountain town. Someplace where no one knows you."

THE PHONE RANG. Saxby DuPont didn't answer. There was no one he wanted to talk to—and yet he listened, waiting for the answering machine to pick up so he could hear whatever fatal message someone might be leaving. The machine had been knocked awry during the struggle with Viktor, but now it was working again. And even as he counted the rings, waiting for the machine to kick in, DuPont took grim pleasure in remembering the savage surprise on the thug's face when he realized that Saxby DuPont was not the weak creature everyone had assumed him to be. That was Viktor's last mistake and he deserved the miserable end he had come to, right there in the apartment.

The phone stopped ringing and then the voice he knew far too well echoed through the empty room.

"Arnold! This is your mother!" And even as he felt a twinge of annoyance—she never would use his new name—that voice slammed him with the misery of his entire childhood: the failures, the taunts, the reek of cabbage boiling in the tiny kitchen. "The answer is No!" she shouted her voice rattling the speaker of the answering machine. "No! You cannot move back here! What are you thinking? You and your fancy career! That ridiculous name. That chin! Hah!" And she hung up.

He curled back into his ball of misery. It was all Viktor's fault.

Yes, he had told the stupid Russian to get rid of that hideous old house—but he'd never told him to kill anyone. He'd never told him to trash PJ's apartment. And he'd never told Viktor to blow up her car. Or to harass Jackson. Or to drag Gunnar out into the snow. It was all Viktor. He'd gone crazy. And with his mother's voice, the voice of Queens, still echoing in his mind, Saxby DuPont thought about that cartoon, what was it? With Mickey Mouse. The Sorcerer's Apprentice. Those animated brooms, carrying endless buckets of water, and no way to make them stop. He could feel the water rising, flooding. He could feel Arnold Firkin washing back over him. He thought about drowning.

And then the phone rang again. He couldn't help counting the rings as he waited for the machine to take over.

And the voice that spoke this time was crisp with anger and authority. The voice of Roger Randall Dictu, terrifying even filtered through the cheap speaker. With a wail of despair and sheer terror, Saxby DuPont scuttled across the floor to grab the pistol that had handled Viktor so well—as if it could protect him from the voice that filled the apartment.

"Arnold Firkin! Yes, I know your real name, you ridiculous fraud. Don't think you can hide behind that answering machine. I know you're there. And I know you are going to come back here to Aspen and you are going to explain everything to the police. That I had nothing whatsoever to do with your unforgettably stupid idea to burn down that house. It was your doing! All yours! You know that is true and for once in your life you are going to tell the truth. You have ruined your life, Firkin. But you are not going to ruin mine. So you will tell the truth. And then you are going to do whatever it is that small people like you do after they have been forced to do the right thing in spite of themselves."

For an instant, the voice teetered, it threatened to tip into territory where Roger Randall Dictu's voice never went. For that instant, there was the slightest edge of panic.

But none of that mattered.

Because the voice was drowned out by the shattering explosion of the pistol. Two shots. The first destroyed the answering machine. And the second obliterated all sounds forever.

And then, although Roger Randall Dictu may have still been talking, Arnold Firkin wasn't listening.

29

JACKSON WOKE WITH THE FIRST RAYS OF THE RISING
sun. He spent a few minutes on the porch, enjoying the morning. Then went inside to set a pot of coffee on the stove and make the bed. As a proud new homeowner, he wanted to keep the place neat and clean—even though he knew that wouldn't last. Louise hadn't been up to the cabin yet and he wanted his house—his!—to make a good first impression.

As he struggled to get the sheets smooth, he focused for the first time on the small night table wedged between the bed and the rough log wall. Only half thinking about what he was doing—most of his mind was still on the prospect of Louise coming up to visit—Jackson opened the drawer in the table. There was a stack of papers inside. On top was a sheet folded double with "Gunnar" written on it in fancy script that looked familiar. But before he could unfold the paper, Jackson's eye was caught by the sheet below it: a clipping from the Aspen Sun, a photo of PJ skiing on Independence Pass in shorts and a bikini top early one summer, years before. Jackson knew the picture well. He'd taken it. And under that clipping were many more: stories from the paper that mentioned PJ—often just her name, buried somewhere down the list in the results of a ski race or a 10k footrace and carefully underlined. And there were more pictures of PJ. Some clipped from the newspaper, with her face in a crowd. Some actual snapshots. It looked as if the old buzzard had a crush on her. Jackson smiled. He knew what it felt like to have a crush on PJ.

He leafed through the pile, remembering some of the pictures, some of the stories. Then he idly squared up the stack, wondering what to do with it all. He felt a little embarrassed, snooping through Gunnar's private life.

And then he took another look at that folded sheet of paper that had been on top of the pile—and he recognized that fancy script: PJ wrote that way sometimes, just for fun or when she was trying to be formal. Again, feeling as if he was snooping, Jackson opened the note. The handwriting was PJ's. No more fancy script.

"Gunnar, sweetie..."

That stopped Jackson cold. It was definitely PJ's handwriting. No question. But "sweetie"? PJ never called anyone "sweetie." Not the PJ that Jackson knew. And the rest of the note didn't help:

"I stopped by to give you a birthday kiss, but you weren't here. I really need to talk to you. Please come down and meet me after work tonight. After last call. I know it's late but please come. Maybe I'll have that special present for you."

And then, at the bottom, instead of a signature, she'd drawn a little heart.

There was way too much wrong. The "sweetie," the heart, the "birthday kiss." That wasn't PJ.

Jackson gulped a mouthful of coffee and went outside to grab his skis.

SKIING DOWN the mountain and then driving into town, Jackson had to stop several times to get control of his thoughts—to deal with the one fact that was keeping him from paying attention to the steep winding road: Gunnar's snowmobile crash happened on his birthday.

Jackson had left it out of the obituary, because it seemed like a trivial coincidence. But now it was part of something he couldn't set aside: PJ had lured Gunnar down the mountain that birthday night, with a note calling him "sweetie" and signed with a heart, a note promising kisses and a "special present."

And then, somehow, Gunnar wound up running his snowmobile into a tree. Going home on a clear night. On a road he'd traveled thousands of times in every kind of weather.

That never should have happened. And he was only there because PJ had left him that note: hearts and kisses.

PJ'S STEP-FATHER WAS standing in the door to her apartment. The last time he and Jackson had been face to face was at the door to PJ's hospital room, two days after the explosion. The hospital was sending Jackson home and on his way out, he'd shuffled painfully down the hall to see PJ. But her father was blocking the doorway. Jackson had tried to see around him, to catch a glimpse of PJ, but the room was dark and her father was large. All Jackson could see were shadows and the blinking lights of the machines PJ was hooked up to.

"Well, Oliver." PJ's father had spoken the hated name firmly. No one called Jackson by that name—his real first name, his father's name, which he'd done his best to leave behind years ago. His by-line and his driver's license both read "Jack Jackson." The last person to call him Oliver had been a lawyer years ago, threatening a libel suit.

"Oliver." PJ's father knew how much Jackson hated the name. "I suppose I have to thank you for saving my daughter's life." He shifted his bulk to block the door more completely. "They told me that if it hadn't been for you, she probably would have died." Something in the hospital room beeped. Jackson tried to see what it was, but PJ's father wasn't getting out of the way. "But if it hadn't been for you, none of it would have happened." He stepped back into the room and closed the door. Jackson was too weak and too sore to do anything except shuffle away.

And now the son of a bitch was standing in the way again. He nodded and said, "Oliver." Just the way he had before. But this time the older man—not really old, just older than Jackson, a burly man with, disconcertingly, the same nose, the same splash of freckles, as his daughter—got out of the way. He had a cardboard box in his arms and he brushed past Jackson, out onto the deck, and lumbered down the stairs to the alley.

Jackson stepped inside. PJ was sitting in the middle of the room, in an armchair that had always been back in the bedroom. Jackson had tossed his clothes on that chair many times. But now PJ was sitting in it, her right leg stretched out on a stool in front of her, a green fiberglass cast on her lower leg and a metal brace on her knee. Her right arm was wrapped in gauze. Her hair was cut short and somehow she was looking strong. She managed a smile.

"They tell me you saved my life, Jack."

"They tell me the same thing. I don't remember any of it."

"Me neither. What did it say in the paper?"

"You know you can't believe..." He didn't bother to finish.

This had to stop, so he stopped it.

"PJ." Just that, but his tone put an end to the chatter. They weren't going to slip back into the old games. "I'm going to say some things you don't want to hear." Her face was blank. "I'm going to ask questions you don't want to answer." Still blank. "But you're going to have to." Blank.

He needed to wipe that blank look off her face and see who was living behind it. And he didn't want to. He knew how much damage it was going to do. He hesitated and in the silence he could hear her father coming back up the stairs. PJ's eyes flicked away from Jackson for a moment. He wasn't going to turn, wasn't going to be distracted—a series of images flashed through his mind: the heart at the bottom of the note to Gunnar, the pictures of PJ in the drawer in the cabin, the police photos of Gunnar's snowmobile upside down in a gully. Then he thought about PJ suddenly telling him to drop everything, to stop caring about who killed Beast or Gunnar and he could feel a few more pieces falling into place in his mind.

He had a cold feeling in his chest.

"I know about Gunnar. I know what you did."

He heard PJ's father walk up to the doorway behind him. PJ cocked her head, looking past him to the door. "It's OK, Dad. Take a break. Get a coffee. Jack and I need to talk." Her voice was tight, harsh. He heard her father walk back across the deck and down the stairs.

Now he had to say the rest.

"You tricked Gunnar into going down the mountain that night. You killed him."

Her face dissolved. It wasn't PJ any more.

That could have been enough. He could have walked away, but he didn't.

"No!" It was more a wail than a real word. "I didn't know. He said talk. Just talk… I didn't… Gunnar just…" Then she was sobbing.

And Jackson still didn't go. He took another deep breath.

"And Harkney House."

The crying stopped. Her voice was raw, but steady. Insistent.

"I didn't know anything about that."

"Yes you did. You had to."

"After." She was crying again. "It was too late. It didn't matter. I didn't have…" Her voice trailed off.

On a late-spring afternoon, once the ski season is over, Aspen can be a very quiet place. That silence filled the room.

"Why?" It didn't matter, but he had to ask.

She thought for a moment, decided to answer.

"Just tired of never having a real place to live." She waved her hand dismissively at the apartment Jackson had always envied. He glanced around and saw that it was almost empty. The walls were bare, the rugs were gone. "Tired of never having a real job, a real life. Tired of slinging drinks for jerks." He recognized the faint echo of an empty apartment. He had been hearing it since he walked in. Now he realized what it was.

"I don't even know you."

"It's still me."

"That's the worst part."

"I'm leaving, Jack. Leaving Aspen. There's nothing here for me."

She was pleading with him to let her go. And why not? She'd just said it: It was too late. It didn't matter.

"I'll go stay with my father for a while," she said. "Until, you know." She gestured at her leg. "And then… I don't know."

And he didn't care.

It was time to go, walk away. But he just had to say it one time. He wrapped everything he felt into a single word. "Dictu." She looked at him. "How could you work for Dictu?"

Her face twisted. "How about you?" She spat it back at him. "You almost wound up working for him too, didn't you?"

Her expression changed, almost the teasing smile she'd always worn when she told him she was better at his job than he was.

Almost, but not even close.

He could have said something, but there wasn't any point. If he pushed her on how much she knew about Dictu and his deals, what could she say? She might lie, she might tell the truth. It wouldn't matter. He already knew enough. Enough that he didn't want to know any more.

Her face shifted again. An expression he almost recognized. It was still PJ after all, still the one face he knew better than any other. She almost said something. Then she didn't. He saw something in her eyes. Then it was gone.

30

"YOU SHOULD OPEN IT."

"Why me?"

"You were the one who found it."

"Super sleuth," said Louise, laughing. "I was just looking for something to read."

In late May, high on the back of Aspen Mountain, summer was still a rumor. The snow was deep all around the cabin. By the end of the day, it was soft, almost slush; every night it would freeze and by morning the crust was icy and thick. It was perfect weather for sleeping late, sitting on the porch in the sun all day and settling down in front of the woodstove at night.

Louise nodded toward the battered metal box on the table. "Just open it."

Gunnar had gone to a fair amount of trouble to hide the box, chiseling out a niche in the log wall behind a shelf filled with a rag-tag assortment of Shakespeare. Maybe he'd figured no one would bother those particular books, with several much nicer sets of Shakespeare nearby. But Louise had a fondness for battered editions—"Why do you think I wound up with you?" she asked when Jackson pointed out that she always chose the worst looking book on the shelf—and when she pulled out the copy of "Macbeth," she'd spotted the box right away.

There wasn't much new inside, mostly confirmation of things he'd already known or suspected pretty strongly. Right at the top, a copy of James Eagleton Osgood's will. Of course Gunnar had that.

There were copies of the Liberty Drift tax records too. Wherever Jackson had gone, Gunnar had been there first.

And then there was a thick sheaf of papers that took a few minutes to figure out. Copies of classified ads from small-town newspapers scattered all over the country. Three a year—one from the East, one from the West, one from the Midwest—every year starting in 1930. And each ad said the same thing: "Seeking any child, or any surviving direct descendant(s) of such child, born between the months of January and March, year of Our Lord 1889, to that particular young woman known as Miss Ernestina Rose, believed to be a native of Kansas City, in the state of Kansas, who was most certainly resident in the City of Aspen, County of Pitkin, Colorado, in the year of Our Lord 1888."

Jackson snorted. "The Trust. A nation-wide search for the heir. Sparing no expense."

"Not very diligent," said Louise.

"Don't think they were in any hurry to pass the money along. Running a trust can be a pretty good gig."

And that was demonstrated by other papers in the box: expense reports from the LD Trust that made it clear that the trustees had been treating themselves very well for quite a long time, as they discharged whatever they decided their duties were. And now it was all gone. Run into the ground and sold to a corporation chartered somewhere East of Borneo.

Near the bottom of the box there was a scrap of an Aspen Mountain topo map, with the tiny vital splinter of the Liberty Drift claim outlined in red. It was an old map, old enough that it didn't show the Skiing Company gondola.

A man can't be too careful with secrets like these. Gunnar had been careful. But he wound up dead anyway. Which happens to everyone.

Dead before he wanted to be. Which also happens to pretty much everyone.

And finally, at he very bottom of the box was an envelope, carefully labeled, "Last Will and Testament."

Jackson hesitated. A revised will? Had Gunnar decided to leave everything to someone else? To PJ, as a reward for her shameless flirting? For an instant he considered tossing it into the fire, unopened.

He handed it to Louise instead.

"You read it."

So she did.

She opened the envelope, unfolded the document inside, paused dramatically and read, "Being of sound mind and body, I, Juliet Finch, do make this last will and testament."

She read the will from beginning to end. It didn't take very long.

Juliet Finch didn't spend any time wallowing in tragedy, but simply noted that, as she approached the end of a long and eventful life, she was pleased to note how little she had accumulated in the way of worldly goods.

"Those who spend their lives grasping and getting will find they have little enough indeed when it comes to that final accounting which we all must face."

And then, because she was after all, Mrs. Juliet Finch, she added, "And my more-having would be as a sauce to make me hunger more."

Louise looked up. Jackson shrugged.

"Macbeth," she said.

Jackson thought he could really learn to hate that play.

Louise held up her hand.

"Here we go. 'And so I bequeath whatever possessions I may have and all that I may own, my estate in its entirety, to my favorite and most annoying student, Gunnar Gustav Magnusson.' "

"Oh shit." It was the only thing Jackson could say, but he said it with wonder and reverence.

"So everything that Finch had was Gunnar's.... And everything Gunnar had is yours." Louise wasn't even half a step behind. "The Liberty Drift!"

"Can't be."

Bu even as he said that, Jackson imagined himself marching into the offices of the Skiing Company and demanding they get their damn gondola off his land! Now!

Then Louise laughed, "Borneo, here we come!" Her voice was cheerful, but that was the end of that fantasy.

The Reverend Osgood had—in the absence of his preferred heir—left the Liberty Drift to Mrs. Finch and Mrs. Finch had left it to Gunnar and Gunnar had left it to Jackson. But the whole process had taken a hundred-year detour to nowhere because no one could find any sign, dead or alive, of that preferred heir, the child born between the months of January and

March, year of Our Lord 1889, to that particular young woman known as Miss Ernestina Rose.

They couldn't find that child because its sad tiny skeleton was lost—along with that of its mother—in the wreckage of a cabin on Aspen Mountain. And, not finding the child, they didn't even consider looking for the former Miss Juliet Rasmussen of Winnetka, Illinois.

Much less Gunnar Gustav Magnusson.

And so, like a football fumbled on the goal line while everyone was distracted by a brawl in the stands, the Liberty Drift just lay there, ignored, until Roger Randall Dictu's shell corporation—chartered somewhere east of Borneo—had snatched it up and run for the touchdown.

So Jackson carefully put the papers back in the box, the box back into its hiding place and the copy of "Macbeth" back on the shelf.

And that night, he and Louise got righteously and joyously drunk and stood out on the porch, as she recited Shakespeare into the dark. Jackson had given Winston all of Gunnar's guns and dynamite, but he thought the poetry was just fine. Even without the explosions.

31

"WAIT." JACKSON WASN'T CERTAIN HE UNDERSTOOD
what he had just heard—even though it was clear and simple, impossible to
not understand. "So he didn't... He wasn't..." He forced himself to say it
clearly and calmly. "He was innocent."

Marybelle smiled and put the miniature tape player back into her purse.

"Roger Randall Dictu was never innocent," she said, snapping the purse
closed. "Of anything."

Jackson considered the tape he had just heard, that instant of despair
and panic. There was truth in that.

"But he wasn't—"

"Oh yes he was," Marybelle insisted. "So completely. In so many ways."

"But no," Jackson protested. "He didn't—"

"Yes he did." Her voice was filled with certainty. And command.

Sitting in his office, Jackson felt as if he was on sheer ice, a near-vertical
slope, going way too fast.

Marybelle continued, calm, assured.

"Don't worry, Jackson. Your story was right, as right as it needed to be."

"That's not the way—"

"And as far as I'm concerned, no one will ever hear this tape again. It's
just between—" she leaned closer, her voice a conspiratorial whisper "—us."

And before Jackson could find any control on that icy slope, she kept
going.

"Now that we're clear" —who was clear?— "we need to settle a little
business." She nodded crisply and, sitting just behind her, Goodie Rawlins
nodded too. Apparently he was he part of that conspiratorial "us."

"I understand, Mr. Jackson" —suddenly formal, no smile— "that you may be under the impression that you have some sort of legal right to the Liberty Drift mining claim."

How did she know that? He saw Goodie's face over her shoulder, calmly smiling. Sure. Enough lawyers and money and you know anything you want.

"So let's be perfectly clear. The LD Trust—I believe you are familiar with all of this, Mr. Jackson? The LD Trust sold all interest in the Liberty Drift claim to the David and Goliath Corporation of Labuan, Malaysia."

Jackson could hear Louise laughing "Borneo!" and he smiled.

"I'm glad that pleases you, Mr. Jackson. In any case, my lawyers and—" she turned her head slightly toward Goodie "— Mr. Rawlins's lawyers, as well, assure us that the sale was entirely proper, entirely legal and, as the saying goes, entirely bulletproof."

Now she smiled.

"So I seriously advise you to abandon all thoughts of pursuing any claim on that property. And I assure you, Jack" —with the smile, she had moved him from Mr. Jackson to Jack, in recognition, he assumed, of his assumed surrender— "our legal position is untouchable and we will support it with whatever resources are appropriate."

She smiled again. Jackson smiled back because he couldn't think of anything else to do.

"And if you wish," she continued, "you may choose to consider this to be part of your personal support for the community. We are about to complete an arrangement in which we will transfer ownership of the Liberty Drift to the Aspen Skiing Company. And they, in exchange, will support rebuilding Harkney House in all its original splendor. You should be proud to be in a position to contribute" —she smiled again— "by doing nothing."

After Marybelle and Goodie left, parading out of the shabby newspaper offices like royalty, Jackson sat engulfed in a swirl of emotions.

Finally, he settled on one and stood up with a smile.

He suspected he had a little more leverage than Marybelle had been willing to concede and he was thinking of a way he could make at least one thing turn out right.

No, make that two things.

ON THE FOURTH OF JULY, Jackson and Louise hiked to the top of the mountain to watch the fireworks from above.

"It feels like they're inside-out," said Louise leaning against him in the dark.

Later, back at the cabin, they sat on the porch, watching stars that seemed almost as bright as fireworks against the absolute black of the deep mountain night. By unspoken agreement, they didn't kiss until, at last, they saw a shooting star.

That morning, they had attended the ground-breaking ceremony for the reconstruction of Harkney House. Goodwin Rawlins had spoken, declaring that the new Harkney House would be built "with the finest materials, to the most exacting standards. And never fear," he promised, "it will be every bit as godawful an ugly duckling as the original!" And the crowd had cheered.

JACKSON AND LOUISE stood silently in the Ute Cemetery on an August morning while the minister said a prayer over the re-consecrated grave. The headstone had been placed back where it belonged, after careful restoration, The process had begun after Arnie Bing had marched into the Aspen Sun and demanded that Jackson take the damn stone—which had spent some time embedded in the wall of Arnie's wine cellar. "Guy who sold it to me claimed it came from the grave of Shakespeare's daughter. Said her name was Juliet. But I was too smart to fall for that. I think he just found it in the river or something. Anyway, I guess it probably belongs back on that kid's grave. Been trying to get through to tell you that ever since that story ran in the paper."

And when the stone was finally settled back on the broken stub, its last line ran smoothly into the line of Shakespeare that had sat alone in the cold and snow for so many months. Together they read, "In loving memory of my dearly beloved daughter Juliet, treasure of my heart... She should have died hereafter."

HIGH ON Aspen Mountain the breeze carried a faint taste of the winter soon to come and the aspens rustled green and gold. Louise brushed fragments of bark and leaves out of her hair and leaned over to kiss Jackson and whisper something in his ear that made him laugh. He stood and stretched and helped her to her feet.

Holding hands, they started up the ridge, then she pulled away and ran through the trees. He chased her down, caught her and kissed her. They went still higher, following the ridgeline and then stopped, looking deep into the mountains, toward Pyramid Peak.

"Where did he try to ski down?"

"You can't see it from here," he said. "It's around on the South Face. Ella May said they're already calling it Dictu's Dive."

"Did he really think he could ski it?"

"He thought he could do anything."

They stood silently, gazing out into the mountains.

Jackson thought about that last tape that Marybelle had played in his office, the tape that no one but Marybelle and Jackson —and Goodie Rawlins— had ever heard or would ever hear.

And he thought about truth.

He knew truth wasn't a word that meant very much to Roger Randall Dictu. And he knew that Marybelle wasn't someone he could trust either. Like Roger Randall, she wanted what she wanted and was willing to cut right through whatever —or whoever— got in her way.

But there was something in Dictu's voice right at the end of that last recording. Something in that one instant of despair and panic that made Jackson think that Roger Randall Dictu might have been telling the truth, even if he was —as Marybelle insisted— "Never innocent. Of anything."

By now, Jackson knew all about the suicide of the man Roger Randall had been shouting at in that last tape, a man whose driver's license said "Saxby DuPont," but whose real name was Arnold Firkin and who had killed himself with the same gun he had apparently used to murder a thug named Viktor Yaroshenko, whose body was found in the apartment with Firkin and whose autopsy showed "near-toxic" levels of cocaine.

A new police reporter had been hired, so Jackson had been able to stay well away from reporting any of that story. And he had been able to keep the rest of what he knew to himself. He knew that Viktor Yaroshenko was the man in the black raincoat who had showed up in Aspen the night of the fire, gotten a pink Cadillac stuck in the snow, sucker-punched a tow-truck diver named Howard and then flown out on a private jet at first light that morning. And he knew that Viktor had flown back into town and that Jenn had spent the last weeks of her life in a hotel room with him, living on room-service food that they rarely touched and tipping the bellboys with blow. And if he didn't really know, still, he was as certain as if he had been there to watch, that Viktor had trashed PJ's apartment, shot out Jackson's windshield and dragged Gunnar out into the snow and left him to die. Near-toxic levels of cocaine indeed.

And he knew Saxby DuPont —or Arnold Firkin or whoever he was— would have done almost anything to get his new museum.

He even knew that the man who had sold Arnie Bing the gravestone stolen from the Ute Cemetery had found it in the backyard of a house he'd rented to a college fraternity over Christmas. Charges had been considered and then dropped.

Jackson knew all of that and the more he knew, the more he still didn't understand.

But most of all, he knew that his big story, the one that had shattered everything, was wrong.

It was completely wrong.

And mostly right.

Completely right and mostly wrong.

And he wanted to know more. He wanted to know what was true. If anything was true. That was supposed to be his job. But in the end, the one thing he knew that was true for certain was that they were all dead. Beast and Gunnar. Dictu. Firkin and Viktor. And Jenn. And Ernestina Rose. And...

He pulled his mind away from that dark swirl.

And he thought instead about the ski season to come, a season he could already see in the snow covering the peaks. He thought about skiing two brand new runs that were there on Aspen Mountain because, in the end, for all Marybelle's legal certainty, Jackson did have a little leverage. One was Gunnar's Glade, a deceptively difficult trail, neatly carved through the trees just past Last Dollar. And the other, so difficult it wasn't even shown on the trail map and its narrow entrance was guarded by a sign that said "Extreme Terrain. Experts Only!" was, of course, named The Beast. Jackson had been there with the trail crew when they were clearing brush that summer. It was narrow and steep and lined by solid aspens. Jackson didn't know if he could ski it, but he knew he was going to try.

Louise saw him smiling and broke into his thoughts with a kiss.

"Come on," she said. "We'll be late."

They climbed higher, cut across the slope and stopped. Below them, a meadow rolled downhill and gathered into a small bowl, lined with aspens, their leaves brilliant gold.

And in the cupped palm of the bowl stood a small wedding party. Maybe a dozen in all. The wind blew and gold showered down from the aspens onto the bride and groom.

The minister, in Native American robes, raised his arms and asked the final question.

And in a moment of stillness, they could hear the bride, gold leaves in her perfect blonde hair, as she smiled and said, "I do."

The minister nodded and the groom, his face breaking into a radiant smile, his hands vigorously patting his enormous belly, leaned his head back and howled his answer into the thin mountain air.

And as the groom leaned toward the bride, Jackson leaned toward Louise. Both couples kissed and Jackson whispered the same gleeful response the groom had howled just moments before.

"Goodie!"

About the Author

Andy Stone first arrived in Aspen on a hippie school bus in 1972, after spending a couple of years wandering around the country putting on psychedelic light shows (sometimes accompanying rock concerts, sometimes in towns that hadn't asked for a light show—or even wanted one). Born in New York City and raised right outside the city, Andy looked around Aspen, realized it was the most extraordinary place he'd ever seen and decided to stay. After two years pumping gas, he wound up, almost by accident, with a job as a reporter at The Aspen Times and now—long story short, as they say—more than 40 years later, he is still writing for the paper, although now he is down to just a weekly column. Over the years at The Aspen Times, he worked his way up from reporter to editor to editor-in-chief and, finally, publisher. He has won more than a dozen awards from the Colorado Press Association for column writing (serious, humorous and, even, sports), feature writing, and editorial writing. He also served as president and, later, chairman of the board of the Colorado Press Association. Despite his alleged loyalty to The Aspen Times, Andy has taken several extended breaks from working at the paper. During one such break, in the late 1970s, he wrote his first novel, "Song of the Kingdom," which was published by Doubleday. In the 1980s, Andy spent three years living in Spain—after being dragged there, kicking and screaming, by his wife, Linda Lafferty, a successful historical fiction novelist.

Now Andy and Linda live "a safe distance" (as he describes it) outside Aspen, with their dog, Rosco, their cat, Jackson, and too many mice (which Jackson apparently regards as close friends, rather than prey).

Aspen Ski company
925-1220